MARK OF THE WITCH

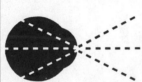

THE PORTAL

MARK OF THE WITCH

MAGGIE SHAYNE

THORNDIKE PRESS

A part of Gale, Cengage Learning

GALE
CENGAGE Learning®

Detroit • New York • San Francisco • New Haven, Conn • Waterville, Maine • London

GALE
CENGAGE Learning·

LIBRARY OF CONGRESS CATALOGING-IN-PUBLICATION DATA

Shayne, Maggie.
   Mark of the witch / by Maggie Shayne. — Large Print edition.
     pages cm. — (The Portal Series) (Thorndike Press Large Print Romance)
   ISBN-13: 978-1-4104-5570-3 (hardcover)
   ISBN-10: 1-4104-5570-X (hardcover)
   1. Large type books. I. Title.
   PS3619.H399M37 2013
   813'.6—dc23   2012041985

Published in 2013 by arrangement with Harlequin Books S.A.

Printed in the United States of America
1 2 3 4 5 6 7 17 16 15 14 13

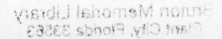

Once in a lifetime, if you're lucky, you'll have a friend like my BFF Michele M. A friend you love so much that when you go out in public together, people mistake you for a couple. A friend you share Stevie Nicks concerts and road trips to the Grand Canyon with, even though it makes your men jealous. A friend who, when you crawl inside an empty crypt and everyone else is yelling "Ewwwww," hushes them all and shouts "Hold still!" and takes your picture. Then she Photoshops your name on the outside of the tomb so you can use it in the back of your next book. A friend who will double-stick tape your boobs into your too-low-cut Romance Writers of America RITA® Award gown on the big night while making you laugh so hard you nearly bust the zipper but forget your nervousness. A friend you would trust with your life — no, more than that: with the lives of your kids. That's the kind of friend I have in my beautiful Michele.

Michele, you are the Thelma to my Louise and I love you more than chocolate. The Portal Series (all of it) is dedicated to you. I even put a treasure chest in it, sort of.

1

Dammit straight to hell, I was being sacrificed *again*.

I stood on the edge of a precipice, the hard ground under my bare feet already warming beneath the rising, scorching sun. The unblinking red-orange eye of an angry god rose slowly over distant desert sands, beyond endless dunes, watching as I paid for the sin of practicing magic without a license.

Just as I had been at every execution before, I was dressed in almost nothing. A white scrap of fabric tied at my hip, covering one leg and leaving the other bare below the knot. Another length of the same stuff was draped around my neck, crossed in front to cover each of my humongous boobs, and then tied behind to keep it there. My hands were tied behind my back. I wore no jewelry. Resentment rose up in me at the notion that Sindar, High Priest of Marduk, had stolen it. And then I wondered how I knew that.

This isn't me. I mean, it feels like it's me, but it can't be me. She's olive-skinned. She's gorgeous. Her boobs are huge. I'm pale and blonde and too thin. No curves here. Not like those, anyway.

And yet it was me. I was there. On that cliff. In that body. No denying it.

There were two other women, dressed pretty much the same way I was, one standing on either side of me. I felt close to them. I loved them.

Three men stood behind us. I felt the one behind me, his hands, warm and trembling, resting softly on my back, low, near my waist, where the skin was bare. My back was screaming with pain I didn't understand, but that man's touch was good. Soothing. I tried to relish it, thinking it was the last time I would feel it or anything good. Ever.

I wanted to turn my head, to look back at him, to see his face, but somehow I could not convince my dream self to do that. It didn't matter, though. I knew what he looked like. In my mind, I saw him clearly: his long black hair, his fine white tunic with a sash of scarlet, the fat gold torque around his corded neck. His arms were banded with steel and coated in fine dark hair. He was strong, and he had ebony eyes.

I didn't need to see him, nor the poor, half-dead man being held captive by soldiers a bit farther away. He'd already been beaten bloody, but he was struggling to break free as they forced him to watch. I'd glimpsed his face as they'd marched us up the cliff, far from our city gates. He barely looked human. His own mother wouldn't have known him.

And Sindar, the High Priest, he was there, too. I knew his face, as well. Eyes lined with kohl, lips darkened with the juices of rare desert berries. The rolls of fat at his neck, sporting layer upon layer of gold. His robes of the finest fabric, imported from the East. His belly so big that the golden cords of those robes had to be tied above the bulge, making him look like a mother about to give birth. I knew he was there, knew the secret lust in his eyes for what was about to happen to us. He was twisted, turned on by violence. Or maybe just by the rush of knowing he held the power of life and death in his hands.

I was going to have to kill him one day.

I tried to look at the other women, because, aside from the touch of those large male hands on my skin, they were the most interesting part of this whole thing. They

9

had dark hair and dark eyes, just like I did. But as I looked at them, they changed, the way a reflection in still water will change when a stone is dropped into it. One briefly became a blue-eyed platinum blonde, the other a fiery redhead, modern women in modern clothes. It was brief, the illusion, and then the High Priest was speaking in some long-dead language, and the hands at my back began trembling harder than before — kneading my waist, I thought — and I closed my eyes in bittersweet anguish.

"Remember, my sisters," said the raven-haired woman who had so briefly been a blonde. "Remember what we must do. We cannot cross over until it is done."

Oddly, the words I heard were spoken in an exotic language I *knew* I didn't know, yet I understood every word.

I tugged at the ropes that bound my wrists, tugged so hard I felt new blood seeping from the welts already cut into my flesh from my struggling. My gaze strayed to the jagged rocks far, far below, and my toes dug into the hard earth as my body instinctively resisted.

But, as always, it was futile — and I knew it. So I relaxed and reminded myself of the plan.

An instant later, my body was plummeting.

There were no screams, not one, not from any of us, as we arrowed downward like hawks diving onto their chosen prey. Our own weight propelled us as our feet pedaled uselessly. The only sounds were the soft flapping of our garments and the arid wind rushing past my face, whipping my long black hair above me. I smelled that wind, sucking it in deeply, tasting every flavor it held in my final breath. I closed my eyes, and awaited my fate. Then I heard the others, their voices chanting a familiar verse, and I joined them. My heart raced faster and faster as I waited to feel the impact of the already bloodstained rocks below.

I felt a sudden jarring blow, like the hit of a powerful electric jolt, in every cell of my body. And then nothing. Blackness.

I opened my eyes and stared through the darkness at the ceiling of my tiny Brooklyn apartment, willing my heart rate to drop back to normal. It was running like a late bicycle messenger on deadline, banging so hard against my rib cage that I thought for a second I might be having a heart attack. I lay very still, afraid to move and make it worse, my eyes wide, blinking at the ceiling.

I'm not in some fucked-up desert. I'm not wearing an I Dream of Jeannie *Halloween costume. I have little boobs. Nice, firm, little boobs. And blond hair.*

I moved my hand carefully, as if I was afraid to set off some unseen trap, and lifted a lock of said hair, so I could see it for myself by the glow of my plug-in night-light.

Yep. Blond. Perfectly blond. Or amber-gold, as my stylist calls it. Crimp curled, only without need of a crimper. And hanging just below my ears, right where it belongs. No long, flowing, ebony tresses in sight.

I took a deep, cleansing breath, inhaling till my lungs wanted to burst, then holding it for a beat or two, before blowing it all out, real slow. And then I did it again. And again. It was a technique I'd learned in the open circles I used to attend, led by my friend Rayne — Lady Rayne, that is — back when I used to believe in magic and shit. Which I didn't anymore.

When I felt it was safe to move again, I turned my head to look at the clock on the nightstand. Midnight. Again. It was always midnight when I woke from the damned recurring dream —

The Witching Hour. And on the night before Halloween, too.

Shut up. I'm not a witch anymore.

12

— and I could almost never get back to sleep.

The adrenaline rush of being shoved off a cliff tended to get a person's blood flowing, I supposed. Sitting up in bed, I pushed both hands through my hair. My spiky bangs were sideswept and tended to fall into my eyes. I thought it made me look mysterious.

My heart was still hammering. I needed a smoke, but like a jackass, I'd quit again, so there wasn't a cigarette in the entire place. No, wait, maybe — I'd switched out handbags just before my latest attempt to go healthy. I might have missed one.

I swept off the covers and got up too fast, then pressed the heels of my hands to my eyeballs to make the room stop spinning. Hell. Another deep breath. Damn, I needed nicotine.

Okay, steady again. Good. I made my way across the bedroom to the halfway decent-sized closet that had been the apartment's one and only selling point — besides it being only two subway stops or a good brisk walk from work — and rummaged around in the darkness within. I stubbed my toe on my antique replica treasure chest and cussed it out for being in the way before I located my most recent handbag, a pretty little leopard print Dolce & Gabbana num-

13

ber that had cost two months' rent.

I had a weakness for shoes and bags, and killer good taste. There were worse things.

Yanking the bag off the shelf by its tiny silver handle, I opened it and had an instant rush of gratification at the whiff of stale tobacco that wafted out. I pawed inside until I felt a crumpled, cellophane-wrapped pack that still held one beautiful, stale menthol.

One. Just one. My precious.

Lighter? Junk drawer. I dragged a bathrobe off the foot of my bed on the way into the living room–slash-kitchenette, then rounded the Formica counter that separated one from the other. The junk drawer — official holder of anything I didn't know where else to put, size permitting — yielded a yellow Bic.

I smoothed the wrinkles out of the slightly bent cig and put it between my lips. It felt good there. Lighter in hand, I speed walked to the bedroom window and wrenched it open. Then, sitting on the sill, illuminated by the moonlight I used to dance beneath, one leg dangling outside, the other holding me firmly in, I cupped my hands at the far end of the cigarette, like any smoker does when there's likelihood of an errant breeze.

But before I could flick my Bic, I went

very, very still, my eyes glued to my wrists, which, I suddenly realized, *really* hurt. They'd been quietly hurting ever since I'd awakened from that stupid nightmare. The pain had seemed like part of the dream, like the pain all over my back and the impact with those rocks. I'd been waiting for it to fade, like the rest, but clearly it wasn't going to.

Clearly. Because there were angry red welts on my wrists, welts that had been bleeding, and that still bore the twisted pattern of rough-hewn rope.

My jaw dropped . . . and my one and only cigarette fell from my lips and fluttered down, *way* down, to the sidewalk below, looking a bit like a girl in white, plummeting from a friggin' cliff overlooking the desert in Bumfuck, Egypt.

Not Egypt. Babylon.

I turned around so fast I almost fell, looking to see who had just whispered the correction. But that was stupid, because it had come from inside my own head.

Father Dominick St. Clair led the way, and Father Tomas, his chosen successor, followed with his heart in his throat. He was nervous, and not ashamed to admit it. It wasn't every day a man was asked to assist

15

in an exorcism. So far, it had all the markings of a made-for-Hollywood production. Creepy old house sadly in need of a paint job, check. Careworn mother, old beyond her years, dressed in clean but faded clothes, check. Narrow staircase that creaked when you walked on it, check. Big wooden door with unearthly moaning coming from the other side, double check.

He stood there and told himself he was a twenty-nine-year-old man with a first-rate education — Cornell, for crying out loud — and a left brain that ruled him. Practical. Intelligent. That part of him did not believe this could be real.

And he suspected that was the part of him Father Dom was trying to stomp out. The doubting side. The doubting Tomas.

The older priest couldn't know it was already too late. Tomas had made his decision. He couldn't keep living something he didn't believe in. He was only waiting for the right time to explain that he couldn't keep living in service to vows that no longer meant to him what they once had.

Dominick paused outside the old wooden door. It had an oval brass knob that had probably been there for two hundred years. "The job I've been grooming you for is coming soon."

He was being "groomed" to keep a witch from releasing a demon from its Underworld prison. Great. He'd often wondered if the Church elders knew about Father Dom's obsession with the ancient legend of *He Whose Name Must Not Be Spoken.* All Tomas had wanted was to be an ordinary priest, to help the poor and hungry and misled, to offer faith to the faithless and hope to the hopeless, to pay back the kindness shown to him by the Sisters of St. Brigit and Father Dom himself, who'd raised him from the age of ten after his faithless, hopeless, addicted mother's suicide.

He'd studied. He'd excelled. College, then the seminary. But unlike every other seminarian, he'd been yanked out of school early and personally ordained by Father Dom. He'd been given special dispensation with regard to Tomas, the old man had said, because of the importance of the mission.

"Did you hear me, Tomas?" Dom asked, sounding impatient.

Tomas snapped out of his thoughts and looked the old priest in the eye. Dom's face was like a white raisin, his body stooped. Yet his eyes were sharp and his perception sharper. Sometimes Tomas thought the old man could see right inside his brain, read the thoughts going on there. But then, he should. He probably knew Tomas better than anyone.

"Your faith isn't strong enough yet to do what will be required of you, Tomas," Dom said, and Tomas realized that he'd already said it once while he'd been lost in thought. "Faith ought not need proof to sustain it. But time is short, and you need to know. Demons are real. And powerful. See for yourself."

He opened the door, and Tomas looked inside. The girl in the bed might have been twelve. Maybe less. She was thrashing, arching her back, grunting and moaning. He froze in place as his mind tried to process what he was seeing. And his initial feeling was that he ought to yank out his iPhone and call 9-1-1.

Dom pushed past him, his black bag already open. He pulled out a crucifix and a bible, small and black and worn, its pages edged in gold. "Get the holy water. Bring it here."

Tomas pushed his doubts aside to be considered later. He took the bag from Father Dom and rummaged inside until he found the vial, pulling it out and uncorking it.

"Use the water and draw an *X* on her

forehead whenever I tell you."

Tomas moved up to the other side of the bed. The girl stank of urine, and it made him want to gag. She was foaming at the mouth like a rabid dog, thick white bubbles erupting everywhere.

"Exorcizo te, omnis spiritus immunde . . ." Dom nodded at him, and Tomas wet his forefinger with holy water and drew an *X* on the girl's forehead. She was hot to the touch, and Dom was still praying. *"In nomine Dei Patris omnipotentis . . ."*

He kept going. Tomas stopped listening. He found himself pulled into the girl's eyes until they rolled back, and he shot Dom a look. "She needs an ambulance. A hospital."

Dom stopped what he was doing and glared at him. Then he lifted one long arm and pointed his arthritically bumpy forefinger at the door. "Get thee behind me." He didn't say "Satan," but it was in his tone.

Tomas didn't argue. He didn't want any part of this. He left the room, head down, and walked down the stairs and out of the house. His trusty old Volvo wagon was waiting at the curb, behind Dom's boat-sized seventy-something Buick. He got in and drove, and he didn't look back.

I sat at the Coffee House. That was the

name of the place, the Coffee House. Its stylized Formica tables were kidney-shaped and orange, with half-circle bench seats curving around the widest side. Stainless steel "pipes" twisted and curved overhead, lights affixed to them, aimed in random directions. Someone once said it was supposed to be retro, but it felt more like "*Jetsons* Chic" to me. The colors were perfect — today was Halloween, and I was at an orange Formica table waiting to meet with a Wiccan high priestess.

I was feeling awkward as hell as I waited for Rayne Blackwood to arrive.

She was one of my best friends, or had been until I'd renounced my witchhood and handed in my pentacle. (Okay, figuratively, not literally. The pent was still in my treasure box, along with all my other witchy stuff.)

I'd started studying the "Craft of the Wise," otherwise known as witchcraft, several years earlier and, being an independent type, I had preferred practicing alone to joining a group. Besides, they still called them "covens," and I just couldn't stop sniggering at the word. Call me a cynic. Whatever. So I'd been what was known in the Craft as a "solitary practitioner." Even now, when I was no longer a believer, Craft holidays still felt like *my* holidays. But there was a lot to be said for celebrating the holidays with others. Banging on a *djembe* drum alone in my apartment just wasn't the same as sitting in a circle with twenty others, all playing as one. I know it sounds lame, but don't knock it until you've tried it.

Anyway, since the only people who celebrated Wiccan holidays were Wiccan people, I'd wound up seeking them out.

Rayne's *coven* (snigger) was a very traditional one in a lot of ways, with secret *oathbound* rites and all that. Rayne was its leader, a Third Degree High Priestess with a Pagan lineage as long as her arm, and therefore entitled to be addressed as *Lady* Rayne. But Rayne had never bought into the lofty title thing, either. None of her witches called her "Lady" anything.

Still, she was a big deal, Wicca-wise. And not a small deal mundane-wise, either — a partner in a Manhattan law firm and a class-A beauty. Green eyes, red hair, killer figure.

Almost as soon as I visualized her in my mind's eye, Rayne came in, waved hello and sent me her stunning smile, then stopped at the counter on the way over, not continuing until she had a cup of high-test in her hand. She wore a sassy little designer suit, black tailored jacket with a short skirt, teal shell underneath, and a tiny, tasteful silver chain around her neck, with matching studs in her earlobes. No giant pentacle pendant. No dangling crystal stars or moons at her earlobes. She was a practical witch. Didn't feel the need to announce her faith on a sandwich board while walking to work. Don't laugh. Have you *been* to Salem?

"Trick or treat," she said, as she slid onto the bench. "How have you been, Indy?"

"Good." I lowered my head, feeling awkward as hell.

"Uncomfortable, are you?"

I looked up to see her smiling at me. She reached across the table, short French-manicured nails gleaming as she covered my hand with hers. "No need to be. I know we've barely talked since you left the Craft, but —"

"What do you mean? I leave comments on your blog every few days —"

"I mean *talked.* Facetime. Not online. It's been eight months since I've even seen you. Do you really think I care what your faith is, sweetie?" She rolled her eyes. "Core Craft tenet, 'to each her own.' "

"You made that up," I said, but I was smiling, relaxing. She didn't hate me for walking away. For not believing anymore. I was glad. Guilt wasn't an emotion I allowed very often, but faith of any kind had been new to me, and leaving it unheard of. Some witches still practiced shunning of those who walked away. Or so I'd heard.

"I made up the wording, for simplification purposes, but not the notion. If I didn't follow it, there would be war in my own family. Your truth is as sacred as mine, Indira."

"Even if my truth is that there *is* no truth?" I asked, watching her green eyes.

"Even if." She patted my hand three times. "Now what's going on?"

"I've missed the shit outta you," I told her.

"Yeah, I'm sure that's all it is." Sarcasm dripped. She flagged down a passing waitress, who had her arms full and looked harried as hell. "Bring us each a big fat gooey glazed donut, would you? But only when you get a minute."

The waitress would undoubtedly have barked at anyone else, with a "this isn't my table" or an "I'll get to you as soon as I can," sort of put off. But she smiled at Rayne. *Everyone* smiled at Rayne. She had the kind of personality that made people love her, no matter what she said or did.

Or maybe it was some of her magic leaking out.

23

Except I didn't believe in that anymore. I lowered my head and caught sight of Rayne's feet. Three-inch stilettos, black leather, ankle-covering uppers that zipped, and open toes. "Oh, my God, I *love* your shoes."

"Thank you. But I assume my shoes are *not* the reason you emailed me. And since I'm on my lunch break, and hence my time is limited, it might be best to skip straight to your problem."

Nodding rapidly, I pulled my head back into the game. I was way too easily distracted. And this was important. But, damn, I had to remember to find out where Rayne had bought those shoes.

Stay on topic, Indy.

I sat up straighter, focused. "I'm sorry I waited for a problem to force me to call. That's pretty rotten of me. I just felt —"

"I know. It's okay."

"And I appreciate you giving up your lunch hour to help me out. And I'm buying, by the way."

"Damn right you are." Rayne winked, and sipped, and the waitress came back with the biggest glazed donuts I'd ever seen.

I took a small bite, followed by a sip of my herbal tea, secretly longing for the caffeine in the cup across the table. Maybe I should give up one vice at a time. Tea and a donut just wasn't the same. Then I swallowed and looked my friend in the eye. "I've been having a recurring dream. Nightmare, really."

"Ahh. All right. Well, I'm pretty good at dream interpretation." She shifted in her seat, crossing one gorgeous leg over the other, settling in to listen. "It's not surprising. I mean, you know the veil between the worlds is thin this time of year."

"Yeah, I know." Samhain, the actual holiday on which Halloween was based, was still a week away. Meaning my problem could only get worse.

"Go ahead, tell me about it."

I nodded and tried to believe that it could get *better,* too. "I don't think it's actually a dream at all."

"No?"

"No."

"What, then?"

"I was hoping you could tell me."

Rayne tilted her head, taking that in, her eyes going serious and contemplative. The effect was ruined when she took a giant bite of the huge donut right after her sincere, "Go on."

"Okay. In the dream, or whatever, I'm standing on the edge of a rocky cliff, wearing clothes from some other era, but not many of them. There's a man that I know is a high priest — not a Wiccan one, mind you — speaking some language that I've never heard before. Two other women stand on either side of me, dressed pretty much the same way I am. We're very close. We love each other —"

"*Love* each other? Is this dream heading for a lesbian three-way?"

I stared at her blankly.

"Sorry. Trying to make you smile. I'm not used to seeing you so freaking intense, Indy."

"This *is* intense. Whatever it is, it's . . . Just let me finish, okay?"

She made a zipper motion over her lips.

"We have some kind of a plan, but I don't know what it is. I mean, in the dream I do, but I don't remember when I wake up. Our hands are tied behind our backs. Three men stand right behind us. I feel one of them — his hands are on my back, and it kind of turns me on, which is really fucked up, since I think he's about to shove me off the freaking cliff."

Rayne had resumed eating her donut, but she stopped in midbite, her eyes going wider as I went on.

"The next thing I know, we're falling. Hitting the ground. Dying on the bloody rocks at the bottom, except things always fade to black before that part."

Rayne lifted her head, met my eyes. I saw rapt interest in hers.

"It's always the same," I said. "We all have black hair, dark eyes, the kind of naturally tanned skin that suggests we're Mediterranean or Middle Eastern or something. I'm pretty sure it's some kind of a ritual sacrifice. And there's always another man, a soldier, being held nearby. He's been badly beaten, and he's being forced to watch."

Rayne blinked. "Any names floating around in your head? Any of the words spoken by the high priest, maybe?"

I nodded hard. "The high priest's name is Sindar. He serves a Sun God, Marduk. I keep getting the feeling I was caught practicing magic and that it was forbidden."

She was nodding. "Any clues in your clothing or the geography?"

"My clothes look like they were lifted from the wardrobe room for *Aladdin*. From the cliff, we're looking out over a vast desert. I can see the shadowy outline of what I think of as my city in the distance."

"Anything else?" she asked, as if fascinated by the story.

"Why? Is this ringing any bells for you?"

"Just tell me the rest."

It was. I could see that it was. "I woke up referring to the city as Bumfuck, Egypt, and I heard a voice in my head say *Babylon.*"

Her eyes flared a little. "And that's all?"

"No. There's this." I held up my hands, pushed back the draping sleeves of my paisley smock top and revealed the rope burns on my wrists.

"Holy shit." Rayne grabbed my hands, turned them over.

"Yeah, that was my reaction, too."

Her gaze remained riveted on my reddened wrists until I lowered them to my lap and let my sleeves fall back in place.

"So? What do you think?"

Rayne shook her head as if trying to clear it. "Are you absolutely sure you didn't get those marks some other way? Some ordinary way?"

"Kinky sex with a bondage freak, you mean?"

"Indy . . ."

"There were no marks when I went to bed. They were there when I got up. There's not a rope in my entire apartment. No one broke in, drugged me, bound me, raped me, untied me and left again, unless they managed to get into a locked apartment and lock it again on the way out, chain and all.

28

I'm telling you, this is . . . it's something else. It's something . . . not natural."

"Supernatural."

"Yes. That." *Which means I was wrong to stop believing, doesn't it?*

Rayne nodded. "All right."

"All right? What do you mean, *all right?* You look like there's more. Do you know what this is about?"

She opened her mouth, then closed it again. "I'm going to do some research, and I'll get in touch, okay?"

She knew something. I could see she did. But she wanted to make sure. Fine. "I can't wait long."

"I wouldn't ask you to. Meanwhile, maybe we should try a protection spell. Would you be willing to let me do that for you?"

By "we" I was sure she meant the full coven. I would have to look all those witches in the eyes knowing that they knew I had turned my back on their faith. On my faith. On the Goddess.

And yet, I needed something. I needed Rayne's cooperation, if nothing else, and sure as shit I would offend and wound her if I didn't agree. Besides, I'd asked for her help. I couldn't very well refuse it when she offered, could I?

Was there some little part of me that had

missed this kind of hocus-pocus bull, too? Yeah, probably, way down deep.

"When?"

"Tonight," she said. "The sooner the better."

I nodded. I wasn't sure if I felt better for having my insane experience validated, or whether that just made it more frightening. "Where? In the park where you usually hold your open circles?"

"No. No, this needs to be private. There's an occult shop in the Village. They have a tiny backyard." She dug in her handbag, pulled out a pen and a business card, flipped the card over and wrote on the back. "I'll get the coven together. Not all of them, just the Seconds and Thirds. If this is what I think it is, it's serious stuff." She slid the card across the table so I could see the address she'd written. "Be there by 10:00 p.m., okay?"

Blinking, feeling a ridiculous burning sensation behind my eyes, I nodded. "Okay. Thank you."

"I'm a high priestess. This is part of my job." She twisted her wrist to look at her watch. "My other job, that is, besides the one I'm late getting back to. But before I do, I need your permission to share what you've told me with one other person.

Someone I trust more than anyone else in the world. You can trust him, too. And he might have information we need. All right?"

"Is he a shrink?" I asked, and when she frowned at me, I said, "Yeah, permission granted. Go for it. Just try not to make me sound too warped."

She was already on her feet, using a napkin to pick up the remaining half of her donut, hoisting her bag, which, I'd just noticed, matched the shoes — same black leather, same silver zipper — higher onto her shoulder. "I've gotta run, Indy. Take care of yourself, okay? And trust me, we'll figure this out."

I tried to smile. "Okay."

And then she was gone, clicking away in her fabulous shoes at high speed. She'd left a half cup of caffeine-laden brew at her seat. Reflexively, I started to reach for it, felt eyes on me, heard a throat clear, and saw a waitress looking at me.

Sighing, I lowered my hand to my own cup of putrid tea. At least I had my donut.

2

"Father Dominick. You asked for me?"

"In the office," Dom called.

Tomas entered and closed the front door behind him. The old priest's entire house smelled like a combination of mothballs and muscle rub that always made Tomas's stomach clench and his nose wrinkle. He forced himself not to allow the latter as he walked through the cluttered living room into what had probably been a den or a library when the old Victorian was built and now served as Dom's office. Crucifix on the wall, books everywhere. Not just on the shelves — and there were lots of those — but in stacks and standing upright along the floor between every piece of furniture that could serve as a bookend. Old books, their bindings and pages overwhelming the smells in the rest of the house, much to Tomas's relief. The smell of books was soothing. It was the smell of knowledge, preserved and passed on.

Father Dom was sitting at his desk, facing his computer. "Come around here, Tomas," Dom said. "I have someone who wants to talk to you."

Frowning, Tomas moved behind the desk. Dom nodded at the big monitor, and when Tomas looked, he saw the girl from yesterday, sitting up in her bed, smiling at them via Skype. "Hi, Father Thomas," she said.

"It's Toe-MAHS," Father Dom pronounced. "Say hello to Dora, Tomas."

"Hello, Dora." He couldn't believe his eyes. The girl looked fine. Oh, a little pale, a little tired, but her eyes were bright, and she appeared perfectly healthy.

"You look much better," he said.

"I know. I feel better. I just wanted to thank you for helping me."

Shame rose, and he bowed his head. "I didn't really do anything. It was all Father Dom."

"No, you were there. I remember. I don't blame you for leaving. Mamma says it was awfully scary. But you came, and I'm better now."

Tomas glanced at Dom, who smiled and nodded at the girl. "Well, we'll let your doctor be the judge of that," he said. "You're

33

seeing him this afternoon, aren't you, Dora?"

"Yes, at two."

"Let me know what he says, will you?"

"Of course. Bless you, Father Dom. Father Tomas." She said it correctly that time, and then the on-screen window with her face inside it vanished.

Dom rolled his chair away from his desk but didn't get up. "Her doctor will give her a clean bill of health. Of course, *he* couldn't find anything wrong with her to begin with."

Tomas nodded. Doubted, but nodded. "I'm sorry I doubted you, Father Dom. I just . . . in my experience . . . I've never seen anything like that before."

"I've seen it a hundred times. Exorcised more demons than any priest in the church. Which is why I inherited this assignment of ours to begin with. This quest."

"And I'm humbled that you chose me to be your successor." He ought to tell him. He really ought to. But no, not yet. The wheels took time to turn, and this was going to be a huge and painful discussion when it happened.

Dom grunted as if he doubted it. "You're the least humble man I know, son. But you were chosen for this. Sent to me just for this. Sit, Tomas," he ordered. "I don't like looking up at anyone."

Tomas sat. The gruff old man was his mentor, his teacher and the closest thing he'd ever had to a father. Yes, he believed in things Tomas had come to consider unbelievable. But even *he* didn't doubt the man with as much conviction as he used to. His doubts were still strong enough for him to know this was not the life for him, however. So he sat and tried to assume a humble demeanor. He loved the old priest, despite the fact that he'd always considered him a little bit crazy.

"Pull your chair around here," Dom said. "We're not through with this machine yet." He was clicking keys as he spoke — slowly. Hunting and pecking with a single forefinger, knuckles swollen from arthritis.

Tomas nodded and moved his chair closer, turning it so he could see the computer screen again. It showed a lengthy series of astrological terms, symbols for the signs, abbreviations for alignments and conjunctions and oppositions at varying degrees. It stood beside a map of the solar system with lines and arrows and more symbols all over it. It looked like an NFL coach's playbook. Astrology had never been his strong suit.

"What am I looking at?"

"This configuration. Right here." Dom

pointed. "In a week it will be exactly the same as it was in the beginning."

"The beginning . . ." Tomas looked up from the screen, meeting Dom's aging but sharp cornflower-blue eyes as he finally got the old man's meaning. "The *beginning? The fifteen-hundred-BC* beginning?"

"More precisely, Samhain Eve, fifteen hundred and one BC. The day a high priest of the cult of Marduk imprisoned *He Whose Name Must Not Be Spoken* in the Underworld. If the demon is going to try to escape into our world again, Tomas, it will be soon. Samhain Eve, in fact. And I'm no longer strong enough to do what needs doing, though it pains me to admit it."

Tomas searched Dom's face. "You're not well?"

Dom shrugged. "I *feel* fine." He turned his head, gazing across the room at the oversized crucifix on the opposite wall. "But the Lord has spoken to me, told me it has to be you. This is the mission I've trained for all my life. Now it falls to my successor before his time. But that's the way it has to be. So sayeth the Lord."

"All things happen for a reason, Father Dom." But inside Tomas was thinking this couldn't be happening. Now not, not when he'd finally made the decision to leave the priesthood and sent in the paperwork making the request formal.

Thank God he hadn't yet told the old man.

"Watch and wait for the signs, Tomas. Watch for the witches of Babylon. The Demon's whores. Each of them bound by oath and by blood to help *He Whose Name Must Not Be Spoken* to escape. Stop the first of them and you stop them all. You must do this, no matter how difficult, in order to keep the demon from emerging and wreaking havoc on the world of man. It is our calling."

It is a fairy tale, Tomas thought. *But I'll humor you a bit longer.* "How will I know —"

"It's written, 'the witch's past sins will rise up to mark her flesh and wake her memory.' Watch, wait, listen, and take heed when you are called. I'll help you all I can, Tomas, but the task, for some reason, must be yours."

Tomas nodded solemnly. He wasn't entirely sure Dom was 100 percent wrong about this, after all. The scrolls were real, and the tale was in them. He had seen it. "And if I locate the first witch and stop her from helping the demon —"

"Then the next will never be activated and our mission is done. Theoretically the Portal won't open again until the next alignment, another three thousand five hundred years from now. But if you fail . . ."

"If I fail to stop the first witch, I have to try again with the second. And if I fail to stop *her,* then I try again with the third."

"And if you fail *then* . . . the demon walks among us and the world of man is doomed." Father Dom gripped Tomas's wrist in his hand, squeezing so hard it hurt. "Do you believe me, Tomas? Have I shown you enough proof of the existence of demons, of the power of them, of the danger they pose, to make you a believer in the ancient prophecy?"

Tomas met the old man's eyes. There was holy fire sparking from their depths. "Yes," he said at length. "Yes, Father Dom. I believe." It was a lie, and he felt guilty as hell for telling it, but what else could he do?

"Hold on to that faith, my son. You are going to need it."

No harm in humoring him a bit longer, Tomas thought. He would play along. But he knew there would be no signs. No witches. No marks. Samhain would pass, and Dom would have to concede defeat. And then Tomas could leave knowing he'd done the best he could for the old guy.

Then his sister called, and all that

changed.

The occult shop in Greenwich Village had a minuscule backyard enclosed by a vine-smothered stone wall and bathed in moon-light. Fingers of dark cloud slithered over the face of the moon, only two days past full. A true Halloween moon — perfect ambiance for a Halloween night gathering of witches. There were fountains and statues marking the four directions. Venus in the west, pouring water from a conch. Brigit — the Celtic goddess of the forge and giver of creative fire to poets — in the south, hold-ing a shallow basin where blue flames floated. On the east wall, the beautiful Eo-stre — Germanic goddess of spring and rebirth — a ring of wildflowers upon her head, incense wafting spirals of fragrant smoke around her. The north boundary was the back of the brick building, and in front of it stood a modern rendition of Gaia. She held a dish of sea salt in her lap.

I sat in the center of it, and five witches stood around me in a circle. They had already performed all the preliminaries and had gone silent now to listen to Rayne as she led the rite.

"We come to weave a web of protection around the solitary witch Indira," she said, her voice deep and compelling.

I wanted to correct her — *former solitary witch.* The words rose in my throat, but I bit my tongue to hold them in.

Rayne wore her long black robes tonight, her vivid red hair loose and moving in the slight breeze, her eyeliner exaggerated, and every limb dripping with sacred jewelry. The other women were dressed much the same way. Everyone jingled when they moved. Even me. I'd dug through my closets and pulled out my old witchy wardrobe. I had chosen white, since this was a spell of protection. A white one-shoulder dress with gold trim that could have been Grecian. But it reminded me, too, of the clothes I wore in that powerful, terrifying dream.

I'd donned my pentacle again. I told myself it didn't mean I was returning to the fold or had started believing again. I *didn't* believe. There was no magic in the world. I'd proven that to myself. I'd cast and cast and cast my spells, but my soul mate hadn't appeared. And I'd been so damned sure he would — so certain he was real. All my life I'd felt this unnamed, unknowable longing gaping like a great big giant hole in my gut. A yearning for the man who was supposed to be by my side, whose absence I felt keenly, even though we had never met. It was real, that feeling. Which meant *he* had to be real, too.

I ached for him. Sometimes even cried for him. Like a real lover I'd had and lost. That's how vivid the feeling was.

Sort of like those damned dreams.

Hey, that was encouraging. Maybe they were as flimsy and imaginary as he was.

Anyway, he hadn't come, so I'd stopped believing. Magic either worked or it didn't. Black and white. Scientific method. Test the theory, prove it right or wrong. I'd tested it. It hadn't worked. Ergo, no magic. Period.

And yet, when I'd pulled out my pretty mini-treasure chest from the back of my closet and opened it, and the smells of sandalwood and dragon's blood resin had enveloped me like a puff of magic from a genie's lamp, I'd felt it all coming back to me. Witchcraft might be all bullshit, but it had felt very real from time to time.

It felt real now.

Rayne was still talking. Her voice was different during a ritual. Deeper. More powerful. "Together with the powers of Earth, Air, Fire, Water and Spirit, and by the unyielding power of the Goddess Herself, we weave this web so that nothing, be it from this world or any other, may harm this woman." Facing me, she said, "Do you have any requests of the Goddess before we raise the cone of power, Indira Simon?"

I nodded and, rising to my feet, lifted my eyes and arms skyward. I felt a tingle flowing through me from the tips of my fingers down my arms, into my spine, and another upward from the ground, through my feet, up my legs and into my spine, until the two energies met and exploded. I pulsed with it and reminded myself it was just a trick of the mind.

"Show me what I need to know," I said, though I was sure no one was listening. I was playing along because Rayne knew something and I wanted her to tell me what it was. "Show me what these dreams mean, what you want of me. More than anything right now, I need clarity. Wisdom. And information."

And while you're at it, that soul mate I've been longing for, forever and a day, would be a really nice bonus. You know, on the off chance you're real.

Stupid. You gave up on that, remember?

"So mote it be," Lady Rayne said.

"So mote it be," the others all repeated in unison.

"So mote it be," I whispered softly. I don't have any idea why there were tears rolling down my cheeks. Maybe my eyes were just

42

reacting to the smoke from the incense that hung in the air. It didn't dissipate like you'd expect it to do, outside like this. And even though it was the end of October, it was warm within the circle, as if it were physically holding our body heat and the fragrant smoke within it, just like it would supposedly hold the energy we raised until Rayne sent it forth to become the magical goal.

One woman hit her *djembe* drum, beginning a slow, steady beat. Another joined in, adding an accent, and then another brought a flourish of her own. A fourth woman shook a rattle in time, and then Rayne began a chant that echoed the heady music.

"She changes everything She touches. Everything She touches changes."

On and on the chant went, and it grew louder, its pace picking up. The witches joined hands, began walking in a circle, spiraling inward until the first of them reached me in the center, then turning to spiral outward again, forming a human snake with no end and no beginning. The drums kept up or led the way, it was impossible to tell which, but everything increased in both volume and tempo until the entire area was vibrating with energy. I felt it in my chest, in the pit of my stomach, all around and within me, until it reached a fever pitch and the chant evolved into a simple, rapid repetition.

"Touches, changes, touches, changes, touches, changes, toucheschangestouches- changestoucheschanges . . ."

Then, like the crack of a starter's pistol at the beginning of a race, Lady Rayne pressed her palm flat to my chest and shouted, *"Release!"*

And I swear to God, I was knocked backward, right off my feet. A witch standing behind me caught me, though, so I never hit the ground as the energy wave — or whatever it was — rushed over me. I sank to my knees in reaction. As I lifted my head, blinking my eyes open once more to look around me, I was not surprised to see several of the other witches sitting on the ground, where they'd settled as they let the power surge from them. I could almost see the result of the spell — the bubble of light around me. I could certainly feel it.

I tended to be a skeptic about most things of a so-called paranormal nature. But in witchcraft, I had believed — had really believed — and moments like this were why.

The mind sure is a powerful thing, isn't it?

"It is done," Rayne said. "Now you'll be safe, at least. And pretty soon, I bet you'll receive the information you've asked for. Watch for signs, Indy."

I nodded. "I was hoping some of that information might be coming from you, Rayne." I searched her eyes.

She averted them. "I have a call out. I might have something for you by tomorrow."

I guessed I would have to be satisfied with that for tonight.

Rayne turned to her fellow priestesses. "Ladies, would you kindly wrap things up for me? I'm drained."

As Rayne took a seat on the cool ground beside me, the other women took over. One thanked the Goddess for Her presence and aid, then each of them bade a hail and farewell to the energies of the four directions. Finally one woman took up the magic circle, the invisible space Rayne had cast. The magic circle was the witches' temple. Sacred space. Holy ground. I knew better than to leave before all of that was complete, but I was eager to go once it was finished, hoping to find a smoke on the way home. I was dying for a cigarette.

Rayne put a hand on my arm and I jumped. "You need to eat something, Indy. Ground yourself. I've got coffee and cake inside."

"Right. Ground myself." I'd forgotten the habitual post-ritual snacking. Always seemed to me that the "grounding" thing was just a good excuse for a pile of sugary carbs. "I know it's rude of me to rush off, but I just feel . . . compelled to get home."

"Then that's where you should be."

"Thanks for understanding. And for all of this . . ."

"Text me in the morning, let me know how it goes tonight. I'll do the same as soon as I have any information for you. Blessed be, Indy."

"Blessed be," I replied automatically.

I headed for the subway stop on the corner, intending to catch the next train to my Brooklyn neighborhood.

But there was something happening to me. A tingling, like an itch I couldn't reach way down deep in my psyche, and a slowly spreading darkness that kept sucking my attention away from the here and now. Like a person running on lack of sleep who almost drifts off, then shakes herself awake, I fought against the somnambulant state trying to overtake me, went down the stairs (*into the Underworld*), dropped a token (*paid the ferryman*) and pushed through the turnstile (*entered through the first gate*). I found a post to lean against on the nearly empty platform and waited for my train to arrive.

A few other people wandered in, most not paying any attention to me. There was an old man who made brief eye contact and smiled, breaking an unspoken rule, probably because in his day it was rude to do otherwise. There was a cluster of pants-hanging-off-the-ass punks, one of whom had a nice crisp unlit Marlboro Light Menthol in his hand, and a nice-looking couple who were too lost in each other to notice anyone else.

Off in the distance, I heard the train echoing closer.

I drifted, pulled myself back, drifted again. I kept almost falling asleep and seeing myself in different clothing. Not quite like in the dream, though. This time I wore a long cloak of black, with a hood pulled up over my hair, bathing my face in shadows.

Stupid dream. Can't you at least wait until I get home?

I jerked myself back to the present. The train was closer. The other people were beginning to edge nearer the tracks. The punks were uncomfortably close to the old man. The lead one was about to light his smoke, lighter in his other hand. But then he paused, pocketing the lighter, smiling at

47

the others, nodding the old man's way. The intended victim seemed to realize it about the same time I did. And just as the flash of alarm showed up in his kind blue eyes, one of the underwear-showing assholes pulled a knife. I felt myself lunging toward them even as I fell into the blackness of my dream world.

I woke groggy, rolled over in bed and pried one eye open to look at the clock. There was a cigarette, a white filtered Marlboro Light Menthol, lying in front of my little alarm clock, pristine, unsmoked, waiting for me. Had the nicotine fairy visited last night?

Then my foggy eyes focused on the illuminated red digits. 11:11. I'd slept way late, which was totally unlike me. My brain reminded me that my shift at Pink Petals, the flower shop sixteen blocks from my apartment, started at noon today, and *that,* more than anything, set a fire under my ass. I bounded out of bed, took a record-speed shower and toweled down in front of the mirror. A handful of mousse and a quick finger comb, and my hair was done. Easy breezy. I was still tugging its natural crimp-curls into shape as I gave my mirror image the once-over, but I stopped moving with one hand still tangled in my hair. My forearm was sporting a black-and-blue mark the size of a pizza slice.

Frowning, I lowered my arm and looked down at my body. Small boobs, still hanging where they ought to, no marks on what I'd always considered a rather boyish figure. I was kind of straight — slender, but straight — long waist that was nice and lean, but no flaring out at the hips. No booty in the back. I was small everywhere. Delicate and slight. I turned and looked back over my shoulder, spotting a good-sized slate-colored blob on one shoulder blade and a maroon one on my butt cheek. Legs looked okay in back. I looked down and cringed at the way the second littlest toe on my right foot was all bent out of shape and discolored. Looked broken. Felt it, too.

I turned back and met my own eyes in the mirror. "What the hell happened last night?" Damn. I was a mess. And that was about the time it hit me that I didn't remember how I got home. In fact, I didn't remember anything except standing in the subway, trying to hold on to the here and now, while something else was trying to suck me in. I remembered the punks and the old guy. I remembered one of them with a knife, and another with a mouthwateringly good-looking smoke in his hands. I remember lunging toward them.

And then . . . nothing.

And now there's a mouthwateringly good-looking smoke on my nightstand. Co-incidence? Or not . . .

I went back to the bedroom, picked up the cig, looked it over. I wanted to smoke it almost more than I wanted to know how I'd gotten home and into bed last night, but I couldn't. God only knew what might be in it. Punks like that, you just couldn't tell — assuming that was where I got it, which was impossible to know.

I picked it up, drummed up every ounce of will in my entire body, took it to the bathroom, dropped it in the toilet and flushed it away.

I almost cried.

I grabbed my towel off the floor, hung it up to dry and rubbed some witch hazel on my bruises. Then I dressed — leggings and a pretty little white camisole with lacy straps, long minty-green sweater over that, with a wide enough neck that it could hang off one shoulder. I added a wide pale brown leather belt that matched my short, kick-ass boots right down to the big gold buckles.

Then I wielded my makeup brushes like magic wands, and in another five minutes I was ready to face the day. Heavy eyeliner, dark shadow, luscious long lashes. I was still wearing my pentacle from the night before, and I decided to keep it on. Hell, it couldn't hurt. And it might help. It had my birthstone, an amethyst, in its center, and ivy vines made of silver twisting around the circle that enclosed it. Each leg of the star was made of a tiny broomstick. I liked it, lapsed Wiccan or not.

Giving one final glance in the mirror, I headed out of my apartment. My boots protected my sore toe so I didn't even limp. None of my bruises showed. No one would ever know what had happened last night.

Apparently not even me.

Sixteen blocks was a good brisk walk, and I loved it. I walked to work most of the winter. I walked it in the rain, when it wasn't torrential. Today was gorgeous. Cool but sunny, and it smelled good outside for a change. I liked the neighborhood, the people I passed on the way, the excuse to get my heart and lungs working a little bit harder than normal. It was all good.

I passed the little convenience store where I used to buy my smokes and almost went inside. I even slowed my steps as I went by the door and, glancing in, saw my beloved Marlboro Light Menthols in their pretty white-and-green boxes, stacked inside a locked, clear plastic case. And the little lighters on the counter. I'd need one of those, too. Maybe just for today . . .

I stopped. I took one step into the doorway, and then I closed my eyes. It's been three weeks. Three hellish, miserable weeks that I never want to go through again. *If I buy a pack now, I'm going to have to go back to Day One. Start over. No. It's got to get easier soon.*

"Lucy?" said someone from inside the store.

My eyes popped open. A man stood just inside the entrance, facing me. And for a long moment I sort of locked onto his eyes and couldn't look away. There was some kind of buzzing in my head, and my skin was cold and prickly.

"Hello," he said.

His voice felt like warm fingers on my skin. *I feel his hands on my back.*

I blinked myself out of whatever sort of idiot-haze I'd fallen into and tried to look at him the way I would normally look at any stranger who called me by the wrong name. He was gorgeous, that was for sure. Italian, or maybe Spanish. Sun-kissed bronze skin, hot Hershey Bar eyes, wide, kissable-looking lips, and a bod to die for underneath an all-black getup with — oh,

52

shit, I was going straight to hell — a white tab at the front and center of his collar.

"I'm sorry, Father. I'm not Lucy. You must have me mixed up with someone —"

"Not Lucy," he said, "Loosie." As he said it the second time, he pointed to the counter, where another clear plastic container held loose cigarettes. The sign above them said, Loosies, $1 ea.

"Is that even legal?"

"I have no idea. If not, it won't last long."

"Still, a buck for a smoke? That's effing highway robbery. Uh, sorry about the effing part. Habit."

"When you're trying to quit, you'd pay five bucks for just one, and you know it," he said, a little humor in his tone and in his eyes.

My knees wobbled. I locked them.

"It's effective, too. You give in to temptation once, but you do it without buying a whole pack and then feeling justified in smoking all twenty. Perfect solution. Weak moment, give in, and you're still okay. Right?"

He made perfect sense. But I couldn't tell him so, because my eyes were on the smooth skin of his neck above the forbidden collar, and the tiny bits of whisker he'd missed shaving this morning. I wanted to rub my

53

cheeks against them.

"So? Loosie? It'll be on me." He pulled a cigarette from the pocket of his clerical black shirt and held it up, much the way I envisioned Eve holding that glossy red apple or pomegranate or whatever it had been, up to Adam.

I took it with a quick snatch. "Imagine a priest counseling me to give in to temptation." *Especially one who looks like he does. 'Cause . . . damn.*

Smiling a little, he pulled out a lighter, and I took a step backward so I could make immediate use of it. I flicked his Bic, smiling at the evil rhyme scheme that brought to mind. The flame rose up and danced like a tiny reminder of hellfire, and there wasn't even a breeze to interfere. I held it to the tip of the slender white confection and drew in my first breath of carcinogenic smoke in three long weeks. Closing my eyes, I let my lips pull up at the corners in sheer bliss and blew the smoke slowly from them.

"Oh, that's good," I whispered. Then I opened my eyes and met the priest's. "Thank you, Father."

"You can call me Tomas."

He pronounced it Toe-MAHS, with the accent on the "mahs." Italian? Spanish? A priest, either way. As in forbidden. Hands

54

off. Don't even think about it.

"Thanks." I took another puff, saluted him with the cigarette between my fingers, and turned to continue my walk to work, smoking all the way and pointedly ignoring the people who waved their hands in front of their faces and coughed big fake coughs when I passed them, even though they had plenty of room to give me a wider berth. "It's still legal on the sidewalk, dumb-ass."

"That's quite a temper you have there."

I frowned, turning around. That gorgeous priest was following me, just a couple of steps behind.

"I'm sorry. Was this your only one? Did you want to share?" *No effing way.* I looked at him, and my eyes tripped over the dimple in his cheek when he smiled. *Okay, I'll share.*

"I have another. Just waiting to get to a spot with a little more room around it."

"Don't tell me you're scared of the fake-coughers?"

"Not at all. Just see no need to offend everyone I pass on my way."

"On your way to where?" I asked.

He hesitated just long enough that I knew something was off. This was not a chance encounter, and given the shit that had been going on with me, and the fact that I had no memory of a long section of last night, I got a little shiver right up my spine. I don't know that I had any specific theory about what he might have had to do with it, but I was pretty sure there must be something.

Then he said, "Flowers. I need flowers."

"Flowers." I sucked in another drag. Half gone already. They really ought to make those loosies in 100s. If someone was desperate enough pay a buck for a smoke, they would certainly pay two for a longer one. "Just by coincidence, I work at a flower shop."

"Which one?" he asked.

"Pink Petals. Four more blocks."

He smiled. "May I walk with you?"

This man was not safe. There were a thousand voices whispering things in my head, and I couldn't understand a single one of them, but being near him made them louder. And yet for some reason I heard myself tell him, "Suit yourself."

So we walked. And the quiet got a little awkward, so I said, "What's the occasion, *Padre*?"

"Occasion?"

"You're looking for a florist. That usually suggests an occasion." I puffed and savored, and figured his company was a small price to pay for the pleasure. Besides, his company wasn't all that unpleasant.

"I just want to send some flowers to a friend. Maybe you can help me with that."

"Bet I can. You looking for anything in particular?"

"I'll know it when I see it."

"And is this for what? A birthday? Anniversary?"

"Samhain Eve, actually."

I stopped dead with my smoke halfway to my lips. He'd even used the correct Irish Gaelic pronunciation, *Sow-en.*

He was watching me, gauging my reaction, I was sure. "Halloween was last night. You're a little late, aren't you?"

"I didn't say Halloween. I said Samhain Eve. It's the original Halloween. This year it falls on —"

"November seventh," I blurted, then barely resisted clapping a hand over my mouth.

I looked up to see him nodding in a self-satisfied way. "So you do know about Samhain," he said.

"I'm a lapsed Wiccan, and yes, I know about Samhain."

"Lapsed?"

I shrugged. "It's all just superstition. So's your path, by the way. I'm an equal opportunity atheist."

"Wouldn't know it by your jewelry."

57

My hand flew to the pentacle hanging against my sweater, between my breasts. "It's a pretty piece. Nothing more."

"I see."

"In addition to knowing about Samhain, I also know that, as a rule, Catholic priests do not follow witches, lapsed or otherwise, around New York City on the day after Halloween. So would you mind telling me just what it is you want from me?"

His smile faltered, and he lowered his head. "I'm not a Catholic priest."

Note to self — he didn't open with *"I'm not following you."*

"Anglican?" I chanced.

"Gnostic."

My brows went up.

"A very-little-known Gnostic sect, actually, known as the Keepers of the Pact."

"Vroom, vroom." I made a twisting motion with my hands, and then, when he didn't smile, sang a few notes. Nothing. He was just staring at me, those dark brown eyes trying to swallow my soul.

And my soul was wanting to be swallowed. Utterly wanting it.

"So you need an arrangement —"

"I don't need an arrangement, Indy. I need you."

I closed my eyes tight, sighed hard. "I was

58

afraid you were going to say something like that." So, he was some kind of stalker, then. I took the last puff of my smoke, looked sadly at the butt, wondering how it had gone so fast, and dropped it down a sewer grate. "Look, I don't know what you're up to here, but —"

"I'll tell you, if you'll let me. Will you give me five — maybe ten — minutes? Will you do that for me?"

"Do I really need the whole spiel, Father? Can't you just hit the highlights? Nutshell it for me?"

"All right." He took my arm and led me off the sidewalk toward a café where they still had a few tables set up outside. It was only another block to Pink Petals. I could see the sign from here. We sat down as if we planned to order breakfast. And then he looked me straight in the eyes. "This is going to sound — well, insane. I didn't believe it at first. But I'm changing my mind." He took a breath, lifted his chin, held my eyes and sort of rushed ahead. "There is a demon who is going to try to come through a portal into our world on Samhain Eve. If he succeeds, he could very well bring about the end of mankind. You are destined to help me stop him."

I tightened my lips, inhaled, nodded

59

slowly, surreptitiously looking around us to see if I could spot a cop. Just my luck, not a single one in sight. "Hoookay. Um, I am pretty sure you have the wrong girl, Father Tomas." (Emphasis on the *Mahs.*) I got to my feet, inching sideways, clear of the table.

"The woman I'm looking for has lived many lifetimes, Indy, including one in ancient Babylon in which she and her two sisters were executed for the practice of witchcraft."

His words slammed into me like a baseball bat in the hands of Derek Jeter. I stopped moving and tried very hard not to look the least bit intrigued, not to meet his eyes as I asked, "Executed . . . how?" Despite my best efforts, my voice came out hoarse and wobbly.

"Pushed from a cliff."

I felt it again, those hands at my back, warm, the touch filling me with utter pleasure and horrible grief all at the same time. I felt the moment when my feet left the solid earth, and the sickening way my stomach seemed to float upward as my body fell. I heard the wind whipping past my ears, tugging my hair.

I sank into the chair again, shook the vision away before I had to relive that horrible impact, and kept my eyes lowered. "I think you're probably a little bit disturbed, and maybe not even a real priest." My voice was very low, very soft, the words delivered in a slow, deliberate monotone. "I'm going to go now, and if you follow me, I'm afraid I'll have to call the police."

He sighed, lowering his head. "Call them with what, Indy?"

Frowning, I started to reach for my Black-Berry in its handy pocket on the side of my French vanilla suede Louis Vuitton bag, but it wasn't there. I must have lost it . . . probably in the subway last night.

When I looked up he held it in his hands.

"Where did you get my phone?"

Touching the screen a few times, he laid the phone faceup on the table and slid it across to me.

"How did you . . ."

"Look," he said.

I frowned down at my phone at the familiar black box of an online video just as it began to play. It took a few seconds for me to realize that I was the star of the piece.

I snatched up the phone and stared in disbelief as I, Indira Simon, wearing the very same clothes I'd had on for the ritual last night, flung my hands out toward a knife-wielding gangbanger and without so much as touching him, sent him flying so hard his pants fell the rest of the way down before his butt hit the concrete. Then I spun around, flinging my hands toward another, and his head bounced back as if I'd delivered an uppercut to the jaw. Only, like before, I'd never touched him.

The way I was moving was like tai chi on fast-forward. Graceful, rapid, powerful. I yelled something at them, but in some strange language that sounded made up. The old man ran away, looking back over his shoulder at me like I'd sprouted horns or something. And then I got nailed from behind and went down hard. But I sprang up again, did a flip — *a fucking flip* — that seemed to defy gravity and every other law of physics and whipped my hands once more, shouting more words in that same foreign language. I missed that time, nailing a big metal wastebasket and sending it flying like a missile. It came apart when it hit the wall, clanging and banging to the floor. And then the punks closed in on me all at once, kicking the shit out of me for a minute, before someone off camera — probably the person holding it — shouted, "Hey, get the hell away from her. I'm calling the cops!"

The voice was female. And familiar, though I couldn't quite place it.

The punks ran for it. Well, two of them did. The third was basically being dragged between them. And then the camera came closer, as if the person carrying it were bending over me. "Are you okay?" a male voice asked.

I heard the woman ordering this guy away, too. Demanding to know if he'd actually been filming an assault instead of helping. I couldn't see her coming closer, as the camera was still on me as I stared up at it. Close up, my eyes were black — jet-black — except my eyes are blue — and then I said, *"Milik ša zanunzê ihakkim mannu?"*

The camera backed away and the video abruptly ended.

I blinked, staring at my BlackBerry, swearing under my breath as I dragged my finger along the bar at the bottom, managing to rewind the video just a little. Then I hit Play and stared again at the close-up of my face.

Yes, my eyes were black. Irises, pupils, everything. Just two black marbles. Dead-looking eyes.

The woman in the video, a woman I still couldn't think of as me, uttered her strange words again, and I whispered along with them, "Who can know the minds of the Underworld Gods?"

"What's that, Indy?"

63

I'd forgotten the priest was still sitting there and looked up at him quickly. "It wasn't me." I barked the words so fast, I didn't take time to think about them first. But once they were out, I knew it was the only possible argument I could make. I turned the phone toward the priest. "Look at the eyes. Those aren't my eyes. This is just some chick who looks like me. My eyes are blue. Not black. All right?"

"But she looks *just* like you," he said.

"No, she doesn't. She has black eyes. And she knows a lot of martial arts shit I wouldn't even begin to be able to do. And how the hell did you get my phone?"

"You left it at your friend's place."

"My f-friend?" I blinked at him, looking like a doe in the headlights, probably. "You mean Rayne?" *I thought that was her voice on the recording.*

He nodded. "She went after you to return it and saw the last bit of the attack. Then she realized that guy was recording it. She tried to get him to delete it, but he told her to go to hell, that it was going to go viral. She took you home and put you to bed, but she was so upset she forgot she still had your phone on her."

"So . . . you know Rayne?"

He nodded but didn't elaborate. "She

64

knows about my . . . mission. That's why she told me about you."

I was feeling horribly betrayed by my friend, and there were tears in my voice when I asked, "And have I gone viral?"

"Thankfully, no. Most people who commented seem to think it's a hoax. But you and I both know it wasn't. Was it, Indira?"

"It wasn't me, and it wasn't real, and I don't want to talk about it anymore, okay?" I got up, hitched my bag higher on my shoulder, turned to leave. "I'm going to be late for work. I have to go." I started walking.

He came with me, damn him. "Trust me, I know how hard it is to believe all this. It took a lot to convince me, too. Took seeing the impossible with my own eyes, and I'm still arguing with my doubting side."

"Your doubting side is right. I'm not a demon fighter. I'm just a simple ex-witch trying to eke out a life in the big bad city. You've got the wrong girl."

"You're a Warrior Witch. One of three. And I need your help."

"You're not getting it." I strode faster, aiming for the big pink sign on the front of the shop up ahead.

"The dreams are not going to stop, Indy."

"She told you about the dreams, too?" No

65

wonder he knew details — the cliff, the location. Everything.

"The dreams have come to call you to action, to make you remember your mission, your duty, your calling."

I reached the door of the Pink Petals, yanked it open hard and looked back at the priest. "My only *calling* is going to be to nine-one-one unless you get the hell out of my face — now." I swung my arm out, aiming my forefinger back the way we had come, and a gust went with it, just as if I'd caused it, blowing over a wastebasket and sending every discarded piece of sidewalk litter airborne all at once.

Could have been a breeze. Had to have been a breeze.

He lowered his head — I hoped in defeat — took a card from his pocket, and a cigarette along with it, and closed the distance between us. "My cell number is here. I'll be in the city for a while. If anything else happens, please call me. I'm the only one who can help you, Indy."

He handed both the card and the cigarette to me. I would have refused to take the card, but I wanted that smoke — badly — and he knew it, damn him. So I took them both.

His fingers brushed over mine.

I jerked as if electrocuted. A flash, white-hot, blinding bright, flesh on flesh, coppery naked flesh on flesh. Thick black hair, bodies entangling through veils of silk.

I feel his hands on my back.

He gripped my shoulders. "Are you all right?"

His touch burned. And he felt it, too, I knew he did. He held my eyes for a long moment, and chills rushed right up my spine. Tears — tears, for crying out loud — burned in my eyes.

He blinked as if stunned, dragged his gaze from mine, pushed a hand through his thick, dark hair, much the way I wanted to do.

Stop it! He's a priest!

I straightened, realizing he'd grabbed me because I'd nearly fallen over backward, knocked off balance by that brief, vivid flash of lovers entwined. "I'm fine."

"No, you're not. And we both know it. It's going to get worse for you, Indy. I'll help you. Even if you refuse to help me, all right?"

I squinted at him, delivering my patented "Who the fuck do you think you are?" look, proudly made in Brooklyn.

But he just turned and walked back the way we'd come, moving in long, powerful strides as I noticed the breadth of his shoulders. He had to be *cut* underneath his black priestly clothes. I wondered if Gnostic priests from the Leaders of the Pack sect took vows of celibacy, then shook the thought away. It didn't matter. I was never going to see the man again.

However, there was a certain high priest-ess who was going to get a fucking earful as soon as I got off work. Because if this guy was her idea of a confidant, she was the most messed-up witch I'd ever heard of.

Then I looked down at my forefinger and wondered if I had really made that phantom whirlwind kick up, and whether I could do it again.

3

Hours later, my workday finished and another long night alone the only thing on my to-do list, I figured I had nothing to lose. If I had somehow tapped into a power beyond everyday witchcraft — which was really not a lot more than positive thinking, focus and luck, or so I'd always thought — then I might as well use it.

I put an old coffee mug I wasn't overly fond of on the counter. It was a putrid yellow shade and had come with a set of four that someone had given me. I'd already broken the other three. Time to get rid of this one.

Standing back a few feet, I focused my eyes on the cup, my arm bent at the elbow, forefinger aimed at the ceiling. When I felt ready, I bought my arm down fast, aiming right at the mug and willing it to explode to smithereens.

It didn't even wiggle.

Huh. Okay, reload and try again. This time I used a sideways sweep of my arms. But nothing. Drawing like a gunfighter didn't work, either. I sank onto a stool for a break, and quickly flipped open my BlackBerry and searched for that video of me, found it, played it, reviewed my moves, tried to find a pattern.

Okay, okay, I had a little more flourish, a little more flair and a lot of anger in my black alien eyes, in the vid. I set the phone down, got to my feet, shook my arms and shoulders to loosen the muscles, cracked my knuckles. "All right, I got this. You're going down, cup."

I attacked again.

And again, the cup just stood there. I think it was looking defiant.

"Well, shit."

I heaved a giant disappointed sigh and decided to resort to the more mundane forms of magic. Maybe I had been just a solitary, but I'd still been a witch. "And a witch knows how to deal with unwanted nightmares and hunky priests poking their nosy noses into her problems. Even if she can't explode innocent coffee cups at will."

I got busy moving furniture.

An hour later I stood back and surveyed my work.

The living room of my three-room apartment was no longer a living room but a temple. I'd pushed the love seat — love seat, what a joke — and chairs past the countertop that divided the living room from the eat-in kitchenette. They filled that tiny space. My psychedelic print love seat had my retro lime-green rocker recliner balanced precariously on top of it. I'd dragged the coffee table I'd rescued from the curb out of the way. It had started out ordinary, but I'd sanded it down, painted it yellow, and then added swirly vines and leaves and blossoms with teeth in them to cover its entire surface. The only thing that I'd paid for, besides the paint, was the custom cut piece of Plexiglas I'd screwed onto the top to protect it.

My living room was bare now, except for the contents of my old treasure chest. I'd laid out seashells and tumbled stones on the beige carpet — God, I hated beige — in a circle big enough to enclose the entire room. I'd set votive candles in tiny clear glass holders at the four cardinal points. I'd placed a black one in the center, inside my old iron cauldron.

I didn't believe in magic anymore. I reminded myself of that over and over again. I was just doing this as a sort of . . . precaution. As a "just in case I'm wrong" thing. All the lights in my small apartment were turned off, except for the little bulb in the tall floor lamp whose base was a tarnished copper mermaid. I'd found it in a thrift store and scored it for ten bucks. It was worth a million to me. I had just enough light to work by, and I would turn even that off once I lit the candles.

My drapes were drawn, door locked, phones turned off. I was naked. I'd taken a quick shower to rinse away any negative vibes that might have been clinging to me from the day. It was tradition, and while I didn't expect any of this to work, *because I didn't believe in magic,* I also wanted to do it right. When the spell failed, I didn't want to wonder if it was because I'd done a slipshod job of casting it.

I took a few deep breaths, and stepped into the circle of shells and stones, lifted my hand and imagined a beam of light drawing a magic circle of energy. I led it backward, following the outline of shells and stones. Counterclockwise. Widdershins, in witch-speak. I opened the quarters in reverse order, too, lighting candles as I went. This was a banishing spell, after all. I didn't have formal coven training, but I knew my shit. I'd only half believed, even when I was practicing. But tonight I was going full throttle. Giving magic one final chance to prove to me that it was real.

I guess seeing myself on that video, wielding what looked like invisible power from my own two hands, had shaken my disbelief. Or maybe I was just wishing it was real. 'Cause, hell, who wouldn't?

With all the candles dancing and sandalwood incense filling the entire place with its exotic scent, I reached for the mermaid lamp and turned it off.

Soft yellow candlelight threw shadows around my feet that danced like little fairies and shadowy gnomes. I inhaled the scent of hot wax and dusky smoke. My body and mind responded instantly.

Because these are all psychological triggers due to repeated use in the past, shifting my brain waves into alpha rhythm. It's not magic, it's post-hypnotic suggestion.

Every ounce of tension left my muscles, my eyes went soft, and my lips pulled into a relaxed, easy smile. My heartbeat slowed. My breathing, too. Every part of me felt easier, lighter. And there was a tightness in my throat and a hotness behind my eyes.

Okay, okay, I miss it. Doesn't make it real. Just makes it . . . nice.

I knelt in front of the black candle inside

the cauldron in the center of the room, my eyes getting lost in the flame until it went out of focus and became a blob of light. "I call upon the darkest form of the Mother. I call upon the Lady of Death and Transformation. The Guardian of the Crossroads. She whose cold hand leads us from this life into the next. Goddess of the Underworld, of the dead, of the past, of every witch who ever lived, and those I have been before. I call you." I closed my eyes, opened my arms, tilted my head back and waited to feel the presence of the Goddess, who I never called by any specific name.

But then, for some reason a name whispered from my lips without my consent. "Ishtar," I whispered. "Ishtar, heed the call of thy priestess." My eyes popped open. *What made me say that?*

A sudden crash spun me around as my big living room window exploded. I fell to one side, reflexively raising my arms to shield my face from the flying glass. The wind, on what had been a perfectly calm night, whipped my drapes inward and swirled through the apartment like a twister. The mermaid lamp slammed to the floor. My Warhol print soared off the wall and hit me in the forearm — aiming for my head.

The candles blew out, and the whirlwind

kept raging.

I jumped to my feet to try to deal with it, though I had no idea how — turn on the light? cover the window? call 9-1-1? — but something stopped me. I held steady, somehow knowing I had to ignore the chaos and finish what I'd started.

I sank onto my knees once again, the windstorm still raging around me, my hair blowing into tangles that would rival Medusa's, and resumed the goddess pose, arms up and outstretched. "Nightmares have plagued me. But they will plague me no more. I banish them!"

The wind seemed to grow even stronger.

"This priest who follows me, thinking I am some relic of a past life, I banish him, as well. He will plague me no more! By the power of Ishtar, I command it!"

Hell, that doesn't even sound like my own voice. . . .

Rising to my feet, I stood in the circle's center, and spun widdershins, slowly at first, then faster and faster. "I banish the dreams, I banish the priest, banish the dreams, banish the priest, be gone, be gone, be gone, *be gone!*" With the final words I let myself sink to the floor, releasing the spell into the universe as the wind kept whipping around me. I closed my eyes to stop the room from spinning and muttered, "So mote it be."

Something growled at me, long and low, like a wolf about to spring.

From my position on the floor, feeling almost too shocked to move, I opened my eyes. "What the fuck was that?"

The cauldron in the middle of the floor was swirling with colors that glowed and shifted and moved. It was the only light in the room. And the growl . . . It came again. From that cauldron.

I crawled closer and looked at the impossible.

The swirling, hazy colors inside the cauldron were real. I stared into them, through them. A shape formed. A torso — nude, male, muscular. And then a head, a man's head, except that it wore a demonically twisted grimace of anger, and its eyes blazed red with an energy that blasted me with pure pain. It hit me hard, and I couldn't look away. And as I stared unwillingly at the image of the beast inside the cauldron, it opened its mouth and released a roar of anguish and rage. It had fangs. Cloven hooves. A tail?

The Devil himself?

But I don't believe in the Devil.

I jerked backward, but it held my eyes. I tried, I really did, to look away, but it was like this thing held me.

And then the image in the cauldron changed. The colors swirled again, overtaking the beast, hiding him, and then changing from oranges and reds and yellows to soft blues and gentle greens as a different face formed. A woman's face this time, a black-haired beauty in flowing robes. Her brows were thick and dark, her eyes like shining chunks of coal.

I know her! She's one of the women from my dream!

Her full lips parted, and she whispered two words. "Help him."

"Who? The priest?"

The beautiful woman lowered her eyes to look down, into the swirling orange and yellow depths at the demon I'd just seen.

"Him?"

"Help him."

"But I don't . . . I don't know how. I don't know what I'm supposed to do. How am I — Wait. Wait!" I reached my hand toward the iron kettle as if I could grab hold of the image inside, but it was fading. The cauldron turned slowly black again. "At least tell me your name!" But it was useless. She was gone.

Lilia.

The wind died with a soft sound that

might have been nothing more than its final gasping breeze. I stayed on the floor, lowered my head to the carpet and tried to hold back the crying jag that was fighting to bust out.

Great. I'm being sacrificed again.

I stood near the cliff, not on the edge yet, but tied between two posts nearby, arms raised and stretched to either side. The goddess position again. Memories — yeah, memories, not illusions — flooded my brain. I heard a crack and felt the brutal slash of a whip slicing my back, and it was as real as anything I've ever felt in my life. And far more painful. It went on until the cutting, burning pain was everywhere all at once. I was shaking all over in agony. It was unbearable, and I longed to pass out, but I didn't.

I screamed until my voice was gone and I could scream no more. My faith went with it, severed along with the ropes that held me as the soldiers cut me down and retied my hands behind my bleeding back. Then I — no, we — were marched closer to the edge of the cliff. I'd seen him again, that other man near the rocks, where soldiers held him. He was more battered and beaten than we were. He'd been forced to watch as we'd been whipped, and he was being forced to watch still, as we were about to be sent plummeting to our deaths on the rocks far, far below. He struggled, though he had to be near death. Hell of a man, that one. Too bad they probably killed him right after us.

I looked sideways at my sister Lilia. She was the youngest, and I was amazed at how straight she stood. How proudly she held her head. She looked like royalty. I was crying softly, almost silently, unlike my other sister, Magdalena, who was loud and sloppy. But little Lilia, the one we'd always thought of as the weakest of us, had been as cruelly tortured as we had, and yet she was the strong one now.

We were at the cliff's edge.

Wakeupwakeupwakeup!

I felt those warm, familiar hands at my back. And again I had that totally fucked-up feeling of liking his touch. His palms warm on my skin, carefully not touching the raw ruin of my flesh. My toes curled instinctively to grip the smooth stone beneath my feet, trying to hang on.

I was going to die on those rocks down there. With my sisters.

Again.

4

Tomas had parked his Volvo across the street from Indira Simon's apartment building, where he had a beautiful view of her windows, and spent the entire night there, trying to keep watch, hoping he would know if something went wrong. He saw other tenants come and go, and at one point, while out stretching his legs, he caught the door before it swung closed and jammed the latch, so he could get in if necessary.

Yes, he'd thought Father Dom was two-thirds of the way to insanity with his obsessive predictions about this demon and its witches. Until he'd seen that subway video. And met *her.* That woman was something else. He could feel it just by looking into her eyes. And when she'd swung her arm in anger, a burst of genuine power had erupted from her.

She'd been as surprised by that as he had.

And now everything he'd been so sure was

just the outrageous exaggerations of an aging priest with delusions of grandeur seemed like it just might be real, after all. Which threw everything else he thought he'd known into question.

His crisis of faith, his decision to leave the church, all of that, he'd decided, had to be put aside until this was finished. Because if he'd been wrong — well, he couldn't undo that. But he could carry out this mission for Dom, at least far enough to make sure it really was just part of an old man's ramblings. Maybe generations of old men. The rest . . . the rest could wait.

He knew already that some things Dom had told him were utterly false. Things about her. She was not evil. No demon's whore. Not that one. She hadn't tried to seduce him or ensorcell him as Dom had predicted she would. She'd run from him instead.

But he'd followed. Because he had a feeling that just wouldn't leave him alone. Clearly some of the things Dom had believed in for so long *were* true. Were, perhaps, unfolding as had been predicted. And the most important thing that meant to Tomas was that she might be in danger. So while this would be his final mission as a priest, it was still his mission — and he *was* still a priest. And he intended to do it right. Maybe that would assuage his guilt over leaving the collar behind, and for not believing in Dom's obsession until now.

He had expected that he might catch a glimpse of Indy moving around behind her apartment windows, though the drapes were drawn. He had *not* expected to see her on the building's rooftop just before dawn.

When he caught sight of her up there his heart almost stopped. She was standing near the brick safety wall, which reached almost to her bare shoulders, her hands along the top of it, the wind blowing through her hair. It looked as if she was getting ready to climb up.

"God, save her," he whispered.

He was out of the car instantly, racing to the building's door and yanking it open, glad he'd thought far enough ahead to disable the lock. He took the stairs two at a time all the way to the roof. Then he slid to a stop. She was standing on the wall now, completely naked. Wobbling dangerously, she held her arms behind her back as if they were tied there, even though they weren't. It was still dark, but there was something staining her back — crisscrossing stripes with scarlet rivulets running from them. And something else, a tattoo on her lower back. Three rows of symbols.

Was that *cuneiform*?

God, what had happened to her? And what was he supposed to do?

Waking a sleepwalker was a bad idea — especially when they were standing seventy feet off the ground. But he couldn't just let this play out and hope she didn't plummet to her death.

Quietly, he approached from behind. She was standing still, her short hair riffled by the wind, her skin pebbling with goose bumps in the cold. She had to be freezing. It was the second of November, for crying out loud. As he crept slowly nearer, she leaned forward, arching her back. No more time. Tomas lunged, snapping his arms around her just above hip level, which was as high as he could reach. The momentum of her body tried to pull him over with her, but he braced one foot against the brick wall and jerked her backward, hard. He landed on his back on the rooftop with her butt on his chest and her lower back against his face. No sooner had he begun to release his pent-up breath in a sigh of relief than she was scrambling off him and onto her feet, turning to look down at him, stark accusation in her huge black eyes.

"Atta bal□ata u anāku mūt amât!" she

shouted.

Then her eyes rolled back in her head and she collapsed straight down, as if her legs had dissolved beneath her.

Tomas got onto his feet. She'd bled on his clothes. On his face. Her back was cut to ribbons. Bending, he gathered her carefully into his arms, then turned to carry her back down to her apartment.

"Owwwww."

I was facedown on my bed and hurting like hell, and when I tried to roll over, a strong male hand on my shoulder kept me lying where I was.

Who the hell is that, and what is he doing in my apartment?

I twisted my head to see. It was him. Of course it was him. Hunky Father Tomas was sitting on the edge of my bed. His face was twisted with what looked like worry, and his hands held gauze and a bottle of something aromatic.

"Father Tomas? What happened? Why are you here? And why the hell am I hurting so bad?" I craned my neck a little farther and got a nice clear view of my own bare ass. "I'm naked!" I tried to roll over again, but his hand held me still.

"It's all right, I'm a priest." He wasn't trying to be funny. He tugged the bedsheet up a little to cover my cheeks. "Lie very still or it'll hurt even more. If you'll stop trying to roll, I'll show you what's hurting in the mirror." The bed moved as he got up and walked to my dresser. I tried to remember whether I'd left anything embarrassing on it. Tampons, undies. I wasn't exactly an immaculate housekeeper. He was back in seconds, holding my silver hand mirror at an angle that allowed me to see my back. And when I did, my stomach heaved and I closed my eyes. My back was covered with deep, long cuts. Stripes. Like a whip would leave behind if —

A whip.

"Shit."

The nightmare or memory or hallucination or whatever the hell it was came back to me so hard and fast I had to jam my face into the pillow to muffle the sob that lurched inside my chest. I was pretty sure he heard it anyway.

"What happened last night?" he asked.

"I don't know." I turned far enough so my words could emerge unmuffled. "I was . . . I was trying to work a spell. You must have seen the living room."

"I saw the circle. The candles. Figured that much out."

Frowning, I twisted my head a little farther. "The circle. The candles . . . that's all?" He hadn't mentioned the shattered window, broken glass, toppled lamp, tangled curtains.

"Furniture piled in the kitchen?"

I blinked. "There was a storm. It smashed the window to hell and gone."

He was staring at me, silent.

"Didn't it?"

He shook his head slowly. "It must have been part of another nightmare," he said. "I spotted you on the roof. You damn near went over the side, but . . ."

"But you saved me." I no longer cared if he saw my tears. He'd seen my bare ass and my living nightmare. What were a few tears?

"I was across the street in my car. I saw you up there and — They're going away."

"What?" I was confused by the sudden change of subject.

"The wounds, they're . . . they're going away." He held up the mirror again.

I ignored it. Pushing past him and his mirror to get to my feet, dragging the sheet with me and holding it in front of my body, I turned my back toward the large mirror on my dresser and looked over my shoulder at my reflection.

The stripes across my back were closing

86

up, forming small pink lines, like battle scars, but then they started fading, too. There was a tattoo, as well, on my lower back, and I knew damn well I'd never had a tattoo in my life. Odd little symbols in neat rows. But they, too, were fading fast. Ten seconds, I stood there. Tomas came and stood right beside me, staring into that mirror. I didn't even care that my ass was exposed again. Ten seconds, and at the end of them nothing remained of those ghastly wounds except for a few smears of blood Tomas must have missed in his ministrations.

I looked at the floor, belatedly pulling the sheet the rest of the way around me.

"This thing — it could have killed you tonight, Indira."

It was true. I shivered with the knowledge that it was absolutely true.

"Next time I might not get to you in time."

"What can you possibly do about it?"

"Take you with me to Ithaca. I'll help you solve this thing. I'll make it go away, I swear I will, if you will just help me keep the demon where he belongs in return. Please, Indy. Before he can hurt you any more."

"Why Ithaca?"

"It's where we need to be. I'll explain more on the way. All right?"

I hated to admit that I was losing my skepticism. I hated to even *think about* believing any of this. But it was real. I'd seen it, right there in my own mirror. I'd seen it. I was still shaking, and it pissed me off. But I ignored that and nodded, a quick, jerky motion that was anything but graceful.

"All right," I said. "You win."

Tomas had told me to take the day to get ready, and to phone if I needed him. I didn't. I made arrangements at work — I had five days' vacation time coming, and if that wasn't enough, I could tack on a few sick days. I didn't need to tell them I was actually talking about my mental health. I packed up my things, enough to last a week, got some cash out of the bank and tried to call Rayne. She didn't answer, so I had to settle for leaving her a snotty voice mail message asking if she'd lost her mind, sharing my most intimate confessions with a demon-fighting priest.

That night, I took an antihistamine along with cold medicine, and for once, I didn't dream. Slept like a rock, in fact. And damn but I needed it.

Next morning I showered, dressed and met him out front as planned, even while wondering if I'd lost my freaking mind to be buying into any of this.

Of course, the bloodstains on my sheets said I wasn't crazy at all. What was happening to me was completely insane, but I wasn't imagining it or dreaming it or hallucinating it — it was real. And who the hell else was going to help me figure it out? Who else would even believe me?

Rayne, maybe. But I'd gone to Rayne. And she had basically handed me off to this priest. As angry as I was at her for that, I trusted her. She wouldn't set some lunatic on my trail. She must believe he could help.

He pulled up right on time to take me off to Neverland in his sagging chariot.

Father Tomas's car was an aging, once-white Volvo station wagon that looked as if it had been through a series of natural disasters. Its color had yellowed to a sort of dull cream that was flaking off in places. He stowed my gear in the back, like he was a gentleman and I was a helpless little female. I stood on the curb just staring at the car, sort of in awe that anything that ancient could still run.

He caught my expression and smiled. "It's a classic. A 1967 Amazon."

"Looks like you *found* it in the Amazon."

His smile didn't falter. "I'm restoring it

myself. It's a . . . hobby, I guess."

"Heaven help me. My savior is not only a priest but a motor head."

He opened a door that looked as if it weighed a ton and held it for me. "Trust me, she runs like a dream."

"She looks like a nightmare." Still, I got in and dutifully buckled up, surprised that the inside looked pretty nice. Definitely a lot better than I'd expected.

In seconds he was behind the wheel, turning the key, smiling at the sound of the engine. "Hear that?"

"Sounds like a car, all right. So it only *looks* like it's going to fall apart on the road, then?"

He rolled his eyes. "Mechanics first, comfort second, cosmetics last of all. It's the unwritten motor head code."

It was comfortable, I had to give him that. There was enough room in the back to transport a small sofa. Okay, that's an exaggeration, but it was big. Despite the super-soft leather and the ultracozy seat, though, I still felt like shit, no matter how I sat.

"Your back?" he asked.

I sent him an almost irritated look, though I was secretly impressed and a little surprised by how much attention the guy was paying to me. "It doesn't really hurt. It's

like a phantom pain, every time I remember
—" I stopped there, because giving voice to
anything more would only conjure it again.
The brutal lashes of the whip. Oh, shit, too
late. "You don't miss much, do you?"

"You're my calling, Indira. I'm not likely
to miss a thing now that I've found you."

"Hell, Tomas, if you weren't wearing that
collar, I'd think you were about to propose."

He looked at me briefly, then pulled away
from the curb. I could have sworn a hint of
panic appeared on his face, but maybe I'd
imagined it. And that was another reason I
wasn't worried about going off with the guy.
He was a priest, and he hadn't done a single
thing out of line. I was the one having
impure thoughts, not him.

I figured I'd give him a break and change
the subject all the same. "So tell me about
your demon fighting thing. You do it often?"

He smiled a little. "Never. And it's just
the one demon."

"Does he have a name?"

"I've only heard him called 'He Whose
Name Must Not Be Spoken.' "

"Are you shitting me? He doesn't even
have a name?" I looked at him, waiting for
the punch line. But he only smiled and
shook his head.

"I know. I know how crazy it sounds. And

to tell you the truth, I was pretty skeptical myself until I saw those marks on your back."

"Yeah. Yeah, I gotta say they made an impression on me, too." I didn't want to talk about that, though. My world had taken a turn for the macabre, and I was trying to focus on the parts that went down a little easier. Those phantom lashes from that phantom whip had left real wounds, and that flat-out scared me too much to dwell on just yet. I'd get to it. But right now, I thought, let's stick to the easy stuff. Stuff about him and this so-called demon of his.

"So how many priests are there on your . . . um . . . anti-demon squad?"

"Two," he said. "Me and the man who trained me, Father Dom. You see, one priest from our sect —"

"The Leaders of the Pack." That's right, keep it light.

"The Keepers of the Pact," he corrected. He gave me an odd look, like he was amused but trying to figure me out at the same time. I liked the way his eyes felt when they moved over my face, probably because I got the feeling he liked what he saw.

Priest, Indy. Priest. Priest. Priest.

"One of us is chosen from each generation as the Guardian of the Portal. Dom chose me. Just as he was chosen by his predecessor."

"And what was *his* name?" I asked. "Father Dom's predecessor?"

Tomas frowned. "You know, he never told me."

"I bet it rhymed. Tom. Dom. Rom, maybe?"

The look he sent me this time was a searching frown, like he was seeing through my plot. Yeah, I was using humor to keep this light, to try to pretend nothing all that serious was happening. But I was also scared half to death. And I was pretty sure it showed. I got the feeling there wasn't much I could hide from those perceptive brown eyes of his.

"When the current Guardian begins to age, he chooses and trains his replacement. That tradition has continued since the time of ancient Babylon."

"Wait a minute, wait a minute," I said, holding up a hand to stop him. "Even I know ancient Babylon is BC, as in Before Christ."

"Fifteen hundred and one BC, to be precise."

"Pre-Christian, either way. Can't have a Gnostic sect, no matter how rare, prior to Christianity, can you?"

He smiled widely, nodding his head not in agreement but in approval. "You're smart. I like that."

"Yeah, yeah, I'm freakin' Einstein. But you didn't answer my question. Nice dodge, though."

"It was a compliment, not a dodge. And it was sincere."

I gave him a thank-you nod and tried not to warm at the praise. He hadn't said I was a knockout, driving him mad with carnal lust. He'd said I was smart. That's all. Down, girl. I tried to focus on the city as he maneuvered the relic through it, instead of on the intense awareness that there was only a foot of space between us. That space, though, wasn't empty. It was crackling and snapping.

"Priests of numerous religions have been entrusted with the mission. From the Cult of Marduk to the Egyptian followers of Ra to the earliest Jews. The calling doesn't end, it just converts. It's only recently that Dom realized the way the stars are lining up on Samhain this year makes it a propitious time for the demon to come through. He probably should have seen it sooner, but he's getting a little . . . unfocused."

He means senile, I thought. I nodded as if that made perfect sense when it actually made none. "You talk about him a lot. Dom."

I spotted the crease between his brows when I said that. Worry? Something. I wanted to smooth it away with my finger, whatever it was.

"Dom took me in when I was a kid."

"Took you in —"

"I was an orphan."

"You were an orphan?" Wait a minute, did my voice just sound like a cheerleader spotting a puppy?

"That's really not on topic at all, though. You were asking why we need to go to Ithaca."

He was changing the subject. And just when I'd decided I was far more interested in his sad childhood than I was in some moldy old Babylonian legend. Even if I *was* somehow intrinsically involved in its fulfillment.

"The Portal is somewhere in Ithaca, at least according to Dom's calculations. By going there, we can not only prevent the demon from coming through this time but destroy him utterly."

"Huh," I said.

"What?" He looked at me, brows raised.

"Well, it's just that —" I shrugged. "I mean, just playing demon's advocate here, but . . . the dude's been in this underworld slammer for three thousand five hundred years now. It seems a little harsh. A lot harsh when you add 'destroy him utterly' to the equation. What did he do, anyway?"

Tomas tipped his head to one side. "I don't know."

"You never asked?"

He shrugged. "It seemed enough that he's a demon."

"Isn't that what they said about witches during the hysteria? I mean, can he even *help* being a demon?"

"You're confusing the issue."

"I don't know that I am. Couldn't he be a *good* demon? Couldn't he have been rehabilitated by now? Open your mind, *Padre.* Think outside the box."

He looked at me as if I'd just sprouted horns and a forked tail.

"There's no such thing as a good demon."

"That's what the witch-hunters said about *us.*"

"What he did isn't as important as what he will do, given the chance."

"And what's that? What's this big bad demon's dastardly goal? No, wait, wait, I remember." I leaned forward, hands on my hips in a superhero pose. "He wants to take over the world."

"I can't believe you're making jokes about this, Indira. Especially given what's been happening to you."

I only shrugged and looked away.

He pulled into the long line of traffic heading onto the bridge, and took the opportunity to turn and stare intently into my eyes. "The goal of every demon is the same. Destruction of all that's good. Perversion of the sacred. Power over the world of man. He could become the anti-Christ, Indy."

I just sat there staring at him, trying to determine whether he actually believed his own words. I mean, he suddenly sounded like a fire-and-brimstone pulpit thumper in a revival tent. I wondered if that was him talking or if he was channeling his precious Dom, and I decided on the latter. "Uh-huh. So we're going to Ithaca to face and annihilate the anti-Christ."

He sighed, lowered his head. "You don't believe me, do you?"

"Not so much, no."

Traffic was at a standstill. His hands gripped the wheel, bumping each other right on top, and I could tell he was squeezing hard.

"And none of it really seems to tie in with what's been happening to me. The dreams. The marks." I touched his shoulder, and he picked his head up fast. "Can you tie it together for me? 'Cause I'm kinda lost."

He nodded. "You and your two sisters lived during the time when he was cast into the Underworld. And you're the only ones with the power to destroy him."

"So it's past life stuff. Destiny stuff. That kind of thing."

He nodded.

I drew a deep breath, blew it out again. "This is scary as hell, you know that?"

"I know." He turned and looked me in the eyes, reaching out to clasp my hands in his. I sucked in a breath and stared down at them. I knew he was only trying to comfort me a little, but it felt like way more. And he felt something, too, I knew he did. The way my hands fit inside his, the warmth of them, and their size and shape and strength. The strangest feeling washed over me as we sat there, facing each other in the comfy front seat of the old Volvo, our eyes locked onto our joined hands as we both began to tremble. It was vivid. Surreal. Dizzying. Like déjà vu.

"Tomas?" My voice emerged soft and raspy, and it didn't help matters. He looked up, into my eyes, and I knew he was as shaken as I was. What *was* this?

Behind us, an idiot laid on his horn, and

we jerked apart. Traffic had moved on without us. I blinked and sat back in my seat, looking anywhere but at Tomas. He pulled the car back into motion, but it bucked and stalled. So he was as flustered as I was. Then he quickly started it again and got moving.

I wanted to change the subject — because really, no matter what was happening to me, it wasn't that big. It couldn't be. I was just . . . me. Not some soldier in a war between God and the Devil or whoever. "I never had breakfast this morning," I said. Damn, my voice had this funny little tremor underneath it. "And I'm starved."

"Okay."

She was afraid, Tomas thought. Scared to death of the horrors he was likely to reveal to her if they kept on talking, and putting off that moment of revelation for as long as she possibly could.

She's arguing for the demon's side, and probably trying to ensorcell you while she's at it.

That was not his own inner voice. That was Dom, lecturing him on the powers of the witch. And while he might have changed his mind about disbelieving the rest of this, he was standing firm on that.

Food was an agreeable distraction, and when he located an IHOP about an hour later and pulled in, he knew by the look of rapture in her eyes that she hadn't *only* been making excuses to end the conversation. She was, by all appearances, ravenous.

And beautiful.

Difficult for him to believe she was one of the three witches whose souls were allegedly bound to a demon. And that was only a small part of what was unbelievable about all of this.

Dom had warned him repeatedly these chosen witches were cagey and clever, and might or might not be aware of their mission, but that he must always presume they were and guard against their tricks. They were powerful women, all three of them. They would sense a man's weakness and use it against him.

Tomas had rolled his eyes at the notion. He'd never thought he had any real weaknesses. Oh, he didn't believe himself perfect by a long shot, but he didn't think he had any particularly lethal vulnerabilities.

Now, though, even *that* belief was being challenged. Because he was attracted to this woman. Sexually attracted. And while he was still a man, a fully functioning one, he hadn't experienced this level of temptation since — well . . . ever. It was growing stronger with every second he spent in her company, and they were going to be together — alone together — for the next week or so.

Was it a spell? Was she, as Father Dom had warned, perfectly aware of her bond with the demon, ready and willing to help him, and using her wiles to enchant and bewitch the priest sent to stop her?

Or was she as innocent as she seemed?

He didn't suppose it mattered, honestly. He had to resist her, had to stop her, and how much she knew or didn't know was irrelevant. Moreover, he had to convince her that her mission, her calling and her key to salvation from the torments afflicting her, were all one and the same: to help him stop the demon from crossing the Portal. When in truth, he was pretty sure her true mission was just the opposite.

The three witches were foretold to be the demon's consorts. They were supposed to help him escape the Portal. But they were also the only ones with the power to stop him.

He supposed he would have to tell her that part of it at some point.

"I'm going to have an omelet," she said as they got out of the car. "A big fat three-egg omelet with a half pound of cheese and ham and mushrooms and — no, wait." She held up a hand, apparently deep in thought. As if the choice was one of the most important of her life. Then she snapped her fingers. "Belgian waffles, with butter melting down the sides and all that whipped cream piled on top, and fruit, and maybe sausage on the side."

She was walking as she was talking, absently rubbing her upper arm. He wondered about that as he held the door open for her and she stepped inside, inhaled, then closed her eyes as if smelling the sweetest perfume. "Coffee," she muttered. "Hail the Goddess Caffeinna."

"That's sort of blasphemous, you know." He was only teasing. He was starting to enjoy her use of sarcasm-laced humor to deflect the things she called scary, even beginning to return it in kind.

"Oh, please, not to the Holy of Holies, Divine Creatrix of the sacred coffee bean." Her attention switched, quick as a heartbeat, to the hostess who'd just appeared to greet them. "Two for breakfast, and a vat of high-test, please. Death to decaf!"

The hostess smiled at her enthusiasm and led the way to a booth.

Indira rubbed her arm again, only this

time she pulled her hand away quickly, as if the arm was sore to the touch. Frowning, Tomas looked at her. "Everything okay?"

"Yeah. Fine." She dropped her hands to her sides.

He wished he could see her arm better, but she'd donned a brown leather jacket with a fake fur collar that looked as if it ought to have a matching helmet and goggles to go with it. Beneath that, she wore a T-shirt that came just to the low-slung top of her skin-tight jeans, so he caught glimpses of bare midriff every time she moved. The jeans were tucked inside a pair of cowgirl-style boots, brown, with stitching and embossing in swirls, loops and flowers, and impossibly high heels.

She looked as if she'd stepped off the cover of some urban style guide. Her T-shirt read Born Again Pagan, and had a triple moon logo that glittered when the light hit it at the right angle. She wore a pentacle, a different one, suspended from a thin silver chain, its star formed in the shape of a gleaming spider's web, with the spider in the center. Its body was a moonstone, its eyes tiny bits of ruby, its legs made of black tourmaline. She had earrings that matched, each with a tiny pentacle web at the earlobe and a thin chain dangling with the spider at the end of it. Same gemstones. Same size.

She might as well have worn a flashing neon sign proclaiming herself a witch. It wasn't a habit he'd noticed in her before, and it sort of belied her claim that she'd become an atheist. Maybe she just felt safer, wearing the symbols of her former faith.

The looks they were getting as they sat at their booth, she in her pentacles, he in his collar, were almost funny. A priest and a witch, having breakfast together. Indira ended up devouring a stack of Belgian waffles and an omelet, washing every other bite down with creamy coffee, and claiming she would quit caffeine again when life returned to normal. He only picked at his own pancakes.

He was too tense to eat, and not only because she was proving to be the biggest test his faith had ever undergone.

Of course, he'd been in a crisis of faith for a while now. And all of this was making him wonder if he'd made the right decision. Because if this was real, after all — if Dom's obsession turned out to be true . . .

But this wasn't the time to ponder those things. That would come later.

Right now, he was about to face a demon. Maybe the devil himself. With a witch as his only ally, a witch who didn't know — or did she? — that she was that demon's friend. Either way, that alliance made her Tomas's enemy.

It seemed unnecessarily risky to take her so near the Portal, since allegedly the demon couldn't pass through without her help. But Dom said it was worth the risk. That she had to be there to help Tomas destroy the demon for good.

He'd trained for this, he'd studied, he knew what had to be done, but that was all back when he thought the whole thing was just an old man's crazy fantasy. But now it was here, real and present. And complicating things further, in all his thoughts on this very topic, he had never counted on liking the woman.

He looked up at her. Sipping her coffee, eyes closed, thick lashes resting on those high-boned cheeks, skin like a ripe peach. He was drawn to her and felt an unbelievable urge to touch her at every opportunity.

She burped, interrupting his thoughts. Her hand flew to her mouth, and her eyes went huge. "Well, that was polite," she said. "Excuse me." Her cheeks were pink with embarrassment, her smile self-deprecating.

She was charming the socks off him, he thought.

He glanced at her plate. Empty. She ran

her forefinger through the syrup on the edge and popped it into her mouth, and he clenched his jaw to keep from groaning out loud. "God, that was good," she said.

"Glad you enjoyed it."

"You eat like a bird, Father Tomas."

"Not normally. Got a lot on my mind."

"Ow!" She gripped her arm again, then frowned and lowered her hand.

"Are you going to let me take a look at that?"

"There's nothing to look at."

He tipped his head to one side. "Clearly, it hurts. You keep grabbing it, then quickly letting go."

"And just as quickly putting it out of my mind. It only hurts if I think about it, so I wish you'd stop reminding me."

"Sorry. It won't happen again." He picked up the check their waitress had dropped, and rose from his seat. "Are you ready?"

The bubbly mood she'd been emanating seemed to burst. Back to reality, he thought. She really was dreading what lay ahead. "Yes. All ready." She got up, too, snatching her mug off the table and taking one last gulp before hurrying to the counter with him. She tugged on his sleeve and said, "Restroom" in a stage whisper. He nodded and tried not to watch her as she walked away.

The restroom was deserted. Perfect. I needed privacy, big-time. 'Cause something *was* going on with my arm, despite my denials to Tomas.

God he was good-looking. And funny. And interesting. So okay, he believed in demons and a fairy tale grimmer than anything the Grimm Brothers could have come up with. *And he's a priest. Don't forget that minor detail.* But no one was perfect.

I pulled off my jacket, wincing as it peeled down over my right arm, then, turned my shoulder toward the big mirror.

My blood rushed straight to my feet, leaving me so damn dizzy I almost fell over. My arm looked as if it had been hacked by a mini-madman with a tiny blade. Little cuts crisscrossed my flesh like a road map, and blood had run everywhere. The inside of my favorite jacket must be soaked in it. Ruined.

Damn it all, Past Self, if you want me to bail on this whole harebrained road trip, you just keep fucking with me.

I looked up at my own face in the mirror, but someone else was looking back at me. Not a pale-faced dirty blonde with a killer sense of style, but a copper-skinned woman with thick black hair hanging long and wavy, heavy brows in desperate need of tweezing, and black, black eyes.

And behind her — no, behind me — stood another woman with similar coloring but a totally different face.

Lilia.

I ought to turn around, see if she's really standing there. I really should.

Too bad I was too scared to move.

She stared at me in the mirror, then suddenly shouted, "Remember, Indira!"

After jumping out of my skin, I yelled right back at her. "Remember *what,* for cryin' out loud!"

"I'll *make you* remember!" I sort of heard her say inside my head. Then she lifted a big curved blade that glinted in the fluorescent restroom lights as she swung it down to carve me up some more.

That was enough to end my paralysis. I spun around, screaming at the top of my lungs. But there was no one behind me.

Before I could even sigh in relief, though, I heard the hissing sound of the invisible blade as it cut the air, and something slashed across my chest. I felt it slicing my flesh, saw the gaping cut opening up like a zipper, saw the blood flowing out of me as I sank to the floor in pain. In terror.

5

The door crashed open, and then Tomas was bending over me. "Indy. Indy, it's all right. It's all right. I'm here. I've got you." His big hand cupped my head, lifting it slightly off the floor as the other one ran over my hair. Wait staff and a customer or two crowded in the doorway to see what was going on, though Tomas's frame mostly blocked me from their view.

Turning their way, he said, "Leave us for a moment, okay? She's had an accident, and I want to get her cleaned up."

"I'll call nine-one-one," a waitress — our waitress, I realized — offered.

"I don't think it's that bad. Let me check her over first, all right?"

"Do you need any —"

"We're fine," he barked in a tone I'd never heard him use before. But it did the trick. The onlookers backed out, and the door swung closed.

Tomas quickly turned his attention back to me. He snatched handfuls of paper towels from the dispenser, soaked them beneath the tap and returned, patting my chest with the icy wet towels. The cold made me gasp and look down. My T-shirt was torn in two, laid open to reveal a long slash across my chest. The blade had sliced my bra dead center, and it gaped, exposing more of me than I liked. Both breasts, almost entirely bare, the bra's lacy cups barely clinging to either side. My eyes shot back to his, but he was intent on patting the blood away from my chest.

"It's not deep, thank God."

I winced at every touch, though he was being gentle. He straightened and then lifted me up and sat me gently on the counter with all the sinks. I had to part my knees so he could get close enough to mop up the blood from my arms, and the feel of him standing there between them was so damn intimate that I noticed it, even amid all the pain and blood.

And fear. I'd never felt so near death as I had when I'd seen that blade flashing down at me. Except in the dreams.

"What happened?" he asked, stepping away long enough to soak a fresh handful of towels.

"I — I — I . . ." *Why the hell won't my mouth work?*

His gaze snapped to mine, and instead of wiping away more of the blood, as I was expecting, he reached around me to lay the fresh batch on the back of my neck. I tipped my head forward, closed my eyes.

"It's all right now. I'm going to wash the rest of the blood away, okay? Are you ready?"

"It hurts." *God, I sound like such a baby.*

"I know, Indy. I know. I'll be careful." He got the towels so wet they were dripping, and squeezed the cool water over the cuts on my arms. I covered my breasts with one arm while he took care of the other, and then switched sides. I tried not to look at the injuries but couldn't stop the tears that burned past my tightly closed lids. Even the trickles of cold water hurt. Finally he tossed the wet towels aside and used his cupped hands to do the job.

"You know how you were telling me the more you think about pain, the worse it is?"

I nodded, the motions jerky, my eyes stinging.

"Well, focusing on something good works even better. So I want you to try that for me. Think about something good, okay?"

"I'll try." I thought for a minute, and then

I almost smiled a little.

"Got something?"

"Yeah."

"Good. You just keep focusing on that, all right? Whatever it is, just —"

"It's you," I whispered.

Tomas went very still. I lifted my head to meet his eyes.

"You're like some kind of superhero, you know that? The way you came busting in here, the way you're trying to take care of me, like I'm the helpless female. Normally that would piss me off, but you do it in a way that doesn't. And you're cover-model gorgeous, too. So I . . ." I shrugged and let my voice trail off.

He sighed and returned to rinsing away the blood.

"I looked in the mirror, Tomas, and I wasn't me. I was someone else. And there was this other woman standing behind me, yelling at me to remember, and then she was slashing me with a blade. Only she wasn't there. No one was there, but it kept on cutting." My voice broke, and I couldn't speak anymore.

Tomas caught my chin in his hands and nodded at my arm. "She wasn't just cutting you. She was writing something. Look."

I was afraid to look, but I did it anyway. I

turned slightly on the counter, checking out my arm in the big mirror behind me. The blood was mostly gone, and the new trickles seemed to have stopped, so the shapes of the cuts were evident. Symbols had been carved into my flesh, odd, ancient-looking symbols that I knew, somehow, were words, letters, writing of some kind. The cuts in my skin weren't deep. They'd bled, and they'd hurt like hell, as if the blade had been hot. But the burning pain was already fading.

"What does it say?" I asked in a whisper.

"I have no idea." Then he blinked. "They're disappearing, they're healing, just like the marks of the whip did."

"Wait," I said, wondering if the other mark had returned, as well. I lifted my shirt in back, looking over my shoulder into the mirror. Sure enough, the tattoo was there, just like before, and fading fast.

He patted his pockets in search of his phone but came up empty. "I left my cell in the car. We need to get photographs before they're gone entirely. Do you —"

I nodded at my gorgeous jacket, lying discarded on the floor, and he quickly picked it up, searching the pockets. He came up with my BlackBerry and fumbled around trying to find the camera function.

By the time he did, and aimed it at my lower back, the marks had vanished, so he tried to capture the ,ones on my arms, but they'd faded to pale pink welts, crisscrossing my skin.

He snapped a shot or two as I tried to hold the sliced edges of my T-shirt together to cover my boobs, then he gave up and shook his head. "Gone. As if they were never there."

"Wish the bloodstains inside my jacket would disappear that easily," I muttered. "Bitch ruined my leather."

He bent and picked up the jacket, turned the sleeves inside out and easily tore the ruined lining out, then tossed it into the garbage. Using more wet paper towels, he wiped the remaining blood from the leather and then handed the jacket to me.

I'd slid off the counter by then but was none too steady on my feet. And there was blood all over the floor.

"I'm going to clean this place up," he told me as I pulled the jacket on and zipped it up. "I want you to go to the car and wait for me. Let the staff know you're all right, and that they'll have their restroom back momentarily. Don't answer any questions, just let them see that you're fine. Okay?"

I nodded, a little surprised by this take-

charge, give-orders, lay-down-the-law side
of him. I hadn't seen it before.

It was sexy as hell.

I stared at him for a long moment as he
washed the blood from the floor. When he
felt my eyes on him, he stopped and looked
up at me.

*Say something, dumb-ass. Don't just stand
here giving him cow-eyes.* "Thank you,
Tomas. I mean . . . really. Thanks."

"De nada."

As soon as we took off again, Tomas asked
if I was ready to hear the rest of the story,
to hear about my mission. I was proud of
myself for looking him square in the eye
and saying, "No. I'm ready to hear some
old school rock and roll and not much else,
if that's cool with you."

He gave an uncertain nod, and I flipped
on the radio and found a classic rock station. We didn't speak again for what felt like
hours.

Leaning my aching head back against the
seat, I watched the world around us change
as he drove. The city fell farther and farther
behind, and in no time we were passing
through farmland, beneath a crystal-blue
sky with barely a cloud in sight. The hills
got bigger the farther we went, and brighter,

115

too. We were heading north, into foliage country, and we passed some breathtakingly vivid displays. And then they started to fade a little. Farther north, the leaves had passed their peak. A few bare limbs at first, then more, and then mostly.

With vintage Aerosmith providing the soundtrack, I could almost have been anticipating a cheerful day in the country.

Except that I wasn't. I was heading toward a showdown with some kind of demon. A real demon. Right?

"Or maybe I'm in a psych ward right now, tripping out on Thorazine and all of this is just a big complex hallucination."

"What's that?" Tomas asked, glancing sideways at me.

Damn, he's so good-looking.

I shook my head. "Nothing, it's all good."

Eventually, we were heading through New York's wine country, and soon after, entering Ithaca. The view on one side was of the campus of Cornell University, sitting high above the tiny city like a crown jewel. On the other, the real jewel, Cayuga Lake, glistening in the late-autumn sun, its mirrorlike surface reflecting the remaining foliage so powerfully that it made me gasp out loud in pure pleasure.

"God, it's beautiful here. It must have

116

been amazing a couple of weeks ago."

"This is one of my favorite places on the planet. I attended Cornell."

"I didn't know that."

He nodded. "And I have a friend there I'd like to contact. Professor Jonathon Yates. He might be able to help us translate the writing that appeared on your arm. If the photos came out, that is. Have you looked at them?"

I blinked down at my cell phone, which I'd dropped on the seat between us. "No." And I didn't reach for it to do so now.

"You know, avoiding what's happening isn't going to make it go away."

I shrugged. "How do you know unless you let me try?" I was only half joking.

His brows furrowed. He was still trying to figure me out. I don't suppose I was easy. The worse things got, the more jokes I made. The scarier things were, the more I pretended they didn't exist. If I could chuck it all right now and head to Disney World, I'd do it in a New York minute.

"Okay," he said at length. "Okay, I got you. For now, keep pretending we're just taking a nice drive in the country. I'll check the photos when we get to the cabin."

"Cabin?"

"Yeah, I have a place here. Just a dozen or so miles from town, around the southern tip of the lake."

I frowned at him. "You bought a place near this so-called Portal on purpose?"

"I bought it before I knew about the Portal. Dom said it was divine guidance. I suppose that's more likely than co-incidence."

"So how did you find out the Portal was here?"

"Ah, that's Dom's department. Astrology, ley lines, magnetic fields." He ran his hand, palm flat, past the top of his head. "I never was very good at that end of things," he said with a smile.

I smiled back at him. I couldn't help it. I was starting to really like this guy. "How far?" I asked.

"Not far."

It wasn't far, not at all. Within minutes he was turning from a side road onto a narrow dirt driveway that seemed to go on forever. It meandered uphill, under a tunnel-like canopy of intertwined bare limbs with a few Technicolor leaves still clinging. The road was coated in their fallen comrades and looked like a painting crew's drop cloth: gold and sun-yellow, rust and scarlet, purple and burgundy, rose and mustard. Sunlight made its way through the branches overhead and dappled everything in brilliance. We bumped over a wooden bridge with a swift-running stream only a few feet below it and then back into the tunnel of trees.

Finally the driveway spilled into a wider space that fronted a house straight out of a dark fairy tale. Cobblestone, with dark wood shutters, window boxes filled with orange and yellow marigolds, and an arching front door made of wide, darkly stained boards. Behind the house, and far, far below it, Cayuga Lake glistened, reflecting the bare-limbed forest and splotches of color like a big stained-glass window in the sunlight.

"It looks like a storybook — but a scary storybook. 'Grimm's Grimmest.' "

"I think it's charming. What's so scary about it?"

I shrugged and got out of the car. He got out, too. Nothing really, I thought. There were no gargoyles, no dead plants, no cobwebs or dusty windows. "I don't know. But it feels scary to me."

"Well, you've been through a lot of scary stuff in the past few days. I guess that must be why."

"Yeah." I stood on the ground staring at the house. "That must be why." But I didn't believe it. As I walked toward the place, I got the creepiest feeling up the back of my neck. As if someone was watching me. But when I looked around to see who, there were only rows of towering maples that spread away from the drive and surrounded the cottage. A little hardwood forest in between me and the road out of here.

I rubbed my arms and looked again at the house. "So is this fairy-tale cottage like . . . sitting right on top of the local Hellmouth, then?"

"No. I promise, the Portal is not under my house. I don't know where it is, exactly, just that it's near. That's one of the reasons I need you — you're going to help me find it."

"Right."

"Would you like to go inside now?"

I looked at the house again, braced my spine and swallowed my fear. "If you insist, *Padre.*"

In his dark world, the demon felt it. The priest was near, and in the company of the witch who held the key to his return. It was happening, just as he had always known it would, though he no longer knew how he had come by the knowledge. He remembered nothing but darkness and hate. He yearned for nothing but vengeance and blood.

And freedom. Freedom from this prison.

His anger had grown over the years. His hatred had festered. He would take that witch and force her to give him the key. He didn't know what form it would take, but he knew she had it.

He would hurt her if she did not comply.

As for the priest, he would hurt him either way. He hated priests of every ilk and would wipe them all from existence if he were able.

And as with most of his overpowering emotions, he did not know why he felt that way, only that he did. He did not question his feelings. He simply felt them, acted on them. There was no thought in between. Only raw hate.

So he would kill the priest outright and the witch in due time.

But first he had to find them.

He could not pass through the Portal until the time was perfect. Midnight on the Eve of Samhain. And he could not pass through without the key the witch possessed. Even then, he would remain in spirit form, not physical. Getting a body would be the second goal. Just getting through the Portal was the first.

But even from this dark place, he could influence beings in the land of the living. The simplest minds would give way to his control most easily. The innocent. So the young, the stupid and, of course, the animals.

They would be his eyes and his ears, since he had no body of his own. They would locate his quarry for him and, if necessary, destroy them on his behalf.

He would deploy his own little army. And now that the priest had drawn near the Portal, it was time to begin amassing his troops.

6

The cottage was cozy enough. There was nothing about it that ought to frighten me. Overstuffed furniture and plants everywhere. Wildlife prints on the walls, huge sliding glass doors that opened onto a rear deck that faced out toward the mirror lake below.

I stood on that deck with the wind riffling my hair, looking out over the railing, just taking it all in. It was a far different view from what I was used to. I didn't think I'd ever seen anything like it. I was a city girl, had been all my life.

Tomas joined me there after a few minutes, a steaming mug in each hand. "What do you think of my place?" he asked as I took one of them from him, felt its warmth, caught the scent of chocolate.

"I can see why you love it here. It's beautiful." I closed my eyes and pulled the cup closer to my face, sniffing. "Mmm. Cocoa."

"Aha. I thought I detected the soul of a chocoholic about you."

"There's nothing chocolate can't fix," I informed him. "I wouldn't be surprised if it could make this alleged demon so happy he grows a halo." I turned to continue gazing out over the water. "You know, this enforced vacation might not be so bad, after all. This is a gorgeous cottage, there's a beautiful lake, what's left of the foliage is breathtaking, and I'm here with one of the best-looking men I've ever met, who happens to indulge me in a smoke now and then. Even if he is a priest."

He blinked. "I . . . Thanks, I guess."

"So have you got one now?"

"One . . ."

I held up my fingers in a backward peace sign in front of my lips. He caught my meaning. "Nope. Fresh out."

"Just used them to lure me here, didn't you?" I accused.

"Is that what you think?"

I shrugged and relaxed, my elbows on the railing, cocoa in hand. "Pretty interesting that you picked this place before you knew this Portal thing was nearby."

"Yeah. I fell in love with the area when I was at Cornell and just never wanted to leave. I was drawn to this place from my first visit here." Then he frowned a little. "Of course, who's to say the Portal wasn't the reason for that? Guarding it is my calling, one into which I was born, according to Dom, so . . . maybe I sensed it even then."

"You ever think he might be wrong?"

"Dom?"

"Yeah. I mean, he's not the Pope. Humans are fallible, and this legend of yours is thousands of years old. You lose a lot over centuries of interpretation and reinterpretation. Just look at the Bible."

He didn't answer me, so I sipped and pretended not to notice. "Well, at least it's pretty here."

He moved to a little round table on the left-hand side of the deck, pulled out a chair and sat down, then waited for me to join him, but I didn't. Just stayed where I was, staring out at the peaceful lake.

"It began three thousand, five hundred years ago, give or take. In Babylon. This demon —"

"I'm not ready to hear this yet." I was tempted to cover my ears and start singing *la-la-la* but figured just telling him was more mature. "Can't we just enjoy the afternoon, maybe toss a couple of steaks on that gas grill over there and —"

"You can't avoid this forever."

"Can I avoid it for now?" I asked.

"Of course you can!" called a booming voice from behind us, beyond the still-open patio doors, inside the house.

I jumped, spun around with my hand to my chest and gasped so hard it hurt. But I relaxed when I saw the man coming out through the glass doors. He wore a priestly collar, like Tomas, but was different in every other respect. He was a tall man, slightly stooped and slender, with salt-and-pepper hair in a slicked-back cut. His smile was wide, and his face reminded me of a very old bloodhound as he came straight to me, one hand extended, his pale blue eyes sparkling. "You must be Indira."

"And you have to be Father Dominick," I said.

"Guilty as charged." He closed his hand around mine, big, but frail and soft, as I looked from him to Tomas and back again.

"I didn't know you were coming, Father Dom," Tomas said.

"You probably think I'm overstepping, right? But I have good reason for being here, Tomas. There's an interfaith conference at the Statler this weekend. One I've been planning to attend. So I thought I might as well stay here with you, in case I can be of any help. And," he added, holding up a grocery bag, "I brought steaks." He shook the bag a little, grinning at me. "Like a bona fide mind reader, eh?"

I couldn't help but smile back. His jovial mood was infectious, and it broke the tension around here, which had been way needed. "Like a mind reader. You're not one, are you?"

"Not at all," he said. "There are few people who wouldn't love a good steak." Then he shot a look at Tomas again and shook his head. "This one, all work, no play. Then again, I guess I've got to take the blame for that. I'm the one who trained him. It's my old job he's doing now." He set the bag on the table, pulling out two magnums of wine. "Tomas, get us a bucket of ice, eh? I'll fire up the grill."

Tomas didn't move right away. Finally, picking up on it, Dom looked at him and sighed. "I know you're up to this job, son. I wouldn't have chosen you if I didn't. But, Tomas, it's been my life's work, too, you know. Training for this time, preparing for it. I just couldn't stay away now that it's finally about to play out, you know? I had to be here. I had to see it through. Tell me you understand."

Tomas drew a deep breath and nodded as he released it all at once. I had the feeling he was going to argue but changed his mind. "I do. I get it." And he seemed to relax as he approached Father Dom and embraced him. It seemed genuine, complete with multiple back slaps on both sides.

As they stepped apart, Father Dom seemed relieved. "All right, now how about that ice?"

"I'll put the wine on ice," I said quickly. "I haven't had a chance to explore the place yet, or unpack, or anything. It'll give you guys time to catch up." I picked up the bottles and nodded at the men as I walked back inside. Frankly, I wanted some alone time, and good old Father Dom had provided a perfect distraction for the hunk. I'd have to thank him sometime.

Tomas waited until she was out of sight, then slid the glass doors closed and turned. "Why are you really here, Dom?"

"Just like I said. It's my life's work. I'm not gonna sit on the sidelines while it goes down."

But Tomas knew the old man too well. "I'm not buying it any more than I'm buying your friendliness toward Indira. You *hate* witches. So what's going on?"

Dom's jovial expression evaporated. His face turned hard, stern. "You need me, is what's going on." He nodded toward the doors. "And now that I've seen the witch, I'm thinking it's a damn good thing I am here."

"What's that supposed to mean?"

"*What's that supposed to mean?* Are you telling me you haven't noticed what she looks like?"

Tomas crouched low in front of the grill, twisting the gas valve open and avoiding his elder's eyes. "I'm human. I noticed."

"I thought so. Believe me, she'll use it. Her looks, her body, she'll use it all. She's in league with a demon, Tomas. You can't forget that."

Rising, Tomas lifted the lid of the grill, turned on the center burner and pushed the ignition button. It snapped three times, then caught with a soft whoosh. "She's not, actually."

"What's this now?" Dom came closer, stood shoulder to shoulder with him, looking his way, but Tomas wasn't looking back. He pretended great interest in the grill as he turned on the other two burners, watching the blue flames light in synchronized order. "She's not what?" Father Dom asked.

"Not in league with a demon." He made his voice sound falsely scary as he said the words and waggled his fingers menacingly in the air. "Or with anyone, Dom. She's just a nice girl who's being plagued by nightmares and phantom injuries, and has no idea why."

"Phantom injuries, you say?"

"Yes. It's happened twice now. At least that I know of. The lashes of a whip across her back, and then a blade cutting her chest and arms. Both times the marks faded within minutes."

Dom was nodding. "It's one of the other two witches, or perhaps the demon himself, trying to stir her memory. And it'll work, too. You mark my words, Tomas, she'll remember, and as soon as she does, she'll return to her true calling. To help her demon overlord escape the Underworld. If she has to kill you to do it, she will. She's a witch, Tomas."

"You say that as if it's synonymous with 'evil.' "

"That's because it is." Dom reached up and closed the grill's lid. "Now let's just let that heat up good before I toss on the steaks. What have you got on hand for sides?"

I stuck the wine in the fridge rather than searching the place for an ice bucket. The kitchen was compact and functional, done in stained wood like the rest of the cottage. Very rustic, with old-fashioned-looking white cupboards and appliances, and a white marble countertop with cream and gold swirls. I was eager to explore the rest of the place, but more eager to do something else. As soon as my hands were free, I pulled out my cell phone, relieved to see two bars appear top left, and called Rayne.

It went straight to voice mail, though. Again. Maybe she was at work and not taking calls. "Rayne, it's Indy. I'm sorry I yelled in that earlier voice mail. I can only assume I pissed you off so much you're refusing to call me back, and I know you were only trying to help. So get over it now, okay, because I need you. I'm in a cottage in Ithaca with that priest you sicced on me, so I hope he's as okay as you said. He seems all right so far, but now another one has shown up, and even though he seems like a cheerful old fart, I'm starting to feel outnumbered. Call me, okay?"

I disconnected and hoped for the best. Stupid of me not to have let someone — anyone — know where I was going and with whom. I was way too old to make those kinds of mistakes. But at least Rayne would know now. It was on the record. If anything should happen . . .

"Think positive much, there, Indy?" I asked myself aloud.

Shaking my head, I walked out of the kitchen and back into the large open, main room, which combined living and dining areas beneath a tall cathedral ceiling criss-crossed by huge barn beams. Two bags sat by the door. One gaped open, and I could see books inside. The other was a small suitcase. Apparently Father Dom planned to stay for a while.

I found that very disappointing.

There was a den, separated from the rest by a closed door, off to the right, staircase to the left. The entire place smelled of wood. It was a soothing scent. There were a couple of other closed doors opposite the kitchen, but I was more interested in the stairway, so I took it. Tomas had taken my duffel up there and probably tossed it into my room for me, so I would soon know which one was mine. The stairs were made of halved logs covered in gleaming layers of shellac. A tiny oval of green carpet had been affixed to each one — to prevent slipping, I supposed. The railing resembled a twisting, knotty, sapling trunk and was like nothing I'd ever seen before. The bedroom doors were lined up along one side of the upstairs hallway and the other side was open, so I could look down into the living room below, with a continuation of that same railing preventing someone from sleepwalking over the edge.

Upstairs was much like down, wood everywhere. A tall fountain stood in the corner near the top of the stairs, slightly dusty and not working at the moment. Tomas must shut it off when he left, and I guessed he hadn't gotten around to turning it back on yet. But it was a beautiful piece, with a flat stone as tall as my head standing upright in a water-filled basin that resembled a stone pond, and cobbles stacked up around it. Crouching down, I inspected the area just behind the fountain, located a power cord with a switch and turned it on.

The thing whirred softly, gurgled and chugged, and then the water began flowing down the face of the flat rock. It could use some more. Still, it worked. I rose and stood back to admire it. "Beautiful." In fact, this entire place was beautiful.

So why did I still find it scary?

I headed down the hall, stopping to open each door I came to along the way. There were four of them, two on the right side and one on each end. The first two I inspected were smallish guest rooms, each done in a different woodland theme. The beds were all knotty pine four-posters, the dressers matched. But each one had a different creature stenciled along the tops of the wooden walls, and on the bedspreads, curtains, framed prints on the walls, and even the bedside lamp. The first was black bears. The second white-tail deer. Neither of them seemed to be occupied.

So I switched my attention to the far end of the hallway, and its single door. I glanced toward the stairs, wondering if there was time to snoop just a little more. I wanted to see what Tomas's room was like. The man fascinated me, and I was itching to know more about him. But no, this wasn't the time. I took a quick look inside the room at the end of the hall and knew it had to be his. Like everything in this place, it was mostly wood, but with a bed made out of an entire white birch tree. The four posts were made from lengths of its trunk, and the headboard was woven in a twisted pattern from its twigs. It was a stunning bed, really. His bedspread was hunter-green plaid, and the art on the walls was all wildlife — but they were photos. In one a doe was curled around her spotted newborn fawn, licking its head, in the shelter of a fallen pine. In another, a huge hawk was feeding something icky to its squawking, wide-beaked chicks.

I heard voices below and quickly backed out of the bedroom into the hall, closing the door quietly and tiptoeing — why, I couldn't have said — on to the final room, the one at the end of the hall near the stairs. It was butterscotch and cream, a far softer look than his. The bed was identical, but everything else was different. The soft chair by the window looked so inviting, I wished I had a good book with me to curl up and read. There were photos in this room, too. Shots of the lake and the surrounding hills taken at various times of year. My bag was on the bed, so I knew this was where I would be staying, and I was glad.

The bathroom was through a door to the right, and it was huge, luxurious and apparently all mine.

I wanted to unpack but figured those steaks must be just about done by now, and my stomach was growling noisily, which was often the case with me. I took only enough time to discard my leather jacket, put on a fresh T-shirt and grab a big woolly sweater from my bag. As I headed back down the stairs, I heard the men talking in low tones, so I softened my steps and moved closer.

They were still on the deck. Tomas held a huge salad bowl in his hands, and he'd apparently left the glass doors open when he'd carried it outside. But it was Father Dom doing the talking as he repeatedly tapped the page of an open book.

". . . we must destroy the amulet the instant she manages to get her hands on it. No matter what it takes, Tomas."

I frowned. What amulet? What's he talking about? One more step brought me into Father Dom's sight, and I pretended not to notice when he slammed his book closed. But I'd had a glimpse at the handwriting and drawings on the parchmentlike pages. It was one of those ancient leather-bound journals that were a staple in movies about possession and the Devil and the end of the world.

He removed it from the table, tucking it somewhere underneath. "There she is now, the woman of the hour. And just in time, too. These steaks are done to perfection." He stood and moved to the grill, stabbing the meat with a long fork and dropping the steaks onto large stoneware plates.

Tomas turned my way, and his eyes looked worried.

Probably wondering how much I just overheard. Not that any of it made sense to me. But what I wouldn't give to get a look inside that journal.

"You made us a salad," I said, because I

didn't know what the hell else to say. Should I demand answers, or play it cool and pretend I hadn't heard a thing? "That looks delicious. Are we eating out here on the deck?"

"If you think you'll be warm enough," Tomas replied.

"I grabbed a sweater just in case. Can I get anything?"

"Dressing for the salad, glasses for the wine."

"Done." I pulled on my sweater and returned to the kitchen. While I stood in front of the open fridge, I saw Dom pass from the deck to the living room, the journal in his hands. Moments later I heard him going up the stairs. When I headed back outside, I saw that his bags were gone.

So we sat like a trio of old friends on the beautiful deck, overlooking the beautiful lake beneath the beautiful twilight sky, eating delicious steaks and gigantic salads. But the cheerful small talk ended abruptly when Father Dom, laughing over something I'd said that hadn't been all that funny, suddenly went dead serious, his eyes holding mine.

"How much, exactly, have you remembered about your past lives, Indira?"

I blinked at him, gaping like a fish sucking air, then giving up as no words seemed to suffice.

"She hasn't remembered anything," Tomas said. "A few bad dreams, but —"

"So you agree with Tomas?" I asked the old priest, holding his gaze without a single flinch. It felt vaguely disapproving, that look. "That this is a past life thing? I mean, that's what Lady Rayne said, but I —"

"Lady Rayne?"

"A friend of mine. A high priestess," I said. I glanced nervously at Tomas, wondering if I'd spilled something I wasn't supposed to.

Father Dom shot a surprised look Tomas's way.

Tomas shook his head — a bit too quickly, I thought. "She's not involved in this."

She is so. She's the one who tipped you off about me, you liar. And why is it, I wonder, that you're lying to your beloved mentor, anyway?

Father Dom nodded, but I sensed his displeasure. Not that I cared.

"Well, in this case," Dom said, "the *high priestess* —"

Was that sarcasm I heard in his tone? Was he *mocking* her status and title?

"— was correct. In 1501 BC and assuming you *are* the witch we've been searching for, you, along with two others, were practicing witchcraft, and for that you were executed."

"Yeah, that I get." I was on my third glass of wine and feeling it way more than I should. "But I don't see how that got us involved in this — this demon stuff."

"Well, you were witches, after all," Dom said. "Communing with demons is part of the tradition."

My jaw fell open. I looked at him, then at Tomas, and then at him again. The old bastard was still rambling on as if he hadn't just insulted my entire religion. Former religion.

"— and while it's not a part of the traditional interpretation, it is my belief that you and the other two can only save yourselves, and redeem your souls, by helping us to thwart this demon's efforts and keep him in the Underworld where he belongs."

Redeem my soul? If I'd had hackles, they would surely have risen in fury. I tipped back my glass, downing the last of my wine, then set it on the table with a quiet clink. "You think I'm damned, don't you? Both of you?"

They looked at me oddly, neither speaking. I stood up and told myself it was just anger. My feelings were not hurt. I don't know why it felt as if they were, but they most definitely were *not.* I didn't give two shits what this pair of priests thought of me, my religion — former religion — or the state of my soul.

"You do, don't you? You think God will send me to hell for something I did in a previous lifetime. And how does that work, anyway? I thought you guys were all about heaven and hell and sometimes purgatory in between? Not reincarnation. What do you do, just pick whichever doctrine fits your needs at the moment?"

Tomas looked wounded as he got up, too, and held up a hand as he came around the table toward me — you know, like you would do if you were walking up to a spooked animal. "I never said that, Indira."

"Then say it now. Tell the truth, Tomas. Do you think I'm going to hell because I'm a witch?" For some reason the words didn't come out quite as smoothly as I'd intended them to.

He held my gaze for a long moment and seemed to be choosing his words, but Father Dom spoke first. "Anyone who practices witchcraft will burn in hell. You know that as well as I do, Indira. But we're not here to try to convert you. We're here because we need your help. Your eternal soul and what you choose to do with it are your own business."

Tomas closed his eyes, lowered his head and shook it slowly. "Dom . . ."

"You know what I just realized, Father Dom?" I asked. My tongue felt strangely thick.

"What?" he asked, brows arching.

"You're a real asshole." I threw my napkin on the table and spun around, intending to make a dramatic exit and stomp all the way to my room. And it worked fine until I was inside. But my head started swimming at the foot of the stairs, and I had to stop and grip the railing to keep from toppling like a spindly sapling.

"Indy?" Tomas was at my side so fast I thought he must've teleported there. He held my elbow with one hand, his other hand at the small of my back.

I feel his hands on my back.

"What is it?" he asked.

"Damned 'f I know."

"Probably the wine," Father Dom said. He was slower arriving but was also looking at me with concern on his face. "I'm sorry if I insulted you. I'm far more dogmatic and old-fashioned than Tomas. I didn't mean to step on toes."

"You insinuate my religion — my former religion, I mean — is so dis'aseful . . . distasteful . . ." I was irritated at the way my tongue got stuck on the *t.* ". . . abhorrent to God that He would sennence me to eternal hellfire for it, and all you can say is you're not trying to sep on my toes?" I frowned hard, my head swimming. I definitely sounded drunk. But I'd only had three glasses of wine.

"Let me help you upstairs, Indy." Tomas was close to me, holding me, and I liked it. "You've had a few rough nights. It's not surprising the wine hit you so hard."

"I c'd drink you unner the table, Priest." Then I blinked. "Hey, you guys din't . . . spike it, did-ja?"

"Of course not," Tomas said. "Come on, let me help you." He draped my arm around his big, solid shoulders. Then he anchored his own arm around my waist, his broad strong hand resting on my hip, and started up the stairs.

I leaned into him and felt a force — like one of us was a magnet and the other one was steel — pinning me to him, pulling me closer, even though I couldn't *get* any closer. The feeling was intense, body to body like that. It buzzed in my nerve endings, filled every empty space inside me. It felt good. And right. And oddly . . . familiar.

I took two steps at his urging before my knees seemed to liquefy and colors swirled in my head. Looking down at me, his expression troubled, Tomas picked me up and carried me the rest of the way. My entire body was enfolded in his strong arms, my side pressed to his chest, my head bouncing softly against his shoulder as he trotted easily up the stairs with me. I tried to link my arms around his neck, but my hands couldn't seem to grip each other and ended up dangling limply at my sides.

In my room, he managed to yank back the covers, and then he lowered me onto the bed.

I tried to smile up at him, but it felt crooked and slightly goofy, instead of provocative and flirty as I'd intended. "This is kinda sexy, you know. Carrying me up those stairs like . . . like Rhett Butler. You gonna kiss me now?"

"No, Indy. I'm not going to kiss you now."

"Maybe later?"

"We'll see." He looked to me as if he was battling a smile, even though there was worry in his eyes. "You get some sleep now, and we'll talk more in the morning."

"I'm scared to go to sleep, Tomas. What'f I have 'nother dream? I could walk right off

143

that cliff outside."

"I already thought of that."

"You did?"

"Of course. You nearly sleepwalked off your own roof. I wasn't going to bring you to a cliffside cottage without taking some precautions. I have motion sensors outside. Anything bigger than a coyote walks by them, an alarm will sound in the house. And just in case, the cottage doors will all be locked. Okay?"

"Why does a priest have motion sensors?" Was I drunk, or was the growing feeling that maybe I was some sort of a prisoner here at all valid? My eyes kept drooping closed, then popping open as he spoke.

"I've had them for years. I had a problem with deer getting into the garden. Haven't turned them on in ages, but I'll make sure they're working before I go to bed tonight. Okay?"

"Okay," I said. "I guess."

"I'll keep you safe, Indy."

I searched his eyes. There was so much sincerity in them, so much honesty. "I believe you." And with those words my eyes fell heavily one final time and I was dead to the world.

7

Tomas had a sick feeling in the pit of his stomach as he stared down at the beautiful woman who was already asleep. She shouldn't be drunk. Not *this* drunk, anyway. Not on three glasses of wine. Sighing, he moved to the foot of the bed to take off her cowgirl boots. Three-inch heels. He didn't know how the hell she stayed upright, much less wore them all day. It took a lot of tugging, but he managed to get them off, and then he peeled off the white ankle socks she wore underneath. Her feet were pale and cool, and he instinctively rubbed them back to life before he pulled the covers over her. He wasn't sure how comfortable she would be in her clothes, but there was no fixing that. At least she'd taken off her jacket.

"Careful, Tomas. She's not on our side, you need to remember that."

Tomas turned, unsurprised to find Dom standing in the bedroom doorway. "She's not on anyone's side, Dom. She's only just learning what's going on here." He swallowed what felt like sand in his throat and forced himself to ask the question that needed asking. "Did you drug her?"

"Of course. We need to inspect her body for signs of the demon's presence. The markings that will prove once and for all whether she is the one." As he spoke, Father Dom moved close to the bed and took hold of the covers to pull them back.

Tomas grabbed his wrist — not forcefully, but firmly. "There's no need." The words on his lips were *over my dead body,* but he managed to hold them in. He had never seen this side of Dom before, and it was freaking him out. He even wondered if the old man had something wrong with him. A tumor, or maybe a ministroke, affecting his brain.

"We already know she's the one. And besides that, I've already seen the marks on her body."

Dom's brows, bushy and white, rose in dual arches. "Have you, now?"

"I did. First the lashes of the whip across her back, from her torture long ago. A tattoo that looks like cuneiform on her lower back that appears and fades away. And then, just this morning, phantom writing cut into

146

her arms. I tried to get a photo before it vanished."

"Show me."

"I . . . It's on her cell phone. My own was . . . out of reach."

Tomas looked around the room for Indira's handbag. It was on the floor, along with her still-packed duffel. Father Dom spotted it at the same time and started forward, but Tomas held out a hand. "I really think we ought to wait until she's awake and not go through her things while she's —"

"Did I make a grave mistake in choosing you for this mission?" Father Dom asked. "Are you going soft on the demon's whore?"

"She's not a demon's anything, not in this lifetime. And I'm only suggesting we respect her privacy while she —"

"Her privacy could get us both killed and unleash the devil's right hand on the world. Is that what you want?" Father Dom shoved Tomas aside with a surprisingly strong arm, and grabbed Indira's handbag. It was unzipped.

Tomas yanked it out of his hand. "I said no."

But as the bag pulled free of Dom's grasp, things went flying out of it, the BlackBerry among them. Dom picked it up, his eyes telling Tomas he wouldn't take no for an answer. A moment later, he was holding it at arm's length and squinting as he scrolled through her photos. He shook his head in frustration. "They're too damned small to even tell what they are!"

"Give it to me," Tomas said, holding out a hand. "I'll email the photos to myself, so we can both get a better look at them on the computer." He didn't bother adding that Dom needed bifocals and was too stubborn to get them. More important, that he thought the old man was out of line. Way out.

Grunting, Dom handed him the phone. "We still have to go through the rest of her things — she might have acquired the amulet already."

"She hasn't." Tomas sent the email, then closed the phone and returned it to Indy's purse, along with the other items that had flown loose. Then he draped the strap over the bedpost and found himself pausing to glance at her as she slept.

Her blond hair was tousled, her thick, lush lashes resting heavily on cheeks that seemed a little too pale. She was still fully dressed. Couldn't be comfortable.

"What did you give her?"

"Nothing that'll hurt her, not that it

should concern you. We must use whatever means it takes to keep her from helping the demon escape his prison. If she gets hurt, too bad for —"

"She's a human being, Dom!"

"She's a sleeper agent in a terrorist plot. Even she may not know yet who she really is, what she was born to do, how many times she has reincarnated just waiting to fulfill her destiny. To help a demon enter our world." His gaze shifted to Indira, but he wore a look of disgust. "Or maybe she already knows. Either way, she's on his side, not ours. Not God's."

"I don't think she wants to help him," Tomas said. "She's not evil."

"She's a witch in league with a demon, Tomas. And you're a priest."

Tomas nodded, unable to argue with that point. He *was* a priest. For now. He pulled a blanket over Indy. "At least she'll finally be able to get some sleep," he said.

I was once again wearing the costume of a belly dancer or something similar: one-shouldered and sheer, my breasts easily visible through the soft ivory fabric. I was glad, because it served as a distraction to the guards who'd just burst into the courtyard where Magdalena and I had been sitting in silent meditation, keeping watch while our sister entertained her lover in the sleeping quarters just beyond.

We saw them coming. I waved Magdalena away and tried to block her scurrying exit with my body, looking the approaching pair of guards up and down suggestively, smiling at them as if in approval of what I saw.

The guards didn't react to my charms at all. "Where is your sister?" one of them said.

Actually, that wasn't what he said at all. What he said was a bunch of gibberish that must have come straight out of the Tower of Babel. But what I heard was its modern-day English equivalent.

"Which one?" I asked, stalling for time. I knew Magdalena would be trying to warn Lilia and her lover that they were about to be caught.

"Lilia."

I shrugged. "I believe she is tending to her . . . personal cleanliness, sir," I said, using a respectful, slightly sexual tone I thought he would prefer. "But I am here, if the king requires —"

His arm swung out, backhanding me across the face so hard I fell to my knees. That was when I knew this was serious. The guards strode past me, their steps harsh on the white stone floors, and I prayed Lilia was up and clothed and her lover hidden. Magdalena had rushed off only seconds ahead of the guards, and I knew there had been little time.

I scrambled to my feet and ran after them. "Wait!" I cried. "You cannot just march through our sanctuary this way, uninvited. The king will be furious. Wait! I'll tell him, I swear —"

"Silence, woman." And then they reached their destination, yanking the curtain down, rather than open, tearing the rich red fabric.

Inside the room, on their feet but still naked, were Demetrius and Lilia. I marveled at my sister's beauty, even then. And Demetrius — he was like a god. He quickly snatched up a coverlet and wrapped it around Lilia, but not before I'd seen the mark on her back. A tattoo, down low. Three rows of symbols. I knew that we all bore them, all three of us, and I knew what they meant. *Daughter of Ishtar.*

Demetrius tried to protect her, standing between her and the soldiers, but then one of the guards marched up behind him and, even as I shouted a warning, swung his mace hard. The ball hit Demetrius in the head, and he went down like a felled cedar.

Lilia screamed and dropped to her knees beside him, but the guard kicked her away,

151

sending her onto her back, leaving her chin split and bleeding.

"Take him to the king," the guard ordered.

The second guard took Demetrius by one arm and dragged him, unconscious, perhaps dead, from the room. Magdalena, who'd been standing to one side of the door, rushed to Lilia and hugged her hard, while I stood there, trembling in fear of what was to come.

The remaining guard began searching our room. He lifted each cushion to look beneath and feel within, and when he felt weight, he used his blade to slash the fabric and pour out the contents.

And there they were for all to see. Our wooden wands, our mortar and pestle, our herbs and stones and our pentacle pendants, which we wore when we worked our magic. Our *forbidden* magic.

He turned to look at us. "Magic is to be worked only by the High Priest. You have broken the law."

"What are you talking about?" I asked, hurrying forward, intent on gathering up our precious items, only to meet with the flat of his hand to my chest, holding me away. "There is no magic here. We only hide our favorite belongings to keep the other girls from stealing them. I suppose they told you we were up to something dark and forbidden, didn't they?"

He looked at me, brows rising. I wished Magdalena would stop sniffling. It didn't help.

"They are only jealous," I went on. "My sister Lilia is the king's favorite. They are trying to hurt us with their ridiculous accusations."

"Mmm. I see," the guard said. "They were lying, then, when they accused you of practicing witchcraft."

"Witchcraft! Is that what they said?"

"Just as they were lying when they claimed the king's most trusted lieutenant was bedding his most beloved concubine?"

"It . . . it was not what it seemed."

"Do not tell me what I witnessed with my own eyes, slave girl." The soldier looked past me, and I was shocked to realize more guards had entered our chambers, along with an apprentice priest with eyes like melted chocolate, who stared into my eyes for a long moment. It was I who looked away.

"Take them," the leader said. "Take them all to the king. I will gather and bring the evidence. Send for the High Priest, as well. We will need his counsel."

The men rushed into our rooms, and

there was no resisting them. I thought of wielding my powers but knew that would only prove our guilt. I hoped, even then, that we could talk our way out of the mess.

I whispered a spell of protection, beamed healing energies toward my injured sister as the guard pulled her to her feet, and decided it was best to go along, pretending to be docile and weak. Perhaps we could still convince the king to believe us.

Though only, I thought, if he were a complete idiot.

As the guards marched us away, I met Magdalena's eyes and saw the tears brimming in them. Lilia cried loudly, sobbing so hard she could barely breathe. I tried to convey to them that they should be calm and watchful, as I was. Awaiting an opportunity, calculating a plan.

But they did not see my message, or perhaps they did not want to. Maybe they already knew we were doomed.

I woke with my sister's name on my lips.
Lilia.

That was the name of the woman I'd seen in my cauldron, after the spell I'd been trying to cast in my apartment. She was my sister! Or had been, in some other lifetime, far, far in the distant past.

She was my sister. And the woman who'd

gotten me killed.

And a witch. There had been three of us. All witches. Just like Tomas and Father Dom had been telling me.

I sat up in the bed, hand to my forehead, because it was pounding. The resurgence of the past was almost too powerful to contain within my brain. I suppose my skull was only designed to hold the angst of one lifetime. No wonder it felt as if it were about to split open.

Still nothing about any demon, however.

Sitting upright, I noticed I was still dressed and lowered my feet to the floor. Bare feet. I saw my boots standing near the foot of the bed, my handbag hanging from a bedpost. Tomas. It must have been.

I was ridiculously glad he hadn't undressed me, and that feeling of relief was followed immediately by the question of why not? Most men would jump at the apparently logical excuse to get my clothes off. Why not him?

Because he's a priest, dumb-ass.

For some reason there were tears burning the backs of my eyes, and I didn't even have the strength to fight them. I just lowered my head into my hands and sobbed so loudly I never heard the door open, or the soft steps of the very man I'd been thinking about approaching me.

But I felt him, oh, I felt him. His hands on my shoulders, squeezing gently, and then just one of those hands moving to my head, stroking my hair, softly.

When I didn't look up, he knelt and tipped his head. "What happened, Indira? Another nightmare?"

I nodded, still crying too hard to speak.

"I'm sorry. I'm so sorry, Indy. Do you want to talk about it?"

Sniffling hard, I lifted my head and met his eyes. His melted-chocolate eyes. Through swimming tears I saw him. And for just an instant he seemed unbearably familiar. It was a wave of . . . something. Déjà vu? It washed over me and tugged me closer to him. My face moved toward his as he stayed where he was, staring at me. I closed my eyes, and then I pressed my mouth against his, sobs still racking my chest.

He pressed back, I swear he did. I felt it, the way his lips pushed back, then parted just a little. I knew he tasted my tears, because I tasted them, too.

And then he pulled back and stared at me.

"I'm . . . sorry," he said.

"I did it. Not you." And somehow my crying jag had eased. The residual hiccup-sobs

156

were still hitting me every few breaths, but my tears had stopped falling.

"Still . . ." He rose to his feet and refused to meet my eyes. "If you're up to it, would you come downstairs? I have the photos we took in that restroom up on the computer. Father Dom and I were looking at them last night, and I'd like you to take a look at them this morning."

"This morning?" I buried my anger that he'd gone into my bag and taken my phone, and glanced toward the bedroom window, saw the sun streaming in through the sheer, gold-tinted curtains. "Wow, I was out all night?"

I looked at him again. He looked away and nodded.

"All right, Tomas. I'll come right down. Just give me a minute to . . . wash my face."

"Take your time," he said, still not looking me in the eye. "And it's *Father* Tomas." Turning, he walked out of the bedroom as if the devil was on his heels.

Maybe in his mind she was.

I was leaning over the computer, looking at a grossly enlarged image of my own upper body, and feeling damned uncomfortable. It wasn't entirely due to the gashes on my arms and back that had been there and then faded to the pink welts covering me in the photos before vanishing like raindrops in the desert. It was also because Tomas was looking at them, too. Father Dom, too, but mostly Tomas. And yes, he'd been there when it happened, but back then he hadn't been staring intently at my magnified pores and lily-white skin. And what the hell was up with that mole on the back of my shoulder? It looked huge! And was that a hair sprouting from it? *A hair? Really?*

I was reaching behind me, absently feeling for the tiny offender, when Tomas said, "It's not much use. The marks were fading too fast to get anything readable. But I'm sure it was some sort of writing. As was the tattoo. Babylonian or Assyrian, perhaps. I just didn't have time to read it."

I blinked at him. "You can read Babylonian and Assyrian?"

"Somewhat, but not Akkadian or Sumerian."

I hadn't realized the true depth of his intellect and was still digesting that when the sound of a motor brought my head around. *God,* I thought, *don't let this be another priest.* "The tattoo on my lower back said, 'daughter of Ishtar,' " I told him.

"How do you know that?" he asked, staring at me as if stunned.

I shrugged. "I don't have the foggiest. But that's what it said."

The engine shut off, and I moved to the window to look outside, then felt the weight of the world rise from my shoulders as if it had just sprouted wings. Rayne was getting out of her Mercedes and heading for the front door. My smile was so big it hurt, and I was yanking the big door open before she even lifted her hand to knock. "God, I'm so glad to see you," I blurted, and I hugged her. Me. The most unfriendly, non-huggy person I know. I hugged her. "What are you doing here? And how the hell did you find us?"

She hugged back. "I thought you could use a friend," she said, coming inside. Her eyes shot past me. "Hello again, Tomas."

"Good to see you, Rayne. You look fantastic, as always."

"Of course I do. I'm a witch."

He smiled at her, and there was something . . . familiar in it. Something intimate. Like a secret the rest of us weren't in on. Father Dom saw it, too. I could tell by his troubled frown and the intense way he was watching the two of them. An odd little cauldron full of something green started bubbling in my belly, even though I told it not to. He was a *priest,* for crying out loud.

She was a *witch*. Nothing could possibly be going on between them.

Are you listening to yourself, Indy? Are you getting how ridiculous your own urge to rip off his clothes and jump his bones is yet?

That's different. That's me. We have a connection.

Uh-huh. Looks like he and Rayne have a connection, too. Maybe he's just kinky. Into forbidden fruit or whatever.

Fuck off, voice of reason. I hate you.

I hate you back.

Tomas and Rayne quickly broke eye contact, and he did the polite-introduction thing. "Father Dom, this is Lady Rayne Blackwood. She's the Wiccan high priestess who first contacted me about Indira."

"I see." Father Dom gave her a nod but ignored her extended hand. "Charmed, I'm sure," he said, loading on so much sarcasm I was surprised the words didn't buckle under the weight. Guess the friendly facade couldn't withstand the weight of two witches. "And you *two* know each other how?"

It sounded like an accusation. And though I wanted to spit on the man for his attitude — and why wasn't he at his conference, anyway? — I was dying to hear the answer.

Rayne and Tomas locked eyes again, and

that intimate something was right back in evidence. Tomas shrugged and said, "Rayne is my baby sister."

Sister? I thought he didn't have any family? I would have to deal with that later. Right now, the weight I thought had lifted from my shoulders dropped from on high and landed there again. The impact nearly floored me this time.

One more member of the enemy team, I thought. This one posing as a friend. As a witch. As a high priestess. My Yoda had lowered her hood to reveal Darth Vader underneath. What the hell? I couldn't seem to catch a break.

Father Dom made some lame excuse to get Tomas alone, probably so he could lecture him. I was pretty stunned myself, and about to do the same thing to Rayne. "You're his sister? And you didn't think that was something I had a right to know?" I asked, as soon as the two holy men had left us alone.

She shrugged and nodded toward the glass doors. "Let's walk outside, shall we? It's a gorgeous morning. Have you eaten?"

Cool, calm, confident. She was everything I wasn't and never would be. Sleek red curls, cute and dignified at the same time. She was the most conservative-looking Wiccan I'd ever seen. No tattoos. Dressy pants with a knife-sharp crease and wide legs. Short-sleeved burnt-orange pullover. Big amber beads around her neck and matching ones at her ears. She looked put together right down to the tan, sensible two-inch pumps. She looked professional.

I gave her a nod and followed her out onto the deck where we'd all enjoyed those steaks the night before, and I winced a little as I recalled Father Dom's obvious dislike of witches. The man was a bigot. If I'd been Tomas, I would never have admitted to having one of us as a sibling.

And apparently he never had. Until now.

We crossed the deck and walked down the steps to the grassy lawn, then followed the path that skirted the edge of the cliff. Mist rose, newborn clouds taking their first flight, from Cayuga Lake far below us. You could barely see the water through its foggy breath.

"So you're angry with me," she said at last.

"When you arrived, I thought you were the cavalry. That you'd be on my side. But it turns out you're the enemy's sister. Yeah, I guess you could say I'm pretty good and pissed."

"Tomas is not the enemy, love." She

162

sighed, walking along the path that ran close enough to the edge to give us a beautiful view. "He's a good man."

"He's a *priest!* His ancestors burned ours, or have you forgotten that?"

"His ancestors and mine are the same people, Indy. We're family."

"Spiritual ancestors, I meant."

"Well, blood's thicker than water and all that."

"Is it thicker than the rack, though? The thumbscrews? The stake?"

She shrugged. "He's not like that."

"They're all like that."

"You're as bigoted as Father Dom."

That shut me up.

Rayne pursed her lips in thought. I was silent, trying to feel the breeze on my face and not the throbbing in my head. "Look," she said at length, "I used to think his beliefs were way out there, even farther than my own." She took slow steps, gazing out at the natural beauty all around us. "But then, when those things started happening to you, the dreams, the flashbacks, suddenly knowing how to hurl telekinetic energy like a pro and how to speak whatever the hell language you were speaking — I mean the marks alone —"

I held up a hand to stop her. "I know."

Because even I couldn't deny the marks in my skin. Everything else could be . . . hallucination, insanity, delusion. But not those marks. Because I wasn't the only one who'd seen them. And there were pictures, for crying out loud.

"You needed help, Indy. And I knew in my gut that Tomas was the only one who could give it to you."

I nodded. "You still could've told me."

She met my eyes and shrugged. "But I came. Isn't that worth something?"

I held her gaze and felt myself soften. "Your big-shot law firm give you a sick day?"

"I took my vacation time. A full two weeks of it. By then Samhain will be a distant memory and this will be over, one way or the other."

"You won't need the full two weeks."

"I figured I might want some time to recover. Goddess knows what a wild ride we're in for."

"Mmm-hmm, I've been getting that feeling myself." I drew a deep breath, and then got lost in the taste of it. Fresh clean air, flavored with the scent of decaying leaves and lake water and morning mist. It was good here — at the moment.

"I'm on your side, even though he is my brother. I'm still a witch, a high priestess. I take my oath to the Goddess and to my sister witches very seriously, Indy."

I wanted to believe her and decided to put it to the test. "Okay, then, do something for me."

"Anything."

I nodded toward the den where the two men had disappeared. "Tell them I wasn't feeling well and decided to take a long hot shower. And don't let them up those stairs."

She frowned at me, tipping her head to one side. "What are you —"

"No questions. You want me to trust you and your brother, how about trusting me in return?"

Slowly she nodded. "All right, I'll do it."

"Promise?" I asked.

She made a backward peace sign and pressed her fingertips to either side of her nose. "Witch's honor."

I smiled. It was genuine, and it felt good. "Thanks."

Then I turned and ran up the stairs to the deck and hurried inside.

Quickly, I darted into "my" room, through it to the bathroom, cranked on the shower taps and closed the shower stall door. I went back into the bedroom, shutting the bathroom door behind me. I grabbed my Black-Berry from my bag, and then, pausing in the doorway, I looked up and down the hallway, and checked the stairs. No one in sight.

I was shaking a little, which was stupid. What would they do if they caught me? Baptize me to death? I darted down the hall. The door to the guest room closest to mine was open, and I could see it was empty. The other guest room's door stood closed. That must be where Father Dom was staying.

My hand was trembling as I twisted the knob, praying he hadn't slipped upstairs in the seconds I'd been in my own room. Bracing myself, mentally rehearsing one lame explanation after another, I pushed it open. No one there. His bags weren't in sight. But the journal was. Right there on the nightstand.

The man had underestimated me. Of course, the minute he realized I'd slipped upstairs alone, he would probably become painfully aware of his mistake.

Quickly I flipped the journal open, whipping out my BlackBerry like a gunfighter drawing his six-shooter. I scrolled to the photo app and began snapping pics. Snap, snap, flip the page. And again, then flip, and again and again.

I tried to resist the urge to look behind me, because that would take more time than

I had. Five pages done. Then ten. And then —

A text message came in. Nothing but an exclamation point, but since it was from Rayne, I knew what it meant.

I closed the book, pocketed the phone and was back into the hallway in two lunges. It nearly killed me to pull the door closed slowly, so it wouldn't bang, but I did it. Two more long strides and I was ducking into my own room, even as someone was coming up the stairs. I peeked out the door as Father Dom's head came into view. I closed my door, dove for the bathroom, closed that door and locked it.

And then I stood there for a long minute, holding my phone to my chest while my heart pounded.

Damn, I thought. *You're pretty good at this.* I pulled the photos up and sat down to take a look. But they were too small for me to make out the words, much less the diagrams and other drawings. I needed to get them onto a computer. Okay, good. Later.

I quickly went to the settings for my phone and set up password protection. I'd have to keep it with me at all times until it was safe to delete the photos. And I needed a damned computer and an hour of privacy.

But right now I needed to take that long

hot shower or I'd give myself away. Not that I needed the excuse. A hot shower would go a long way toward soothing my headache. At least I hoped it would.

I took my time about it, and forty minutes later, give or take, I was feeling greatly refreshed. I was decked out in brown leggings, a long green sweater dress and a wide brown belt. My hair was dry and, since I'd moussed and scrunched it, excessively curly. I chose a pair of tall, sexy suede boots and poured all my stuff into the bag that matched them. I did my makeup to perfection, looked as good as I ever had, and turned to give myself one final glance in the mirror.

She was there, standing right behind me, and I instinctively spun, raising my arms defensively.

Nothing. No one. Still, I kept my arms crossed in front of me as I glanced warily at the mirror again.

She was there. But I wasn't.

She was my reflection and, I realized, not Lilia, the same dark-haired, dark-eyed woman who'd hacked me to bits in the IHOP restroom. Nor was she the other woman who'd stood beside me on the cliff, Magdalena. So that meant she had to be . . .

I lifted my hand and watched the mirror image lift hers.

I leaned closer, and she did, too. I stared into her eyes, and she stared back into mine. She had taken over my reflection, this raven-haired, copper-skinned beauty. She was even wearing my clothes.

"Don't trust the priest," she said. And I realized my lips were moving, as if *I* was the reflection of *her.* My mouth formed the words, but I wasn't speaking them aloud. I was hearing them inside my head. "He has to kill you. He has no choice. Just like before."

Then the image wavered like water rippling, and I was me again. She was gone. I was still standing there, my stomach queasy — not in a sick way, but in a way that only happens when you see something you know is impossible. It's a shock to the system, and it rocks you right to your core. It was impossible for my reflection to turn into some alleged past version of myself and talk to me.

It was also impossible to believe what she had said. Tomas would never . . . Unless she was talking about Father Dom? That man gave me the creeps.

But could he really be that dangerous? He

169

was an old man, and a priest, for crying out —

A sound stopped my thoughts dead — a blast, an explosion, and close enough that it rocked the house. I gripped the sink when the floor shook, then quickly turned to look out the window. A cloud of thick black smoke was ballooning in the distance over the city of Ithaca.

"Oh, my God." I raced out of my room, down the stairs and through the house onto the deck, where the others were already gathered. They were shielding their eyes from the morning sun as they tried to pinpoint the spot, which was on a hillside kitty-corner to our own, around the curving tip of the lake.

"It's near Cornell," Tomas said. "I think it's —"

"It *is* Cornell," Father Dom said. He was bent over and wheezing, hands on his thighs. He must have run outside at the sound and was still out of breath. He looked at Tomas, and his eyes seemed to swim with moisture. "The conference. Jesus have mercy, it's the conference."

8

Tomas had thought he was prepared, but nothing could have prepared him for what he saw when the four of them got to the university. The Statler was a working hotel and conference center where students got hands-on experience in running the business and planning events. There had been some five hundred clerics, representing over a hundred religions and denominations, gathered there for a forward-thinking, open-minded exchange.

Now there was rubble.

Rescue vehicles and police cars blocked access to that section of campus. Clouds of smoke and dust darkened the air, and if you looked hard enough, you could glimpse the walking wounded as they stumbled away from the blast in search of help. People with sooty faces and stand-up hair, torn clothes and broken bones, helping one another or alone, staggering out of the cloud toward the flashing lights that signaled help had arrived. Others, including students and faculty, stood around the perimeter, weeping, shouting, shaking their heads, pointing.

And Tomas still wanted to doubt what had so clearly happened.

"It was him," Father Dom said in a low tone. "It was the demon."

Tomas looked at the old man, momentarily rocked by the pure hatred he saw on his face. "We don't know that for sure. Maybe it was a gas line explosion or . . . something."

Father Dom's fury-filled eyes shifted to Tomas's, but only briefly. He quickly looked around, noting, as Tomas had, that Rayne and Indy were a few yards away, deep in conversation with another woman. He kept his voice low. "What other conclusion can we draw? The demon knows where the Portal is located. He's far ahead of us on that. He knows there's a witch here to help him," he said with a quick glance at Indy and Rayne. "Along with a priest who will try to stop her. And with so many faiths — including Gnostic and Wiccan — represented at this conference, all together near the Portal . . . naturally he attacked here first. Who else would have motive?"

"He wouldn't risk destroying the witch.

Without her, he can't get his hands on the amulet, and without the amulet, he can't escape the Underworld."

Father Dom reached up and tucked the white tab of Tomas's priestly collar out of sight. "I'm right. You mark me, son, I'm right. It was him. No priest is safe here until this is over. Best not to advertise our presence too loudly." He tucked his own collar out of sight in the same way.

Tomas felt a chill run right up his spine. "Come on, Dom. The demon would sense us by our aura more than by our clothing."

"Maybe. But there's nothing we can do to disguise our auras, now, is there?"

"Actually, there is," Indy said from behind them.

Both men turned to look at her. Tomas saw the devastation in her eyes, the trauma of what they were all witnessing, and moved closer to her, instinct urging him to offer comfort, to keep her close. To keep her safe.

Which instinct, though? That of a priest, or that of a man?

"Even a lapsed solitary witch knows about shielding."

"Invisibility spell," Rayne said with a nod. "We could teach you."

"I think we'll pass on taking lessons in the black arts," Father Dom said before Tomas could answer. "Who was that you were talk-ing with?"

"A high priestess," Rayne said. "She was here for the conference."

Dom's eyebrows went up. "She wasn't injured?"

"No. She and the other Pagan leaders had a breakfast gathering downtown."

Dom looked at Tomas. "So no witches were harmed in the explosion."

"She thought they were all at the meeting. Of course, she's not sure. No one is," Indy said.

"I am," Father Dom muttered, shooting Tomas an I-told-you-so look.

"God, who could have done this?" Indy stared at the rubble, shaking her head slowly.

"The demon did it." Father Dom's tone was as certain as his words.

Indy sucked in a gasp, and her wide eyes shot to Tomas.

"It looks likely," he said. His instincts continued to push him toward her. She looked so frightened, so shaken, that he wanted to put his arms around her, remind her that he was going to keep her safe. The urge was almost irresistible, and it felt . . . old. As if he'd done it many times before.

Before he could decide whether to obey

it, Rayne did it for him. She moved closer to Indy, put an arm around her shoulders and told Tomas with her eyes that she'd seen his inner struggle. "We should get out of here," she said. "There's nothing we can do, and —"

Her words were interrupted by a voice from the crowd.

"Tomas?" someone said. "Tomas Petrosa, is that you?"

He lifted his head, scanning the onlookers, recognizing the voice and spotting Professor Jonathon Yates, a friend from long ago, making his way toward them.

"By God, it is you," Jonathon said when he reached Tomas and the others. His straw-yellow comb-over was thinner and grayer than Tomas remembered, but his eyeglasses were exactly the same, soda-bottle-thick with black plastic frames. He gripped Tomas's hand and pumped hard. "Good to see you again."

"Good to see you, too, Jon, though I wish it were under any other circumstances," Tomas said softly.

"You people need to get back," a firefighter called from a dozen feet away. "Everyone back off at least a hundred feet. Let's go. Move it!"

"Come with me," Jon said. "There's nothing we can do here. Other than pray." He included Tomas's entourage with his eyes, and then turned and led the way across the lawns to the glorious red stone Sage Chapel, which wasn't far from the devastation and yet remained miraculously undamaged. Its arched stained-glass windows and the statue of Jesus above the front door were untouched. And as they entered through the tall wooden doors, Tomas felt the same awe he had always felt when he stepped inside this building.

He'd seen a lot of churches, a lot of cathedrals, all over the world. But in his heart, this one held its own and then some in comparison. Vaulted ceilings, the inverted ship-rib design of churches of old, the sheer magnitude of the place, took his breath away. It was holy here, regardless of one's belief system. And that was, he thought, the very point.

It was a place of power. And he felt safe within its walls.

"Sit, sit," Jon said, as they slid into the pews, Father Dom sliding in beside him and Jon, while Indy and Rayne took seats in the row just ahead. He glanced at Indy, then got stuck staring at her face. She was looking around, taking in the chapel he'd always considered one of the most beautiful ever built, and her eyes showed appreciation, admiration, maybe even awe.

"Tomas? Are you listening?" Jon asked.

He jerked his gaze away, focusing again on his friend, but not before noting the stern look of disapproval on his mentor's face. "I'm sorry. This is just so awful."

"Especially given what your friend Jon just told us," Father Dom put in. "He overheard one of the officers saying something about a bomb."

"A bomb?"

Tomas shot a look at Indy, who looked as shocked as he did. She'd missed hearing that, too, lost in the beauty of the chapel, while he'd been lost in the beauty of her.

"Of course they won't release that information anytime soon," Jon was saying. "But yes, a bomb. Were you two at the conference?" he asked suddenly. "Is that why you're here?"

"No," Tomas assured him. "Dom was planning to attend later, but we were at my place, above the lake. You remember."

"Of course." Jon looked at the women, then back at Tomas, reminding him that he had yet to introduce anyone.

"I'm sorry. Jonathon, meet my friend Indira Simon and my sister Rayne Blackwood. And this is Father Dominick."

177

"Sister?" Jon shot a surprised look at Rayne, then back again.

No wonder. When Jon had known him, Tomas had no family. Only Father Dom. "We found each other only a few years ago," he said, then quickly changed the subject. "Everyone, Jon is a professor here at Cornell. Ancient linguistics."

"Oh, you're the one," Indy said with a nod. "Tomas, he could look at that video and maybe see what's —"

"I was thinking the same thing."

She met his eyes, and he felt a connection, a knowing, as if they were on the same page, finishing each other's thoughts like a couple with twenty years behind them.

"What video?" Jon asked, breaking the moment.

Tomas sighed. "Since there's really nothing we can do here . . . do you have a few minutes and a computer we can use?"

"Yes, of course. My office is across campus, though. Are you up for a walk?"

Others were filing into the chapel by then, many of them kneeling to pray, others weeping.

"I'd be glad to get away, to tell you the truth," Indy said. "There's so much death here."

"I feel it, too," Rayne said softly.

As the five of them left the chapel, Tomas looked back toward the rubble, and saw body bags lying along the pavement. He lowered his head and whispered a silent prayer, wafting a blessing toward those souls.

When he looked up, he noted that his sister was doing exactly the same, in her own way.

Indy looked from one of them to the other. "They're dead," she said. "Or buried alive awaiting help. Only the rescue workers can help them now." Her tone was almost challenging.

She almost stomped as she walked away, following Jon, who was obliviously leading them to his office. Rayne lunged after her, but Tomas caught her by the wrist. "Let her be. She's making a last-ditch effort to retain her skepticism right now. The alternative means that what's happening to her is real, and she's just not ready to handle that yet."

"She'd better get ready soon. If Father Dom is right and the demon is responsible for this, then he's more dangerous than I knew."

But not more dangerous than Dom knew, Tomas thought.

I was becoming tired of being surrounded

by people who saw everything as a sign, as some otherworldly message, a clue. People who blamed everything on gods or devils, and who considered praying or casting spells to be the maxed-out top of their personal responsibility. I'd forgotten for a while there just why I'd walked away from organized religion of any kind.

Religious people were all alike. Every one of them. Leaning on crutches that were inventions of weak minds. There was a logical explanation for what was happening to me. I had only come here to rule out the illogical ones. And yeah, maybe I had also let myself be swayed by those milk-chocolate eyes and the urge to drag my fingers through that thick, dark hair.

At least that was what I was still trying to believe. Admittedly, that meant that what was happening to me was some kind of mental breakdown, which wasn't a much more pleasant prospect than past lives and a vengeful demon. But a little.

Okay, maybe deep down inside I knew better, and maybe that knowing was growing bigger by the minute, but I wasn't ready to concede.

Not just yet. It scared me to realize how close I had come to buying into the crazy. But demons didn't plant bombs. People did.

Ordinary human dirtbags. Often in the name of religion, which was another reason I disliked it.

We headed into another gorgeous building — the architecture on the Cornell campus was still blowing me away with every freaking building we passed — and wove through a couple of hallways and up one flight to Professor Yates's office. He booted up his computer and looked over at Tomas.

As Jon stepped out of the way and Dom looked on, Tomas sat down behind the desk and began tapping keys. Jonathon looked up and met my eyes. "There's coffee — only about an hour old — if you want," he said, nodding toward a small table in the corner.

I went for it. Now that I was back on the juice, I got grouchy if I didn't get enough of it. He had a few heavy mugs, white with green stripes around the tops. I filled one, searched for creamer and wondered why coffee always tasted better out of just the right kinds of mugs. Like these.

"Mini fridge," Jonathon said, reading my mind and nodding toward another corner.

I was stirring the thick cream — not half-and-half, real cream, because clearly the prof knew how to live — into my mug, watching its golden swirls transform my coffee, when Tomas said, "It's gone."

"What's gone?" I asked.

"The video of you kicking the hell out of those subway muggers without ever touching them, and screaming at them in what I think was ancient Babylonian."

I sighed in relief, taking a drink and knowing that any second he'd be asking for my phone, where the video was saved.

I was licking my lips, savoring the taste of what had to be some kind of exotic blend, when blackness descended like a heavy curtain dropping faster than an ancient Babylonian witch from a cliff. I heard the cup break on the floor at my feet. A momentary feeling of utter remorse for the wasted delight washed through me as hot liquid spattered my boots. But other than that, I pretty much checked out at that point.

Tomas had been just about to ask Indy for her phone when suddenly she dropped her mug and stood with her arms pulled behind her back. Her feet were together, body tilted slightly forward as if she was standing on a precipice and about to fall over. And damn if there wasn't a breeze moving her hair. *Inside* the office.

He shot out of the desk chair. Everyone else in the room had frozen in place, just staring at her. She stood there, eyes closed, hair wafting in a breeze that seemed to grow stronger, lifting it higher.

"What the hell is —"

"Shh," Tomas said, cutting Jon off, then gesturing to include them all in the command. And then he approached her, carefully, cautiously. "I'm here to help you," he said softly.

"Atta baltata u anāku mūt i-ta-x!"

Tomas shot a look at Jon, who quickly scrambled back behind the desk, turned his computer around so the screen was facing outward and hit a button on the keyboard. "Babylonian," he said. "Early period. God, this is tough. I've heard it spoken by linguists trying to re-create the language, but this is . . . this is raw. This is authentic. The accent . . . everything! It's . . . it's like it's real. All right, uh, I think she's saying, *You are alive . . . but I am dying. . . .*"

Tomas nodded, though he hadn't taken his eyes off Indy for more than an instant. "You're not dying. I'm here to help you. To save you. Can you . . . can you tell me your name?"

Her eyes flashed open and met his, and the power they held hit him in the gut, nearly doubling him over. He felt its force

183

in every part of his body, and it was intensified by the shock that her eyes were dark,
dark brown, perhaps even ebony, now. Yes,
black. He couldn't distinguish the irises
from the pupils. She glared at him, her hair
blowing even more in the nonexistent wind,
and she said "In-DEE-rah!"

Jon peered at his computer screen, then at
the girl whose image was reflected in it, its
built-in camera recording her every move.
"Tomas, what the hell is going on here?"

Tomas held up a hand for silence, but
Indy answered for herself, not in her own
voice, but in English that seemed to be a
strain for her to speak, laden with a thick
accent. "He ees aboud to keel me." She
nodded toward Tomas. "To . . . poosh me
over." She looked down, no doubt seeing
not a carpeted floor but a vast emptiness
with jagged rocks at the bottom.

"No," Tomas said. "Not me. I won't hurt
you. I would never — I wasn't there then."

"Yes, you are dere. Your hands upon my
back. You are de one. You keel me den. You
keel me now. *You!*"

He stared at her, not knowing what to say,
but she went on, the words foreign, his mind
not even registering them this time until
Jon whispered, "Even though I loved you."

And then, with a bloodcurdling scream,

184

Indy pitched forward and fell facedown onto the floor.

9

I remembered it all when I awoke. Every last bit of it, in startlingly clear and vivid detail. I remembered standing on the edge of that cliff far from the city, with my sisters on either side of me. And the arrogant high priest Sindar giving orders from a safe distance. He'd stood on a tall boulder, above us all, shiny bald head painted in designs of red and black. The wind was snapping his red robes, and there was malice in his eyes. I'd hated him then. I hated him now. The emotion filled me and flowed like acid from my pores. It burned, my hate for that bastard.

And that other man, my sister's lover, beaten bloody, being held and forced to watch. Him, I pitied. And even admired. Even though he could barely stand upright on his own, he struggled against the bastards who held him. He'd murdered the king in his rage, trying to escape and save us. Or her, at least. Lilia.

I knew his name, that tortured man. It was Demetrius.

And I remembered Tomas. Not his name — that hadn't been his name then. But it was him. There was no doubt in my mind it was him. He was a servant of the temple, as were the two men who stood behind my sisters. Apprentice priests, learning at the feet of the master. It was Tomas who had stood behind me with his hands on my back that terrifying, fateful day.

How I knew, I could not be sure. He hadn't looked the same. Oh, his hair was similar, dark and thick, though it had been longer then. His eyes had been darker, and closer set. They were a lighter brown now, set farther apart. They were also wiser, deeper somehow. His jawline had been harder then, his lips thinner. Today the jaw was strong but not cruel, and his lips full and thick. He did not look the same. He did not occupy the same body. And yet I knew him. Sensed him.

Loved him.

He'd been a young priest, obeying the commands of Sindar. Blinded by his faith? I felt his hands — hands that had once caressed me in passion — touching my back as I prepared to die. But I knew his betrayal must have broken my heart and my spirit long before my body was broken on the rocks below.

It was so cruel!

Tears burned, squeezing their way from beneath my lashes and spilling hotly onto my face, then sliding down either side toward my ears and my pillow.

My . . . pillow?

I was in a bed. I squeezed my eyes tighter, frowning, trying to get a grip on where I had wound up — and how I'd wound up there. I'd been at Cornell with Tomas and Dom and Rayne, and we'd met that professor . . . Jonathon Yates. And then I'd been on the cliff about to die. In the past. Not a dream. Not a hallucination. It had been real.

No, no, no, I don't really believe any of that. Do I?

"Indy?"

His voice. God, his voice. No, I couldn't bear it.

"Indy, are you awake?"

I blinked my eyes open and met his. A sob racked my chest, and I clapped a hand over my mouth to try to catch the sound it made before it escaped, but it was no use. My tears were streaming, my chest heaving with the power of heartbreak.

"It's all right," Tomas said softly. His hand

was stroking my hair, his eyes on mine, and so filled with concern and . . . and feeling. "It's okay, I'm right here. Tell me what's happening. What are you feeling? What do you remember?"

I stared at him, searching his face, knowing that the utter heartbreak unfolding inside me was completely irrational. It made no sense. It wasn't real. And yet the words that stumbled brokenly from my lips were, "How c-c-could you? Oh, Tomas, how could you?"

He was apparently stunned into utter silence by my question, and he lowered his head, unable to look me in the eyes. I noticed odd things then. The darkness beyond the bedroom window, how purple-gray it was, so I couldn't tell if it was day or night, or judge how long I'd been out. I could only tell that there was a storm building.

"Then it's true?" he asked softly. "What you remembered, it's true?" His fists were clenched on his knees. "I wanted to deny it. To say you were imagining it all, but your memories haven't lied to you yet. Indy, I can't imagine myself, in any lifetime, ever being capable of hurting you." He lifted his head and met my eyes again. "I'm so, so sorry."

As a fresh flood of tears washed over my face, I turned my head toward the wall. "It was just a dream. It's not real."

"It *is* real. And if you remember that we were lovers in that lifetime, Indy, I have to say, it explains a lot. The feelings I've been . . . wrestling with since I first set eyes on you . . . It's no wonder, really. It's —"

"It was just a dream." I snapped the words that time, angry at him. Angry over something that, even if it had been real, had happened thousands of years in the past. Furious. *And how much freakin' sense does that make, Indy?*

About as much as the rest of this, that's how much.

"It wasn't a dream," he told me.

I shot him a look, let him see how pissed I was at him, no matter how illogical the feeling was. "Yeah? Well, if it wasn't a dream, then it ought to be a very big lesson to you in what religion does for people. Blind faith. Murdering those who challenge your beliefs or break your rules. Stupid obedience to some man-made cleric who deems himself closer to God, whatever the hell God is, than you are. What kind of a weak-willed idiot would —"

The look of absolute pain in his eyes made me lose my train of thought and bite back the rest of my words. I blinked and looked away from him. Took a breath. Swallowed hard. Started over.

"Obviously I'm still overwrought. The dream was powerful. And it seemed very real. And my emotions are apparently convinced it was, no matter how little sense that makes. I'm feeling right now as if the man I loved murdered me. And I'm feeling as angry at you as if you really were him. I'm sorry, Tomas. You don't deserve that." I looked away again. "It's all freakin' ridiculous, but that's what's going on in here right now." I patted my head as I said it, and realized I should have been patting my chest. This was all happening in my heart. My head knew better.

"I'm sorry, Indy. I'm so very sorry."

"You didn't do anything. Not really."

He lowered his head, and I could have sworn I glimpsed a hint of moisture on one dark eyelash. "And I have to say this," he went on. "You know as well as I do that religion isn't evil. Religion is beautiful. Mine is. Yours is. They're sacred paths to understanding the Divine. When individuals do ugly things in the name of their chosen faith, it says nothing about the faith. Only about the individual."

I lowered my head, ashamed of myself. "I

know. I'm sorry."

He nodded. "Regardless of what happens here, with this quest of ours, I give you my word, my solemn oath, that I will spend the rest of this lifetime trying to make up for the horrible wrong I did to you then."

With an aggravated sigh, I slapped my hands down on the mattress, then pushed myself up into a sitting position. Angrily, I knuckled my eyes dry. "Don't beat yourself up, *Padre.* It's not real."

"Then how were you speaking perfect Babylonian?" he asked softly. "And why the hell does it feel more real than the floor under my feet right now?"

I stared into his eyes, a snappy comment on my lips, and then forgot what I was going to say. He lifted his hand to the back of my head, fingers tangling in my hair, and drew me nearer. My eyes fell closed, and I swayed toward him as his other arm came around me, pulling me tight to his chest as his lips caught mine. He kissed me.

I held on for dear life, clung to him, and felt a firestorm in my chest that just wouldn't die down. I kept reasoning with myself, but my self wasn't listening.

It isn't real. None of this is real. It was just a dream. Magic isn't real, God isn't real, religion isn't real, witchcraft isn't real. There are no curses, no demons, no angels, no reincarnation, no past lives, no —

His mouth opened and closed over mine, in a gentle yet demanding rhythm that was born of nature. And my arms twined around him, palms flattening to his powerful back and clinging there as I opened to him. His tongue swept into me as if he were feeding from my mouth, like a hummingbird drawing nectar from a lily.

Love isn't real. No, no, no, this feeling expanding my heart like a balloon about to burst isn't real. It can't be. . . .

I clung hard, falling back onto the pillows and pulling him with me. We shifted and clung, and wound up completely in the bed. His body was stretched out on top of mine, his hips moving in a pattern as old as time. I arched mine in answer. And the answer was yes.

There was a powerful flash of lightning that lit the entire bedroom, a crash of thunder on its heels. And Tomas stopped moving. Slowly he drew his mouth away from mine. And then his body followed, easing his delicious weight off me. He got up from the bed and stood beside it, staring down at me. I was lying there with my hair all tousled, still staring at him hungrily and longingly — willing him with whatever power lived in me to return to my bed. To my arms.

He pushed his hands through his hair. "God, what am I doing?"

I closed my eyes, ashamed of trying manipulative magic on him. "I'm sorry," I whispered.

"You? It's not you, it's me. You have no vows to uphold. You remember what we were to each other then. It's no wonder you're acting on those memories now. I don't have that excuse. I don't even remember what happened between us, what we felt. . . ."

"Part of you does." I sat up as I spoke.

"I'm a priest!"

"You were then, too. Didn't I mention that part? You were a priest, and I was a harem slave. We were both breaking the rules, Tomas." I bit my lip, shook myself. "Or would've been, if it was real."

"Didn't work out so well for us, did it?" he asked. "If it was real, I mean." He shook his head slowly and turned away from me, staring at the rain that had, at some point, begun pounding down outside. It was darker than before, telling me night had fallen, and that fact startled me as it made its way into my brain. It had been morning, last I remembered.

"I'm sorry, Indy. This can't happen."

"Because having sex is a big no-no, right? Worse than murdering in the name of God. Worse than betraying a woman who loved you." I closed my eyes tight. "God, I think I'm losing my mind. None of it's real. None of it."

I hugged my waist, the sheet trapped between my arms and my nightgown, lowered my head.

Why does it feel as if it's the most real thing in my life?

And who the hell changed my clothes?

Rayne. Had to be Rayne.

"We *will* get through this, Indy. All of it. I'll help you."

"Sure," I said. "Whatever you say . . . Father Tomas."

He nodded at the nightstand. "I had to run back out for supplies while you were sleeping. I bought you a journal. Rayne thinks it might help you to start recording your dreams as soon as you wake up."

I didn't look at it, just kept my head down. "Thanks. I'll do that."

"Can I get you anything else?"

Yeah, I thought. *A day's worth of calories, a vat of coffee and a fucking bus ticket home.* But aloud I only said, "No. I'm fine."

"I'll go get some sleep, then."

"All right."

"Good night, Indy." He was willing me to look at him. If I did, I thought, I would die. Every time I looked into his eyes the emotions of some make-believe other lifetime welled up in me, and I wanted to wrap myself safely in his arms and never come out. Stupid.

And yet, he was making me look, tugging at me with his eyes, and I obeyed as if hypnotized. Lifting my head, I met those brown eyes. *I love you* danced on my tongue and knocked on my teeth, and I clamped my jaw to prevent the ridiculous declaration from leaping out.

When it was safe to speak, I managed to say, "Good night, Tomas."

But to my own ears it had sounded just the same as the words I'd refused to say. And from the look on his face as he left me there, I think it sounded that way to him, too.

Tomas went to his own room and asked himself what the hell he'd been thinking to bring her here, under the same roof with him.

He took a bracing shower, cold enough to help him regain his focus, but he couldn't shower forever. After that he pulled on a

196

pair of pajama pants and paced until he found himself with his arms braced against the windowsill, staring into the storm-ravaged night sky. Impulse lowered his head, long practice moved his lips. Habit, not faith. His faith was on the bench, sitting off an injury. His faith had taken a beating followed by an open-ended vacation that had begun before he'd even met the woman next door. And yet, out of habit, Tomas prayed.

"Help me see clearly. Help me know what's right. If I failed that miserably in the past, how can I trust my own judgment now? What seems like an obvious sin in hindsight must have seemed like my duty at the time. It *must* have. Or I would never —" His chest heaved, throat tightening until it hurt. "I could never — God . . . how could I have killed her?"

His knees bent — not habit this time but pure weakness — and he wound up resting on them, head still bowed against the cool glass while the rain pounded against the other side. He had never fully believed that this task was his calling. He had never believed he was destined to prevent a demon from crossing into the world and wreaking havoc on mankind. But now . . . now he was seeing things he couldn't deny. He had been inextricably entwined in this

197

curse, in this prophecy, in this madness, since the very beginning. He'd thought he was just picking up the story where the last Guardian of the Portal had left off. But instead he was continuing a story he himself had started centuries and centuries ago. The other Guardians Dom had told him about had been nothing but placeholders. Tools, used by God, to ensure he would inherit the information he needed to find her again. To make this right somehow.

"Maybe Dom's right," he whispered. "Maybe by keeping her from helping the demon I might save her from this nightmare and make up for taking her life. That has to be it."

Then why did his theory feel so incomplete?

He lifted his head, opened his eyes, and then jerked backward so fast he fell on his backside on the floor. Just beyond the glass a raven was sitting on a tree limb, hunched against the rain and glaring in at him. Its eyes were lifeless and cold, like black marbles, its feathers ruffled and beaded with water. It didn't look away. It just stared.

It wasn't right. Wasn't natural. Neither was the icy chill dancing down his spine. His breath stuttered out of him, and he saw puffs of steam as he shivered. With every thing in him, he knew he was in the presence of evil.

"Get thee behind me," he whispered. Habit again. But it didn't work.

Forcing himself to his feet, he squared his shoulders and yanked the window upward. Then he leaned outside into the pouring rain, waving his arms at the thing. "Get away! Go on, get out of here. You've got no business here!"

With a furious squawk and a flapping of huge wet wings, the bird took off. Tomas drew back inside the room and reached up to close the window. But as he grabbed hold of it, he glimpsed the lawn below.

A fox, its mouth open as if panting, tongue lolling out, eyes fixed on him. Movement caught his eye, a furry white flash in the storm. A whitetail buck a few yards to the fox's right, standing there staring up at him, angrily pawing at the earth, flicking his tail. Tomas forced himself to look away. To scan farther. A raccoon, a coyote, three pigeons, a woodchuck, a chipmunk. All scattered across the lawn, staring up at him in the moonlight with lifeless eyes. He stood straighter, chills racking his entire body.

And then Dom's voice boomed, "Thou art an offense unto me! In the name of Jesus Christ, be gone!"

Tomas jerked his head around to see his friend standing in the bedroom doorway, then quickly back again. The animals were scattering into the trees. In seconds the lawn lay empty, raindrops pelleting the grass.

"You should've done that yourself, Tomas."

Tomas turned again, stung by the disgust in Dom's tone. The old man was looking at him as if waiting for something.

As if he knew.

"Why didn't you?" Father Dom asked softly. "Are you worried that you've . . . lost favor with God?"

Tomas averted his eyes, refusing to answer Dom's subtle charge. He couldn't answer to anyone but God Almighty. Not on this one. "Why would I worry about that?"

Dom broke eye contact but seemed to be listening intently as he paced a few steps one way, then the other, rubbing his chin as he spoke. "Well, Indira, of course. Now that she's got you believing you were lovers in another lifetime I —"

"More important, that I killed her in that other lifetime," Tomas interrupted.

"Well, either way." Father Dom nodded toward the window. "What do you think you saw out there tonight?"

Tomas turned to gaze out into the pour-

200

ing rain. "Animals. Animals everywhere, staring up at me. It was . . . unnatural. And cold. I could see my breath." He frowned and blew into a cupped hand. "But I can't now."

"It was him," Dom said. "He Whose Name Must Not Be Spoken. He's found you."

Tomas lifted his brows.

"He knows there will be a witch who's meant to help him, and a priest who's sworn to stop her, in the vicinity of the Portal in the days before he can cross. That's why he attacked the conference."

"I still don't understand how he could have done that. He's still on the other side. A spirit being, not a physical one."

Father Dom's face softened. It always put him in a better mood when he was asked his opinion, and he was never humble about giving it. He sank onto a chair near the window. "He can't do anything physical himself, of course. But he can influence some minds. Only the weakest of humans are vulnerable. The young, the mentally ill. But for a demon to exert influence over animals is easy. Common. He can see through their eyes, hear through their ears, for brief periods." He nodded toward the lawn. "What you saw were his eyes and ears.

He's watching us through them. He's found us, Tomas. None of us are safe on our own. Only God's grace and protection are keeping him at bay right now."

Tomas shivered and gave serious thought to bringing the shotgun up to his room for the rest of the night. "But what about the conference?" he asked. "No animal planted that bomb."

"I just heard it on the television. They've picked up an escaped mental patient. This formerly docile inmate just up and walked out of the hospital. He stole a truck, drove straight to a hardware store for fertilizer, then to a gas station for diesel fuel, and from there —"

"Straight to Cornell."

Father Dom nodded. "Weak mind." He tapped his head.

Tomas tended to think some of the mentally ill had more receptive minds than the supposedly sane people of the world. He believed it was more about wavelength than illness, frequency on the proverbial dial. They were simply more in tune with the spiritual realms than every one else.

But of course, that theory could be taken wrong, like some sort of blasphemy, so it was an opinion he seldom voiced.

"Where was the witch when the animals

appeared?" Dom asked.

"In her room sleeping, as far as I know. But if you're suggesting she was behind this, forget it. Indy wouldn't know how to control the mind of a field mouse." He smiled briefly as her face showed up in his mind's eye, and then he frowned as her expression turned from teasing to afraid. "As a matter of fact, I think we shouldn't even mention this to her. She's scared enough as it is."

"I think it best we don't tell Indy anything beyond what she needs to know," Father Dom said. "She's not on our side in this, Tomas. Not willingly. And you must not forget for one moment what she is."

Tomas looked away. *Here we go again.*

"She's a witch who made a pact with a demon over three thousand years ago, and who has lived lifetime after lifetime with only one goal — to keep that promise, fulfill that pact. She's a powerful witch. She can seduce a man without laying a hand on him. They all can. And she's already trying to seduce you. She's homed in on your weakest point, your overly caring heart — made weaker, I might add, by your long denied libido."

Tomas averted his eyes.

"Don't be ashamed. Desire weakens every man. It's a test of your faith, Tomas. It's not supposed to be easy."

"My faith is fine, Father." But it wasn't. It hadn't been in a long time.

Dom shook his head as if he knew better. "She's convinced you that you've wronged her, that you owe her, that you loved her once. For the love of God, be strong, Tomas. Remember it's all an act, a game. You're nothing to her! Nothing, that is, but the enemy." He rose from his chair and clapped a hand onto Tomas's shoulder. "If it came down to you or the demon, she would think nothing of killing you, you know."

"I don't believe that," Tomas said.

"Well, you'd better believe it. If you hope to succeed in your quest, you had better, by God, believe it." He drew a deep breath, wheezing a little as he exhaled, and turned to go. "I'll pray for you. For all of us."

But not for her, I'll bet, Tomas thought. And he wondered again if he was on the right side in any of this, and doubted it more than ever. Oh, sure, the side of the demon was the wrong one. But was Dom really any better? Was there a third option no one had seen or even bothered to look for?

After Tomas left the room, I slipped out of bed and tiptoed to Rayne's bedroom. After tapping softly on the door and getting no reply, I opened it slightly. "Rayne? You in there?"

She wasn't. But I heard her shower running, and I spotted her laptop on the nightstand. Precisely what I needed. I slipped inside and picked it up, scribbled a note promising to return it in a couple of hours, or sooner if she needed it, and thanked her for the loan.

Then I took it back to my room. I emailed myself the photos I'd snapped from Father Dom's journal, then accessed my email account from Rayne's computer and opened them one by one.

The first photo showed a drawing marked "Amulet." It was a disk-shaped piece about two inches in diameter, with twin gemstones almost where eyes would be, if it were a face. It wasn't a face, though. There was a tiny ring on the top with a chain through it.

Frowning, I opened the next image.

In order for He Whose Name Must Not Be Spoken to escape from the Underworld, he must have the amulet. The witch who served him long ago secreted something of his within it. We know not what. Only that, without it, he cannot escape.

"But I don't have any amulet," I whispered. Maybe the priests had the wrong witch, after all.

When the first witch is activated and her memories of that long ago lifetime are stirred anew, she will recall how to attain the amulet, which she herself hid in the astral plane. Only she can retrieve it. And once she has it, she will attempt to pass it on to the demon. She is bound to help him, by word and by vow, and nothing will stop her. Besides, stopping her would only keep him imprisoned until conditions are right for him to make another attempt. Instead, the priest in charge must allow — even encourage — her in her efforts. Bring her to the Portal. Assist her in remembering. Allow her to retrieve the amulet from the astral plane.

As soon as she does, it must be destroyed, no matter the cost. If this is done, the demon will be doomed to remain in the Underworld for all eternity.

The remaining pages were filled with things I already knew or rambling sermonettes in Father Dom's shaky hand. I deleted all the images and returned to Rayne's room. I peeked in and saw that she was sound asleep, so I just left the laptop on the floor inside her bedroom door and tiptoed back to my own room.

I was beyond disillusioned. Tomas had lied to me. He'd told me that my destiny was to help him. But the truth was, I was supposed to help the demon.

And what kind of a woman did that make me, anyway? What kind of witch had I been back in Babylon? Had I *deserved* to be pushed off that cliff?

Hell, I didn't know. I couldn't sleep, though. I sat up in bed for a long time before I finally decided to make use of the gorgeous leather-bound journal Tomas had brought me, and then I wrote and wrote and wrote until my eyes were drooping and my vision swimming.

The sun rose hot and unforgiving, slanting in through my bedroom window and burning my eyes. I looked up from the journal, still open on my lap, with one hand at my forehead, like a military salute, and squinted against the light. It didn't do any good, though, so I set the embossed journal on the nightstand beside me and slid out of bed to close the curtains. Then I looked back at my rumpled covers and the clock beside the bed. 9:15 a.m.

"Dammit, how do I keep losing so many hours?"

Someone tapped on my bedroom door, and then it opened. Tomas peeked in at the empty bed, and then at me. "Damn," he said. "You look rough."

"Gee, thanks."

"Oh, come on. Even rough, you're beautiful, and I think you know it."

I almost gaped at the unexpected compliment. He seemed embarrassed by it, too. "Are you okay?" he asked.

"Up all night," I said. "But I guess that's because I slept the day through yesterday."

"Probably." He nodded at the journal. Lilies were cut into the leather, a dragonfly landing on one of them. "Writing?" he asked.

"After a while."

"Anything you want to share — in the journal, I mean?"

"Not with *him.*" I didn't mean it to sound as nasty as it did, and I wished I could take it back, but it was too late.

"And you think anything you say to me is going to go straight to Father Dom, is that it?"

I met his gorgeous brown eyes. He had been on my side, or at least I'd thought he was. "Wouldn't it?" I asked, watching his face.

"No. If you want to talk confidentially, I promise I'll keep it to myself." He sat on the edge of my bed. "You can trust me, Indira."

Could I? I really did want to talk about

some of the things from the dreams. More and more had come back to me as I'd been writing, almost as if the act itself was a form of hypnotic regression or some shit like that.

Walking toward the bed, I picked up the journal and closed it, running my hand over its tooled leather cover. "It's a beautiful book."

"Rayne thought I should have gone with a black one, with a pentacle cut-out. But I thought you'd prefer this one."

"You were right." Did he know me that well so soon, or was it more? Or maybe it was just a lucky guess. My stomach growled out loud.

"You're starving," he said. "Dom and Rayne have already eaten, but I waited for you, so I'm starved, too."

"You waited for me?"

He nodded, averting his eyes.

"Where are they now?" I asked. Behind him, beyond the still-open bedroom door, the house had an empty feeling to it that I was only just now noticing.

"Rayne wanted to make a grocery run, and she somehow managed to talk Dom into going with her. I think she wanted to give us a break."

I smiled as my face got warm. "She's an even better friend than I realized."

"So it's just two of us for the next couple of hours. In a well-stocked kitchen, on an utterly gorgeous morning. I say we enjoy a big fat breakfast on the deck."

I waited for him to say more. He didn't, so *I* did. "And talk about the demon?"

"Not unless you want to." He got up and started for the door. "So what'll it be? Eggs? French toast? I make a mean French toast. Or another Belgian waffle?"

"That was our first meal together," I said. "Belgian waffles at IHOP." Maybe it was a little wistful sounding. Because I was feeling wistful, and also twisted and conflicted and confused about the man. Maybe I'd loved him once. Maybe he'd killed me once. Maybe he was lying to me now. He was forbidden. Maybe a danger to me. And yet I wanted him so much it was like a knife in my belly.

He stopped, hand on the doorknob, and looked over his shoulder at me. "I know you sense Dom's . . . dislike of witches," he said. "I don't share it. I think you're a terrific human being, Indy, and I did even when we were basically strangers."

I blinked. He was winning me over. "We're not strangers anymore?"

He shrugged. "You feel more like family now. I know Rayne feels the same way."

I closed my eyes, smiled easily. "Thanks, Tomas. That means a lot to me. You and Rayne . . . No, never mind. It's none of my business."

He shrugged. "Go on and ask. I know you're dying to."

"Okay, I will. I didn't think you had any family. Why are your last names different? She's never been married."

"Well, we're not full brother and sister. We just have the same father. My mother committed suicide when I was ten, and hers OD'd. We both went into the system, not even knowing each other existed. Rayne wound up being raised by a halfway decent aunt on her mother's side. I spent most of my childhood in an orphanage run by nuns. Until Father Dom took me in."

"And sent you to Cornell. How did he afford it?"

He lowered his head. "I had a pretty sizeable scholarship."

Holy shit, he must be even more brilliant than I thought.

"My plan was to attend a seminary after that, and I started, but Father Dom pulled me out early. Said it was urgent that he begin one-on-one training with me."

"And you went for that?" I asked, surprised.

211

He nodded. "Father Dom was the closest thing I had to a father. I never knew my real one. So when he told me God had spoken to him, and that the Church had given him a special dispensation to ordain me himself immediately — well, what could I say? I was handpicked by God for this, Dom said. And you know, given what we're learning about the past, I'm starting to believe it."

I was mesmerized, soaking up every revelation about Tomas as if I were starving for information. In my mind's eye I could see him as a child, and then as a young man. And now. I could definitely see him as he was now.

"When did you find each other?" I asked.

"One of the sisters in the orphanage sent me a letter right after I was ordained. She said she'd held on to the secret as long as she could and thought I had a right to know. She sent Rayne a copy, too. I have no idea how that nun knew, and she died before I had a chance to ask her, but she'd known about us all along. She thought she was doing us a favor not to tell us when we were still too young to do anything about it. Rayne's aunt didn't want any more kids, and we lived on opposite sides of the country. So knowing just would have made things harder, she thought."

"Wow."

"You wouldn't believe my surprise when I found out my sister was a witch." He smiled when he said it. Like it was a term of endearment.

"Or hers, I'll bet, when she found out you were a priest."

He lowered his eyes. "You know, she never passed judgment. Never condemned me. I even started reading books on the Craft so I could understand her better. And she started sitting in on mass to learn more about me. He sighed, shaking his head slowly. "She's not your average witch, Indy."

"And you're not the average priest. Not even . . . the average man," I whispered before I could stop myself.

I love him.

Shut up.

He was staring at me as if I'd just revealed more than I ought to. Was my voice all raspy when I said that? Were my eyes all dreamy? I thought so. Was it possible all my casting and conjuring had finally paid off? My soul mate had finally shown up, only — surprise, surprise — it turns out he's a priest. Not only that, but apparently, my sworn enemy and former murderer. Nice.

If the Goddess is real, She's a total bitch.

Sorry. A total Bitch. Capital B. Out of respect. And why the hell am I feeling like crying again?

"I'm going to take a shower. I'll be down in twenty minutes for that breakfast you promised me," I told him. "French toast sounds perfect."

I left him there staring after me, and I took the journal with me when I went to take my shower.

10

I sat on the deck in the sunshine, my belly pleasantly full, embracing a warm coffee mug, watching Tomas flip pages in my journal, which I'd been discussing with him. I would never know if I could trust him or not unless I gave it a try. Besides, he knew things. He was the kind of man I had aspired to be with one day, back when I believed in gods and goddesses and magic. A spiritual man, deeply intelligent, curious, open-minded, apart from his rather blind devotion to Father Dom. And now that I knew how much the old man had been to him, I couldn't even hold that against him, could I?

Maybe I was starting to believe again. A little bit.

He flipped another page and paused. "What's this?"

I reached for the book, turning it to face me. "Just a drawing of a tree. I keep seeing it in the dreams. Over and over. And it always feels . . . important. Like it means something. But so far, I don't know what."

I studied the image of the gnarled old tree, but it didn't mean anything more to me now than when I'd drawn it.

"What kind of thoughts or feelings come to you when you see it?" he asked.

I sighed, shaking my head. "Excitement. And fear. And a kind of . . . knowing, except I don't know what it is I'm knowing."

He pulled the book back to him, staring down at the picture. "It looks kind of like an old man, doesn't it?"

"I thought that, too," I said, glad he was seeing what I had. Maybe that meant I wasn't completely insane. "There's his head, that big knot near the top." I pointed to the spot. "The swirls in the bark there look like wrinkles, and you can even pick out eyes."

"Yes, I see them. And that root almost looks like a crooked foot."

"Yeah. And this one limb is like an out-stretched arm. Even has a finger at the end. That sharp twig. Like it's pointing at something."

"What is he pointing at, Indy?"

"I don't know. I wish I did."

He sighed. "It's a good start. Keep doing

this, keep drawing what you see, writing about those dreams. It's bound to help."

"Oh, I will. I *am.* There are several other things that make me feel the same way the tree does. A boulder with writing on it. A medallion on a floor. A dark doorway underneath a statue. Oh! And a castle with spires. Look at it." I flipped pages, showing him my drawings as I listed them, glad to have someone to share things with.

Glad to have *him* to share it with was what I really meant. And I wanted to share a lot more with this man. I looked up then, caught him staring at me instead of the journal, and I could have sworn his eyes reflected the same senseless longing.

And then I looked away, because what the hell else could I do? "I just wish I knew where all this was going to end up."

"Well, that much I can tell you, Indy. You'll help me. The demon won't be able to come through. Samhain will come and go, and the Portal will close. And the world will be safe for another three thousand years." He touched my hand sending shivers up my spine. "If Father Dom is right about this, your dreams and flashbacks will go away, and you can get right back to living your life the way you want to."

"Yeah?" I asked. "And what if he's

wrong?"

He looked at me. "You know something you're not telling me?"

I wasn't quite ready to admit to him that I had snuck a peek at another journal last night. Father Dom's. But I did want to see his reaction to what I had learned — to test him a little, I guess. "Tomas, what if it turns out that I'm supposed to help the *demon*, not you and Dom?"

He frowned, and looked away from me. "Dom would see that as validation of his own prejudice. To him, witches are *all* in league with demons."

"I guess." I swallowed hard. He already knew all this, and he hadn't told me. Why? I wondered. Why would he lie to me? I stared at him, willing him to open up and tell me the truth.

Finally he tipped his head and said, "You know, even if you were on Team Demon in that past lifetime, it's not like you still would be now. You're a good witch. You would never want to help some demon take over the world."

I sighed, disappointed that he hadn't revealed more. "I guess you're right. I just can't help wondering . . . If that's true and Dom knows it but hasn't said anything, then what else might he — or even both of you

— be keeping from me? I don't like being lied to."

"I don't blame you." He reached across the table, clasping my hand in both of his. "Keep listening to your dreams, Indy. I think they're pointing the way, I really do."

"Something else has been niggling at me," I said. "That tattoo. 'Daughter of Ishtar.' If we were harem slaves, it stands to reason the king would have had plenty of chances to see it. Wouldn't it have given us away as witches?"

"Not at all," he said. "Ishtar was one of the goddesses of the Babylonian pantheon. Today, only witches and Pagans worship her. But back then, everyone did."

I nodded. "I should have known that. I just didn't think that —" I heard a car pull up out front. Our respite was over. And I regretted it to my toes.

Later that morning Tomas sat in Jon's office, uncomfortably aware of Dom standing judgmentally off to the side, fighting to keep his own face impassive as Jon did his bit with the subway video. He'd asked Indira for it, but she'd claimed to have deleted it from her phone. Which had him worried. Because he hadn't believed her. She'd seemed off this morning. All through breakfast. Quiet, watchful. He kept getting the feeling she was trying to see through his skull into his brain, trying to get him to tell her the things he hadn't yet revealed. Because she was right — she was supposed to be helping the demon. At least according to the legend. But she couldn't know that.

Unless she'd remembered.

No. She would have said so. Besides, she'd just learned that he had probably been the guy who'd pushed her off that cliff thirty-five-hundred years ago. He supposed that might have something to do with her wary demeanor.

Fortunately Rayne had saved a copy of the video on her hard drive at home, then accessed it from her phone and emailed him a copy, which he had in turn emailed to Jon Yates.

Jon was just as theatrical as ever, he thought. The guy could have just typed up the translation and sent him a copy. But no, it was considerably more dramatic to play a little bit of the video and then interpret Indy's foreign words, and then play a little more. He had the giant monitor turned toward them so they could follow along, and he stood, as if he were the star of some a.m. newscast, pacing as it played, then pausing it, and standing beside the screen to recite the lines in modern English.

"As you can see, she's just repeating the same phrase over and over again. 'Where is the Portal?' " He leaned over and tapped the mouse, and Indy started moving again. She spun in a beautiful martial arts move, threw her hand out in a punch at the end of it, then spun back the other way and did it again, followed by a flip. She thrust both hands out as she landed. Each time she punched the air, men went flying, but it was obvious she never touched them. She was throwing them around with some unseen power.

Then, just before the thugs ran off, she spun around to face the leader and shouted something else. Again Jon paused the recording.

"Here she says, 'Attacker of innocents! Just like the priest who killed us. Where is the Portal, damn you?' "

He hit a button and the images ran forward. This time he let the video play out almost to the end, where she was panting in exhaustion. Everyone else had fled the scene except the man recording it, who had finally gotten around to asking Indy if she was okay. She lay on the concrete, looking at the thugs as they ran off, and she spat out a sentence with so much hatred that Tomas

221

almost felt it burn. Jon paused the video and said, " 'I will find that priest. I will kill him.' "

Tomas got to his feet. "That's enough."

"There's one more line. 'Who can know the minds of the Underworld Gods?' It's right —" He was fast-forwarding as he spoke, but Tomas reached past him and stopped the playback.

"Enough, it doesn't mean anything." And yet, he was remembering that she'd recited that same line when he'd shown her the video for the first time. So she knew what she'd been saying. . . .

"Considering that a hotel full of clergy got blown to hell and gone yesterday, Tomas, I beg to differ," Jon said. "Was this woman out of your sight at all that day?"

"No, she was not. And I don't even see how that's relevant, since the police have already arrested the bomber."

"A young man without so much as a speeding ticket —"

"A mental patient," Tomas inserted.

"He was there for depression."

"I don't care if he was there to quit smoking. He did it. There's no doubt about that, is there?"

Jon sighed. "The only question is whether he acted alone. The police can't find a motive, and he claims not to know why, either. Kid's back in the hospital and on suicide watch now." He looked from Tomas to Dom and back again. "If you two know anything about this, or if your . . . friend is involved in any way —"

"We don't and she's not," Tomas interrupted. "Then why are you here in town? And why is she with you? And how the hell did she do all that stuff in the video. And —"

Dom held up a hand for silence. He had stayed in the back of the room, saying not a single word the entire time. Tomas thought he was trying to let him take the lead, to make him feel as if he were the one in charge of the mission. But he knew that would only last until he disagreed with the old man.

"Could you get anything else from the tape?" Father Dom asked.

"Tape?"

Dom waved a hand at the computer. "Pardon. Digital-whatever-it-is."

Sighing and, Tomas thought, finally seeing he would get no answers from them, Jon returned to the desk and hit the mouse. Tomas watched as, on the screen, Indy crawled into a corner and huddled there. Tears streaming, she moved her lips, but if she said anything, it was inaudible. He had totally missed that before.

"What was that?" Father Dom asked.

Jon held up a hand, clicked a few buttons. "Let me enhance the sound. I think I can get it." The video playback screen was reduced to a small box in the corner, and an audio box came up. As Jon clicked the Play arrow, vertical lines appeared, spiking and dipping as Indy's voice rose and fell.

Jon looked at the other men. " 'Where is my beloved? How much longer must I wait to feel his touch again?' "

Tomas closed his eyes. God, could she be talking about him? The man who'd pushed her from the cliff all those lifetimes ago? And yet hadn't she just promised to kill him if she found him? It made no sense.

Despite that threat, the anguish in her voice, in her face, as she expressed her longing for his return was real. And heartbreaking.

And it got to him.

When he opened his eyes again, Father Dom was shaking Jon's hand. "Thank you. We'll be in touch if we get any more . . . anything." He glanced at Tomas, and his eyes said, *I told you so.*

As they walked across the beautiful campus, far from the area that was still bar-

224

ricaded with crime scene tape, and crawling with investigators and journalists, Dom put a heavy hand on Tomas's shoulder. "At least now you have no doubt whose side she's on. Do you?"

"She didn't know what she was saying."

"Part of her did, son. The part of her that lived then."

"But that's not who she is now. No more than I am the same man who pushed her from that cliff three thousand years ago."

"But you are that man. And just as you did what you had to do then — what God demanded you do then — you will do what He demands of you now."

Tomas stopped walking and lifted his eyes to meet those of his mentor. "Did you know, when you chose me for this task, about my past-life involvement in all this?"

"No, Tomas. I didn't know. I chose you because God told me to choose you. He led me to you. He knew. He knows all."

Tomas's heart twisted into a knot of pain. "I want to remember."

"What?"

"I want to remember that past lifetime. I want to know what I knew then, to understand what brought me to the decision I made." He didn't know if he could bear it, but he knew he was on the right track. "I need to know, Dom. Is there a way?"

Dom's expression was like a door slamming. "No, Tomas. The past is gone. Only the future remains, and that's where you need to keep your focus. On the future. And your part in ensuring that there is one." He sighed, then strode onward. "We're going to have to come back here. We can't let your friend Jon keep any of his notes, much less that video. We should have taken it with us today."

"He won't share it. I've already told him to keep this between us."

"And you trust him to do that? With something this explosive?"

"I do," Tomas said.

Dom lowered his head. "Then you're a fool. Come on. I think it would be a good idea for us to have a talk with that bomb-making mental patient, don't you?"

I recounted the entire breakfast discussion to Rayne, only I told her the truth about having had a look at Dom's journal, and what it had to say about me being on the demon's side and having to find some kind of amulet Past Me had hidden in the astral plane in order to set him free.

I told her, too, while letting her flip through my journal, that I thought Tomas

226

knew all that and was keeping it from me. And she insisted that if that were true, he must have a damn good reason. But I knew she loved her brother. She wasn't exactly unbiased here.

And yet I wanted so much to believe in him, too.

Heaving a heavy sigh, I said, "I need to stop thinking about this for a while." I took my journal from her and closed the cover.

She smiled and jumped to her feet, not even seeming regretful at the change of subject, and I felt an immense surge of relief and gratitude for that. "I have just the thing to perk you up. How about we take a gorgeous, refreshing walk to the lake?"

My head came up. "That sounds really good right now."

"Oh, it will be. Better put your journal away first. Tomas wouldn't snoop, but that Father Dom —"

"Is a total asshole."

She laughed softly. "Bring your phone. You're going to want to take pictures of this."

"Okay." I clutched the journal close, and jogged back inside and up the stairs to tuck it away beneath my mattress. Then I rejoined Rayne, who was by then in the kitchen sticking a note to the fridge with a hawk-shaped magnet. The note told the others where we'd gone, in case they returned before we did. She had filled two water bottles, which were now dangling from her shoulder on long straps. "Ready?"

"Is it far?" I asked with a nod at the water as I took one bottle from her.

"The direct route isn't. But there's a more meandering path through the woods with a waterfall on the way. You'll love it. We'll bask in the sunshine and what's left of the autumn leaves, and have nature all around us. Not a word about demons or amulets the entire trip, I promise. Perfect, right?"

"If I had a smoke it would be," I said.

I almost jumped up and down at the look that crossed Rayne's face then. Her brows went up high, then she quickly lowered them again, avoiding my eyes.

"Rayne?" I said in a slightly menacing tone.

She sighed. "Oh, all right. I suppose you've earned it." She pulled a stool away from the breakfast bar and climbed up to reach on top of the kitchen cabinets, coming down with a pack of cigarettes — menthol, too. She took one out and tossed it at me.

I caught it, feeling better by the minute, and rummaged in the drawers until I found a lighter. "You do know your brother well."

"That I do. He keeps telling me he's quit. But he always has a stash." She replaced the pack, got down and put the stool back where it belonged. And then we headed out for a leisurely, blissful morning hike.

At least, that was what we intended it to be.

11

Tomas stood outside Marty Swenson's room at Tompkins County Mental Health, looking at the nineteen-year-old through the slightly open door. His stomach knotted with pity for the poor kid. He looked haggard, obviously laboring under the influence of whatever anti-psychotics had been pumped into him. His eyes were circled in more rings than Saturn, puffy, and so blue they looked bruised. The whites were bloodshot and dry. He was in restraints, though he didn't seem to notice. He just lay there, very still, staring at the ceiling, no expression in his lifeless gray eyes.

"You can talk to him, *Padres.* Just try not to upset him."

That was the officer stationed at the door. Father Dom had decided they should show off their collars rather than hide them on this particular visit. He'd given the police officer some line about the church's unofficial inquiry into the bombing, and his explanation had seemed to make perfect sense to the cop.

"Don't be in there too long," the cop added. "And quit if he gets agitated. His doctors don't want him upset. I'm enforcing their rules as much as anything else here. So I'm going for a coffee. You have until I get back. That sound good to you?"

"Of course," Father Dom said.

It occurred to Tomas that though he agreed with the officer, Father Dom would do whatever it took to get the information he wanted and wouldn't care if he upset the patient or not.

He's not always a very nice person, is he? Why haven't I ever seen that before?

He's just focused on the mission, that's all, he told himself.

But since when does the Bible teach that the end justifies the means?

Father Dom opened the door farther, and the two of them stepped inside, letting it close behind them.

"Hello, Marty. I'm Father Dominick, and this is Father Tomas. I hope it's all right if we talk with you for a few minutes."

The kid's eyes didn't move. He just maintained that unblinking focus on the ceiling so steadily that Tomas was surprised when he answered. "I don't care." He hadn't thought the kid had even heard Father Dom's question.

There were no chairs in the room. Nowhere to sit down, not even a table or a window ledge. Tomas stood awkwardly, watching the young man, content to let Dom do all the talking.

"I know that you aren't the one responsible for what happened."

The compassion in Dom's tone actually surprised Tomas into looking at him.

It apparently got to the patient, too. He blinked. It was the first time his eyes had moved at all.

"I know that someone else — something else — somehow got inside your mind and made you do what you did."

Another blink. "How do you know?"

"I just do. It's true, isn't it?"

Slowly, the young man in the bed nodded.

"Do you remember any of it? Buying the chemicals? Building the bomb? Taking it to the university? To the Statler?"

The boy's breath escaped in a slow stuttering sigh. "No. I didn't even know there were ministers and priests there."

"Can you tell me what you do remember?"

Tears welled in Marty's eyes. They coated

232

the dull gray, making it shine like wet concrete. "I fell asleep in the hospital. I woke up standing in the middle of a dust cloud, staring at a pile of rubble."

Dom's eyes shot to Tomas's, then darted back to the boy. "What about before that, Marty? What kinds of things were happening to you that landed you in the hospital to begin with?"

Marty closed his eyes slowly. "I can't . . ."

"We might be able to help you, if you'll tell us."

"We?" Finally his eyes shifted away from the ceiling, and when he saw Tomas, his expression made it clear that despite Dom's introductions, he'd just realized that the old priest was not alone. Then he focused solely on Tomas, and something changed. His eyes widened, and dark clouds seemed to gather in their gray depths, darkening them. "You," he whispered.

Tomas felt a cold chill go through him, and then realized it wasn't coming from inside but from without. His breath formed a cloud in front of his face.

"Where is she?" Again a whisper.

Tomas's throat was dry as he replied, "Where is who?" But he already knew.

"Bring me the witch! She is mine!" The kid's voice had broken, then deepened, emerged strong and bestial, with a growling undertone. "Bring her to me, or I will destroy you and all you love!" Marty tugged against the restraints, managing to sit up in the bed, trying to reach for Tomas. "Bring her to me, dammit. Bring me the witch!"

Tomas gripped Dom's arm and backed toward the door, but before he made it there, the kid suddenly relaxed and smiled very slowly. His look was pure evil. And then the deep growl subsided to a low whisper once more. "Never mind. She's coming to me. I see her now." Then Marty collapsed on the bed, eyes rolling back into his head for a moment before he went limp and unconscious.

Tomas looked at Dom. "What the hell does that mean?"

"It means we'd better get to your demon-serving witches before he does," he said.

"It's beautiful, isn't it?" Rayne had to shout over the roar of the water.

I nodded in emphatic agreement with her statement of the obvious. The waterfall was narrow, pouring down from about thirty feet above where the two of us stood and plunging into a small pool at our feet, a brief, frothy pit stop on the way to the lake another hundred feet below, cutting deeply into the sheer stone face on the way down. As the water roared down from above us, it hid a rift in the face of the rocky mountainside, a rift that widened as it reached ground level where we stood, a deep darkness cloaked behind the waterfall.

I stood watching the water for long moments, basking in the natural beauty, letting serenity wash over my body and soul. The mist that dampened my face felt good, cool and bracing in the sixty-degree temperature of an autumn afternoon. It was warm for this late in the season.

Rainbow prisms appeared and blinked out again as droplets arced in the sunlight. Beautiful stones — some glittering like quartz, others striking in their pink and deep gray striations, some with fossils on their faces — lay at the bottom of the pool, visible wherever the water wasn't too foamy to see. And where the fall hit the surface, the riotous bubbling froth was almost hypnotic.

And yet my eyes kept darting to the darkness behind the waterfall. I didn't know why, but I couldn't seem to keep my focus from that place.

"It's a cave," Rayne said, stating the obvious again.

"Have you ever gone inside?"

She didn't answer, but when I looked at her, she was staring at the cave and shaking her head slowly.

"Why not?" I asked.

"I don't know." She dragged her eyes from the darkness behind the waterfall, met mine and tried to pull off a sarcastic grin. "Maybe 'cause I'm not six?"

"That's not it, and you know it," I told her, and watched her fake grin die a slow death. "There's . . . something . . . You feel it, too, don't you?"

She shrugged and looked away from me. But I knew she felt it. She was a witch, how could she not? There was something back there. Something . . . conscious, maybe? I felt eyes watching me, watching us both, from somewhere in that darkness. And I felt whatever it was calling me . . . pulling at me with some unseen force.

"I want to go inside."

"No, you don't, Indy," Rayne said quickly. "Look, okay, I admit, I feel something, too, but whatever it is, it isn't good. It feels . . . icky."

She tugged my shirtsleeve when I kept staring at it. "Come on, there's a great vantage point right over here. You can smoke your cigarette and enjoy the view."

She knew how to distract me. I'd forgotten about the treat in my pocket because I'd been so entranced by our walk. The woods were wet, the path we took, slick with mud from the recent rainstorm. And I thought the falls were probably running at a higher intensity than usual, too.

I followed her to a big flat rock. She perched on it, so I climbed up after her, took a comfortable position and lit my cigarette. Inhaled, exhaled, closed my eyes. Damn, that was good.

"The view from here is the best I've ever seen."

I looked at her, glad my smoke was blowing away from, rather than toward, her, and followed her blissed-out gaze. And then a long, slow "woooow" came out of me. Because it was beautiful. Beyond beautiful. Cayuga Lake spread out below us, choppy and dark today. Moody. The way our rock jutted, it was almost like we were flying over the water. Floating, at least.

I pulled my cell phone from the pocket of my denim shirt, which I was using as a jacket, and took a couple of shots that I knew wouldn't do it justice. "Wish I had a real camera and a wide angle lens," I muttered.

"It still doesn't come out the same. I've tried it. There's nothing like being right

237

here. It sort of feels like — like an energy place. You know? A place of power?"

"It does." I looked at the photos on my phone, realized she was right — none of them did it justice — and set it down on the rock beside me. "Speaking of power . . ."

"Were we?"

I met her eyes, saw the teasing light in them, realized how much I truly liked this woman and nodded. "Yeah, we were. So, speaking of power, why haven't I been able to repeat what I did in the video?"

"Have you been trying?"

"Of course I've been trying. Hell, who wouldn't? I keep going back and watching the damn thing, trying to move just the same way, you know? But nothing."

Rayne nodded. "Well, you know power is never about 'stand here and hold your hand this way and say these words.' I mean, that's rote. Magic comes from within."

"I know that."

"The words we say, the ways we move, those are just tools — tricks, really — to make our psyche relax enough to let the true power flow."

"I know that, too. I read all the same books you did, you know."

She smiled, nodded. "So then I guess the pertinent question is, why do you think you can't repeat it?"

Because it's not real.

But I'm way past that now, aren't I?

I took a deep drag, enjoying the hell out of my smoke and wondering if they trained high priestesses to act like shrinks, because she sure seemed to know how to make me find the answers inside myself. "I think it's because I'm not that person. I think she's the one with the powers. Not me."

" 'She' being . . ."

I was looking toward that cave again. Rayne's voice got lost on the breeze.

"Indy?"

"I'm sorry, what?"

"Who is she?" she asked.

"My past self. The one who was shoved off a cliff in Bumfuck, Babylonia, a gazillion years ago." I smoked some more. My cigarette was burning away while I was talking, and I hated like hell to waste it.

"But you are her. Part of you is, anyway."

"I guess that's where the disconnect is for me. Despite the dreams, I don't feel like I'm her. Even partly her." *Trying pretty hard to convince yourself, aren't you, Indy?* "I feel like she's a person I wouldn't even like all that much. Like if I met her, I'd want to backhand her, you know?"

"Well, that might be it. If you feel conflict

239

with her, then you're not accepting the part of you that *is* her. And if you can't accept her, then you can't accept her powers. But they're *your* powers, too. And you can tap into them if you just let yourself. That video proves it."

I lowered my head, took the last few puffs and then rubbed the cigarette out on the rock. I tucked the butt into my pocket. Far be it from me to go polluting such a beautiful spot.

As if I couldn't help it, I looked at the cave again, then forced my eyes back to Rayne. "She was . . . is . . . in love with your brother," I told her. "If I let her in — I'm afraid I will be, too."

She was silent for a long moment. I was looking down at the boulder beneath me, studying the patterns in the stone. Or pretending to.

And then her hand covered mine. "I think he's having doubts about continuing in the service of the Guardians, and maybe in the priesthood itself. And I think those doubts were happening before all this started. At least, that was the impression I was getting from our conversations."

"Really? Because I sure as hell don't want to be the cause of him doing something he thinks will damn his soul to hellfire."

"Oh, come on, we both know there's no such thing."

"Do we? There's a freaking demon trying to get out of some sort of underworld. Doesn't that sort of shake your confidence in everything you thought you knew before? 'Cause it sure as hell shakes mine."

She hesitated, nodded. "Yeah, I guess it does." Then she sighed. "He can leave the priesthood and not be damned, though. I know there are ways . . ."

"He will never do that."

Last time he killed me rather than give up his calling, after all.

The dark cave drew my eyes like a magnet. I couldn't even resist it long enough now to hold Rayne's gaze. I tried, several times, but my own kept shifting back to that black maw behind the falls. "I have to go inside."

And with that I slid off the rock and started forward, skirting the bubbly pool until I got as close to the cave as I could, and then sloshing through the icy water the rest of the way. I had to walk straight through the waterfall. There was no other way to get to the darkness behind it, and I did, even while Rayne was shouting at me to come back and calling me a friggin' idiot, among other things.

I entered the cascade, darting quickly

through it, but feeling the jolt of the frigid water all the same. It soaked me to the skin, and I emerged shaking myself and rigid with the shocking cold. And then I stood there, looking into the pitch-darkness, my entire body leaning forward, my feet itching to walk deeper inside, as if they had a will all their own.

"Dammit, Indy, I don't want to take an ice-water shower today!" Rayne shouted from just beyond the falls.

"Just wait out there!" I called, turning back and becoming momentarily transfixed by the sight of the waterfall from this perspective. It was beautiful, like looking at the world through a crystal prism. I could see her on the other side, a blurry form done in muted colors. She looked a lot like the depiction of loved ones waiting to greet the newly dead at the far end of the proverbial tunnel.

That thought gave me a shiver that was unrelated to the cold.

"I won't be five minutes, okay?"

"Fine. Whatever." She sounded pissed, not like an angel guide for the dear departed.

I turned away and started walking. The darkness was almost heavy, closing up around me, enfolding me in arms of black. The perception of "density" wasn't so much due to the presence of anything but more to the absence of everything. There was no light. The roar of the waterfall drowned out all other sounds. There was no scent here. And the walls of the cave were beyond the reach of my hands as I groped in the pitch-darkness. The air was so still I couldn't feel it on my skin. I felt cold, and I felt my feet pressing soundlessly against the floor beneath me. Nothing else. There was just nothingness. Even the sound of the rushing water faded behind me as I ventured deeper.

I moved slowly, my hands out in front of me now, until I felt the cold stone wall against them and wondered if I'd reached the back of the cave. But then something caught my eye from the left, and I turned to see a slightly lighter shade of black, as if there were some faint source of light in that direction.

Keeping one hand on the wall, I moved that way, inching my feet ahead of me, in case the ground fell away suddenly. But it didn't. I kept going, and then I was standing in front of the unimaginable, staring right at it and still not believing it was real.

It was a little taller than I was, and oval in shape, widening to about two feet in the middle. Its surface was watery, only not made of water. It rippled with translucent strands of gray — pale gray, and paler gray, and darker gray — and violet and blue, and seemed not to be backlit but lit from within by its own swirling colors.

"What the hell is it?" I asked aloud.

It looked as if it was made of some combination of smoke and water. It looked as if I could put my hand right through it if I wanted to.

And I wanted to.

I reached out. My fingertips inched closer and closer. I was almost touching it, swallowing my fear and forcing myself onward.

And then a face appeared on the other side, and I screamed and jerked my hand away, stumbling backward and falling on my ass on the hard stone floor.

It stared at me. A shapeless, formless being whose only clear feature was its eyes. And they were eyes I'd seen before, but I was damned if I knew where. Human eyes, though. Very human. Very . . . beautiful. And roiling with pain.

I saw them in my cauldron. And somewhere else, too . . .

And then I heard a female voice, not from the thing on the other side of the fog-and-water curtain — that thing was most certainly male — but from above. And it, too, was familiar.

He needs your help, Indira. You must find the amulet and return it to him.

I blinked, shaking my head and returning my gaze to the soulful eyes gazing back at me. Tomas wanted me to find the amulet, too. To hand it over to him so he could destroy it, preventing a demon from crossing through some portal and —

I examined the misty, watery oval again. *This is it. This is the Portal.*

And then I looked again at the being beyond it. *And this is the demon? This blob with eyes that look like they belong in some rescue-the-kids commercial? This is the big bad threat to mankind?*

You must help him, the woman told me again, and knowledge washed over me. *My sister. Lilia.*

"I don't fucking know how, and frankly, I'm getting sick of all these mind games. If you can talk to me like this, why not just tell me how to call forth the freaking amulet so I can get this the fuck over with?" Assuming I wanted to, of course.

Don't you think I would if I could?

Her answer came in an angry shout that seemed to echo from the walls of the cave like an explosion, deafening. I clasped my hands to my ears, but it did nothing to dampen her volume. She was screaming at

245

me now. *You hid the amulet in the astral plane! Only you can call it forth! You have to remember!*

And at that moment I felt as if a blade were being drawn across my skin. And again, and then again. I felt hot blood seeping, and I screamed in pain as I felt the shreds of my blood-soaked blouse falling away.

Remember! Remember, damn you!

Why would my one-time sister attack me this way?

But I knew, didn't I? Yes, I knew on some level that she had no choice, that she had to make me remember. That it was vital somehow. And that she wouldn't go too far . . .

Or maybe that last part was wishful thinking. I *hoped* she wouldn't go too far.

If you kill me, I'll never be able to help anyone.

I clutched my arm and, turning, stumbled back the way I had come, only belatedly thinking to press one hand to the wall so I wouldn't get lost. I made my way to the place where I thought I should turn right and head toward the entrance again, but I couldn't see the falls or even hear their roar. The slashing continued, and the pain was excruciating. I fell to my knees, crying out for help.

And then I fell forward, my cheek slamming into the cool, unforgiving stone floor. It was so dark, so utterly devoid of any sensual stimulation, in the cave that I didn't know if my eyes were open or closed, whether I was conscious or unconscious. Whether I was still alive or finally, mercifully, dead.

Maybe she'd gone too far, after all.

Tomas broke every speed limit getting back to the cabin, which was completely unlike him and clearly made Dom nervous. To his credit, though, Father Dom never once told him to slow down, at least not in so many words.

Once he made it there, his relief was short-lived. The second he burst through the front door and called Indy's name, he knew the place was empty.

Father Dom was still making his way up the front stairs when Tomas found the note on the refrigerator.

Taking the scenic route down to the lake, with a stop at the waterfall. Back soon.

Rayne & Indy

"Well, son? Where have they gone?" Dom asked.

"Down to the lake." He paced nervously to the sliding patio doors and looked out over the lake below. "They're probably all right."

"I've no doubt they're all right. Demon's not likely to do harm to his own servants, now, is he? But if the witch figures out how to get her hands on that amulet, and he convinces her to give it to him instead of you, well . . . that's a whole other matter. That puts us all in danger. Her included."

Tomas was irritated with Father Dom for being more concerned over the amulet than the safety of Indy and Rayne. But he let it pass for the moment — partly because he knew that was exactly the way Dom expected *his* priorities to fall, too. The way they would fall if he were putting the mission first. But they didn't fall that way. Never had.

Rayne was his sister, and he loved her. He was already regretting that she'd become entangled in this dangerous situation. And Indy was . . . Indy was . . . amazing. And not the devil's mistress Father Dom was so damned determined to make him believe she was. Not even close to that.

"She's getting to you, isn't she, Tomas?

The witch?"

He shot a look at Father Dom but didn't answer. "I'm heading down to find them."

"I'm coming, too."

Tomas almost snapped at him to stay behind, then caught himself. What the hell was happening to him? Dom might be a few bubbles off the beam about the demon and his plans for world domination, but he was his friend — family, really. "Best grab a jacket," he said instead. And then he crossed the room, opened a closet door and took one for himself. It was big and made of faded denim, just heavy enough to keep out the chill. As he pulled it from the hanger, he spotted the old shotgun leaning against the rear corner of the closet. It had come with the house, and he'd had it inspected and repaired, and kept it around for emergencies. Rabid raccoons, or wounded animals in need of putting down.

He'd never had to use it. Had often wondered if he had it in him to do so. Impulsively, he reached in and pulled it out.

Father Dom raised his brows. "I didn't know you owned a gun."

"There was a rabies scare a few years back," he said.

"Ah."

"Forgot I had it, to tell you the truth."

"You have . . . bullets?"

"Yeah." He handed the shotgun, a twenty-gauge pump action with a long barrel and open sights, to Father Dom, then turned back to the closet, reaching onto the overhead shelf and digging through piles of winter hats and various other items. Eventually he felt the heavy, cardboard box and pulled it down. "Just five slugs."

"We shouldn't need more than that," Father Dom said.

"Let's hope we don't need *any.*" Tomas put the slugs in the breast pocket of his jacket, held the gun in one hand, barrel tilted downward, and headed out the back door and onto the trail.

"Don't you think you ought to load it?" Dom asked a few yards later.

He was already breathless, and while Tomas felt sorry for the pace he was setting, he was also feeling more worried by the minute.

"Like I said, I hope we don't need it."

"But if we do, it would be more helpful loaded than empty."

Tomas just kept walking. The trees were nearly all bare, but the sunlight was warm for this late in the season. The light breeze carried the scent of apples from the cluster of trees in the tiny orchard off to the right

250

of the cabin.

"And given that thirteen priests were murdered by this demon only two days ago, I would think —"

"Thirteen clerics," Tomas corrected. They'd just heard the numbers that day: thirteen dead, twenty-three injured. It would have been much higher, but a number of attendees had been at an off-site function when the bomb went off. "They weren't all priests." He crossed himself and thanked God again that the death toll hadn't been higher.

"Load the gun, please, Tomas."

Dom was looking at him as if he'd noticed Tomas's burgeoning tendency to argue with his every suggestion, so he nodded. But even as he reached into his pocket for the slugs, he caught movement from the corner of his eye, and when he turned, he saw the wolf.

It was crouched low, its teeth bared in a menacing snarl. A low growl emanated from it as it kneaded the earth.

"Tomas —"

"I see it." He flipped the gun in his hand, then fished a slug from the box in his pocket and slid it into place, but there was no time to pump the slug into the chamber before the animal sprang at him. Its forefeet hit

251

him square in the chest, knocking him onto his back — hard — and the gun flew from his hand. With snarling, growling jaws snapping at his neck, he buried his hands in the beast's fur to hold it away.

Dom was scrambling, panicked, snatching up the gun, trying to work the pump action.

Hot saliva, hotter breath on his face. The wolf pushed so hard that Tomas's elbows bent, allowing it closer. Teeth scraped his neck. And then, with one massive, all-out effort, he straightened his arms again and sent the wolf flying off him and into a tree. It yelped in pain.

He jumped to his feet, crouched and ready, as he watched the wolf regain its footing.

It stared right back into his eyes, looking confused. Dom rushed to Tomas's side, shouldering the gun.

Tomas put a hand on the barrel, pushing it down, and the wolf turned and ran off into the forest.

They stood there, both panting, Tomas from the battle, Dom from excitement. "Should have let me kill it," the old man said.

"Why? It wasn't the wolf's fault." Tomas shook his head. "Hell, I didn't even think there were wolves anywhere near here."

"Not just wolves, either." Dom looked around, and Tomas followed his gaze. The older priest was looking into the trees to the left of the trail, where a coyote, smaller than the wolf, scrawnier, but just as dangerous, stood with his tongue lolling, staring intently at them.

"They're flanking us," Dom said, nodding toward the other side.

Tomas turned to look, and sure enough, there was a second coyote, powerful and potentially deadly, on the opposite side of the trail.

He quickly took the gun from Dom and shoved in three more rounds, then pumped one into the chamber, making room for one more. The box in his pocket was empty. All five slugs were in the gun. That was not only all he had, it was all it would hold.

Caw! Caw! Caw!

He jumped, startled by the nearness of the crow's throaty call, then spotted it sitting on a limb only a few feet above his head. Staring at him. He stared back. "You're one of God's creatures, crow. Don't let a demon use you. You're too good for that."

He glanced left and right. "That goes for you two, as well," he told the coyotes. "Go on, get out of here before I change my mind and shoot you all." He waved his arms, one of them still holding the shotgun, and the coyotes scurried away as the crow left in a heavy flapping of black wings. Tomas angled the gun downward again. It was growing heavy as he kept on going.

A half hour later Dom was puffing like a steam engine and Tomas was feeling more worried by the second. Dom was slowing him down, and his gut was telling him to get to Indy and get to her now.

But the old man was going to keel over if he didn't ease off on the pace.

Tomas stopped, pointing out a stump where Dom immediately sat. Bracing his hands on his knees, the old priest leaned forward, panting. "I should have stayed behind," he admitted between gasps.

"Yeah, and going back up will be a lot worse, you know." Tomas looked back the way they had come. "Maybe you should just wait here."

Dom lifted his head and probably saw the urgency in Tomas's eyes. "Yes. If you'll leave me the gun. I don't want any more demon-eyed wildlife coming around."

"Don't kill anything unless you have to," Tomas said, handing him the weapon. "You know how to use it?"

"I'll figure it out."

"There's a bullet in the chamber. All you have to do is turn off the safety —" he showed him the button with a forefinger "— aim and shoot. If you need more than one, you'll need to —"

"I saw what you did. I know what to do next." Father Dom patted his hand, which was still holding the weapon, then drew the gun closer to him. "Go on."

"I'll be back for you soon. If you feel like heading back to the cabin, just stay on the path. There are a couple of forks, but if you keep going right, you'll be fine."

"Thank you, Tomas. Be safe now. And keep your mission in mind above all else. Your duty. Your calling. Remember that."

"Always." He said it, but he didn't mean it. He was relieved to leave Dom behind, relieved because it freed him to do whatever he had to do to protect Indy and Rayne, without the old man's watchful, judgmental eyes on him.

He gave Dom a final nod, and continued down the steep and twisting path. In a few minutes he could hear the waterfall in the distance. Encouraged, he picked up his pace and finally emerged from the forested path into the clearing at the edge of the cliffs. The gorgeous waterfall came into view, taking his breath away — but only for an instant. He glimpsed Rayne sitting on a boulder near the edge of the waterfall, staring at it as if trying to see through it. He lifted his hand, about to call out to her, then froze when he heard a scream.

Rayne heard it, too, and jumped off her makeshift seat. "Indy?" she called.

Tomas ran the last dozen yards, grabbed his sister by the arm and heard a second scream. "She's in the cave?" he demanded.

"I couldn't stop her. She said she had to go. Tomas, get her. Help her!"

He nodded. "I left Dom halfway up the trail," he said, yanking off his jacket, then his shoes. "Go back for him, get him back to the cabin. And for God's sake, make some noise so he knows you're coming. He's got the shotgun, and he's spooked."

"I don't want to leave you."

"I don't want you here." He clasped her neck, drew her closer and kissed her forehead. "I love you, sis. But this is my mission. *My* problem. If anything happened to you —"

"Oh, go get Indy already."

He did, wading into the water and hissing at the cold, then pushing straight through the freezing cascade and into the darkness of the cave beyond it.

256

About thirty feet in, he found her, his feet bumping against the softness of her body on the cave floor. Quickly dropping to his knees, he felt around to find which end of her was which, and immediately realized that she was nearly naked from the waist up. His hands slid over the warm skin of her belly, his knuckles grazing a rounded breast, before he drew them away and reached for her arms.

He found them, along with the sticky blood that coated them. He wiped his hands on his pant legs and touched her again, seeking her face this time, and finding it.

"Indy?" he asked, cupping her cheeks, patting one of them. "Indy, wake up now. Wake for me, okay?" He slid his fingers over her neck to feel for a pulse and heard the whisper of her breath in the process. "Good. You're alive."

"Tomas?"

"Yes, it's me." He shifted her up off the floor, holding her against his chest to warm her. She was shivering.

"I . . . I found it, Tomas."

He blinked in the darkness. "You found . . ."

"The Portal."

He looked deeper into the cave but saw nothing. And yet he did not doubt her. "I need to get you out of here, Indy. You're hurt, and I can't even see how badly."

"Okay," she said.

He slid his arms beneath her and picked her up. Her body nestled close to his, naked skin against his shirt, beneath his arms. Every part of him was reacting, feeling her, wanting her, raging against whatever force had caused her harm or pain. He was reacting to her like a lover, not like a priest, and he knew it.

But if Father Dom could accuse her of manipulating him, of casting spells that would cut her to ribbons just to elicit his protective instincts, then he was a fool. This woman was an innocent. There wasn't an evil cell in her body.

He lowered his head to kiss her forehead, but she tipped her chin up, and he caught her lips instead. Her hands immediately dove into his hair and held him to her as her lips parted. He tasted her with his tongue, and the kiss heated, deepened, intensified, until he was feeding from her mouth and she from his.

He was aroused — powerfully, almost painfully, aroused. And it was wrong. Yet he couldn't stop kissing her. And then a flash, an image — a memory? — entered his mind. He was kissing her, and it was him, and it was her, but it *wasn't.* She had long dark hair and wore flowing skirts below a tiny scrap of fabric that barely covered her breasts. There was thick dark liner around her eyes. He wore a tunic of white, with a gold sash. His hair was long, and his heart was damn near bursting with emotion.

With love.

For her.

He broke the kiss, shaken, and certain that his vision was true. They'd been together before. In that other lifetime. And he remembered it now.

But given the intensity of the feeling that had just swept through him, could he really have killed her?

He lifted his head and, saying nothing, strode forward. When he carried her back out through the freezing waterfall it was a painful relief.

12

Cold water shocked me back to consciousness, but consciousness brought pain. Hot, burning pain so bad I hissed through my teeth before I even opened my eyes.

Tomas had me in his arms, carrying me. He was dripping wet, and so was I, and we were moving toward the flat rock where Rayne and I had been sitting before. Behind us, I saw the waterfall and realized he'd carried me through it. He must have come into the cave after me. I was briefly amazed that he would do that. And then I wondered how much farther he would have come to rescue me. What if I'd gone through the Portal into the Underworld itself? Would he have come after me then?

Reaching the big rock, he lowered me onto its cool surface. I could feel mist from the waterfall hitting my skin, and though I was cold and already wet, that soft shower felt soothing somehow. I tried to meet his eyes.

He wasn't looking at me, though. He'd spotted something to the left and quickly grabbed it.

My cell phone. He pointed it at me, and I realized he was snapping photos.

"What . . . are you doing . . . that for?" I could barely speak, the pain was so intense.

"It's happened again, Indy. Look at your arms."

I did, only then remembering that my shirt was missing. I was lying there in my demi-bra and cargo pants. And before I could object, he was snapping more photos. Automatically, I crossed my arms over my chest — though I was the furthest thing from shy, and my bra covered as much as a bikini would have. It was more or less a reflex action. But as I moved, wincing at the new pain the movement caused, I looked down and saw the reason for his urgent picture taking. My arms were once again crisscrossed with cuts — the symbols of some forgotten language. Blood trickled from them, and still he snapped away.

"Do you give a shit that I'm bleeding to death down here?"

He lowered the phone, met my eyes at last. "You're not. But one of these days you will be if these episodes keep up, and the only way we can stop them is to get the answers we need and end your involvement in this thing for good." His eyes softened as tears brimmed in mine, and he reached out to touch my face.

That was when it came rushing back to me — kissing in the cave, holding each other, and the feeling, just for an instant, that the two of us were madly, deeply, in love. Not just the memory but the feeling itself returned to me. In that moment I adored him, knew he was my soul mate, had no doubt he loved me just as much. I would have died for him without a second thought.

His eyes met mine, and he whispered my name and leaned closer. As our lips met again I was whisked back in time, until I was once again on that cliff, and he was behind me, his hands on my back.

The reality of it was there and then gone, like the brief glow of a lightning bug on a summer night. And then I was back in the present, lying on the cool stone, feeling the autumn kiss on the air, and the pain on my arms and back fading fast as his mouth possessed mine.

I twisted my head to the side. "Tomas, the marks are fading. I feel it. Take your photos."

He sat up, shifting away from me, blinking as if he, too, had been momentarily transported to another place and time. Nodding, he lifted the phone and took a few more pictures. I rolled onto my stomach, because I knew there were already healing marks on my back, too. Almost as if his kiss held some kind of magic.

I heard the phone clicking with each shot, heard him moving around, and heard someone whisper, *Remember.*

A flash. Symbols drawn on thick parchmentlike scrolls. My own hand held the inkreed. I wrote them — the same symbols that had carved themselves into my flesh in the cave. What the hell did they say?

The clicking had stopped.

I rolled onto my back, blinking up at Tomas. His intense brown eyes, deep-set and mesmerizing, stared into my very soul. "They're gone," he said softly. He slid the phone into a pocket, then offered me his hands. I took them and let him help me to my feet, then immediately rocked sideways, dizzy as a drunk, and swore under my breath.

"It's all right. I've got you." He picked me up again, and then, turning, began striding back the way I had come what seemed — and in a way had been — a lifetime ago.

"You can't carry me all the way back to the cabin, Tomas. It's not only uphill, it's steep."

"Watch me." He looked down and tried a gentle smile, but it died quickly. "You were right about our shared past, Indy. I . . . I've been having flashes of memory, too."

"You have?"

He nodded, his eyes shifting away from mine again. "I remember. . . . a love more powerful than I knew anything could be. And I remember being there with you on that cliff." His brows crunched together as if he were in pain. "And I don't know how I can ever make up for what I . . . now believe I did to you in that lifetime."

"I'm not sure it matters," I whispered. Lifting my arm, surprised at how much effort that took, I pressed my palm to his cheek, drawing his eyes back to mine. "I'm here. I'm alive. We're together. Doesn't that seem to you to sort of . . . mean something?"

He nodded. "It means God wants us to finish what we started back then."

"Yes, that's what I think, too. I mean, I know you're a priest and all, but maybe that was just the path you had to walk to find me again, and now that you have, you can —"

"Indy, stop."

I bit my lip, realizing by the look on his face that I had jumped the track — his track, at least — and landed on my own.

"The mission God wants us to complete is the vanquishing of a demon that threatens us all."

"Oh." *Why do I have the feeling he doesn't believe that any more than I do? Wishful thinking?*

He looked into my eyes.

Does he see the disappointment, the heartbreak, I'm feeling right now? Probably. And he probably finds it as stupid as I do. I mean, okay, I'm changing my mind about not believing in anything woo-woo, because clearly there's some major woo-woo shit going on here. And reincarnation is a huge part of it, a part I can't justify doubting any longer.

But in this lifetime, we barely know each other. Even if it feels like we do.

"What happened in that cave, Indy?" he asked.

"Change the subject much?" I was being petulant, and I knew it. So I heaved a sigh, pressed my hands against his chest and said, "Put me down. I can walk from here."

"You're still too weak. I can —"

"Put me the fuck down, Tomas."

Startled, he stopped walking and gently lowered me to my feet. Yeah, I was furious with him. As furious as if we'd been married this whole thirty-five-hundred years and he'd just forgotten our anniversary. I wanted to smack him. Kick him. But I strode uphill instead, head down, eyes on my feet.

"I found the Portal. It's in the cave. And I saw him. And I'll tell you right now, Tomas, what I saw was no demon. It was more like a . . . a wounded animal pleading for help. For mercy. Mercy, isn't that right up your priestly alley?"

"He's a child of Satan, a demon, Indy. He's one of the great deceivers."

"Yeah? Then why do you sound like you're trying to convince yourself as much as me?"

"He wants your help."

"And I swore I would give it to him. All those years ago I made a vow to help him, and you knew it and didn't even tell me."

He couldn't even hold my accusing eyes. "I was going to. I just —"

"And this amulet I somehow magically hid in some other plane? The one I'm supposed to retrieve and give to him? Were you going to tell me about that, too?"

He lifted his chin. "Of course I was. Because if we can find it and destroy it, it ends his chances of ever escaping."

"And what if I decide that's not what I want to do, Tomas? What if I decide to keep my promise and help this being who looks so freaking sad and tormented to me?"

266

"Indy, you can't mean that."

He stared at me. I stared back. We didn't speak. And then he said, "I should have told you everything. I know that. But you can't believe what you saw in that cave, Indy. Naturally he's not going to appear to you as he truly is. He's trying to elicit your sympathy, make you doubt your true role in all this."

"Naturally." I rolled my eyes. "You act like this is everyday shit to you, when you know, and I know you know, that you're as lost as I am. You've never dealt with a demon before, have you?"

He shook his head. "No. But Dom has. And I've been studying, preparing for this my entire lifetime."

"Several of them, as a matter of fact." I was being sarcastic and snotty, and I couldn't seem to help it. "Look, holy man, hasn't it even occurred to you that I was the *victim* thirty-five centuries ago? I was murdered, thrown off a freakin' cliff, for 'communing with demons' or practicing magic without a license, or being too sexy for my own good. And you were apparently on the side of the guys who ordered it." I stopped and turned to stare up into his eyes, and I saw him flinch. "I mean, doesn't that give you a little pause? A little doubt about who's on the right side here?"

He looked away, said nothing.

"You do have doubts! I saw them in your eyes just now." Turning, I continued stomping uphill. "At least that's something."

"You've found the Portal," he said. "That's something, too. I intend to return here and close it permanently."

I blinked. "You know how to do that?"

"Yes, I know how to do that."

"And what happens to . . . him . . . when you do?"

"He stays where he is. Where he belongs."

"Suffering in Hell?" I asked. "Is that where he is?"

"Demons have no souls, Indy. Only souls can suffer in Hell."

I kept going, kept walking, mulling that over for a while, and finally I shook my head firmly. "No. I may have changed my mind about reincarnation, but wherever that de — wherever that being I saw is, it's not Hell. Because I still don't believe in Hell. It's never made sense to me."

He muttered something under his breath. It sounded like "me neither," but when I called him on it, he said he'd only been clearing his throat. Right.

"Did you get the photos this time? The writing on my body?"

"Yes. I think so."

I nodded. "I think we need to get it translated, Tomas. I need to know what those words are. I'm compelled to know what I died for. I mean, what the hell could possibly be more important than. . . . than a love like we must have had? Because it felt . . . it felt . . ." I stopped. I couldn't say more, because I was choking back tears.

"I know. I felt it, too."

I braced my hand against the smooth white trunk of a young poplar tree, my head hanging. "I wonder if we could feel it again? When all this is over, I mean, and your mission for God is accomplished."

He touched me. It was just a hand on my shoulder, but it was enough. I turned suddenly, and the act brought my body flush against his. My hand curled around his nape as if of its own volition, and I gazed into his eyes, willing him to want me as hard as I could and forgetting all about the fact that I had given up the practice of witchcraft. And that he was a priest. "Why would we feel this way if we weren't supposed to do something about it, Tomas?"

He stared at me. I could see the war going on inside him. And I didn't care. He belonged to me, I knew it suddenly, fiercely and surely. He was mine. His eyes darkened with desire. His lips parted, and he stared at my mouth.

I rose onto my toes and pressed my mouth to his, but only briefly. He shivered in reaction as I lowered myself again. And then his arms snapped around me, one hand cupping my backside, and jerked me hard against him as his head came down and his mouth took mine.

We were mashed together, body to body, mouth to mouth, tasting, devouring each other, our pulses pounding in sync, when voices on the wind reached us and a twig snapped like an exclamation point.

We pulled apart, both of us looking up the trail toward the sound.

Rayne was standing in the path, blinking at us as if she'd just spotted a unicorn. And as I met her eyes, wide with confusion and surprise, Father Dominick appeared just behind her.

I took a guilty step away from Tomas. "I'm sorry," I said, keeping my voice low, for his ears alone. "I didn't mean to push you like that. It's powerful, whatever's there between us. It's ancient, and it's powerful, and I honestly don't know if I can resist it much longer."

"I don't know if I can, either."

I shot him a look. It was so good to hear

him say those words. But I wanted more. So much more. Then he put a hand at the small of my back . . .

I feel his hands on my back.

. . . urging me forward to meet the others.

I slept. I slept out the remainder of the day and straight through the night. It was morning again when I blinked my eyes open and slowly focused away the blurriness of the clock on the nightstand. Glowing red characters. 8:45 a.m.

I closed my eyes.

"So . . . you gonna tell me what the hell is going on between you and my brother?" Rayne asked me.

She was sitting on a padded stool that had been over by the window last time I checked.

I wonder how long she's been there? She couldn't have sat there all night, could she?

I thought back to the day before. I'd gone straight to my room to collapse facedown on my bed and try to recover from the . . . the attack. Or whatever the hell it had been.

It was an attack. No other word for it. And I don't know if anyone else has noticed this yet — hell, I'm only just figuring it out myself — but every single one leaves me feeling weaker,

271

sicker. I'm starting to think this shit could kill me.

I rolled onto my back with a heavy sigh, faced Rayne, and tried to decide if her eyes were accusing or merely shocked.

"Good morning to you, too. I'm feeling terrible, thanks for asking."

She blinked, pursed her lips, gave a nod. "How bad is it?"

"I don't know how many more of these episodes I can take, is how bad it is." I inhaled deeply and sat up in the bed, leaning forward over my legs and pressing both hands to my spinning head.

"I'm sorry. You need anything?"

"Coffee. Food. Ibuprofen, but only if there's nothing stronger on hand."

She moved, but I wasn't looking. And then I smelled something heavenly that made me raise my head and blink blearily into the mug she was holding under my nose.

I closed my hands around the mug, absorbing its warmth, bringing it to my lips with all the dramatic gratitude of a man who'd just crossed the desert tasting his first sip of water.

And then I sipped again. And then once more. And then I lifted my head and opened my eyes, finally feeling able to face the morning.

There was a plate with a silver lid sitting behind the alarm clock on my nightstand. She put the plate on my lap.

"The food might need a warm-up."

"Is this your brother's French toast?" I asked. Then I took off the lid and smiled. It was.

"He wanted to bring it up himself, but Dom is reading the absolute worst into his every move, and besides, I wanted to see you first. To talk about . . . what happened."

I blinked at her in sheer amazement, and even though the French toast, which had a scoop of scrambled eggs and two sausage links flanking it, was calling to me, I managed to resist diving into it for one more second. "Do you know that you're probably the best friend I've ever had?"

Try the only friend I've ever had.

"Just probably?" she asked, making a big phony wounded face at me. "Did I mention I brought ibuprofen, too?" She picked up the plastic bottle and shook it like a rattle. "Extra-strength."

I laughed softly, and she did, too. Damn, it felt good. I held out my hand, and she shook two tablets into my palm. I washed them down with the coffee, then set the mug aside and went for my fork.

I wolfed down three bites — these episodes not only drained me of energy and made me feel sick as a hangover, they made me ravenous — and then I managed to take a long enough pause to say what I knew needed saying.

"I know how bad that must've looked. That kiss. God, I know. I tried to tell you what I've been feeling . . . or what my past self has been feeling or — but it doesn't matter. It was wrong. He's a priest, and he's your brother, and you're my friend. I'm sorry, Rayne."

She got up from her chair and paced to the window. Staring outside, she stood deep in silent thought for a long moment, giving me time to devour more of my luscious breakfast. Then she finally turned back toward me and shook her head.

"I don't know if you should be sorry. I really don't think it's . . . wrong. You know? But . . . if this is what's been going on with you two, you should at least have told me."

"There was nothing to tell, Rayne. Nothing's really . . . happened until now."

Okay, that's not quite the truth. But I'm not giving her a full account of every kiss, touch and smoldering glance. I mean, really, some things are just too personal, even for a best friend, high priestess and confidante. Even for the guy-in-question's sister. No, make that especially *for the guy-in-question's sister.*

I kept eating until I had cleaned the plate, then set it on the nightstand and slid up until I could rest my back against the headboard. "It was just a kiss."

"He was sucking your face off, Indy. That was not *just* an anything. That was . . . that was freaking hot."

I had to look away, because my face was getting warm and, I figured, pink, too. I sipped the coffee, putting all my focus on that. "Did Father Dom see?"

"Damned if I know. The guy gives me the creeps, I'll tell you that much."

An icy chill shot briefly up my spine at her words, but I couldn't have said why. "I don't like him much, either. And for what it's worth, I think it's mutual."

"He's a zealot," she said. "He'd probably vote to reinstate burning at the stake for the likes of us, given the option." She rubbed her arms as if she, too, felt the chill. "If you're the reincarnation of a girl who was executed and my brother is the reincarnation of her lover, then is it possible Father Dom is the reincarnation of the high priest you hate so much in all those dreams?"

"That would be the obvious conclusion, wouldn't it?" I could look at her again now that she'd changed the subject. "It was certainly my first thought. I mean, once I started believing that any of this could be real. That any of us were really connected to those past lives playing out in my dreams. But no. I've thought about this a lot, and he's not. There's nothing about him that reminds me of that bastard Sindar."

"Are you sure?"

I nodded, sipped, nodded again for emphasis. "After all, not everyone I know was involved in that alleged past lifetime. I mean, you for example. You weren't there."

She looked at the floor. "I guess you have a point. I had to ask."

"I'm glad you did." I smiled at her a little sheepishly. "It changed the subject."

Her head came up again, eyes serious and probing. "Not for long. I want to know what's going on between you and my brother, Indy."

I lowered my head, then raised it again, because it would be more believable if I looked her squarely in the eyes while I lied to her. "I don't . . . I honestly don't know what to tell you."

She lifted her hands, palms up. "Uh-uh! Tell me how you feel about him, for crying out loud. Tell me what he's saying about all this. Tell me how far it's gone. Tell me how far it's going to go."

"That would take a psychic — or a witch. You tell me."

"You're a witch, too, Indy. A powerful one, and I think we're way past the stage where you can keep denying it and expect anyone to believe you. Hell, *you* don't even believe you at this point."

I lowered my eyes, unable to hold her gaze when she said something I knew was absolutely true and wished was not.

"Have you slept with him?"

Without looking up I said, "Of course not!"

"Of course not *what?*" she asked.

Right, right, right. Look her in the eyes. "Of course I haven't slept with him."

She moved closer to the bed, sat down on the edge. "I didn't ask that question out loud, Indy."

I frowned hard. "What do you mean? I heard you —"

"I only thought it."

"No way. No fucking way. Rayne, stop messing with me."

"I'm not messing with you. I thought it, but I didn't say it." She shook her head slowly. "But you heard me. You answered me. You're a witch. You found the Portal. You saw the Demon. And I think, deep down, you know more than you're letting yourself acknowledge."

Swallowing hard, I nodded. "Tomas and I — we were lovers in that other lifetime. And God knows how many in between. It was forbidden then, too."

"And you wound up dead," Rayne said softly. "Maybe the Universe is going to keep throwing you together until you figure out that love is more important than anything else and treat it that way. And maybe you're both going to keep suffering until you finally learn it."

My throat was dry, my skin clammy. "I don't know if what I'm feeling now is real or just leftover emotion from thirty-five hundred years ago."

"If you feel it, it's real. Time is an illusion. Everything is happening now. If you've studied the Craft at all — and I know you have, Indy — then you know that."

I swung around sideways, so I was sitting right beside her. "It feels real. It feels like the most powerful thing I've ever felt."

"A love that lasts lifetimes? Are you kidding me? That is the most powerful thing you've ever felt, dummy."

I smiled a little at her loving insult. "I don't know what to do. I mean, how can I ask him to give up his . . . calling? To break his vows?"

"Will you listen to yourself and think a little bit?" She reached across to me and pushed my bangs out of my eyes. I wondered if my hair was standing up all over and realized she wouldn't care. "Do you have any idea how many impossible things had to fall into place for the two of you to find each other? Among all the billions of people living on this planet right now? For him to find you again, after more than three thousand years — the chances must be like finding a single grain of sand in the desert. And for you to live in the same city as his own sister . . . for you to be born in the same century as him . . . and for you to remember. Do you really think our Goddess or his God or both of them, arranged all that and then expected him not to love you again? It wouldn't make any sense to believe that, Indy. Would it?"

I lowered my head, tears brimming in my eyes. "He's obsessed with this demon thing."

"Then get the damned demon thing over with and out of the way. Because I'm more and more convinced it's not about him anyway. It's about the two of you. It's about love, babe. All the rest is just the window dressing the Goddess threw in to force you two together again."

I tipped my head sideways. "When did you

decide all that?"

"Right now. It just came to me. Things do, sometimes. But it feels true. I trust it."

I met her eyes and saw the conviction there. "I wish I could believe it, too."

"But you don't, do you?" Rayne asked.

"I don't know. I need to think. But I do know that Tomas doesn't believe it. Not any of it. And that makes everything else sort of moot, don't you think?"

"You two looked as guilty as teenagers caught in the act on that trail yesterday," Father Dom said softly. He'd poured them each a few fingers of whiskey over ice, after requesting a private conversation in the den.

Tomas had managed to duck him last night until he could reasonably take refuge in his bedroom. But this morning there had been no escaping his friend's dogged persistence. So he took his small glass, emptied it in a single gulp and relished the burn. It gave him time to compose an answer. He was waiting for a call back from Jon. Last night he'd uploaded the newest photos and emailed them to his friend, who'd replied that he would get to them first thing this morning. Tomas was willing the damned phone to ring before he was forced to answer Father Dom.

But it didn't. And his glass was empty. He set it on the coffee table and stiffened his shoulders. "I'm a man, Dom. She's a beautiful woman, and we have a powerful history. Maybe if I'd been warned about this aspect of it I would have been more prepared, but it's hitting me out of left field. I wasn't ready for this." He looked at the empty glass again. It was still full of perfectly good ice cubes. "Fuck it, I'm having another one."

Dom gasped at the profanity but bit back whatever condemnation he'd been about to offer in response, a fact for which Tomas was absurdly grateful. The old man sipped his own whiskey while Tomas got up, crossed the room and refilled his glass.

Eventually Dom said, "I know it's not easy for you, Tomas. And I respect your honesty about this."

"It is what it is. No point lying about it."

"Precisely. It is what it is. Lust. Carnal and human. And flawed, as all human things are."

Tomas studied the amber liquid in his tumbler. It reminded him of Indy's hair. "It feels deeper than that, though." Why the hell was he discussing this with Dom, of all people? Dom, who would never understand. Hell, he wasn't sure anyone could understand. How many people loved the same soul over thousands of years, through dozens of lifetimes?

How many people had their soul mate's blood on their hands?

"Feels deeper? Like what?" Dom rose from the sofa, glass in hand. "Like love?" he asked, loading enough sarcasm on the word to make it feel dirty. "We both know the only real love is love of God, Tomas." He walked across the room and clapped Tomas on the shoulder. "Just hold steady, son. Just hold steady. Keep your mission in mind, your assignment, given to you by God Almighty, who chose you from among all others to carry this out because He knew you could handle it. He had faith in you, Tomas. All you have to do is have faith in Him. Stay strong. Don't let the charms of a witch sway you from your sacred duty, nor from your holy vows."

Tomas nodded, listening, hearing, but not feeling the words as deeply as he felt his need for Indy. God, he had so many questions. How could he believe Dom was wrong about all of this when he'd seen the power of the old priest's faith with his own eyes. The exorcism — Dom hadn't faked that.

But that wasn't the question that spilled

from his lips. It was another. "Why would God choose me for this? Why, when I was so close to her in the past? It makes no sense. Why not some other priest, one who has no history with her?"

Dom stared at him, his eyes deep and wise and knowing. "It's a test of your faith, my son. Vanquishing this powerful evil, this demon we now face, requires an act of supreme faith, an act of absolute belief." He sipped, contemplated, then nodded as if the answer had come to him. "In truth, Tomas, you should be on your knees in gratitude that God has so much faith in you. It's just like when He commanded Abraham to sacrifice his beloved son, Isaac. That's exactly what this is!"

An icy chill raced down Tomas's spine at those words.

"It's just that sort of test of faith. And it is a test you must pass, Tomas. Do not be swayed." Dom was on a roll now, pacing the room and getting more and more fired up, sounding like a Pentecostal preacher in a revival tent. "Faith, my son, is far stronger than any other force in existence. You must believe — believe with everything in you. With your whole heart, your whole soul, your whole mind, you must believe in your calling, in your duty. Put that above all else and you cannot go wrong. You can trust me on this. I know it to be true. Nothing is more important than faith."

The telephone rang as Tomas searched his soul for a deeper understanding, because there was something . . . off . . . and yet familiar about the words, something that was like a puzzle piece that didn't quite fit. But the ringing cut off his contemplation, and he vowed to ponder this more later as he picked up the cordless receiver and walked to the far side of the room.

"How is she this morning?" Jonathon asked without preamble.

"She slept like the dead, straight through the night. I think she's awake now. My sister's upstairs with her, took her some breakfast."

"The . . . injuries?"

Tomas sighed, unsure how much to reveal and deciding secrecy was probably useless at this point. Father Dom was already ranting about Jon having seen too much, but there wasn't much to be done about that now. "The cuts are gone. Healed as if they'd never been there. But it took a toll on her, all the same." He felt Dom's eyes on him as he spoke and looked up to see him walk over and hit the speaker button on the phone base.

Tomas wanted to roll his eyes, and the thought moved through his mind that apparently God trusted him more than Dom did. Still, it wasn't worth an argument. He set the receiver down and continued the conversation. "Do you have anything for me, Jon? Are the marks writing, like I thought?"

"They are. Akkadian," Jon said. "It's in two parts. Something like an incantation on her left arm, and something more involved on the right arm and back. An account, a history. The first line — which I'm interpreting as a sort of title — is The Truth I Must Remember."

Dom looked at Tomas sharply, his attention caught.

Jon went on. "I'm working on the full translation now. I've got to tell you, Tomas, it's wild stuff. Harem slaves being sacrificed to a sun god. The murder of a king. A high priest with questionable motives."

"Really? Questionable how?"

"Can't say yet — it's only hinted at. But I'll be done by this afternoon."

"We'll come over," Tomas said. "What time do you want us there?"

"Three work for you? I should have it finished by one, but I have meetings in between —"

"We'll be there at three, then."

"We'll be where at three?"

Indy's voice, coming from the living room, sent shivers of desire flaring through Tomas's body to settle in his groin. He was almost hard just at the sound of her innocent question.

Maybe Dom was right and this *was* some kind of spell.

Turning, he allowed himself the absolute pleasure of looking at her, which only made him want her even more. She looked worn-out. There were circles under her eyes, and her hair resembled the feathers of an agitated rooster. She was hugging her terry bathrobe around her, had silly fuzzy slippers on her feet, and was clutching a coffee mug in her hands as if it were a life raft in the middle of an empty ocean. And she was the most beautiful thing he'd ever seen.

Her eyes devoured him in return, and he wondered if the mutual lust fest they had going was as obvious as it felt like it was. He tried to paste a casual smile on his face to cover up the longing that had to be visible in his eyes.

Dom reached past him and picked up the telephone receiver, speaking softly to Jon before hanging up.

And even though he was aware of the old

man's movements, he was entirely focused on Indy.

"Where are we going at three?" she asked again.

"Cornell," he said, finally managing to master the art of speech. It was worse today, this feeling. He'd dreamed of making love to her last night. Only it had been more like a memory. Not their bodies, not their clothing. Outdoors in what felt like a desert oasis hidden among the dunes, bathed in moonlight. Now that he'd remembered being with her once, loving her once, it was as if a floodgate of feeling had broken wide open. "Jon's translating the symbols from those cuts. Says there's a history having to do with — with what you've been remembering written on one arm and your back. And that there's an incantation on the other arm."

Her eyes widened. "An incantation? Do you think. . . . do you think it might be the key to me figuring out how to get hold of that ever elusive amulet?"

"I'm hoping that's what it is."

"And the history?"

"It was titled The Truth I Must Remember."

She nodded slowly. "My sister — at least I think it's my sister — keeps telling me to

remember. Screaming it at me. I wonder if
—"

"We'll soon find out."

She lowered her head with a sigh. "God,
maybe we're actually getting closer to the
end of this . . . this nightmare."

"Maybe."

"We'll all go," Father Dom said. "This
afternoon. We'll all go together. Find out
exactly what that writing was about." He
looked worried as his eyes darted from one
of them to the other, but they lingered long-
est on Tomas.

Tomas's gut was telling him to leave Dom
and Rayne behind, but he knew what that
would look like to the old priest. And
besides, having them along would provide a
buffer. Maybe keep him from falling prey to
his own weakness where Indy was concerned. He needed to keep his head clear,
be objective.

Indy was looking at him, silently begging
him to tell Father Dom no. To make the old
man stay behind. Additional evidence that
he probably ought to do the opposite. Being
alone with her was not a good idea, not even
on a busy university campus. "All right," he
said, with a nod at Father Dom. "We'll all
go."

"Good. Good. Now, in the meantime, I

have somewhere I need to be, things I need to do that I've been seriously neglecting."

Tomas saw Indy and Rayne frown, but he was the one who asked, "Dom, what are you talking about?"

"Well, the reason I came here to begin with, of course. The Interfaith Conference."

"Is that still going on?" Indy asked. "I would've thought, after the bombing —"

"Of course the conference itself has been cancelled. But a lot of the clerics stayed in town. Some are still hospitalized, but others have arranged a memorial service for those who died. It's . . . it's by invitation only. I really should be there, Tomas."

"Of course you should," he said softly. "Where's it being held?"

"Sage Chapel." He picked up a sweater he'd left lying on the small sofa. "Don't worry. I'll be finished in plenty of time for our meeting with Professor Yates."

"Good," Tomas said. But he didn't mean it.

And he felt guilty as hell for the surge of relief that washed over him as Father Dom went out the front door, got into his oversize bronze Buick and roared away.

13

As tired and as drained as I was, I was almost giddy at the prospect of having Tomas and Rayne to myself for the next few hours, without the glowering, buzz-killing presence of Father Dom dragging us all down. And you know, even though he didn't say it out loud, I thought Tomas felt that way, too. He seemed to grow lighter the second the old goat's car growled out of earshot.

Okay, there was a minute or two where I sort of wished Rayne would find somewhere else she had to be, as well. But I bounced myself right back from that. Because when we were alone together, there was too much between Tomas and me. It was intense and deep and emotional, and yes, sexy, too. But neither one of us was ready to take this thing any further. And having Rayne with us would keep things from going down that road.

We needed a break.

I clapped my hands together and glanced at the clock. "So? Am I the only one who feels like a kid at recess all of a sudden?"

Rayne smiled. Tomas averted his eyes, but I saw the glint of agreement in them first.

"Okay, well, I've had an exquisite breakfast already — thank you for that, Tomas. I could eat your French toast every day for the rest of my life and be happy."

He looked at me with a smile that was pure impulse, completely honest. "I'm really glad you enjoyed it. Are you okay, Indy?"

"Of course I'm okay. But I need to take a shower and throw on some clothes. And then I think we ought to . . . try to have some fun today. Just for a couple of hours, while Dom's gone. Maybe get our minds off all this demonic, life-and-death, end-of-the-world stuff and just do something . . . stupid fun."

"I am so with you on that," Rayne said, smiling. "Go ahead, take your shower. My brother and I will come up with a plan while you do."

"Okay." I met Tomas's eyes. "Make it a good one. Nothing heavy, nothing dark."

He sent me a salute, and I thought he looked as relieved as I felt. "I promise."

And then there was that long tugging

process I had to go through every single time I wanted to tear my eyes away from his. But I managed it and headed up the stairs.

As soon as I reached my room I kicked the door closed behind me and went straight to the bathroom, cranked on the taps and shed the heavy bathrobe. I was still tired. Worn down. But better than earlier. And as I stood under the pounding, hot spray, one arm braced against the tiled wall, head down, I felt the heat easing some of the aches from my body, relaxing some of the knotted-up muscles, soothing the tension from my nerves. I felt the headache easing.

I wonder what that translation has to say? I wonder if this is going to be it? The way to get the amulet.

Stop thinking about that! You need an easy day for a change, dumb-ass, or you're headed straight for a breakdown.

Tomas, I thought. Tomas, Tomas, Tomas. His mouth on mine, his arms around me, his body pressed up against me. The feelings of love came rushing through me.

Through me.

Huh. Interesting that I was feeling them as if they were my own emotions. Not leftovers from some past self clouding up my heart, but real, now, sorts of feelings.

Maybe. Maybe these feelings *were* real. My own.

Of course, that didn't solve the problem of his priesthood.

Will you get your mind off problems, just for this morning?

I lathered up, rinsed down, washed my hair and called it good. This was not the day for a long, lingering shower, no matter how good it would feel on my poor battered bod. Today I wanted to spend every minute I could with Tomas, and with Rayne, too. It was going to be a mental health day, and damn, did I need it.

I opened the shower door and stepped out into the steam-filled bathroom, tugging a towel off the rack and wrapping it around me, under my arms, tucking it in front to keep it in place. I padded over to the little sink and cranked on the faucet, reaching for my toothbrush with one hand, then giving the steamy mirror a palm-swipe with the other.

She stood behind me in the mirror, black hair waving like every strand was a living thing. Black eyes. Beautiful. She looked at me in that mirror, and I stared back, absolutely transfixed, inwardly cringing in case she started up with the slashing again and hoping to the Goddess that she wouldn't.

He's a dangerous man.

I blinked. "Who?" I wanted with everything in me to turn around and face her, but it felt as if something was literally holding me still, right where I was.

The priest.

"Which —"

You are very close now. Very close.

"And you're a pain in the ass. Why don't you just carve me up in English next time and save us all the hassle?"

I am not the one cutting you, Indira.

"Then who the hell is?"

You are. Your past self, your higher self, knows. You must remember.

Oh, well, that was an interesting piece of bullshit, wasn't it?

"How about you just leave me the fuck alone today, Lilia? How about I get a few hours of peace from you and all your crap today?"

You must not give the amulet to the priest.

"All right, let me put it this way. Either leave me alone for the next few hours or I'm walking. I'll leave. I'll go right back to my apartment and my job and my life, and if the world ends because of it, too fucking bad. How's that sound to you?"

Do not give the amulet to the priest. Return it to the one to whom it belongs.

I closed my eyes, clenched my fists and literally tore my body free of her hold, forcing myself to turn around. When her grip on me broke, it broke fast, and I whirled so suddenly I almost tipped over. Without opening my eyes I flung out my hand and drew the shape of a Banishing Pentagram in the air before me. "Be gone!" Then I pushed with my open palm, and the door crashed open as if I'd kicked it.

I opened my eyes, blinking in surprise.

There was no one there. I'd blasted the bathroom door wide open without touching it. I looked at my hands, and I smiled a little.

I did it.

I was still shaking like a leaf, half expecting the slashes to start striping themselves across my back again.

Not gonna happen. I banished her ass. Maybe I should've been embracing my inner witch all along.

I told myself that I felt just a little bit more in control, and that it was not as big a freaking lie as it felt like, and then I brushed my teeth.

"She's going to end up in the hospital if this keeps up, you know." Rayne was digging through the giant closet as she spoke, though digging for what she hadn't yet said.

295

It was a big closet, with boxes stacked behind the hanging rods, and shelves overhead. She'd stored various things there over the years since he'd bought this place, stuff she dug out whenever she came to visit.

"I noticed how weak she seemed this morning," Tomas said.

"Pale, too," Rayne said. "And did you get a load of the dark circles under her eyes?"

"Yeah."

She poked her head out of the closet, stabbing him with her eyes. "If this keeps up it's going to kill her, Tomas."

"You think it's that serious?"

"You trust my instincts?"

He nodded. "Yes, I do."

"Where she's concerned anyway," Rayne finished for him, diving back into her excavation project. "I wish you'd listen to me about Father Dom."

"You've never liked him."

"There's something very wrong with that man, Tomas. Something very wrong about this whole secret one-man-per-generation subsect of the Church devoted to fighting a demon that no one is even supposed to know about."

He sighed, glad he wasn't looking her in the eyes. "You can't deny it's real. Not anymore, not with all we've seen."

"Something's happening. But you can't be sure Dom's interpretation is the only one, much less the right one. The guy's seriously warped, Tomas. I mean, have you ever even talked to anyone else in the Church about this?"

"You know I haven't. I wouldn't know who to talk to. Dom says very few people even know we exist." He'd always taken Father Dom's secret mission with a grain of salt, until he'd seen proof of the existence of demons at that little girl's exorcism. But frankly, now that he'd met Indy, he was having more doubts than ever before about what was right and what was wrong, and even what was real.

Again Rayne popped her head out of the closet. "Aren't you even curious about what the hell a bigot like Father Dom is doing at an interfaith memorial service?"

"I was hoping his interest in the conference was a sign that his mind was starting to open a little more," he confessed.

"His interest in the conference was a sign that he needed an excuse to come out here and make sure you did what he thought you should do about Indy and the so-called demon."

"Now you don't think it's a demon?"

"Indy saw it. She didn't think it was a

demon." Rayne emerged fully from the closet, holding his old acoustic guitar. "The word of a fellow witch is plenty for me to go by."

"She keeps telling me she's not a witch anymore." He tried to ignore the way his fingers were itching to get hold of that guitar. He'd packed it away almost a year ago, when Father Dom had told him that such pursuits were wasteful, frivolous and displeasing to God. He hadn't agreed. But he *had* obeyed. What the hell had he been thinking?

"Once a witch, always a witch. I'm going to initiate her. If she'll let me."

He raised his brows, attention distracted from the guitar. "Really?"

She nodded. "Granted, she's never been formally Dedicated to a coven, nor done the required year and a day of dedicant-level lessons and practice. But I think her life experience is more than she would have gained from any of that. And really, the initiations are given by the gods. We just observe them through ritual. And what is all this, if not an initiation? A death and rebirth for her?"

"Death and rebirth. That's what initiation is to you?"

"It's what it is, period." She handed him

298

the guitar. "In my opinion, brother, you're going through one of your own. The second-degree initiation is a symbolic descent into the Underworld. A dark night of the soul."

Taking the guitar from her, he looked at it instead of his sister's eyes. How had his life gotten so far off track? How had he fallen in with what seemed more and more clearly to be Father Dom's private obsession?

"I think you'll get through it, though," she went on. "Anyone can get through anything, as long as they know the one sacred truth. The one thing that underlies everything in creation."

"And what's that?" he asked.

"That love isn't just the most important thing, it's the *only* thing. The only real thing. Everything else is made up. So when all the extraneous stuff confuses you, just take a step back and focus on love. It's all you have to do. It's always the right answer."

He had a brief flash of Father Dom saying much the same thing, only in his version the word *love* was replaced by the word *faith.*

Was that what this was? A choice he had to make between love and faith?

Just like Abraham, Father Dom whispered in his mind.

"Tune that baby up," Rayne told him,

nodding at the guitar. "I'm gonna build a little campfire outside, even though it's still daylight, and then scour the cupboards for marshmallows."

I had no idea that Tomas could play guitar. He knew all the songs that people these days considered campfire classics. John Denver and the Eagles, even John Prine and Kris Kristofferson. I knew them all, too, because we had satellite radio at Pink Petals, and we listened to a lot of Americana and country and seventies hits. So I sang along a little. Mostly off-key.

Rayne sang, too, like a freaking songbird. She could really carry a tune. And every now and then Tomas would jump in with a little deep harmony, and I just sat there in utter bliss. The smells of burning firewood, of smoke, and underneath them the autumn leaves decomposing on the ground, were like brushstrokes of sensory color, painted on the air. The music, his voice, and hers, too, punctuated by the snapping and crackling of the campfire, surrounded me like an embrace. And the sun filtering through the trees, dappling the ground beneath a baby-blue sky, made my eyes water in joy.

When I was practicing witchcraft regularly and casting spells to summon the man of my dreams, my soul mate, I'd done an exercise where I described him as if I were standing there looking at him, even though I wasn't. The things I had written about him then came rushing back to me now.

He is handsome, with a smile that is never fake. It's genuine, coming right from his heart.

He has brown eyes that can melt me like a chocolate bar in the hot sun.

He's deeply spiritual — he believes in magic.

He doesn't care about flashy cars or money.

He's happiest in the country, where I want to live once my life gets started.

I guess I'd kind of been thinking his arrival would be the starter's pistol for that. My life. I'd been crouching on my mark, getting set, for three years, waiting for that gunshot. It hadn't come.

He plays guitar.

No shit. I'd actually written that. In my vision of my soul mate, he always played guitar. I don't know why. I used to see it just as plain as . . . as I was seeing it right now. Except his face was always a little blurred. But everything else was clear: a man in black, strumming a guitar by a campfire in the country.

And suddenly a feeling of déjà vu washed over me, a feeling so intense that I got dizzy and thought I might throw up.

Oh. My. Goddess. It's him. It's really him. He's the one I saw in all those visions, those dreams. He truly is my soul mate.

There was no longer any doubt in my mind. Or in my heart.

A few hours and a dozen toasted marshmallows later, the old priest returned and the beautiful enchanted afternoon came to an end, like a dark curtain falling at the end of a play. He descended, and bam. Done. No more lightness or music or laughing.

The guy was like a living, breathing pall.

It was time to head out to meet Professor Jon Yates anyway, though, so our fun had to end either way. We put out the fire, and Tomas brought his guitar inside, leaning it carefully in a corner of the living room.

I didn't miss the disapproving look Father Dom sent him. And I noticed that Tomas didn't back down from it, just returned the old man's cranky gaze with a smile and asked how the memorial service had gone.

Dom huffed. "Sad, of course."

"I'm sure. Who spoke?"

Father Dom's eyes danced away from Tomas's. "Several clerics of different bents. Few with any true understanding of life and death and what it all means, of course, and none who knew what truly happened." He shrugged. "But I can tell you more on the way. We don't want to be late."

Tomas took his keys off the rack near the door, and we all went out. I was heading for the front passenger door of his old, once-white Volvo when the holier-than-thou-king managed to speed-walk past me. Odd how old and frail he could seem when it suited him. Shuffling along slowly, fighting to catch his breath, maybe pausing to lean over, one hand braced on his knee, the other up in the air, waving in a "give me a minute" gesture. But only until there was a reason to move. Or until he *thought* there was a reason, anyway. He was in the front passenger seat beside Tomas before I could even blink.

Rayne saw it. I knew because she put a hand on my arm and, when I looked at her, rolled her eyes. "Guess the *Padre* called shotgun," she whispered.

"I'm surprised he's not on your brother's lap," I returned, catty and not one bit ashamed of it. I opened the rear door and got in, sliding all the way over, so I was right behind Tomas. Rayne got in beside me and closed the door.

Tomas looked into the rearview mirror and met my eyes. I stared into his, silent, willing him to stop listening to Father Dom and start thinking for himself. He must have felt it. He had to feel it. I willed him to feel it. I willed him to turn away from Father Dom and toward me instead.

Rayne said, "Tomas, would you mind turning on the radio? My addiction to modern media is causing me serious withdrawal up here."

I frowned at Rayne's request, knowing she was up to something but not sure what. Sure enough, as soon as the music came on and Tomas had found a station playing Bob Dylan, she spoke to me, keeping her voice low and soft. "I saw that" was all she said.

I lifted my brows in a show of innocence.

"We do not use manipulative magic, Indy. You know better."

I tilted my head to one side. "I wasn't —"

"Yes, you were. On my brother. And you have to know I'm not gonna put up with that."

I sighed, lowering my eyes. Her hand closed over mine. "Besides, you don't need to. The power of love, remember? He's going to come around on his own."

"You think so?"

"I know so. He's already there, he just doesn't know it yet. His brain is all mixed up with demons and demon fighting, rite and rote and doctrine and vows, and the guilt trips being heaped on his head by the old goat up there."

Father Dom's head came up from his in-depth study of the notebook computer he'd brought along. Images of the symbols cut into my flesh earlier filled the screen. It made me shiver to have Dom looking at my skin. He glanced back at us as if he'd sensed he was the topic of our discussion.

We both smiled, and I wondered if mine was as phony as Rayne's.

Father Dom returned his attention to the computer.

After a moment or two Rayne looked at me again. "Aside from all that, I'm glad to see you embracing your witchy side again. Welcome back to the Craft of the Wise, Sister."

I lowered my head and realized that I had indeed begun believing again. With all I'd seen and experienced lately, I couldn't very well continue claiming not to believe in magic. In gods and goddesses. In demons and spells and curses. Not when they were all around me.

"How did you know?"

She looked at me as if I'd asked how she knew that day followed night.

"You need to be initiated," she whispered. "It'll connect you spiritually with every witch who ever lived, the long line of those wise women who came before you. Will you let me do the honors?"

I met her eyes, humbled to my core. A year and a day of study was normally put in before initiation. Testing, practice and lessons, but above all experience, were required. I felt like a fraud. "I haven't earned it."

"You're ready, Indy. In fact, you're ready for all three levels of initiation. Though performing them all at once might be too much to take — especially in your current physical condition. So one at a time. To connect you. To empower you."

I didn't feel worthy, and yet, here was an experienced High Priestess of the Craft, telling me I was. Offering to make me an official witch. A priestess of the Goddess.

I bowed my head and nodded my acceptance. "I'd be honored, Rayne. Thank you." Then I whispered, "When?"

"Tonight," she whispered.

Tonight! My stomach knotted in nervousness. Initiation was a Very Big Deal, even to a solitary witch like me. Former solitary witch, I added mentally.

Already we were pulling onto the Cornell University campus, making our way amid the beautiful buildings and perfectly groomed grounds toward McGraw Hall, which housed the Archaeology and Anthropology Departments. And every parking space we passed was filled.

Rayne elbowed me. "Go on, get us a spot. Long unused muscles get weak. They need exercise."

I smiled, as so much of what I'd learned came rushing back to me. I opened my chakras and closed my eyes, and felt the power coursing through me, sending shivers of energy up and down my spine. "By my will and Lady's grace, I now create a parking space," I whispered. Then I snapped my fingers.

"There's one," Father Dom said, pointing.

I opened my eyes and saw a little VW Beetle — original, not new — backing out of a spot directly ahead of us.

"So mote it be," Rayne whispered with a secret smile.

"What's that?" Dom asked, turning the radio volume down.

"I said Amen," Rayne replied. It wasn't even a lie.

I had to keep my head down, because I was feeling something that would have shown in my eyes. I was feeling the surge of my own power, the return of something I had lost, something I had missed more than I had even realized. Only now that I was connecting to that higher source again did I understand the emptiness its absence had left in my soul. God, why had I stopped believing in magic?

But I knew why. It was because so much of my work, my studies, my practice, had been in the service of one goal. I wanted to find my soul mate. The man who would love me forever. And it had failed. No matter how much I cast or conjured, how much I meditated and visualized and wished for him, he had not come.

And so I had decided that magic didn't work. That it was all just make-believe. And I had been very glad I'd resisted the urge to join a coven and commit myself to the Craft, because it would have been harder to walk away had I taken the solemn vows of an Initiated Witch.

As hard, I thought, as it was going to be for Tomas to walk away from the vows he had taken. But he would. I knew he would, because the pattern that had been invisible to me before seemed so clear now. I didn't choose witchcraft in this lifetime. I chose it long, long ago. And him. I chose him, as well. Both of those choices were still with me today. It was my witchy spirit that had led me back to him. And the so-called demon's machinations, for better or worse, had brought us back together.

And his calling, too, I thought slowly. Tomas's vows and his mission had also been essential elements in reuniting the two of us.

He needed to see that, too. He was going to have to realize that we were meant to be.

We all climbed out of the car and started up the sidewalk toward the building where Jon was waiting. But as we moved forward, the oddest feeling began creeping up my spine. As if someone was watching us. I glanced over my shoulder, but there was no one. Students coming and going, most with white earbuds dangling. And then I spotted the squirrel. He sat on a low limb of a nearby tree, so motionless he appeared to be stuffed, and his eyes stared unblinkingly at me.

I reached up to touch Tomas's shoulder, drawing his attention. He'd been walking just ahead of me — Dom, as always, at his side — but he stopped and looked where I indicated.

"Over there, too," Rayne said, nodding in another direction.

Canada geese, a whole flock of them, were marching toward us in single file, all of them staring at us as they drew closer.

A growl drew my head around, and I saw three dogs — two pugs and a poodle — straining their leads to watch us, growling, their eyes like marbles, their little bodies quivering as their owners tugged and commanded them to come along.

And then, remarkably, Tomas slid an arm around my waist and pulled me up beside him. "They're only watching. They won't attack."

"How can you be so sure?" I asked softly. As I looked around, I wasn't entirely convinced that some of the passers-by were not also acting as the demon's eyes. A couple of them seemed to be in possession of the same vacant-eyed stare as the animals.

"Because he wants us to find the incantation that will enable you to call forth the amulet. He needs you to get it so you can return it to him. Without it, he can't hope to succeed. He won't try to stop us from getting it."

"He won't try to stop me," I reminded him. "But what about you, Tomas? You intend to destroy the thing once I get it. The demon — or whatever he is — has every reason to want to take you out."

He seemed to get stuck in my eyes. "Destroying the amulet is the only way we can prevent this from ever happening again. If we succeed, Indy, we end this forever. No one will ever have to fight this battle again. And you'll finally be free to move on when the time comes, either into the afterlife or another incarnation if that's what you believe in, without all this baggage from the past holding you like an anchor."

I swallowed hard, seeing again the pain-filled eyes on the other side of the Portal. Eyes that had seemed to be begging for my help. It would be like kicking a puppy to squelch the hope in those eyes. They couldn't have seemed less demonic to me.

At the same time, I saw the genuine caring in Tomas's eyes and knew he was not lying. He honestly thought destroying the amulet would be the best thing for me, as well as for mankind.

I swallowed my fears and tugged myself away from Tomas's side. "Wait here," I said, and I walked off the sidewalk into the grass, toward one of the snarling pugs. It stared at me, teeth bared as I approached.

The owner, an impossibly thin waif with flat-ironed blond hair to her waist, said, "I swear, I've never seen him act this way. He's usually so friendly, I —"

I flicked my hand up, palm out, in the universal sign for *Stop,* and she went instantly silent. Then I crouched near the dog and stared into his eyes, and I whispered to him.

"Are you seeing me? Are you seeing me through this innocent creature's eyes? Hearing me through its ears? Then listen up. I haven't decided yet if I'm going to help you or not. But I promise you, if you hurt Tomas, I will destroy the amulet myself. Do not put me to the test, Demon — or whatever you are. I love that man. I'll kill you with my bare hands before I'll let anything happen to him. Are you hearing me? *Are* you?"

The dog blinked, whimpered and sat. His tongue came out as he started panting happily, and his little head tipped from one side to the other as if he were puzzled, trying to decipher words he'd never heard before.

Smiling in relief, I scratched his head, and he gave me a completely nondemonic doggy smile. Then I rose and walked away as the skinny girl scooped up her pug and hurried in the other direction.

Father Dom was saying something to Tomas, leaning close and speaking behind his hand. I had no doubt he was telling him how I was obviously in league with the Demon and must not be trusted.

Frankly, I wasn't so sure he was wrong.

The Demon seemed to hear me and obey me. I was a witch who could command a demon. I was a walking stereotype of the worst possible sort.

And yet I didn't feel as much fear of this so-called demon as I had before. It was a priest who'd ordered my execution all those centuries ago, after all. Not a demon. A priest who'd stood behind me at the top of the cliff, his hands on the bare skin of my back as he prepared to push me over. A priest.

My priest.

The man I loved.

A siren's wail dragged my attention away from my thoughts as a police car came to a screaming halt right in front of the building we'd been planning to enter — the building where Jon Yates's office was.

All four of us ran toward the door as the officers emerged from the car. A weeping woman came running down the steps toward them. She gripped the first cop by his upper arm. "He's still there. God, he's still there. I wanted to cut him down, but I —"

"All right, ma'am, all right, calm down. Your nine-one-one call was impossible to understand. You need to tell us what's going on."

"It's Professor Yates!" she sobbed. "Jonathon Yates. I found him in his office. He's . . . he's hanged himself!"

14

Tomas stood there, shock washing over him as he saw one of the cops walk the hysterical woman back into the building. The other one took up a position at the doors and spoke into his radio.

Tomas lunged up the steps, intending to follow the first cop and the woman inside, but the cop at the door stopped him, a hand to his chest. "Sorry, Father. You'll need to wait out here. This is an active investigation."

"He's a friend. I need to know what happened."

"So do we. But if you want to help . . . Do you have any idea what's been going on with the professor?"

Yeah, Tomas thought. *He was helping me interpret messages from a demon. And now he's dead. And I don't for one minute believe it was a suicide.*

But if he said any of that, he would wind

up detained for questioning or, worse, a psychiatric evaluation. And there was no time for any of that.

"No. I'm just . . . I'm shocked. I want to know what happened."

"I'm very sorry for your loss, Father. But I can't let anyone in. And I have to question anyone coming out, so you're going to have to wait."

"How long?"

The cop swallowed. "It'll be a while."

A heavy hand clapped down on Tomas's shoulder, and he turned to see that Father Dom had joined him at the top of the steps. "Come on, son. We have to let the officer do his job."

Turning, shell-shocked and almost dizzy with it, Tomas walked back down the steps to where Rayne and Indy waited, wide-eyed, as stunned as he was and probably scared, too.

As they approached the women, but before they got too close, Dom leaned nearer. "Things are getting very dangerous, Tomas. And it's clear to me that the witch has no intention of cooperating with us," Father Dom said. "Did you see the way she spoke to that dog?"

Tomas nodded, but he didn't want to hear it. Jon was dead. His friend was dead.

"And not just the dog, either," Dom went on. "They all went back to normal. The squirrel. The birds. Even the students. She's a far more powerful witch than either of us knew, Tomas. She not only communes with demons but commands them."

"This isn't the time, Dom."

"This is the *only* time. How do you know she didn't orchestrate this herself? Jon was translating something — maybe she's remembered the incantation on her own and didn't want us to know. Maybe —"

"Enough!" Tomas snapped loudly, angrily, and Father Dom fell silent, maybe in shock. But silent all the same.

Tomas continued toward the women, who both hugged him hard when he got close enough. Their arms, their warmth, were a comfort at a time when not much could be.

"There's no way Jonathon hanged himself," he muttered.

"So says every friend or relative of every suicide that has ever been," Father Dom said, standing back from the group hug.

Rayne stepped away, but Indy pressed closer, hugged longer. "What if the demon did it?"

"Dom says he can't do anything physical — not directly, anyway. He has to influence humans or animals to —"

"He managed to influence someone to plant that bomb." Her face was pressed to his chest. The movement of her lips, the vibration of her words, the heat of her breath, seeped through his shirt, and his arms tightened convulsively around her.

"I know," he said.

"We need to end this, Tomas. Too many people are dying."

"I agree with you."

Finally she backed away from him, blinking away tears and then, quite suddenly, frowning at something behind him.

He turned to see what had caught her attention, but he didn't see anything other than a nearby boulder. It had a bronze plaque on its face, apparently bearing an inscription. It was only a few yards away, but the way Indy was staring at it seemed to indicate it meant something to her. Without a word, she began walking toward it. Frowning, Rayne went with her.

Tomas started to go, too, but Dom gripped his arm, stopping him.

Father Dom preventing me from going to Rayne and Indy. It's a literal representation of what's happening to me on all levels. A living parable.

"Tomas, I am rethinking our plan of action. To have her retrieve the amulet and then allow us to destroy it for all time seemed the best possible idea, and in many ways it still would be. But if she intends to turn it over to him instead, we will have failed utterly. Maybe it's better if we simply prevent her from acquiring the amulet at all."

"And let this thing keep going on, lifetime after lifetime? She's trapped in this cycle, Dom, don't you see that? It's like a curse. No, we have to end it. We have to break it now."

Dom lowered his head. "Thirteen clerics have died. And now your old friend. The world is at stake, and your chief concern is still with the witch?"

"Yeah," he said softly. "I guess it is."

"I pity you, Tomas. I pity you for the torment you're inviting into your life by your lack of faith."

Tomas tugged free of Father Dom's restraining hand, and hurried toward Rayne and Indy. Dom followed. Looking at the rock, then at Indy, Tomas said, "What is it?"

"That's the one I saw in my dream," Indy said. "It was sort of . . . glowing."

"Are you sure it was the same one?"

She shrugged her bag from her shoulder and pulled out the journal — the one he had bought for her. Then, quickly, she flipped the pages and turned the book face-out to show him the drawing.

She had sketched a boulder exactly like the one before them. It even had the square plaque on its face, with tiny lines to indicate writing, and a silhouette of a male face a lot like the one actually engraved there.

"It means something. It has to."

Rayne nodded in agreement. "Indy, maybe you should look around for the other things you saw in your dreams."

"Yes, the other things you drew," Tomas agreed excitedly.

Indy nodded hard. "I sketched everything. I mean, I'm no artist, but —" As she spoke, she riffled pages. "Let's see . . . There's the tree that looks just like an old man, bent and stretching out one partly broken branch, like it's pointing a finger at something."

"Like *that* tree?" Rayne asked, pointing herself.

All eyes turned that way, and Tomas heard Indy gasp. A moment later she had found the page with the sketch of the tree in question. It was a perfect image of one in the distance, across a sloping green lawn. Men were already gathering around it with chain saws and a pickup truck to remove the broken branch. But until they did, everything about it, even the larger knots in the tree's trunk, was identical to her sketch. There was even a small bird's nest on the broken limb, accurately depicted.

"This has to mean something," Tomas said.

"I . . . I have to follow the signs, Tomas. I know you've lost a friend and you need to stay here, but . . ."

Tomas shook his head. "I'm coming with you."

"Me, too," Rayne put in. "You might need me."

Father Dom opened his mouth, but Tomas spoke before he could. "I need you to stay here, Dom. I need you to find out what happened to Jonathon. And what he did with the translation, if you can."

"But suppose you need me?"

"It'll be too hard for you to keep up." He met the old man's eyes, looking at him steadily and deeply. "You chose me for this, Dom. You were guided by God to do that. Maybe it's time for you to trust that God knew what He was doing when He made you pick me." And as he said it, he thought it made more sense than anything else ever had. Maybe there really *was* a reason why he'd been chosen for this mission. Maybe it was because Dom had things too twisted up in his mind, with his preconceived notions and prejudices clouding his vision.

Dom closed his eyes for a moment, then looked up. "Maybe I can convince the officer to let me deliver the professor's Last Rites before they move the body."

"Good idea. See if you can get a look at his notes, especially the translation. Slide the pages under your shirt if you can."

The old man nodded. "I'll meet you back here by this rock whenever you've finished. Agreed?"

"Yes, good," Tomas said. "If anything else happens, call me." He patted his cell phone, which was attached to his belt.

"I will." Then, turning, Father Dom started slowly toward the building.

Tomas noticed that his old friend was limping. Very clever, he thought.

Together with Rayne and Indy, he headed for the broken tree. They followed its pointing "finger" while Indy flipped pages in her journal. Suddenly she stopped, looked up and blinked in what looked like amazement.

"I . . . I thought it was a castle," she whispered.

And no wonder, given its huge rough-cut stones, its gothic arched windows, its elaborate, pillar-flanked entrance. The clock tower beside it could easily be mistaken for a castle spire.

But it wasn't a castle. It was Uris Library. They stood outside the building, staring at the beautiful entrance, as students with backpacks strode purposefully in and out.

"Now what?" Tomas asked, looking down at Indy and noticing again how beautiful she was. How stunningly beautiful. Almost otherworldly.

"Now," she said, meeting his eyes, and nodding as if feeling completely sure of herself and rather proud of it, "we go inside."

I couldn't believe the confidence that was surging in me. I mean, it seemed really inappropriate at a time like this, you know? With Tomas's old friend apparently hanging dead in his own office.

There was something off about that. I didn't know what, but I was letting it ferment a little, way down deep in my subconscious, because something wasn't right. The timing. It was too coincidental. It had to be connected to what we were doing here. And while I knew you couldn't tell much about a person by meeting them once, I hadn't picked up any depressed vibes from the late Professor Yates. Hell, he'd seemed happy. Vibrant, even.

But despite the tragedy of that, and the oddness surrounding it, there was still this feeling bubbling up inside me. A feeling of . . . of power, really. Ever since Rayne had offered me the honor of initiation at her own hand, the feeling had been growing. And then, when she challenged me to do a simple parking-space spell and it had worked instantly, the feeling had grown even more.

Why was I even surprised by that? I'd always had fairly decent success with minor magics. Finding lost items, snaking my way through traffic jams. Making unpleasant customers suddenly remember somewhere else they had to be. It was the big stuff I'd never been able to do.

The big stuff. Like the one spell I had cared so much about: the one to bring my soul mate to me.

But now it was all coming back to me, all my studying and practicing, all my casting and conjuring. As I looked at the image given to me in my own dreams, sketched out by my own hand and accurate to the tiniest detail in the objects now revealing themselves on campus, I was almost high on my own power. Every time I saw proof that it was real, it became more real. I was feeling ten feet tall and bulletproof by the time we entered the hallowed halls of the Uris Library, standing in the shadow of McGraw Tower. My drawing's castle spire.

"Now what?" Tomas asked.

Rayne looked at me expectantly. I just shrugged. "I don't know."

We walked through the library for a while, exploring it while I waited to feel . . . something. Eventually we wound up in the elaborate and breathtaking A. D. White Reading Room. I blinked like a doe in headlights as I took it in.

"Students call this the Harry Potter Room," Tomas whispered. It seemed natural to whisper in a place like this. Like in a church.

There was ornate bronze-colored metal-work everywhere, levels of books rising on two sides, deep red carpet on the floors, and gleaming antique hardwood desks and stands. It was like something ancient and sacred. Mystical and powerful, this place.

I was looking for something, anything, else to match my sketches. There were only a couple left. A decorative design I thought was a medallion on a floor. A dark doorway beneath a statue — a bust, really — and a very old treasure chest, which didn't count, because it was my own. It was home in my closet with all my magical supplies.

My confidence was waning.

"Don't give up yet, Indy," Rayne said. "We haven't been here that long. Why don't we climb up to the higher levels, browse the stacks, see if we hit on inspiration?"

She was staring upward as she spoke. From the level we were on, you could look up and see the stacks on either side of us rising two more levels. Catwalks with railings in that same bronze-colored metal with its twisting swirling scrollwork stretched along two sides of the room overhead. More of those ornate metal railings protected the aisles in front of the elevated stacks, creating safe areas to walk, all carpeted in red just like the main floor. This design left the center open all the way to the vaulted, cathedral-like ceiling. Between the stacks, huge arched windows let the sun pour through. The place was a work of art in itself.

I nodded, and we headed up a metal staircase. No one questioned us or stopped us as we scanned the stacks and made use of one of the catwalks to cross to the other side. I was determined to see every inch of this place, all the while straining my senses to find some clue. Rayne took one side, Tomas and I the other, as we moved up to the third and final level.

Tomas put a hand on my shoulder as I scanned the place so intently that my eyes hurt. "Stop trying so hard, Indy. Relax. Let the revelations unfold on their own."

I blinked at him and got caught in his eyes like a fly in a spider's web. I saw so much there, caring and concern and a heavy grief. "Are you all right?" I asked softly.

"No. No, I'm not all right at all. I don't believe for one minute Jon would've taken his own life."

"No, I've been thinking the same thing. But what I can't figure out is why the demon would want to hurt him when he was just about to give me the incantation that would allow me to retrieve the amulet. That's what he wants, isn't it?"

"We don't know for sure that's what he translated."

"I'm sure," I told him. "I felt it in my gut as soon as you got off the phone with him this morning. And not just the spell we need, but more. *The truth I must remember.* God, Tomas, you don't know how badly I want to read that part."

"I know. It might have answered all your questions."

"And maybe shown me what the hell I'm supposed to do."

He frowned. "You mean . . . with the

amulet?"

I nodded firmly and held his eyes, and I'm pretty sure my newfound inner strength was beaming from mine. "Yes, Tomas, that's what I mean. I've seen the face of this so-called demon. It's pain-racked and tormented. And I've heard the voice of my . . . my sister from that long-ago lifetime, commanding me — pleading with me, even — to help him. All that is pulling me in one direction. And then I've got you pulling me in the other. You, a man I once loved and who I'm starting to love again . . ."

He blinked hard when I said that, even flinched a little, but otherwise he stood still and kept listening.

". . . but also a man I'm pretty sure helped to murder me, a man who chose his religion over his love for me. And at your side, pulling your strings like a puppeteer, there was — and maybe still is — an old priest I trust less than I'd trust a black widow not to bite."

I shook my head slowly. "I gotta tell you, Tomas, my feelings for you are the only thing coming down on your side in this. Everything else, including my own gut, is telling me to help the demon."

He sighed, lowering his head. "Thank you for being honest with me about that."

"What are you going to do, Tomas?" I searched his face. "What are you going to do if I decide to help him instead of you and Father Dom?"

He dropped his gaze. "I don't know."

That hurt. I wanted him to say he would respect my judgment, let me make my own choice and protect me from Dom when I did. But no. Instead I got an "I don't know." Which in my mind translated as "maybe kill you again."

That's not what he said, dumb-ass.

No. He didn't say anything, really. Even though I just basically told the idiot that I'm falling in love with him.

I had to turn away from his eyes, because they saw too much in me and I didn't want him spotting the hurt. This wasn't the time for this, anyway. We were close to something. I felt it. I started to pace away from him, one hand sliding along the railing, when I glimpsed something on the floor below us and came to an unsteady halt.

"Oh, my God."

"What is it?" Tomas walked quickly to where I stood, trying to follow my gaze. "Do you see something?"

I nodded, opening my journal to the page where I'd drawn the intricate medallion shape. I pointed at it, then at the red carpet far below us.

The same shape was right there. Right there on the carpet.

"But . . . but that's just a shadow." Tomas turned, and I did, too. "See? The light is pouring through that window, angling downward so it passes through the railing —" He turned again, his finger tracing the path of the sunlight to the metal rail with its twisting patterns. "The railing is what's causing the shape. It's just a shadow, Indy."

"Maybe so, but it's identical to my drawing."

He looked at the book, looked at the floor. I heard the shoes-on-metal sound of Rayne crossing the catwalk. Clearly she'd seen us pointing and was coming to investigate, and a few seconds later she was looking over my shoulder at the sketch and then at the shadow on the floor.

"That's amazing," she said. "And even more so when you stop to think that if we'd been here an hour earlier or later, we'd never have seen it."

"Just like the tree," I whispered. "The men were right there, ready to remove that branch. If we'd been even a few minutes later, it would have been gone."

She nodded slowly. "You're channeling. The Goddess is guiding you with a steady hand, Indy. I've never seen anything like this."

"Neither have I," Tomas admitted. "You're amazing."

I warmed at his praise and tried not to show it. "Let's get down there." I closed my hand around his. It was an impulse. I did it without stopping to think and was about to pull it away when he squeezed and kept my hand right there.

"Come on. What are we looking for next?" he asked.

"A dark doorway behind the medallion design," I said. "There should be a statue near it." I turned the page and revealed the next drawing even as we were hurrying down the stairs to the shadow on the floor, still holding hands, with Rayne right behind us.

The place had only a handful of people in it. Students, maybe, or professors, visitors, researchers, who the hell knew? Ignoring them all, the three of us walked to the center of the medallion-shadow and stood there looking around.

But there was no dark doorway. "It should be just above the curlicue in the medallion," I said pointing it out in my sketch. "Just to the left of the clock."

"There's no doorway there," Rayne said,

pointing, then jerking her hand down to her side again with a quick look around to see if anyone had noticed our touristlike enthusiasm. We did *not* want to draw attention. "Just the clock and the statue."

I looked back at my drawing. Why was everything there but the door? Suddenly Tomas swore under his breath, and my eyes shot to his. "What?"

"The time, Indy. Look at the time."

I looked at the clock again. "Ten after five? God, have we really been wandering the campus looking for clues for two hours? Father Dom's going to think we abandoned him."

"But look at the time," he said, tapping my book, and I looked where his finger was. I'd drawn the exact same time that showed on the clock right now. The hands on my drawing were at precisely five and ten. But instead of feeling excited by yet another validation of my powers, I felt a little sick to my stomach. This was getting surreal.

"But there's no doorway," Rayne said. "Just the statue."

The three of us moved toward what turned out to be a bust of a man, Andrew Dickson White, Cornell's co-founder and first president, and the man for whom this part of the library was named. Tomas looked behind the bust, even ran his hand over the wall, and shook his head.

I lowered my own in abject disappointment, and then froze. "Tomas, the floor," I whispered.

He looked where I was looking. The plush red carpet was solid everywhere else, but there was a break, a seam in the shape of a large rectangle, around the pedestal on which the bust rested. As if there were a doorway under it, in the floor itself.

"Could this be it?" Tomas looked at me.

I nodded. It was. I felt it right to the roots of my hair.

"Then there must be a way to open it," he whispered.

I turned the page in my journal. But I was all out of drawings, except for the one of my "treasure chest" at home. And then I looked at the bust itself.

Rayne nodded at me. "That's it, Indy. Use your inner eye. Try to see it through the eyes of magic, the Eyes of Spirit."

"Come on, Rayne. You and I both know the Eyes of Spirit are transferred as part of the third initiation. I haven't even had my first yet."

"The Goddess gives the power, Indy. We only hold a ritual to acknowledge and honor it. The power is already there. You've been a witch for more than three thousand years. I have no doubt you made it to the Third Degree during at least one of those lifetimes. Maybe all of them."

I lifted my head and looked into her eyes. What I saw there was absolute belief — in *me.* Then I looked from her to her brother, and he was gazing at me with something even more powerful. Something I didn't dare analyze.

But it filled me with belief. A belief stronger than any I'd had before.

I stepped back several feet and stared at the bust, deliberately allowing my eyes to go blurry as I opened my energy pathways. I didn't look directly at the statue, just let it fade and relaxed my mind.

The man's face was wise, with crow's feet at the corners of his eyes. He had a full beard and an impressive mustache. Folds of fabric made of white stone draped from his neck over the lapels of a stone suit jacket and a loop of twisted cord. It was all part of the bust and all made of the same white stone. But that loop seemed, in my eyes, to glow.

"People are starting to stare," Tomas whispered.

I lowered my head, blinking my eyes clear, and wandered over to a nearby shelf to pretend to peruse the titles there.

Tomas and Rayne were beside me in seconds. "Well?" Rayne asked.

"It's in that piece of the bust that looks like a loop of cord. There's a switch or a lever or something. But how are we going to try this in broad daylight with all these people around?"

Tomas looked over his shoulder, then back at me. "Return by night? After hours?"

"No," Rayne said. "With the bombing, and now what happened to Professor Yates, security here is going to be tight. And we sure as hell don't want to upset any nervous cops on the hunt for terrorists."

"Then what?" I asked.

Rayne met my eyes. "You two find the restrooms, duck inside and wait five minutes. I've got this. Meet me back at the boulder when you're done. I'll catch up with Dom there and set his mind at ease."

"What are you going to do?" Tomas asked, looking worried.

She leaned up and kissed her brother on the nose. "Just trust me. See you later."

And she turned and hurried across the red carpet, and within seconds she was gone.

Tomas looked at me and shrugged. "I

think I saw some restrooms before. Come on."

He led me back through the stacks and out of the reading room, wandering in what I was sure were random directions before stopping right in front of a pair of restrooms. "It shouldn't be long," he said, with a glance at his watch.

He looked back at me, and then impulsively leaned down and kissed me quickly on the mouth before ducking through the gender-appropriate door.

I blinked away my nervous smile and followed suit.

Moments later the fire alarm went off. I closed my eyes and said, "Lady Rayne, you're a freakin' genius."

Only minutes later we were back in the A. D. White Room, standing alone in front of the bust. The library was even more mysterious and awe-inspiring now that it was entirely devoid of patrons.

Tomas put both hands on my shoulders, as if to lend me his strength, as I reached out to touch that loop of twisted cord on Mr. White's vestments. I ran my fingers over the cool, bumpy shape of it, pushed and pulled on it, but it didn't move.

Of course it didn't move. It's stone!

But I kept trying, until my forefinger slid

off the cord and into the circle at the center of the loop, and something clicked. Suddenly the entire bust, marble pedestal and all, began to move. I jumped backward, landing flush against Tomas's chest, and his arms closed around me, holding me there. It was sexy as hell, and I wanted nothing more than to turn and look up into his eyes, maybe see passion starting to simmer there. But I couldn't take my eyes off the statue.

The pedestal rose slightly, maybe an inch, shoved upward as part of the floor also rose directly beneath it, then swung to the side, pivoting on one corner. Beneath it, a stairway spiraled downward into absolute blackness.

15

"What I wouldn't give for a flashlight," Tomas whispered.

"There's an app for that."

He looked at me with a puzzled frown as I pulled out my BlackBerry and turned on its LED light. It wasn't as bright as a real flashlight, of course, but it would do in a pinch. And we were definitely in a pinch. I held it out in front of me and started down the steep metal staircase. The steps were narrow, but surprisingly solid for as old as they had to be. Even so, they wobbled just enough to make me uneasy, and they made enough noise to wake the dead.

Tomas stopped behind me and called out in a harsh whisper, "Hold up a sec. Turn that light this way."

I did, and in a moment he took it from me, exploring the underside of the floor surrounding the door until he found what he was looking for. He touched something, and the floor above us moved itself back into place, lowered itself and blocked out the world.

We were alone. Utterly alone, in absolute silence. The only sounds came from the two of us, our breathing and, in my ears, the pounding of my heart. He looked at me, and I at him. How long had I been waiting for a moment like this, a moment of absolute privacy with him?

And yet, I couldn't indulge myself in fantasizing about what would happen if I leaned up and kissed him just then. This was too important.

God, I was sounding just like him. But I was feeling more and more as if I had been born for a reason. I'd been given powers, a connection to the other side, for a reason. And the reason had to do with this so-called demon — and with my own murder so many lifetimes ago.

A murder in which my beloved Tomas had been my killer. My executioner. It didn't seem possible.

Sighing, I turned away from him, taking my phone with me. Aiming its light ahead of me, I started moving down the noisy stairs again. I saw nothing beyond the meager reach of the light. Only blackness. Our steps echoed and creaked and clanked.

I hoped to the gods we reached the bottom before the firefighters arrived to answer Rayne's fake alarm, though I knew the chances of them hearing us were slim. The air felt cool but surprisingly dry on my face, and I could smell earth and rock and soon . . . books.

Yes, books. That unmistakable aroma of ink and paper and bindings. The same smell that had permeated the rooms above. It was, I realized, one of the best smells on the planet. Books.

The stairs seemed to go on and on, and we just kept descending, but finally they ended at a flat stone floor. I held my light up, shone it around us, revealing a series of archways forming a circle around the base of the stairs, which had ended dead center. Five arches, I realized, each one with a symbol over the top.

"They're the Aristotelian symbols for the elements," I whispered. I'd learned about them in my studies of the Craft of the Wise. I highlighted each of them with my light as I spoke. "Earth," I said, aiming the beam at an inverted triangle with a line crossing through it. Then I shifted to the next archway, marked by the same symbol, only with the point upright, for Air, followed by the symbols for Fire, Water and Spirit over the remaining archways.

"So which way do we go?"

"I don't even know what we're looking for, Tomas."

"Information from the past. About a demon."

"Information would be Air. But the past, that might be Water. Demons are definitely spirit, though. Or maybe Earth . . . or . . ."

"Can't you . . . you know, use your . . . powers?"

I met his dark eyes and felt the same stirring in my belly that I always felt when our eyes met. It was like connecting to a current when we touched gazes. Or lips.

As I stared at him and forgot everything else, I said, "Truth. We're seeking truth. That's fire." And I knew I was right. I moved toward the archway with the simple upright triangle. "This way."

He took hold of my hand. "Stay close, Indy. I'm feeling very antsy down here. I'm not sure it's safe."

I let him clasp my hand in his, relishing his touch, his protective attitude, his caring. "I feel safe with you, Tomas."

"I can't imagine why," he said softly, and I realized we were both still whispering, even though we had to be far out of earshot of anyone. Anywhere. This place, though, like the library above, resonated with a sacred energy, and it was that energy we were responding to with our respectful tones. Dark stone walls surrounded us, and combined with the stone floor to ensure that every footfall, every word, echoed.

Even our whispers.

I stepped beneath the fire arch and stopped, staring into the darkness beyond. I lifted my BlackBerry and aimed its beam ahead of me. It did little good. The light only reached a few feet.

"I'm sorry, Indy." I could tell from his voice that Tomas was close behind me. "I'm so sorry for what I did, the part I played in the past."

I stopped, my entire focus on those words, and a response spilled from my lips without me even knowing what I was about to say. It just came out. "I told you to do it. I begged you to do it, Tomas." I blinked, as surprised by the words as his gasp indicated he apparently was, but at the same time knowing I'd spoken the absolute truth.

I turned and stared into his eyes, lit from the glow of my phone. "You . . . you remember that?" he asked.

Searching my mind, I realized that I did. "It just bubbled up out of me like some underground spring finally finding a path to the surface. You didn't want to do it, even though you knew you'd be punished, maybe even executed, if you refused. They didn't know about us — the powers that be, the high priest. They would have killed you, too, if you'd refused. And I would have died anyway. I couldn't have borne it if you died, too."

"You loved me that much," he whispered.

Tears were burning in my eyes. The emotions of another lifetime, the heartbreak, bursting forth again, as fresh and sharp as if they were brand-new. "You loved me enough to condemn yourself to die with me. I couldn't let you."

"God help me, I should have," he whispered. "The memory feels so real to me, so present. Not like something that happened three thousand years ago, but like something that's alive right now."

"I know." My words caught in my throat. I had to take a breath, swallow to relax the muscles enough to go on. "It feels the same way to me."

He stared into my eyes and gently brushed my hair away from my face with one hand. His mouth was close to mine, so close that his breath fanned my lips, warm and soft. Something felt like raging waters, rising and pounding against the walls of my heart from within, swelling it and trying to break through. I fought to hold my feelings in, but I knew somewhere inside that it was a battle I could not win. Nor even keep fighting for very long.

"Tomas," I whispered.

His mouth closed over mine, and he held me hard against him, our bodies practically melding. I felt him shudder as my fingers twined in his hair and his arms closed even tighter around me. One hand moved upward to cup the back of my head as he bent over me, feeding from my lips like a hummingbird feeds from a lily, and we turned like dancers as we kissed.

And then there was a sound, like stone scraping over stone, echoing all around. We pulled apart only a little. Our lips stopped mating, but his arms stayed around me as we both searched for what was making that dark, deep sound.

Some of the stones in the domed ceiling were moving, and light came spilling through from somewhere beyond them, filling the room. I tried to peer into that light, knowing it couldn't be coming directly from the sun, since we were down far too deep in the earth — that stairway had been endless. And yet what looked like natural light beamed, from five equally spaced openings, forming a circle enclosed in the larger circle of the domed ceiling itself.

"It must be some kind of mirror system," Tomas said. "We must have triggered it when we stepped through the arch."

"And look, five again. Five points inside a circle. Just like a pentacle." I drew my eyes away from the light and looked around the newly bright room. It was lined with shelves, which were in turn lined with books. Moving to the nearest one, I touched a spine with great reverence, gently pulling the volume from its spot. The cover was very old, the lettering on it foreign to me.

Tomas walked up and looked over my shoulder at the cover. "That's Hebrew. This is *The Lesser Key of Solomon the King.*"

"Ceremonial magicians use the rites in this book," I said and stopped. Then I jumped in headfirst. "For summoning angels and demons."

"We're in the right place, then." He scanned the rest of the books, his eyes eager and sharp. There were perhaps a thousand titles, or at least that was my best guess. "But how do we even know where to begin?"

I walked around the room slowly, my gaze moving up and down the shelves. The books' spines were all illuminated now, but none of them seemed to jump out at me any more than the rest.

And then I paused. Because one high shelf held something that wasn't a book at all. It was a small wooden chest, with a rounded top and a small antique iron lock dangling on the front.

I stopped in front of it, staring, my heart tripping over itself in surprise. It was my chest, or its twin, anyway. "Whatever it is, it's in that box," I told him.

"How do you know?" he asked, coming to stand close beside me.

"Because I have one that looks exactly like it. Not old or anything. A replica. Cheap. I bought it at a flea market years ago. I was never sure why I liked it, but I did. It's where I keep all my magical supplies."

He nodded.

"Can you get it down for me, Tomas? I can't reach."

Standing on tiptoe, he was able to just reach the bottom of the chest. He inched it out over the edge of the shelf with his fingertips, and then farther, until its own weight tipped it forward into his waiting hands.

The chest was about two feet wide and maybe eighteen inches high at the top of its arching lid. Mine was maybe a third its size.

He carried it to the center of the floor and set it down. "The next thing is to get it open." He tugged experimentally on the lock, an ancient-looking iron padlock without any keyhole. "It's solid. It's not going to give."

"Then we'll have to take the whole thing with us."

He looked up at me and swallowed hard. "It's going to be hard enough to get out of here undetected, Indy. The firefighters will have declared the library safe by now. People will have come back in. We can't exactly come popping up out of a hidden passage beneath a statue carrying a stolen artifact from a hidden sublevel."

"Then we may be stuck here until after hours. Maybe we can sneak out in the dead of night without drawing too much notice."

His lips pulled tight at that notion. "I don't like leaving Rayne out there with no one but Dom to protect her. She's too close to all this."

I looked at him, looked at the box, looked at the light shining down around us. "Maybe there's another way out." My eyes were back on that box again. It felt as if it was pulling me to it. I was itching to get at it — alone.

Why don't I want him here when I open it?

It didn't matter why. My gut had led me

true so far, I had to go with it. "Tomas, why don't you take a look around, see if you can find another exit? I can take a closer look at this box while you do."

He studied me for a moment, tipping his head slightly to one side before apparently making up his mind. "Okay. Yell if you need me. I won't go far."

"All right." I held up my BlackBerry. "Take this. You might need it."

"Thanks." His hand brushed mine as he took the phone from me and our eyes met, and his beamed something into mine. It felt like tenderness. Like . . . more.

I watched him walk away, then sat down with the box in front of me, turning it this way and that, and examining it all over. Its sides were smooth wood, broken only by the metal-lined seam of the lid. Metal bands divided the lid into thirds, black iron and clearly old. The lock on the front was intricate, decorated with embossed swirls and vines. And then I tipped the box onto its back and caught my breath.

The underside was painted — and brightly, too. There was a black-and-white grid, like a tic-tac-toe board, with gold borders and colorful symbols in each square. Nine of them, and one more at the head of the board.

I touched that lone symbol, the most familiar one — the Eye of Horus, with its curlicue eyeliner and vacant stare — drawing my fingers over its smooth surface.

And it lit up.

I caught my breath, jerking my hand away. I heard a rumbling sound then, either around me or inside me, I wasn't sure which. I pressed one hand to the floor, looking up in fear of the room collapsing around me, but the rumbling died slowly away.

Okay, okay, something is definitely up here. I stared at the glowing eye for a full minute, as it slowly faded and finally blinked out again.

Then I studied the other symbols, and I realized what they were. They came from the major arcana of the Tarot. Death. The Hanged Man. The Lovers. The Hierophant. The Tower. The Magician. The High Priestess. The World. The Empress.

As I studied them, I knew what I had to do. The cards were like chapters of the story of my past life. Perhaps if I touched them in the right order . . .

What was I first? Not a lover, a witch.

Rayne's words echoed in my mind. *You've been a witch for more than three thousand years.* Okay, then. First, the High Priestess. She sat on a throne between black and white pillars, the crescent moon at her feet, a sacred scroll in her arms.

I touched her.

She lit up.

The Lovers had to come next, for I had fallen in love then and was in love still. Yes. I pressed my fingertips to the image of the nude male and female forms standing beneath the sheltering arms of a benevolent god.

It lit up, too.

Which one next? The Hierophant? That had to be the High Priest who ordered my death. Death, skeletal and frightening upon his white horse? No, the Death card stood for change. My eyes lit on The World. In some decks it was The Universe, and it symbolized death far more than the Death card did. It stood for death and rebirth. And that fit.

I touched the woman who stood amid an endless circle with the elements surrounding her in all directions.

The third square lit up, and I heard the distinct snapping of the ancient padlock. As I set the box into its correct position once more, I saw that the lock was now hanging open. Carefully, shaking with anticipation and more, I removed the lock and lifted the lid.

A blinding beam of white light blasted at me from inside the box, and I instinctively averted my face, throwing up one arm to protect my eyes. Then, as it faded, I lowered my arm, dared to look inside.

I saw an array of parchment pages rolled together and secured by a leather tie. Inside the raised lid, there were words.

I read them aloud. "For the Eyes of Spirit alone."

"How did you know what that said?" Tomas asked softly.

I was startled by his presence, not to mention because I hadn't even heard him return, but I didn't turn, couldn't look away as my focus sharpened and I realized that the words I was staring at were not in English.

"That's Akkadian," he said softly.

"But when I looked at it just now, it looked like English." I took the scrolls from the box and held them to my chest. "I can't read them until I see Rayne."

"Why not?" he asked.

"The Eyes of Spirit are given to a witch during the third initiation. I don't have them."

"But Rayne said that sort of thing is given by spirit."

"I don't care. Look, I've come this far. I'm not looking at these until I'm sure I'm supposed to." I lowered my head. "Okay, it's stupid, but I keep visualizing the Nazis when they looked inside the Ark of the Covenant in *Raiders of the Lost Ark*. You know. Indiana Jones."

"Your namesake."

I rolled my eyes, feeling as if I was slowly emerging from a trancelike state. I closed the lid and turned to look up at Tomas at last.

Just the sight of him made my heart seem to swell up in my chest. God, I felt a lot for that man.

"I found another way out," he said. "Great timing, huh?" He offered his strong hand and I took it, dropping the scrolls back into the chest with the other. "Let's go."

I surged to my feet, stumbled and sort of slammed into him. His arms shot around me, an automatic reflex to keep us both from falling over. But then they stayed there. I laid my head against his chest — I just couldn't resist the urge. And when I felt his heart beating there, it did something to me. Poured gasoline on the sparks that had been flying between us since the day we'd met.

"Tomas." I breathed his name so softly I didn't know if he'd heard me. It wasn't like me to be all soft and whispery. Not like the old me, anyway. Being around him seemed to have unearthed a new me. One who was all about hearts and flowers, whispers and softness, and the warmth of skin against skin.

"I can't stand this much longer," I confessed, lifting my head.

He looked straight down into my eyes. "Neither can I."

"Then kiss me already."

His lips rose a little at the corners. Like he wanted to smile, but he didn't. Not quite. And then he lowered his head and his mouth found mine, and we kissed like teenagers after prom.

I was shaking all over, and that surprised me. I hadn't expected it. But the kiss didn't end, and I didn't want it to. Ever. So when my knees got all jellylike, I just let them melt and held on tighter. We staggered around a little, turning in slow circles, his feet shuffling, mine just going along for the ride, while our mouths kept each other busy. I wound up with my back against a stone wall. It felt cool, and his chest and his arms felt warm. I used the wall to hold me up and held him tighter. I would not in a million years have planned to wrap my legs around his waist like a spider monkey, but that was exactly what I did.

And that took things deeper. Hotter. He was moving against me, and I was writhing and moving, too, until the only thing keeping it from being actual sex was our clothes. His mouth slid off mine and traveled a path along my jawline and down to my neck, and damn if that wasn't the hottest thing ever. His lips moving over that sensitive skin, nipping now and then like the world's sexiest vampire, just teasing his way to the big bite at the end.

He cupped the back of my head with one hand and bent his head lower, nuzzling his way into the scooped neck of my tank top, pushing impatiently at the fabric and managing to get a mouthful of breast, though not the best part. Not yet. But even that made my skin tingle, my nerves jump. I clutched his head with both hands, thinking, *more, more, more.*

And then my breast was fully exposed and he was lapping at the peak while I panted.

I love you!

What the fuck? I went still. *Whose voice was that? And did I say those words out loud or only in my head?*

Seeming to pick up on my sudden jolt of ice water, Tomas lifted his head, met my eyes, and then slowly, gently, lowered me to my feet again. "I want you so much I can't think about anything else," he told me.

"Me, too."

"But I can't."

I almost rolled my eyes, but I couldn't. "I know your vows are important to you."

He lowered his head, turned away from me. "There's something I haven't told you."

"So tell me."

He met my eyes, and his were dark with emotion. "I faxed a request to leave the priesthood, and for a dispensation from the vows of celibacy."

"Oh, Tomas, tell me you didn't do that for me." I moved closer to him, sliding my palm up over his back, to his strong shoulder, still shivering with need and arousal. His head was low. As if he were ashamed of what he was admitting to me.

"I did it before I met you. I explained everything in my letter, including Dom's belief that I was chosen for this mission and my intent to fulfill it before leaving the priesthood. But I knew this life wasn't for me even then." He lowered his head. "You're the first person I've told."

"I'm touched you felt you could share it with me." I didn't know what to say. "I left my faith, too, you know."

"You weren't a priest."

"Or even a priestess. But I am now."

He nodded. "And to be clear, I'm not leaving my faith. I love my belief system. I just don't think I was cut out to be a priest."

"I can say without doubt, Tomas, that if the Goddess Herself told me that I had to give you up for Her, I'd tell Her to take a flying leap."

His head came up, and he was smiling. It was a pained smile, but a smile all the same. "Aren't you afraid she'll strike you with lightning for saying things like that?"

"She'd be laughing with me and telling me she liked my spunk."

"I like your Goddess," he said.

"I'm pretty fond of your savior, as well."

His face softened. "I've been tearing myself up wondering if this was the right decision. I'm allowed to withdraw the request right up until it's approved, and every morning I wake up wondering if this is the day I make that call. But every time I look at you, I'm sure it was the right decision."

"So . . ."

"So I'd feel better about this if I could manage to keep my hands off you until I've been officially excused from my vows."

I drew a deep breath and let it out slowly. I didn't want to say what I was going to say, but I would feel like a total ass if I didn't.

"This is a big decision, Tomas. Are you absolutely sure you're not doing it based on leftover memories, or guilt, or any of that crap from this past-life thing we had to-gether? I mean, even though you weren't aware of it, on some subconscious level you might have remembered it all. Felt guilty."

He thought for a long moment, his eyes roaming my face in a way that was almost like a touch. "I'm not sure of anything right now, Indy. Except what's between us. That's real."

I lowered my eyes, because suddenly there were tears in them.

He slid an arm around my shoulders. "Let's get out of here, okay?"

"Yeah. Okay."

16

They followed the tunnel Tomas had located, heading toward the wafting, autumn-scented air and ever-growing pool of light. It hit Tomas that this journey was just like the one his soul had been taking. He'd walked through darkness, accepting a life that seemed like the one that was expected of him. Believing in Father Dom's insistence that he had a calling while never truly feeling it himself. Always, he'd been waiting for that passion, that fire to light his way toward his purpose, to light a fire in his soul. But it had never come.

Until he'd met Indy. And that was a whole different kind of fire.

He'd been drawn to the light of that fire, and it had only grown brighter. She'd breathed delicious, fresh, living air into his life. And he'd felt like he was inhaling for the very first time.

He was making the right call. He was

more sure of that now than ever.

The literal light they were following through this dark underworld turned out to be coming from a streetlight near what resembled a storm drain grate above the place where the subterranean passage came to an abrupt end. The sun had set by then. A ladder with only three rungs was affixed to the facing wall.

Tomas stepped up onto the first rung, hooked his fingers through the grate and pushed experimentally. The thing rose without even token resistance, because it turned out to be hinged on one side. *Who'd have thought?*

He lifted it only a little, then lowered it again and looked down at Indy. She was holding the box to her chest, looking up at him and tempting him to get lost in her eyes again. "Ready?" he asked, indulging himself in just looking at her.

"Yeah. Ready."

"I have no idea where we're going to emerge, so let's do it fast and hope to avoid notice."

"Okay."

"Okay." He drew a breath, swallowed hard, and pushed the grate up and over onto its back, rapidly climbing out but maintaining a low crouch. He took a quick look around. They were near the boulder where they'd been supposed to meet Father Dom hours ago. There were people around, a small crowd milling outside the building where Jon had been found. But mostly their backs were to him, and the boulder made for a good visual distraction. Still crouched, he reached back down first for the box, which he set behind the rock, and then for Indy. Her hand locked onto his, and he helped her up and out. Then he replaced the grate. They got to their feet, brushed themselves off and looked around casually, trying to determine whether they'd been seen.

But no one's attention was on them.

There were four police cars parked on the grass outside McGraw Hall, as well as an ambulance with its back doors standing open. As they looked on, two EMT's came out of the building, a black body bag strapped onto the gurney they rolled between them. It jounced down the steps, but the body stayed aboard.

"I still can't believe it," Tomas said.

"It doesn't make any sense. There's no reason for the demon to target him. He's not a priest, and he might have been about to give us exactly what the demon's supposedly waiting for. A way for me to get that amulet."

Tomas knew she was right. "We're missing something. We have to be."

"I see them," Indy said quickly. "Father Dom and Rayne. Tomas, I don't want Father Dom to know about the scrolls we found. At least not yet."

He was silent for a moment.

"Please?"

"He's going to see the chest."

"Not if you give me the car keys right now," she said.

He swallowed hard, then nodded once and handed her the keys. She took them and went jogging over the rolling lawns, taking the shortest route to where they'd parked the car.

He dragged his eyes from her and turned his attention back to the crowd. Spotting Rayne, he lifted a hand and waved. Relief relaxed her face when she spotted him, and she came plowing through the onlookers toward him. She was halfway there before he noticed Father Dom shuffling more slowly behind her, muttering apologies as he shouldered his way amid the throng.

As soon as she broke free and crossed the grass to meet him, Rayne flung herself into Tomas's arms, and he held her hard. "God, I'm glad to see you!" she said. "I was getting so worried. I don't know what's happening around here."

Her words were muffled by his shoulder, but he made them out. "I can't believe the cops are still here. It's been hours."

"Given the bombing, they're being extremely careful not to miss anything," Father Dom said. He looked around. "Where's Indy?"

Tomas's reality had undergone a profound shift while he'd been underground with Indy. He realized it as soon Dom asked where she was, because it made him tense up and feel defensive. As if Dom were the enemy.

"She went to get the car," he said. "I was concerned about your leg." It was an absolute lie. He'd known Dom long enough to know his limp came and went as suited the occasion. "What have the police said about Jon?" he asked, to shift the subject away from Indy.

The ambulance was pulling away now. A pair of cops were making the rounds, questioning people, taking notes. Rayne backed away from him, her hands still on his shoulders, her eyes damp. "They're not saying much of anything."

"Not to the general public," Dom said. "One of the officers told me — off the record, of course — that it looks like a straightforward suicide to him."

"He used an extension cord," Rayne whispered.

Father Dom placed a heavy hand on Tomas's shoulder. "The secretary found him hanging from a light fixture in his office. No one else appears to have been there, but I have no doubt this is yet another death on the shoulders of He Whose Name Must Not Be Spoken."

"I don't know," Tomas said. "Indy was just saying how that makes no sense. Jon was about to give us the incantation that would let her get her hands on the amulet. The very tool he believes he needs to escape his underworld prison. Why would he kill Jon before he gave it to us?"

"Why does a demon do anything?" Dom asked. "Maybe he's figured out that she's going to give the amulet to us instead of him, and that we intend to destroy it for all time. Maybe he prefers to let it go for now, until the stars align again in another three and a half millennia rather than risk never having another chance at all." He shrugged. "But it doesn't matter. I got the incantation." He patted his breast pocket.

The Volvo pulled to a stop along the nearby campus road, and Indy jumped out

363

and trotted toward them, keys in hand.

When she got there, Tomas said, "Dom got the incantation."

Her eyes widened as she handed him the keys. "How did you manage it?" she asked Dom.

"This collar buys me a lot more access than your normal Joe. I asked for privacy to deliver the Last Rites before they moved the body and took a quick look around his desk. He'd already printed it out for us."

Rayne frowned at him. "I never saw you go into the —"

"It was while you were still with Tomas and Indira," Dom told her.

She lowered her head, but her frown remained.

"What about the rest of it?" Indy asked quickly. "The text he said was titled *That Which I Must Remember.* What about that?"

His eyes shifted away from hers. "He hadn't printed anything but the incantation. I didn't have time to look through his computer files. That would have been pushing it." He shrugged. "Doesn't matter. We have the incantation. That's all we need." He started heading toward the Volvo. "Samhain is tomorrow night, Tomas," he said with a glance over his shoulder. "We're nearly out of time." He reached the car, went around to the front passenger door and pulled it open.

Tomas was about to get in the driver's side when Rayne hurried up behind him, clapped him on the shoulder and held her other hand out, palm up.

"Keys."

He frowned.

"You just lost a friend. You're so distracted you're almost walking into things. I'll drive."

It took him a moment, but he realized she was right. His brain seemed to be operating in slow-mo. He slapped the keys into her palm, muttered his thanks and got in the back. Indy was already there, and she met his eyes and told him without a word that it was going to be okay.

He wondered how. Because he couldn't squelch the feeling that Dom seemed almost relieved by Jon's death.

Dom was all about secrecy, about telling no one of the mission, about destroying every hint of evidence once it was done. Jon was a snag in all that. He'd seen the photographic evidence and translated it. "He'd seen more than that. A lot more."

"You haven't told us about your end of things," Dom said. "Did you find anything?"

Tomas met Indy's eyes, saw the plea in them, made his decision. "No. It was a . . .

365

very long wild-goose chase."

He saw the relief and gratitude in her eyes before she shifted her attention to Dom. "Can I see the printout?" she asked, leaning forward in her seat.

He twisted, taking the single folded sheet of printer paper from his coat pocket as he did, then handed it over to her without even an argument. Tomas noticed that Indy's hands trembled as she took it.

He wondered if there was something in that translation that might have driven Jon to suicide somehow. But he couldn't even imagine anything that powerful.

Indy was unfolding the sheet, looking at it, frowning. Then she sighed heavily. "It's so simple."

"My thoughts exactly," Dom said.

Indy handed the paper to Tomas, and his eyes skimmed the lines.

By the powers of earth and sky,
By the forces of Goddess and God,
Return to me that which I gave you for safekeeping long ago.
That I might restore it to its rightful place
And reset the balance once more.

It didn't rhyme. It wasn't pretty. It was simple, straightforward, and yet somehow so powerful it made him shiver.

He looked up and met Indy's eyes. She

looked a bit shell-shocked. And he understood. All they'd gone through, just for those few simple lines. He put a hand over hers.

"I can't believe we're this close to ending it," she said. "I just have to say the spell, and the amulet will . . . what? Just magically appear?"

"I don't know. Maybe," Tomas said, but he quickly realized that she wasn't asking him, and he handed the sheet over to Rayne, who skimmed it quickly while they were stopped for a light.

"We'll soon find out," she said as she started driving again. "We'll do the spell tonight, as soon as I've given Indy the proper initiations. That way she'll be stronger, better able to handle whatever happens next."

Indy nodded, but she looked scared to death. "Initiations? Plural?"

"I think we'd better do all three."

"Don't worry," Tomas said, closing his hand around hers. "I'll be right there with you."

"No, you won't, Tomas." Rayne drove a little faster, as if eager to get on with things. "The Wiccan Ceremonies of Initiation are oathbound sacred rites, not spectator sports. You are not allowed to watch." She shifted her eyes to Dom. "That goes for you, too." And then she glanced up at Indy in the rearview mirror. "But I'll be right beside you. And we'll be in the safety of a sacred circle, surrounded by the Guardians of the Watchtowers, in the presence of the Lord and Lady. You will be safe. I promise."

Indy nodded, but the fear in her beautiful green eyes didn't dissipate even a little bit. And Tomas thought he knew what she was thinking. Sure, she would be safe during the ceremony. But what about after? When she had to face a demon and decide whether to help him — or destroy him?

I was afraid to let the ancient scrolls out of my sight. I couldn't have said why, but I couldn't even bring myself to hide them in my room, the way I had been doing with my journal. The box, yes. I tucked that into the back of the closet and threw a pair of jeans and a T-shirt over it. But the scrolls themselves — I couldn't part with those. I mean, really, how were you supposed to truly hide anything in a house that wasn't your own? Anyone who cared to hunt hard enough would find it under the mattress or tucked in the back of the closet. I could have locked it inside my suitcase, but let's face it, luggage locks are a joke.

I'd told Rayne about the scrolls and the words under the lid of the box saying that they were for the Eyes of Spirit alone, which had strengthened her decision to perform all three initiations together. I had to take a shower, Rayne said. She instructed me to make it a sacred one, rinsing away negative energies and vibrations, cleansing my spirit as well as my body, in preparation for the ritual. I took the ancient scrolls into the bathroom with me and locked the door. I would have taken them into the shower if I wasn't so afraid of ruining them. They were important. Ancient. And they held a message for me. *For me.* It had been written Goddess only knew how many centuries ago. For me.

It was mind-boggling. And while part of me was dying to take a peek, the rest of me was embracing a newfound respect for and belief in the ways of magic, the Craft of the Wise and even the rules of that path, though I still believed that they, like any dogma, were man-made and therefore not to be trusted. At the same time I harbored this superstitious belief that if I looked at the message without being properly initiated first, something very bad would happen.

I needed to see it with the Eyes of Spirit.

Unable to let the scrolls out of my sight, I

managed to take the prescribed shower by leaving the stall door open just enough to provide a clear view of them resting on the counter beside the sink. Facing them, I stood beneath the spray, sudsing and rinsing my hair and body, and then standing still and quieting my mind. I tipped my head back and imagined the warm water infused with spiritual light. And in a few seconds it actually gleamed gold and white, like sparklers on the Fourth of July, showering me in purity. It wasn't visualization. Or imagination. It was real.

I'm really a witch. I'm a real live spell-casting, magic-making witch!

Nothing bad could survive such a bath, I was sure of that much. And yet, even with my entire being drenched in the giddy wonder of a kid at Disney World, I never once closed my eyes. I kept them on that scroll the whole time.

When I emerged, I didn't dry off with a towel. I let the water evaporate naturally from my skin as I ran a comb through my hair, fluffed it with my fingers and put on a stretchy white headband to give it a bit of life. No mousse. No gel. My face, like my hair, was au naturel. I donned the huge white cotton pashmina Rayne had left in my room, wrapping it around my body, beneath my arms, then around again, knotting the ends of the fabric over one shoulder.

My scrolls cradled in my arms, I went barefoot down the stairs.

Tomas was waiting there, his gaze sliding from my head to my feet and back again, stopping at my eyes. "You look beautiful."

I smiled and lowered my head in a completely uncharacteristic moment of shyness. "Thank you." I wondered briefly where the old goat was and decided I didn't care.

"I'll be here when you've finished."

"All right."

"Rayne said to send you right out. She's in the apple grove to the left of the deck, near the cliff."

I nodded, my eyes shifting away from his toward the door. This was important to me, I realized. I had butterflies in my stomach and was more intent on where I was going than on the man standing with me just then. And that was saying something. I was in love with him, after all.

He leaned down, kissed my cheek and whispered in my ear, "Blessed be, Indy."

My lips parted as my throat suddenly tightened. For him to whisper that beautiful Pagan greeting to me on this night, of all nights . . . well, it took my breath away and made my eyes go damp. "Don't go making me cry before I even get started."

"No makeup to run. Cry if you want to."

I stood on tiptoe and kissed his cheek. "Thank you, Tomas."

"For dragging you into a war, risking your life . . ."

"For all of it." I put my hands on his cheeks. "Because it led me to you. And to this, and it turns out . . . this means something to me. More than I knew when I left it behind."

"You never left it behind. Not really."

"No, I guess I didn't. And you're not leaving your beliefs behind, either, Tomas. Remember that. God loves you, no matter what."

He reached up and squeezed my hands, then let them go, but I thought he was tearing up a little. "Go on now. Lady Rayne awaits."

Nodding, I turned, not so much as sparing a glance for the glaring old priest as I finally spotted him looking on from the big desk, where he sat clicking computer keys. I felt him, though, felt his hatred and disapproval and judgment. I felt all of it. And then I took a deep breath and blew it all away. No negativity. Not tonight.

I left through the sliding doors, walked across the deck and headed down the steps to the lawn. As I moved toward the small grove of apple trees, I saw the soft glow of candles lighting my way. Rayne had put votives in glass jars she must have rescued from her brother's recycling bin and made a path for me to follow. It was dark outside, except for those candles. The moon had not yet risen. But though dark, the night was far from quiet. The chill autumn breeze hummed through the trees in countless harmonies, raising goose bumps on my arms with its cold breath. Far below, the slapping of water on rock joined in the chorus. Bullfrogs provided the bass line, and every now and then a night bird launched into a high-pitched diva-riff. I loved the cold tickle of the still-green grass and the occasional crunch of dry leaves beneath my feet. Every one of those crunches released a whiff of autumn's unique aroma, a smell like no other.

The line of candles ended right between two gnarled old apple trees whose low, twisted limbs formed an arch. Rayne stood directly beneath them, waiting for me, heavy red apples hanging over her head. Her face was dark, her dagger pointed directly at my chest.

"Better you should rush upon this blade than enter this circle with fear in your heart," she said to me. "Tell me, then, how do you enter?"

I panicked for a second, realizing I didn't know what I was supposed to say and racking my brain to recall.

"Do you enter with fear?" she asked me softly, brows lifting.

"I feel no fear."

"What *do* you feel?" she asked.

I closed my eyes and knew I trusted her, and I recognized the feeling spinning wildly in my heart. Love. And then I knew the proper response, a familiar phrase among students of the Craft. "Perfect love and perfect trust."

She smiled and lowered her dagger, welcoming me with a kiss to both cheeks, then stepping aside to let me walk beneath the arching limbs of the trees. As soon as I did, she drew a line in the air with her blade aimed at the ground, closing the invisible energy door she had opened to let me enter the magic circle.

More candles in jars demarcated the four quarters of the sacred ring, casting a soft yellow glow that made the magical sphere even more real to me.

From there on, the rites were long and involved, and I knew Rayne had combined the elements of the Initiation to the First

Degree with the elevation ceremonies to the Second and Third Degrees of traditional Wicca. I was led around the circle, introduced to the powers and energies of the four directions. I was marched along a spiral path into the symbolic Underworld, where I faced and spoke to Death Herself. I was laid out on the ground, my body serving as the original sacred altar. I was censed with smoke and asperged with holy water. I was asked to repeat a solemn oath of service. I was given the Eyes of Spirit, as Rayne stared unblinkingly into my eyes and I into hers, until they seemed to grow bigger and bigger, and I felt myself falling into them. It felt so real. I was spiraling, falling, but not like in my dreams. There was no fear, no pain waiting at the bottom. No death.

There's no such thing as death.

Moments later, when Rayne laid her hands against my chest to transfer the power into me as it had been transferred into her from her teachers — as it had been transferred into them by theirs, and on and on back as far as memory could go — it was like an explosion in my chest, in my head, in my heart. I was shaking all over when it was done.

Rayne wrapped a braided cord of three colors — silver, gold and white, one color to represent each of the three degrees — around my waist and knotted it there.

I was then introduced to the quarters again, and then to the God and Goddess, this time as a Third Degree High Priestess of Wicca, as Lady Indira.

Only this time was completely different from any ceremony I had participated in before. This time . . . *I saw them.*

I'd lost track of the time, had no idea how long it had all taken. But when it was done, I felt . . . different. Taller. Stronger. More powerful. And I felt, too, the hot touch of something on my lower back and was fairly sure what it was.

"Rayne, I feel something. Will you take a look at my back and see?"

Nodding, she shifted the pashmina enough to see down my spine. And then she gasped. "You have a tattoo?"

"I didn't until now," I whispered. "Not in this lifetime, anyway." It would remain now. I don't know how I knew that, but I did. I was a witch, a priestess, now, and Ishtar was my goddess. She had chosen me.

I turned to face Rayne again, surprised when she handed me the scroll. I didn't remember surrendering it. I'd forgotten both it and its importance.

"You can read it now," she said.

I stared down at the pages, running one hand over them, listening to the newly awakened knowledge inside me. "No. I'll read it tonight. First I want to try the spell. The one to retrieve the amulet."

She nodded. "Meditate and prepare," she said. "I'll get Tomas. He has the incantation. And I know he'll want to be here for this."

"Dom can't come into the circle!" I blurted. The words burst from me before I even knew what I was going to say.

She smiled. "He probably wouldn't want to, anyway. But I'll have them both stay out, just to be diplomatic. Be right back . . . Lady Indy."

A lump rose in my throat, but I forced words past it. "Thank you, Lady Rayne."

I sat in the center of the circle, promptly deciding to tuck the scrolls under my "robe" and tighten the cords to hold them there. Father Dom didn't even know about their existence, and I wasn't about to take a chance of him finding out. Something inside told me that I was right to want to keep him in the dark.

Once that was done, I tried to quiet my mind, to meditate, but there was just no way to achieve that state of mental silence.

There were too many things rushing through my head. Would the spell work? Would I actually utter an incantation and make a real, physical object appear out of nowhere? And what then? I still didn't know what I would do with it once I had it. Give it to Tomas and let him destroy it? End this entire thing once and for all?

That notion felt worse than it ever had before. How could something so sacred, so special and so important that it had been hidden for over three thousand years, be destroyed as if it didn't matter? It seemed a sacrilege to me. Why would I have hidden it with so much care if it was supposed to be destroyed?

And what about after I made my decision about the amulet? Would Tomas and I just . . . go our separate ways? Could I honestly return to my old life as if none of this had happened?

I couldn't. I'd left all of that so far behind me now that the thought of going back seemed ludicrous to me.

Before I could think much further, Rayne was back, beaming, Tomas by her side. I slid my gaze from her to her brother, and saw that he was staring at me as if he'd never seen me before. His eyes expressed surprise. Did I look so different, then?

"Congratulations, Lady Indy," he said.

"Thank you, Tomas." He took the folded paper from a pocket, handed it to Rayne, then stayed where he was as she cut a door and re-entered the circle, closing it behind her. Father Dom had arrived and now stood beside Tomas, pouting in his chronic state of disapproval. Then I saw him clasp Tomas by the wrist and heard him say, "Steady, my son."

No, I didn't hear him say it. Because he'd muttered it under his breath while shielding his mouth with his other hand. And yet I knew what he'd said.

Eyes of Spirit. Good shit. And tough luck for you, old man. Tomas is on my side now. You might as well go home.

I nodded, accepting the folded sheet of paper from Rayne. I opened it, reread it three times, then handed it back to her. The two of us moved to the center of the circle, and I stood there and extended one hand upward, toward the energies of the Great Above, and the other downward, into the realm of the Great Below.

And the power came. The wind picked up and lifted my hair, and there was a light softly illuminating the circle, a light I knew was emanating from me. The words came then. They were not the words written on the paper, but I knew as I spoke them that it wasn't the words that mattered. It was the power.

Power I was wielding now. I felt it surging inside me as the words spilled from my lips in a voice deeper than my own.

"Hear my words and know me," I said to the stars. "I am Lady Indira, daughter of Ishtar, the Queen of Heaven. Give heed to my call!"

I felt heat in the palm I had raised to the sky and suddenly saw where the light was coming from. A beam of radiance was blasting from somewhere beyond the endless sky and into my palm, down my arm, into my torso.

I looked down. "Hear my words and know me. I am the daughter of Ereshkigal, Lady of the Underworld. Obey my command!"

Instantly a shaft of glowing black luminescence shot from the earth itself into my lowered hand and up through my feet, then into my midsection, where I felt it meet and entwine with the white light and empower every cell in my body.

"Hear my words and know me." My voice was even deeper now. "I am she who hid the amulet and that which it contained, and I call it forth now, for the time has come. So mote it be!"

It felt like an explosion from within, expanding my chest like a heart attack on crack. Or maybe the big bang had just happened in my sternum. There was a flash of blinding light in my eyes, but it came from the inside, and it knocked me right off my feet.

And then everything went silent and I sat up, blinking.

There on the ground in front of me was a flat, gold disk, maybe two inches in diameter, with two gleaming stones that looked like diamonds in its face, glinting in the candlelight. A long chain of silver was attached to it.

Holy shit, it really worked.

I pushed myself up onto my knees and stared down at the amulet. Then I looked up again, a smile splitting my face as I sought Tomas's eyes. He was looking stunned and bewildered as he stared back at me. Why wasn't he smiling? "I did it," I said. "I did it!"

But his shocked expression remained as he moved forward, his legs oddly stiff. Bending, he picked up the amulet. I caught myself wondering what he was about to do.

Destroy it?

He straightened. I was still on my knees, but I lifted my head, met his eyes and begged him to trust me without saying a word.

"Destroy it, Tomas! Do it now!" Dom was shouting.

But Tomas, my Tomas, didn't even seem to hear the old man. Instead he held my eyes and slowly lowered the chain over my head.

Looking down again, I saw the ancient, magical amulet resting upon my chest and lifted my hand. My fingers caressed it. "Thank you, my love," I whispered, for Tomas's ears alone.

And then my brain exploded in another white-hot flash. Everything went blindingly bright and then velvet, silent black.

When Indy had moved to the center of the circle, extending her hands, one up and one down, Tomas had been able to focus on nothing else. God, she was like a divine being, an angel. She literally glowed from within, lighting the dark circle beyond the ability of the small candles lining it. She'd changed, visibly changed, from before the ceremony. He watched, he listened, and he was even more stunned when at last she began to speak, because she wasn't speaking English. It was Babylonian flowing flawlessly from her lips.

But that was just the beginning. She paused between words, and a bolt from the sky hit her. His first thought was lightning — a bolt from a clear sky. But it wasn't lightning. It wasn't anything he could identify. A beam of white-gold light entered her body through her upturned palm.

And then she lowered her head and started talking again. Deep, deeper than her normal voice. And richer, somehow.

He was a little more prepared this time, but just as stunned when another bolt of light — only it was black light this time, he couldn't describe it any better than that — shot up from the ground and into her other hand.

A heartbeat later she was emitting an even brighter glow than before. It came from her body, beaming out of her like an aura. He tried to look at Rayne to see if she was as shocked as he was — because surely this didn't happen every time witches cast a spell, did it? Surely she would have told him if it had. Anyway, it didn't matter. He couldn't look away.

And then there was a flash and Indy hit the ground. The lights shut down, and there was a golden disk lying on the ground in front of her.

It had worked.

She looked at him, smiling, telling him as much, but he was still in shock over seeing her as the center of a laser light show. Despite that, he moved into the circle, though his knees kept trying to buckle, and he bent and picked up the amulet.

He had a choice to make, and he had to make it right then. To trust her with what was, after all, *her* destiny. Or to trust Father Dom instead.

There was no competition. He looked down at her and met her eyes, then lowered the necklace over her head until the amulet lay on her breast. She thanked him with her eyes and lifted a hand to touch the golden disk.

Suddenly she froze, her eyes going blank, her body, rigid, paralyzed as the amulet's golden glow flashed unnaturally brighter.

"Indy?"

The amulet wavered and began to fade.

"Grab it, Tomas!" Dom shouted. "It's vanishing again!"

But it continued to fade, until all at once it disappeared and Indy's head rose. Expressionless, she faced him, and her eyes flashed. The diamonds from the amulet were there, *right there,* in her eyes. And then her eyes fell closed and she collapsed on the ground.

Tomas fell to his knees beside her, cradling

her, lifting her. "Indy! Talk to me. Wake up."

A heavy hand fell to his shoulder. Tomas looked up. Father Dom was there, staring down knowingly. "This was supposed to happen."

"What?" Tomas searched his old friend's face, noting vaguely that his sister was rushing around releasing the energies of the four quarters and performing the other closing rites. He knew they were important or she would be there with him. He shifted his attention back to Father Dom. "What do you mean by that?"

"The amulet has melded with her. She has taken it into her own body. 'Only she who created it can call it forth, and only to return it to the one to whom it rightfully belongs,' " he quoted. "It won't emerge from her again except by her will, and only then to go to the Demon. To enable him to cross back into our world."

"And you knew this would happen all along?"

"I did. I was hoping you could smash it first, but . . ." He lowered his head briefly, gave it a rapid shake.

"I don't understand, Dom. If you knew she would . . . absorb the damn thing, then how the hell did you think we'd be able to destroy it?"

Dom leaned closer, lowered his voice and said, "There's only one way, Tomas. There's only ever been one way. And it's the same solution that you enacted long, long ago. You have to kill her, Tomas. That is your true calling. You have to kill the witch."

17

"You've lost your mind, Dom!"

Tomas refused to listen to anything further; in fact, he was still unsure he'd heard Dom correctly to begin with, as he carried Indy back toward the house, her beautiful white robe trailing almost to the ground. Rayne, having finished the closing rites in what must have been record time, raced along beside them, holding up the edges of her own identical garment, held in place by braided cords just like the ones wrapped around Indy's waist now.

"What happened?" Rayne asked. "Where's the amulet?"

"I think it's . . . inside her."

His sister clapped a hand to her mouth and raced ahead to open the sliding doors, then up the stairs to open the bedroom door. She yanked back the bedcovers, and Tomas laid Indy down and pulled them over her again. Sitting on the edge of the mattress, he stroked her cheek, pushing her hair back over and over, searching her face for any sign of life. She was breathing, but the pulse in her throat was beating soft and fast, like a hummingbird's.

"It was too much for her. Too much," he whispered.

"Not for her," Rayne said. "She's amazing, Tomas. I've never seen such a powerful witch."

He shook his head. "Dom says . . ." And then he stopped. Indy might be a super-witch, but his sister was no slouch, and if he told her what Dom had said out in the apple orchard, the old priest might be sitting on a lily pad catching flies before morning.

Or worse. Rayne had a temper. And she was fiercely protective of her fellow witches. "Dom says what?" she asked.

"Never mind. I need to make him leave. This is over, this is . . . over. It's done. I'm sending him home. Stay with her?"

"I will."

Tomas nodded, but he couldn't seem to take his eyes off Indy. His heart ached for what this had cost her, was still costing her. And at this point, he just wanted her to be all right. She'd done her part. It hadn't worked, and there was no way he — or anyone else — was going to kill her to make it work. Dom had crossed the border from zealot to lunatic. It ended here.

"I'll be back as soon as I can," he told his sister, finally dragging his eyes from Indy and rising from the bed.

Rayne wrapped her arms around his neck. "You're making the right decision, Tomas. I don't know what the answers are, but I don't for one minute believe that out of the four of us, Dom is the only one who has it all figured out. He's the least-holy holy man I've ever met."

He hugged his sister. "I love you, Rayne. Thanks for being here for me."

"Where else is a sister gonna be when her big bro's out fighting demons and saving the world?" She moved to the bed and sat down, her entire focus shifting from him to Indy. "Damn, did you see it out there tonight? The power coming into her from above and below? Did you see it?"

"Yeah. I saw it."

"I've never seen anything like that before."

Well, that answered one of his questions.

"She's really something special, Tomas."

"Yes," he said softly. "Yes, she really is."

He left the room reluctantly, but he'd made up his mind. It was time to confront Father Dom and politely retire from this insane mission. And while he was at it, he might as well break it to his mentor, the man who had performed *his* initiation rites — only they called it ordination in his neck of the woods — that he'd decided he could no longer remain in the priesthood.

It was going to devastate Dom. But Tomas thought the old man had bigger problems than being disappointed in his apprentice. He needed help. And Tomas was going to make sure he got it. Dom had been the only father figure Tomas had ever known. He would see to it that he got better.

"Hey, there you are."

Rayne was stroking my hair when I woke. I'd felt the soft caress in my dreams and had hoped it was her brother. But no, it was Rayne. And that was almost as good.

I smiled, though I felt tired. "Hey. Where's Tomas?"

"Having a sit-down with Father Dom. I think he's finally ready to bail on this mission of his."

I sat up straight in the bed, my brain coming fully awake. "Really?" Was he actually telling the old goat that he was hanging up his collar? Or just giving up on this particular demon quest? "Did he say that, or are you guessing?"

"Oh, he said it. I had the feeling there was

more, but that's all he gave me. Still, it's a good sign."

"Yeah, I guess." I lowered my head, feeling sort of let down. "It's a pretty anticlimactic ending to all this, though, wouldn't you say? I mean, we went through so much to get the amulet, and now that we have it, he doesn't even want it?"

"Well, we don't actually have it." Rayne pursed her lips and seemed to be searching for words. "I mean, you do, but . . ." Shrugging, she sighed. Like she'd just given up on trying to convey something she didn't understand herself.

"I have it?" I put a hand to my chest to see if I was still wearing the thing on a chain, warming at the memory of Tomas putting it around my neck. I patted myself down, pausing on the shape of the scroll at my waist. "I don't have it." I lifted the covers to see if the amulet had fallen off underneath them while I was asleep or passed out or whatever I'd been, but it wasn't there. I gave up the hunt and began untying the cords at my waist, which were only supposed to be worn during ritual.

Rayne pursed her lips, started over. "You sort of . . . absorbed it."

I had tugged the cords out from beneath the covers and was holding them out toward her. But I froze at those words. "I . . . what?"

"Absorbed it." She took the braided cords from me and gently twined them into a coil as she walked away from me. She put them into a black drawstring sack she must have taken from her own things, tugged it closed, and then brought it back and hung it from the bedpost. "The amulet vanished, the diamonds flashed in your eyes, clear as day, and then you passed out cold."

"But . . . but I don't understand."

"Me neither," she said softly. "Maybe you'd better read the scrolls now."

I drew a breath and reached under the covers. When I'd removed the cords, the scrolls had slid from their spot at my waist, but now I fished them out from under my makeshift toga and laid them on my lap. "I'm exhausted. I don't know if I can stay awake long enough to read them."

"I'll tell you what. I'll go make a pot of strong coffee and bring you some carbs to go with it. You need to ground some of that energy you absorbed, anyway."

"Sweet carbs, please," I said with a smile. "If I've got a good excuse to eat them, they might as well be packed with sugar."

Rayne nodded. "That's what I always say. Be right back, hon."

She left me alone. My hands were shaking

as I lifted the rolled-up bundle and carefully untied the strand of leather that held it together. I moved in slow motion as I gently unrolled the parchment pages. There were a dozen, give or take, and I smoothed them onto my lap, holding both ends to keep them from curling right back up again.

At first all I could do was frown down at the lines and shapes that seemed entirely nonsensical to me. But as I kept staring at the pages my eyes went out of focus, and the symbols blurred and shifted . . . and became the letters of my own alphabet, words in my own language. And I began to read.

Did I ever really think magic wasn't real? How could I have been so blind?

"Here," Dom said, picking up a glass of whiskey over ice and handing it to Tomas. "Drink it, you're going to need it."

Tomas had come into the den looking for Dom, mentally preparing himself to break the news. But now that he was face-to-face with the man who'd chosen him as his own successor, trained him for the job, ordained him personally and practically raised him to boot, words failed him. So he took a deep pull from the glass, crossed the room and, bracing one arm against the darkly stained window frame, stared outside. "It's starting to rain."

"Seasons are changing," Dom said. "Going to be nasty for the next few days. Creek was already high from that last big storm, too."

Tomas took another drink, draining it this time.

Dom walked up beside him, pouring in a little more. "What I said before, it shocked you," he said.

"Then you really did say it?" Tomas asked. "I've been telling myself I must have heard you wrong, or that you were speaking figuratively or . . . shit, I don't know what. Something. Anything."

"Believe me, I understand. But I have always known it would come to this, Tomas. I didn't tell you, because I didn't think you were ready to hear it. And then . . . with this alignment, and the Demon forcing us to act . . . Hell, Tomas, I thought I'd have more time to prepare you —"

"For murder?" Tomas asked, turning to pin him with his eyes. "I can't believe you're actually asking me to take a life, much less her life! You're a priest, for God's sake."

Dom didn't even flinch, only sipped his drink and paced away. "This is a test of your faith, Tomas. It's not me asking you to do this. It's God. And He's not asking. He's commanding."

"No."

"Just the way He commanded Abraham to sacrifice his child, Isaac. I told you that earlier."

Tomas turned away, remembering again the shiver of unease that had tiptoed up his spine at that comparison. It had been an inner knowing. He should have listened to it. "Well, you were right to think I wasn't ready. I will never be ready for . . . that."

Dom moved closer and put a hand on Tomas's shoulder, but Tomas flinched away from his touch. "Sometimes, my son, drastic measures are necessary. A single life is not as valuable as the thousands, perhaps millions, that could be lost should the Demon make his way through the Portal into the world of man. My God, Tomas, do you think this mission, this quest, has been handed down from one holy man to the next for three thousand five hundred years for nothing?"

The man was nuts, Tomas thought. His mind was completely gone. "I think you've been too focused on the . . . mission for too long, Dom. I think maybe — I think maybe this whole thing has had an impact, mixed things up in your mind a little."

"I'm not insane."

Tomas stared at Dom, not blinking, looking him dead in the eye to show his old friend his sincerity. His honesty. His concern. "You're talking about committing murder."

"Sacrifice. For the greater good."

"It's murder." Maybe if he just kept repeating it?

"She's going to hell otherwise. She's a witch, Tomas. But giving her life for this noble cause, to save her fellow man from the claws of the Demon — it might very well be the only way she can escape damnation. You'd be saving her soul!"

"Her soul? It's her soul you're worried about? What about yours? What about *mine,* Dom?"

Dom held his gaze. "You killed her once already."

He flinched, because that blow hit home.

"It's your destiny, Tomas. It's your fate. You have to do this."

"I refuse. And I'm done with this. Whatever this demon does, he does. If God wants to stop him, He's powerful enough to do it without my help, and without murdering an innocent woman." He swallowed hard and set the half-empty tumbler down, wanting to keep his head clear. "And I might as well tell you, I've put in a request to leave the priesthood, and I've requested dispensation from the vow of celibacy."

"She's corrupted you!" Dom accused, wide-eyed, trembling now with rage. "I knew it! I knew she was bewitching you with her —"

"You know *nothing.* I did this before I even met her." Tomas picked up the drink again, then slammed the glass back onto the table without taking a sip. He didn't need liquid courage. The more he thought on this, the more certain he was. "This is over now, Father Dom. You can stay until morning. Then I want you out of here. And I want you to know, I think you need help, and I'm going to do everything in my power to see that you get it."

Dom sipped his own drink, nodding slowly. "I hope you're prepared for the repercussions of your actions, Tomas. To turn your back on a sacred calling, a task for which you were handpicked by God Almighty — you risk divine retribution, my son. And I would just as soon be far from you when it begins to unfold." Another sip drained the glass, and he set it down, then, turning, left the den.

Tomas sank onto the sofa. His body felt weak and yet, somehow, lighter. Like he'd been traveling uphill with a thousand-pound sack over his shoulder and had finally decided to just put it down.

Just put it down.

He closed his eyes, eyed his half-empty glass, thought about refilling it and getting good and drunk, but he couldn't even summon the energy to get up off the leather sofa to find the whiskey. He was emotionally and spiritually drained.

He found himself sliding forward from the couch, dropping heavily to his knees, folding his hands and lowering his head. He tried to pray, but when he moved his lips, no sound emerged. His throat closed tight, his eyes burned with tears he hadn't known were waiting to spill over, and his chest heaved when they finally did.

"Just show me what to do, Lord," he muttered when he managed to speak. "Send me a sign. Something. Anything."

The cell phone chirped. The wind outside howled. A low rumble of thunder came over the horizon. It was going to storm like hell. The bridge would wash out again for sure. He looked at the caller ID. Private. No matter, he picked it up.

"This is Tomas Petrosa," he said.

Static . . . "— ation . . . for Divine Worship . . ."

"Congregation for Divine Worship?" he asked. "Yes, yes. I didn't expect you to get back to me so soon."

"got . . . your . . . quest."

"You got my request, yes. Good."

". . . fusion."

"I'm sorry? You'll have to speak up, and talk slowly. There's a storm coming in and you're breaking up pretty badly."

"You . . . not a priest."

He blinked, lifted his chin, swallowed hard. "I'm not a priest. Am I understanding you correctly?" *Could it be over and done that easily? Wouldn't there be more to it than just —*

"You never were."

The static had suddenly cleared. The words came through crisp and perfectly audible. "What does that mean?"

"We have no record of your ordination. You don't need the dispensation or the release. There are no vows to break, as far as the Church is co . . . erned. It . . . on't . . . oh . . . ee . . . at —"

Silence. He glanced at the screen. Dropped Call.

He felt . . . numb. He didn't know what to make of what he'd just been told. Had there been a paperwork snafu?

Then he looked at the closed door and

knew better. For the love of God, could this possibly have been one more of Father Dom's manipulations?

It was entirely possible, he realized. Dom had yanked him out of seminary, told him he was needed, chosen by God for a mission so important he'd been granted special dispensation to . . .

"To ordain me himself. Oh, my God. It was never real. It was never real. . . ."

He put down the phone and sat there for long moments, staring into nothingness. He didn't feel regret. He didn't feel sadness. He felt . . . empty, confused about who and what he was, if he wasn't a priest. At the same time, he felt . . . relieved. And guilty for feeling relieved.

A tap came on the closed door of the den.

He lifted his head slowly and pulled himself to his feet, checking to be sure his eyes were dry before going to the door and pausing for a moment with his hand on the knob before pulling it open.

Indy was standing there. She'd put on blue pajamas with bunnies all over them. Her hair looked like she'd been running her hands through it repeatedly. She had a giant plateful of assorted cookies surrounding two glasses of milk in one hand and the parchment scrolls in the other. He looked from the cookies to the scrolls to her face.

She was smiling as she said, "It's going to be okay, Tomas. I know what happened now. This has all been a terrible mistake."

Send me a sign, he'd prayed. He'd thought the phone call had been his answer. But no. Now he thought maybe his sign was wearing bunny pajamas, and carrying cookies and milk.

"So? You gonna let me in so I can tell you about it?"

He looked into her eyes. They were so familiar. This was just the way he imagined an old man felt when he looked into the eyes of the woman he'd spent his entire life loving. It felt that intimate, that deep, that real.

That old.

He opened the door wider. "Never could resist cookies and milk."

"Why the hell do you think I brought them?" she asked with a grin. She came into the den, kicked the door closed behind her and set the plate on the table, frowning at the glasses and the whiskey bottle that were already there. "That's a really bad idea, Tomas."

"I know."

"We need to stay sharp, stay alert, until we make it through this."

"I know."

"I mean, even if the demon isn't really the villain you think he is, he's still powerful. Maybe dangerous."

"The demon's not a villain?" he said.

"Not even a real demon, I think. But he still thinks we're the enemy. Or that you are, at least."

"Well, he's got that right."

"But you're not. You'll see." She sat down on the sofa and unrolled the scrolls. "I'm going to tell you a bedtime story, Tomas. And I want you to listen with a completely open mind. Can you do that? Can you forget all Father's Dom's indoctrination and pretend you know nothing about any of this as you hear the truth?"

Frowning, Tomas sank onto the leather sofa next to her. "What makes you so sure it's the truth?"

"It was written by an eyewitness."

He blinked, stunned, part of him wondering if she was as crazy as Father Dom. But no. He knew better. He'd seen her power with his own eyes.

Then again, he'd seen Dom's, too, with that possessed little girl. Power did not necessarily indicate sanity. Good tip to remember.

He reached for a handful of Oreos and

one of the glasses of milk. Then he leaned back and closed his eyes. "I'll do my best. I'm listening, Indy. Talk to me."

"I've already read every line of this tale," I told Tomas, making myself comfortable. I turned and leaned back against the arm, curling my legs beneath me, and though I unrolled the sheets of parchment, I didn't intend to read them to him. I didn't have to. "It's a bit under twenty pages, and there's a lot of extraneous information. Not to me, of course. It's all important to me. I figured out about halfway through that I knew the next line, the next word, before I read it. And I realized that was because I was the one who had written it."

His eyes popped open, and he sat up quickly. "You wrote it?"

"In that other lifetime. I trust it."

"All right," he said.

"I was Indira then, too. Indira, daughter of the potter, at first, and later, once I was taken with my sisters into the royal harem, I was known only as the King's Indira."

He nodded, and he didn't lean back again but instead leaned forward for another cookie, his eyes on me, eager, but also a little bit fearful. "Go on."

"My sisters were Magdalena and Lilia.

Lilia was the king's favorite, but she fell in love with his first lieutenant."

He lifted his brows. "Like Lancelot and Guinevere."

"Exactly like that. But the ending takes its own turn. His name was Demetrius."

I gave a quick look around me as I said the name aloud for the first time, half expecting some sort of repercussion to speaking the name that 'must not be spoken.' But nothing happened. And I thought again that Tomas's mission was all bullshit propaganda, perpetrated by a long line of so-called holy men.

"Magdalena and I tried hard to protect the two of them from being found out. But I never told my sisters about my own secret liaison with a young Priest of Marduk, the sun god, whose name I never wrote down, for fear someone would find him out and punish him."

He stared into my eyes.

I stared right back, then lowered mine to read a passage. " 'He loved me like no man has ever loved. I never doubted it. And I loved him just as fiercely. And yet our love, like my sister's, was forbidden.' " Hot tears came to my eyes as old, old emotions rose up in my heart. I couldn't look him in the eyes just then.

"Someone ratted out my sister and her lover. Soldiers raided the harem quarters and caught them together. Demetrius fought to protect her — to protect all of us — but he was outnumbered, and in the end we were all arrested. As they searched our quarters and questioned our harem mates, they learned another secret we'd been keeping."

He searched my eyes, riveted by the story.

"We were practicing magic. Witchcraft. And that was strictly forbidden. Only the high priest of the Temple, Sindar, was allowed to cast and conjure. He was the one who said that we should be offered as sacrifices to Marduk to appease his anger. Demetrius, when he heard what our fate would be, broke free of his chains and went on a rampage. He killed the king, along with several of his soldiers, and was beaten nearly to death by the rest."

Tomas closed his eyes, lowered his head. "Poor bastard."

I knew then that he had no idea what I would tell him as my story went on.

I lowered my head, flipping pages that were filled with what no doubt appeared to him to be ancient symbols and glyphs but were, to me, as clear as they had been on the day I'd written out my tale. "The high

405

priest loved the king beyond all others. I wrote that I always suspected it was the same sort of love I felt for my young priest and just as forbidden, but that Sindar would never admit that, even to himself. Still, he was determined to inflict the worst sort of punishment he could imagine on Demetrius for killing his beloved king."

Tomas nodded. "He was the man who was forced to watch while the three of you were executed, wasn't he?" he asked.

"Yes. But that was kind compared to what Sindar had in store for him next. He was sentenced to be cursed. Immediately after we were pushed from the cliff to our deaths on the rocks below, Demetrius was to be taken into a dark cave by Sindar alone, where he would undergo a spell that would strip the soul from his body. Then his throat was to be cut. His soulless spirit was sent to the Underworld, where he would be held captive in the land of the dead forevermore. His stolen soul would be destroyed in an elaborate ritual that the high priest would perform solo."

Tomas's eyes widened. Yeah. He was starting to get it now.

"No one bothered keeping their intentions secret. I think Sindar liked us all knowing what was going to happen to us. Torturing us with the knowledge. Torturing Demetrius by letting him know Lilia would be killed. Torturing Lilia by letting her know Demetrius would be sentenced to a fate far worse than death. Eternity in darkness."

"It's hideous," Tomas whispered.

"My sisters and I made a plan. We cast a spell of our own, and we meditated and focused all our will on carrying it out, not even knowing if it would work. When we crossed the veil between life and death, the instant our bodies hit the rocks below the cliff and our souls were torn from them, we planned to fly into that dark cave and snatch Demetrius's soul before Sindar could destroy it. We intended to divide it between us, hiding it within whatever sacred objects we could find — because a soul needs to be bound to the physical realm to keep it from being reabsorbed into the whole. We planned to then bind the objects to ourselves, taking them with us into the afterlife, where they would remain until we called them forth again in a future lifetime."

He was blinking as if exposed to a sudden bright light. "And did you succeed?"

I shrugged. "I couldn't very well have written it down if we had, since I would have been dead by that point. But I do know that the entire plan hinged on the help of one living being. The man I loved, the young priest. You, Tomas. I had planned to give you a vial containing three drops of my blood and three drops of the blood of each of my sisters, and ask that you somehow get it into that cave to enable our spirits to find our way there so we could accomplish our task."

He closed his eyes. "It's doubtful I did it, though. I couldn't have pushed you from that cliff if I truly loved you, Indy."

"Then why is it that there are three witches, each one supposed to call forth a magical tool from the astral plane? Why is it that those tools are supposed to help free a so-called demon from the Underworld?"

"I don't know. I don't . . . I don't know, Indy. I admit it fits pretty well —"

"It fits perfectly. Dom got it wrong. And that's because he's been going by the version of the story written by Sindar and handed down by centuries of priests. Sindar wouldn't have made himself the bad guy, would he?"

"No, I don't suppose —"

"History is written by the victors, isn't that what they say? But I wrote a history of my own, before they killed me."

"Before *I* killed you, you mean."

"Let it go, Tomas. It doesn't matter. What

matters is that I'm not supposed to help free a demon to wreak havoc on mankind. I'm supposed to return one small part of an innocent man's soul to him, to help release him from an undeserved sentence."

He met my eyes. I could see he was hearing me. Perhaps even believing me.

"Tomas, destroying the amulet means destroying an innocent man's soul. Don't you see that?"

He stared into my eyes for a long moment, and then suddenly the clouds in his own seemed to clear. "I've been misled," he whispered.

"Dom is just a tool. He's been used by a higher power, just not in the way he thinks. His job was never to destroy Demetrius or keep him imprisoned. It was to bring us together so that we could find the truth. And we have. His work is done, Tomas."

He nodded.

I blinked, because he wasn't arguing. "Do you . . . do you agree with me?"

"Yes. I do. You're right. This makes sense. It all fits."

Man, that was way easier than I expected. I swallowed hard, squared my shoulders and jumped back in for round two. "I want you to send him away now."

"I already have. He's leaving in the morning."

I smiled slowly, letting the beautiful pages roll up again. I gently tied the leather cord around them and set the scrolls on the small stand beside the sofa. "You sent him away even before you knew . . ."

"Yes."

"But . . . I thought you believed he was right about the demon."

"Not as much as I believe in you," he said. "And not as much as I believe that what I feel for you is real, and vital, and too much a part of me to ever deny, and that there's no way what's between us can be wrong or . . . or evil."

Tears burned in my eyes as his hand came to my cheek, resting gently there. And then he kissed me, and I knew it was all going to be all right. Together we would go to the Portal on Samhain Eve — tomorrow night. We would go, and I would say the incantation that would come to my lips as if on its own. It would free the amulet from my body, freeing Demetrius's soul-piece from the amulet and returning it to him. It was all I had to do. And then this — or at least my part in it — would be over.

It was the right thing to do. I felt it right to my toes.

410

Tomas was seeing it now. Thank the gods, all of them, I thought, and then I stopped thinking as his kiss changed into something deeper. He cradled my head in his hands, his tongue dipping and tasting my mouth as he lowered me backward onto the sofa.

I pressed my hands to his chest. "Not yet, Tomas. Not until you've been released from your vows. I don't want you to —"

"I'm not a priest anymore. It's official."

"You mean we can —"

"Yes." He kissed me again, and this time I let the flames that had been licking at the tinder of my soul take hold. And they blazed *hot*. We kissed, and kissed, and tugged and pulled at each other's clothes as we did. He unbuttoned my shirt.

Everyone else was in bed. The den was quiet, private, its door closed tight. He pushed my pajama top from my shoulders, and his eyes roamed lower, gleamed with pure appreciation, and then he was kissing, caressing, my breasts. His hands moved down my back, and then he turned me and his lips followed their path.

But he stopped at the base of my spine. "The tattoo is back."

"I know. It's been there ever since my initiations. I don't think it will fade away again."

He pressed his lips to it, then turned me around again and kissed his way up the front of me. I arched off the sofa so he could push down the pajama bottoms. As soon as I was out of them, he rearranged us, pulling me down on top of him.

I tugged his shirt up, impatient, until he stripped it over his head and gave me full access to his magnificent chest. He was so perfect, broad and strong, a few dark hairs, not too many. Just enough to entangle my fingers as I stroked and touched and kissed his chest the way he had kissed mine.

I lost myself in the past. We were in a nest of pillows, and sheer curtains surrounded us. My hair was dark and his was long, and our bodies, our limbs, were nude and entwined. I heard soft whispers, sighs of pleasure, words of love.

And then I was back in the here and now. His pants were gone. I didn't remember taking them off. He was bare and hard and warm, and nudging inside me. I closed my eyes and helped, and when he slid into me there was this moment of such intense, exquisite relief. . . .

Finally. By the gods, it's been so long.

And I knew it was true. This was old. This was real. We belonged together. And we had waited too damned long to find each other again.

I don't know if he felt what I did. But he'd gone still, too, in that same moment. And his eyes seemed as stricken as mine must have been.

But then we began to move again in a rhythm as old as time, in a love almost as old, carrying each other to the closest place to paradise this side of heaven.

18

Tomas felt like a new man in the morning. He woke smiling, despite the gloom outside. Rain was pounding down; it had been all night. Indy's beautiful face was completely relaxed and mostly in shadow. Just for a moment he looked at her lying across his body, her head on his chest, one small, perfect hand resting over his heart.

God, she was beautiful.

He felt blessed and yet vaguely guilty. Probably to be expected, he thought. He'd taken a vow of celibacy, and even though it had apparently never been "official," he didn't think God cared much about record keeping. One did not overcome years of subtle indoctrination with one night in the arms of an angel. No matter how sure or right it felt.

Sighing, he slid quietly out from under the brown faux-fur throw they'd pulled off the back of the sofa to cover them during the night, then straightened it back over her beautiful body. He pulled on his clothes from the day before, hesitating at the black shirt with its white collar insert. He couldn't wear it anymore, he realized. He'd found his true calling, and it was not the priesthood.

And apparently never had been.

He set the shirt aside, and wearing only a pair of well-worn jeans, he picked up the plate of leftover cookies and the half-empty milk glasses, turning toward the door to carry everything to the kitchen.

As he stepped out of the room he spotted Father Dom standing near the front door, a suitcase on the floor beside him. Dom saw him, and the look on his face told Tomas that he knew exactly what had happened last night. Whether he'd been spying or had accidentally seen or heard them, he didn't know. But the knowledge was written all over his mentor's face. And Tomas supposed his current shirtless appearance confirmed it. Dom might even have caught a glimpse of Indy as the door had swung closed behind him.

He lifted his chin, met Dom's eyes and refused to feel sorry or to apologize, knowing he was in the right. "I learned some things last night, Dom."

"No doubt," Father Dom said with disgust.

Tomas felt his jaw twitch in anger. "About the past — about all of this. We've been fighting on the wrong side."

"The Devil truly is the great deceiver. To have fooled even you. But rarely have I seen him appear in quite so tempting a guise as he has this time." He shrugged. "Then again, greater men have fallen. Greater priests, even."

"I'm not a priest. And apparently I never was. At least, there's no record of my ordination. Can you tell me why that is, Dom?"

Dom glowered at him. "Need I quote your sister to you? Ordination is given by God, not by man." He threw his hands in the air. "They don't have paperwork on me, either. Booted me out of the Church ages ago."

Tomas gaped in shock. So much made sense now.

"Do I let that stop me from doing God's work? Of course I don't."

It was worse than he'd thought. Dom was a fraud? Had he even fooled the sisters at St. Brigit's? He must have been a real priest at some point.

"How long ago were you —"

"Doesn't matter. I'm leaving." Dom

416

gripped the doorknob.

Tomas wanted answers. "Dom, you need to listen to me." Then he looked past him at the pouring rain and was hit by another realization. "And you may as well stay. You know as well as I do that with all that rain last night, the bridge is probably washed out."

"No, Tomas. I do not need to listen to you. You've made up your mind. You'll free the Demon, and he will destroy the world of man. I will awaken to the sound of trumpets in the house of the Lord. And you will awaken to eternal hellfire. *I* have no regrets. I doubt you will be able to say the same."

Tomas watched as Dom turned and reached for the doorknob, apparently choosing to ignore the warning about the bridge. But Tomas didn't need to see it to know it was under water. He'd been petitioning the highway department to raise it for years, but since his was the only place up here, it was way down on their list of priorities.

"Dom, you're not going to be able to leave today," he said again.

His old friend looked at him as if hearing him for the first time. And then a bloodcurdling, positively inhuman scream came from the second floor.

Tomas felt his blood go cold.

Rayne.

He lunged into a run, taking the stairs two at a time. He sped along the hallway and slammed through her bedroom door. And then he froze as he caught sight of her, lying there in the bed with foamy spittle around her nose and mouth. She was kicking, her arms thrashing, her body twisting, as guttural sounds emerged from her throat.

He couldn't believe what he was seeing. Images of the little girl at the exorcism flooded his mind.

Shaking himself free of his momentary paralysis, he moved to Rayne's side, clasping her shoulders and shaking her gently. "Wake up, honey. Come on now, wake up and talk to me."

Her eyes popped open, nearly bulging, bloodshot. He felt a whisper of relief. And then she shrieked in his face, and her breath was so fetid it almost knocked him over as her back arched off the bed. Suddenly her eyes rolled back and her body went completely lax. At least she'd stopped thrashing.

"My God," he whispered, staring down at his now unconscious sister in shock. "My God, what the hell is this?"

"You know what it is, Tomas. We've both seen it before."

He turned slowly. Father Dom was standing in the doorway, and beyond him, shaking like a leaf, wrapped up in the sofa throw, stood Indira, her eyes wide and glued to Rayne.

"You betrayed God," Dom decreed, pointing a gnarled but steady finger at him. "You broke your vows in the arms of a demon's whore."

"Hey, watch it, pal, I'm standing right here!" Indy snapped.

Father Dom ignored her and kept speaking to Tomas. "And so the Lord has withdrawn his protection. Now your sister is possessed by the very demon you were sent here to destroy."

"Bull. Shit." Indy shouldered her way into the room between Dom and the door frame. "That's not what this is, and you know it. Don't listen to him, Tomas."

He couldn't look at Indira. Not now, not knowing what he had to do. His eyes were drawn back to his sister in the bed. He had to protect her, and it if meant hurting Indy, well, she was just going to have to forgive him when it was all over. Or not. Either way, it couldn't be helped. There was no other way out of this.

"Tomas?" she whispered.

But he couldn't look at her.

"Tomas, we were going to return a piece of Demetrius's soul to him. Why would he attack your sister when we were going to help him?"

"Because he could," Father Dom said. "Young lady, I'm beginning to believe you might not be aware of just how deceived you are. But I have expelled demons before. Many, many times. Tomas was with me not long ago when I exorcised a demon from a young girl. We know a possession when we see one. And we know the devil and his workings. He only seeks to harm, to destroy. Even his own servants are not safe. Until you seduced Tomas away from his true calling, God provided him with protection, and that protection extended to his beloved sister, despite her fallen ways. But as soon as he broke his vows, that protection was removed. As witches, you court the Devil every day of your lives. I'm surprised you don't know that."

Tomas looked at Indy. He couldn't help himself. She looked right back at him, her eyes wide with disbelief, her expression asking him if he was truly naive enough to buy into Dom's delusions. He had to look away, back to his sister, unconscious and helpless.

"There's only one way to save her, Tomas."

He turned to look at Father Dom. If Dom had reason to save her, she would be all right.

"We must perform an exorcism, son. Today. Now."

"Tomas, don't be an idiot!" Indy shouted. "She needs a hospital, not a priest! You can't possibly —"

"Don't." Tomas held up a hand, stopping her words midstream. "Indy, you don't have a clue what this is about. I do. Dom's right, I have seen it before. Whatever else he is, he's an experienced exorcist. This is for real." Thunder clapped as if to punctuate his words.

"Then why aren't you looking me in the eye?" she asked him.

So he faced her and forced out the words. "He's right about this."

"Tomas —"

"Stay out of this, Indy!" he barked, and then he looked at Dom again as lightning flashed across the old man's face. "Will you help me, old friend? Help me save my sister?"

Dom's lips thinned, and then he spoke. "Have you seen the error of your ways, Tomas? Have you seen what happens when you let anything come before your faith?"

"I have. I swear, I have."

Dom nodded slowly. "Then I'll try to save her. But remember, all I can do is *try.*"

"This is fucking ridiculous." I turned and headed back downstairs. I wasn't about to let Rayne die from whatever the hell had suddenly taken her over while the two men played exorcist. I was going to call 9-1-1 for an ambulance. And while I was at it, I thought, I'd tell them to send some cops along with it, because those two white-collar criminals were not going to let Rayne go easily.

They were both freaking nuts.

And it hurt. God, it hurt so bad that after the night we'd shared Tomas had turned on me like this. I mean, okay, Rayne was his sister and she was in bad shape, and he loved her and was obviously afraid for her. But still . . .

Hell, I love her, too. You don't see me buying into some madman's hallucinations over it. She needs real help. What the hell is the matter with Tomas?

The rain was pounding down outside. I shivered, crossed the little kitchen and reached for the cordless phone, only to find there was no dial tone whatsoever. Nothing but static. *"Dammit."* I slammed the thing back into the base and noted that the power was still on.

Has to be the phone lines, then. Probably this damned storm.

And if the phones were down, so was the Net.

I headed back upstairs, undaunted, determined to get help for my friend. I couldn't resist going past my own room to take a quick glimpse at the two maniac priests in Rayne's room. They'd gathered up some of their magical tools by then. Oh, they would rather be tortured than call them that, but that's what they were. They had their sacred book, their crucifix, their holy water, their vestments. They didn't seem to be hurting Rayne any. Just praying over her and sprinkling her with the holy water every now and then. She was still unconscious. As I peered in at them, Tomas looked back at me, his eyes intense. And maybe a little angry.

Just leave it alone, they seemed to be saying.

Just go piss up a rope, I glared back at him.

I was hurt, but damned if I'd let him see that, so I broke eye contact and strode away, ducking into my own room and digging through my purse for my cell phone. Found it, score. Battery good. Signal?

Hell. There were no bars on its face, just

the message that it was searching, followed by the dire notification No Service.

I flung the phone onto the bed, then looked toward the window, desperate now, certain that Rayne needed medical help and that she needed it soon. And it was up to me to get it for her. Entirely up to me.

Rivulets of rainwater streamed over the glass, while gusting wind sent new bursts of droplets pounding down. I swallowed hard, moving closer, staring out into the storm. *I'm just gonna have to go find help then — or a phone or a signal, whichever comes first.*

Nodding in affirmation, I yanked warmer clothes from the dresser. A pair of jeans, a hoodie, heavy and warm. I put on thick socks and hiking boots, and then slipped from my room to the stairs, not taking the time to look in on Rayne again. The sooner I got my beautiful sister-witch out of here, the better. Those two working over her could not be good for her. Not in any way. Waving a crucifix over a witch, ordering the devil out of her — no, that was just wrong on too many levels.

I tried to walk quietly down the stairs, despite the weight of the boots, and managed not to disturb the monotone muttering of the priests in the other guest room. I checked the little bing-bong device that was supposed to signal if a door or my bedroom window were opened during the night.

It won't be turned on. Tomas set that up to protect me, so I wouldn't sleepwalk out the door and off the cliff. Only at night, he said. But I was with him last night, so he wouldn't have bothered to —

The green light was glowing on the control box. It was turned on. I wondered who'd done that?

I examined the thing to decide my best move and found that it had a volume control on the side. I twisted it all the way down, hoping they would be too busy with their ritual to hear anything else, then checked that the green light was still on. Good. If I turned it off, they might notice.

Then I went to the closet nearest the front door, located an oversize yellow rain slicker and put it on. I took the keys from the key rack and, as silently as I could, opened the door, ducked outside and closed it softly behind me.

Cold rain smacked me in the face, driven by merciless gusts. Some of it even felt icy, as if it were beginning to freeze into sleet. So much for our warmer than normal fall. I tugged the slicker's hood around my face, holding it in place with one hand, and bent forward to push my way through the wind to Tomas's old Volvo.

The storm was fierce, howling wind, deafening thunder. It didn't let up. Probably would, soon, but I wasn't going to wait. My only regret was that I hadn't stolen another smoke for the drive down off this cursed mountain.

I made it to the car, diving behind the wheel and closing the storm outside where it belonged. I didn't even try to mute the slam of the car door, knowing the storm itself would drown out any noise. I turned the key.

Nothing. Freakin' nothing. I clenched my fist and shook it at the sky. "A little fucking help here? I mean, come on. No phone. No cell signal. Now no car?"

And then I stopped and blinked slowly. That was a hell of a lot of failure in one fell swoop, wasn't it? Yeah. Maybe a little bit too much.

I wanted to take a look under that Volvo's hood, but I'll tell you what, I wouldn't have known what the hell to look for. I eyed Father Dom's big brown car, though. It was parked around the side of the cabin, just its ass end sticking out my way. I hadn't seen his keys inside on the rack by the door. He'd either left them in it or he had them on him. Or maybe they were in his room.

I hoped they were in the car and, ducking, I ran that direction, my feet making slapping sounds on the wet earth as the storm raged on. The wind pushed me from behind now. I reached his car and yanked on the driver's door.

Locked. I cupped my hands and peered through the glass, but there were no keys inside that car, and the other three doors were locked, as well.

Hell.

I was out of options. Unless I wanted to walk out of here.

I thought maybe I should give one more look around for Dom's keys before I resorted to that, and knowing the men would be too busy with Rayne to pay much attention, I thought I'd have a fairly good chance of finding them so long as they weren't actually on him.

God, I hated like hell to go back into that cabin. I'd been so close to free. I wondered if Dom was crazy enough to try to stop me from leaving, if he knew what I was up to. I wondered if Tomas was crazy enough to let him. Or help him.

Dejected, I went back inside. I peeled off the raincoat, shook it and hung it way in the back of the closet where I'd found it. I put Tomas's keys back on the rack, then took off my damp, muddy boots. My jeans were blotted with rainwater, my hair and face damp. At least my shirt had stayed dry.

Not wanting to make it obvious that I was planning to get the hell out of here and bring back help for Rayne, I set my hiking boots inside the closet, as well, then closed it and eyeballed the stairs again. I'd have to walk right past the two priests to get to Father Dom's room. And past them again on my way back to the stairs.

I swallowed hard.

Just do it, chicken shit.

Okay, okay.

I pulled my hoodie off and used it to wipe off my face and soak some of the water from my hair. And then I stiffened my shoulders and strode up the stairs, lifting my chin, and trying to keep my expression placid. Instead of sneaking past them, which would have raised their suspicions if they'd seen me, I walked right in on them, as if that had been my destination to begin with, interrupting them in midspell. Er, prayer.

"This is insane," I said. Both men went silent and swung irritated gazes my way. "We should get her to a hospital. Right now. We should take her and go."

Dom puckered up like a prune.

"Look, you're priests. They'll let you pray

over her there. But they'll also have her tested for other causes and hooked up to life-sustaining fluids, maybe even put her on a heart monitor."

"She does have a point," Tomas said softly, shifting his eyes to Dom.

"You told me yourself not an hour ago that the bridge had certainly been washed out by this storm. Didn't you, Tomas?"

Tomas blinked and lowered his head, but somehow I got the idea that he hadn't forgotten that for an instant.

"Is that true? Is the bridge underwater?"

"Yes," he said.

"You've seen it?"

"It always is when it rains like this. It'll be impassible for at least a day. Maybe longer, depending on when the rain stops."

Not to a determined witch with her foot to the floor, it won't.

"Your sister is dying due to the influence of the Demon," Dom scolded Tomas. "Yet you waste your time answering to his mistress."

I bristled right up. "Fuck you, Dom. I know who that so-called demon really is. And the high priest who cursed him was probably a guy a lot like you." I shot my eyes back to Tomas. "It's your sister's life we're talking about here. Don't you want to at least cover all your bases?"

He looked at me then, and I thought his eyes were not just telling me to let it go but pleading with me to do so.

"Get out!" Dom shouted.

I damn near jumped out of my skin, because his tone was so violent. I didn't even stop to look at Tomas, I just left the room, giving the door a good slam on the way out. I was shaking all over once I was in the hallway again, but I reminded myself that this was exactly what I'd wanted. To close the door, so I could go into the bastard priest's room and — I hoped — find his car keys.

I was no longer sure I wanted to leave Rayne behind when I left this place, though. Maybe I should just wait until dark and sneak her out of here in the dead of night.

Might be good. Might not. Better check the bridge first. See if it's even safe. But first, keys. I needed a vehicle.

I padded down the hall, tossing my hoodie into my own room and slamming that door for good measure. Let them think I was in there stewing. Then I ducked quickly into Father Dickwad's room and quietly pushed his door closed behind me.

The bed was neatly made, and there was not so much as a paperback out of place.

You wouldn't have known anyone was even using the room, except for the tiny black plastic comb on the dresser.

I paused over that comb, tempted to take a hair from its teeth, hunt down some rusty nails and graveyard dirt, and cast a whopper of a curse on that old son of a bitch. But that was not what I'd come here to do.

I didn't see the keys anywhere. So I opened each of the four dresser drawers and went through his neatly folded clothes. Since I'd seen his suitcase by the door earlier, apparently he'd unpacked before starting the exorcism. I opened the closet, and searched the pockets of his two shirts and two jackets. Empty.

I knelt down and felt inside the only pair of shoes I saw there. Nothing.

I checked out the adjoining bathroom, and found only a handful of hotel-sized shampoos and conditioners, pilfered from a Holiday Inn.

What happened to "Thou shalt not steal"?

Medicine cabinet. Nothing. Antacids, individually wrapped packets in a nearly empty box. They were the plop-plop, fizz-fizz variety. Hardly any left. Lowering my head in defeat, I spotted lots of little wrappers in the wastebasket.

Frowning, I bent down to pick one up.

Same stuff. Plop-plop, fizz-fizz.

Six wrappers. Why had he needed so many?

And weren't you supposed to mix them with water and drink them down? Where was his glass?

I supposed he could have taken it down to the kitchen. He was a fastidious old goat, after all.

And then something jolted in my brain, like a tiny electrical charge, and I was seeing the foam oozing from Rayne's mouth.

Just for the hell of it, I unwrapped one of the tablets and put in my own mouth, then just closed my lips and held it there as it began to tingle and sort of sizzle on my tongue. In a few seconds I was foaming at the mouth. Just a little. Not as much as Rayne had been doing earlier.

But then, I'd only used one. There were six wrappers in the trash.

Six.

I couldn't take it anymore and bent to spit the shit out, cupping my hands under the tap and doing my best to rinse the residue of the stuff out of my mouth. It took several big gulps. When I finished, I straightened and met my own eyes in the mirror.

Okay, so maybe you manufactured that much, you sly old bastard. But what about the rest? How the hell do you induce convulsions and unconsciousness?

I looked around the bathroom much more thoroughly then, even peeking beneath the lid into the toilet tank. Then I went back to the bedroom to see where else I could search.

Under the bed.

I knelt down and lifted the comforter, which hung down to the floor. Nothing under there but a plain dark blue suitcase, the old-fashioned hard-shell kind. I pulled it out and flipped the latches — unlocked, good — lifted the lid and stared at its utterly empty interior.

It's not empty. I can feel it's not empty. Come on, Eyes of Spirit, don't let me down now.

Aha! Nothing really sinister, like a false bottom. Just a panel to keep things separate, like lots of older suitcases had. I unsnapped it, lifted it, and there underneath were three brown plastic bottles. The kind prescriptions came in. But I knew the pills and labels didn't match as soon as I twisted the cover off one, because there were numerous shapes, sizes and colors of drugs inside. Not just one.

And I knew right then, even though I didn't have proof — yet. I knew that bastard had drugged Rayne. If these drugs were innocent, then why would they be hidden here, instead of sitting in the medicine cabinet next to the antacids?

I poured a handful of pills into my palm, then pocketed them to take to the hospital with me later. The doctors would need to know what she'd been given. Then I put the cap back on the bottle, lowered the panel, closed the lid and slid the suitcase back underneath the bed.

Rayne wasn't safe here. I was going to have to wait and find a way to take her with me when I left. But where the hell were the keys to the old bastard's car?

I was still on my knees beside the bed when I heard them talking in the hallway. Footsteps — coming this way. The doorknob twisting.

I flattened my body facedown on the floor and scrambled sideways like a crab on crack, slipping under the bed. Quickly I reached out and yanked the comforter back down. In the nick of time, too, because the door opened just as I snatched my hand back out of sight.

Had they seen it?

"In here," Father Dom said softly. "I don't want to risk her listening in."

"She's not going to listen in. She thinks we've lost our minds, Dom. And I'm not entirely sure she's wrong. We really ought to take Rayne to a hospital. It's clear our efforts aren't working."

Good job, Tomas. Now just get a tiny bit saner. Come to the light, jackass.

"No, our efforts aren't working. Do I really need to tell you why?"

The old priest's shoes came into view in the inch of space between the bedspread and the carpeted floor. He was walking away from Tomas, pausing to stare out the window into the rain. "You betrayed your God. You broke your vows. You caved in to temptation." The black shoes turned around, pointing back toward Tomas again. "You slept with the Demon's whore."

"Don't call her that." Tomas's tone was low and dangerous.

"You gave up the protection God had granted you, and your sister because of you. You made her vulnerable to attack by the very Demon your girlfriend serves."

"I've repented, Dom. Surely God will forgive me."

"You've repented by word alone. But not by deed. I'm afraid your sister's condition is going to get worse."

Tomas's voice was low, emotionless, when he said, "Tell me what I have to do to save Rayne."

Father Dom was still for a moment. Then he said, "Your Indira is going to help the Demon. You know that. She's going to slip away from us. She's going to go down to the cave, to the Portal, and utter the words that will return the amulet to him. And then he'll be able to pass through. And you know there's only one way to stop her."

Tomas faltered, his voice even softer than before. "I can . . . lock her in her room, stand guard over her, keep her here until Samhain has passed and the veil —"

"And in three thousand five hundred years, it will all happen again. There's only one way to stop her, Tomas. We must destroy the amulet just as we've planned to do all along."

My throat tightened as I listened to them.

"And there's only one way to destroy the amulet." The shiny black shoes moved closer as the old priest stood toe to toe with Tomas. "You have to kill her, my son. You made the right decision once — the only decision you could make at the time. Maybe now you're starting to understand why. You have to do it again, just as you did before. You have to kill her to save the world. To save your sister. You have to kill the witch."

19

I pressed a hand over my mouth to silence the gasp that tried to erupt from the core of me. My God, had that been his plan all along? Not just Father Dom's but Tomas's, too? And what about last night? Had it meant anything to him, or was it just a slip, a weakness? Did he honestly believe he had fallen prey to the spell of a witch? To the temptation of a demon's whore?

I wasn't going to wait around this loony bin to find out. I was out of here just as soon as I had an opportunity. And somehow I had to find a way to take Rayne with me.

Tomas said nothing. Not a word in my defense. Not a denial. Not an argument.

And then Dom went on. "We'd best keep a close eye on her in the meantime — if she gets down there without us, she'll return the amulet before we have the chance to stop her. Where is she now, anyway?"

"I don't know," Tomas said softly. "I don't know."

The two of them left the room, presumably to go looking for me. I figured they'd start in my bedroom, which gave me time, I hoped. I slid out from underneath the bed and glanced up at the clock on the nightstand. And an idea began to take form in my mind. I grabbed the clock, set it ahead an hour, replaced it on the stand, then hurried to the door to peer out. They were in the hallway outside my bedroom door, tapping it and calling out my name.

I quickly yanked the suitcase out from under the bed, dug out those three pill bottles and jammed them under my blouse. Closed the case, shoved it back under the bed. No way was I risking him carrying out his threats against Rayne.

And that was exactly what it was, I realized. A threat. He might as well have said, "Either you kill the witch or I kill your sister." Only he was disguising it as, "Either you kill the witch or God is going to kill your sister."

Was Tomas really buying into such bullshit? Did he really think that was the nature of God? Blackmail? Murder?

I was back in the doorway again five seconds later, trying to figure out how the hell to get ahead of them and downstairs without them knowing. They opened my bedroom door and stepped inside. I took that moment to dart out of the old priest's room and down the hall, ducking into Rayne's room before they came out again. I sat in the chair beside her bed, reaching out to take hold of her hand, and wondered what on earth I could do to help get the poison out of her system.

At least the old bastard wouldn't be giving her any more.

Unless he's got another stash somewhere. Like in the car.

Damn, but I need those keys.

I heard them calling for me but stayed right where I was, saying nothing. *Let 'em search, let 'em get the idea that I'm not gonna answer even if they yell till they're hoarse. Let 'em wonder where I am and go down the mountainside in the rain looking for me. Let 'em fall off the face of the motherfucking earth, over the cliff, and let the lake swallow them whole. Both of them. Bastards.*

I'd been betrayed by the man I loved for the second time. He wasn't going to get a third chance. I noticed there was a clock in Rayne's room, too, and I quickly set it ahead an hour, replacing it on the nightstand just before the door opened and Tomas stood

439

there looking at me. I noticed he wasn't wearing his clerical collar.

"Didn't you hear us calling?"

I shrugged. "Heard. Didn't give a shit."

He couldn't hold my eyes, looking instead at his sister. I wanted to tell him that she'd been poisoned, show him the evidence, but I was too afraid he wouldn't believe me. Or that his mission, his faith, would be more important to him than the truth. Besides, Father Dom would just come up with some lame explanation, and he had Tomas so twisted up inside that he'd probably believe him. And I would have given myself away before I'd even had a chance to flush the drugs. So I said nothing, got slowly to my feet and moved past him into the hallway.

He put a hand on my shoulder. "Indy —"

"Don't touch me." I stood motionless, waiting.

He lowered his hand. "It's going to be all right," he told me.

"You're damned straight it is."

He glanced toward the stairs. Father Dom was on his way up. "We need to talk. Alone," he said.

"Right." So he could kill me. "I've got nothing to say to you, Tomas." And yet my throat was tight with tears I refused to shed. I walked away, into my room, slamming the

440

door behind me, then leaning back against it and blinking away the tears in my eyes. A couple of gulps of air, though, and I beat them into submission. I had work to do. Moving to my nightstand, I quickly reset the clock.

By my count there were two more downstairs, and one in Tomas's room. Neither man wore a watch. I was lucky there.

It was getting dark. I was antsy and wanted only to slip away from the two lunatics and try to find a way out of here. All day I'd been reading and rereading the words I'd written so long ago, the words of the tragic story of Demetrius, the man who'd made the mistake of falling in love with the king's favorite harem slave. And who'd paid a price far more dear than his life for his crime. He'd paid with his soul.

A piece of that soul lived inside me now, in the amulet I had absorbed into my body in order to protect it from the two priests. I felt it there. I felt his pain when I read about what had been done to him. I felt his torment, and his rage.

I didn't blame him for it.

Rayne still slept. There had been no more convulsions. I'd flushed the pills, all but one of each variety, which I held on to for the

E.R. staff. Those were in my pocket. No more foaming at the mouth, either. Maybe once was enough with that particular special effect. But she was still unconscious. I didn't know if Dom had more pills on him and was keeping her drugged or not. I tried to be in her room every time he looked in, but I had to go to the bathroom every now and then.

Mostly they'd left me alone with her. And I'd read from the scrolls mostly in private, though they kept watching me, and I noticed Dom was trying real hard not to leave Tomas alone with me even for a minute.

I wondered if Tomas had told him about the scrolls. And if not, why not? I didn't suppose there was any hurry. I'd be dead soon, according to their plan.

I'd found that if I focused on the story and on Demetrius, holding his name in the forefront of my mind, I could feel him so clearly that I could almost talk to him. And I thought maybe if I kept trying, I'd manage to actually do so.

He was not a nice guy. Not even human anymore. All I sensed of him was pain, confusion, rage, fury.

And grief, though it was buried way down deep.

Maybe returning the piece of his soul I

now held would assuage that, restore a little bit of humanity to him. I hoped so. Because right now there wasn't anything human about Demetrius. Maybe releasing him from his Underworld prison truly would be a mistake. But it was the only right and just thing to do. And it was, I knew now, my mission. My reason for being. My calling. It was more important than anything else. More important than Tomas, and more important than my own life.

And it was time. I was sitting on the sofa in the living room, where I'd been for the past hour, pretending to read a book while they hovered over me like vultures. Tomas was wearing his collar again, his all-black clothes. They even *looked like* vultures, I thought.

They were watching me. I knew they were. I'd managed, though, to set every clock in the house ahead by an hour. It was a quarter to midnight now, at least as far as they knew. Fifteen more minutes and they would believe my opportunity was gone. Even now they undoubtedly thought it was too late. Fifteen minutes wasn't even enough time for me to make it down the path to the cave — especially in the dark — much less perform the ritual.

I lowered my eyes. "Are you happy now?

You've won. You've sentenced an innocent being to God only knows how many more years in an unbearable prison. Your God must be so proud of you." I sent them hateful looks. "I'm going to bed."

Tomas nodded. "All right." His eyes held mine for a long moment, and I could have sworn I saw something in them. Longing? No. It couldn't be. He believed I was the enemy, had let himself be brainwashed by the old priest.

I couldn't afford to trust him. He wanted me dead. That would end only when I returned the amulet to Demetrius. And I still had a little over an hour to make that happen. I went upstairs and looked in on Rayne, who was sleeping soundly. Still no more thrashing or foaming. Thank Goddess.

Dom doesn't have to torture her anymore. He thinks he's won. That he's convinced Tomas to kill me. As long as Tomas doesn't balk, he'll leave her alone. I hope.

Could I even blame Tomas all that much for doing whatever it took to save his sister?

Yeah. Because there has to be a better way than murder. My murder. Not that I'm biased or anything.

I went into my room, closed and locked the door, opened my bedroom window and climbed out into the rain. The wind had let up. The rain still fell steadily, but it wasn't pouring like it had been before. Dangling from my fingertips, I whispered a spell, and then let go.

I hit the ground hard, driving a grunt from my chest and creating a splat when I landed that I was sure must have been audible inside.

Apparently not in the rain. I got up onto my feet from the mud-slick ground and looked back at the house. If they were still in the living room, they wouldn't see me, because my bedroom window was on the opposite side of the house. I didn't see any faces peering out.

Good.

I headed into the woods and then kept just inside the tree line until I found the path down toward the lake.

I felt eyes on me and, startled to hell and gone, spun around, half expecting to find those dark-suited hypocrites following me. But no. It was just the animals. A squirrel and a raccoon, standing in the rain and staring at me with huge, hypnotized eyes.

And then I heard a deep tormented voice echoing inside my head. His voice.

Hurry.

I picked up my pace.

■ ■ ■ ■

"It's time," Dom said softly, looking at his cell phone.

Tomas lowered his head.

"The time for hesitation is over, Tomas. If you needed proof she was on the Demon's side, intending to help him, rather than us — rather than your sister, a fellow witch she claims to love — you have that proof now. She set all the clocks ahead to give herself time. We're supposed to believe it's midnight, but it's only eleven. And she's gone, right on schedule. While Samhain still holds open the Veil."

Tomas nodded. "I'd hoped she wouldn't go."

"But she did. At your request, Tomas, we've given her every chance to redeem herself, but she has not. This is the moment when you must choose between good and evil. This is the moment when you, like Adam of Genesis, must decide whether to obey God Almighty or turn away from Him in favor of the forbidden fruit offered by the temptress. This is the deciding moment of your entire life, Tomas. And the only chance you will ever have to save your sister, not just from death, but from eternal damnation. From the very jaws of the mouth of hell. Go. Go down the mountain and do what must be done."

Nodding, Tomas rose from the sofa and, with a heavy sigh, went to the closet for his raincoat. "I'm sorry I doubted you, Dom. And I'm grateful you waited, that you gave her the chance to change her mind. I won't let you down again."

Pulling on the slicker, he went to the back door, slid it open and stepped out onto the deck in the steadily falling rain.

The path was steep and slick with mud, and not even my heightened senses could make passage easy. My feet slipped and slid, and I fell on my ass more than once as I moved way faster than I should have. I didn't know exactly what I was supposed to do when I got there. I didn't have words or a spell to chant. It would just be me, my own will and my power as a witch. But those were things I had confidence in now. I'd been given the power of a long line of traditional witches, passed down through centuries of practice. From teacher to student, from old priestess to young, from woman to woman, from Rayne to me.

It wasn't my power alone. Not anymore. There were covens of witches behind me,

447

living and dead, bound by spirit.

I would never be alone again.

I'd used that power to cast a spell of protection around Rayne before I'd left her room tonight, quietly, silently, unnoticed by the priests.

I hoped it was enough.

I slipped once more as the rain came down harder again and a gust of wind seemed to push my feet out from under me. My shoes were coated in a thin layer of brown that had spattered onto the legs of my jeans, and the seat of my pants was wet from my repeated stumbles. I gripped a low tree limb to pull myself up and pressed on.

It seemed to take forever. Like one of those dreams where you run and run, but can't get anywhere. But finally — finally — I emerged from the woods and found myself staring at the waterfall and the pool that spread out below it. Rain hit the surface of the pool so hard that the drops appeared to be dancing. It was dark as hell outside, the sky blanketed in clouds, no light. And yet I saw everything clearly. I wondered why for a second, then I realized there was a glow, soft, but persistent, coming from behind the cascade. Coming from the cave.

Coming, I realized, from the Portal.

Come to me. Bring me that which is mine!

"I'm coming," I replied, speaking aloud, as if it — he — could hear me that way. Maybe he could. I started forward, then spun around when I heard footsteps behind me.

Tomas emerged from the trees, appearing on the path where I'd been standing only seconds earlier. Our eyes met in that odd, spectral glow from the cave, raindrops like a curtain between us. A curtain neither of us could ever pass through again. We were on opposite sides.

I shook my head. "You shouldn't have left him alone with your sister, Tomas. He's insane, you know."

"I locked her door, took the key."

That took me off guard. "Then you know?"

"I —"

"It doesn't matter. I know now what I have to do. And I won't let you stop me."

"I'm not going to try." He started toward me, but I backed away fast, holding up my hands like stop signs.

"Don't come any closer!"

He stopped, and his brow furrowed. "Indy, you don't have to be afraid of me."

"Don't I?" I shook my head, took another step backward. I'd put the pond between us now, but it also stood between me and the cave. Behind me there was nothing but the sheer drop-off and the rocky lakeshore far below. And yet I didn't look. I couldn't look. "I heard what Dom told you to do, Tomas. And I didn't hear you refuse." I took a deep breath, released it. "Hell, you didn't even argue."

His face was stricken and also confused, as he tried to figure out how I'd overheard them. And then he pushed that question aside as if it didn't matter. "If I had told him I wouldn't do it, he would have tried to do it himself. I never fell for any of it, Indy. Look, I knew the bridge was washed out. I knew he'd done something to Rayne. I was just trying to con him, to keep him from hurting her any more — or hurting *you,* for God's sake — until I could get us all to safety."

I wanted to believe him. Maybe he saw that, because he went on.

"I thought if I could con him for one more day — the rain's letting up. The water should recede by dawn. We can get Rayne out of here."

I shook my head. "I'm the one you're try-ing to con."

"No." He sighed heavily. "I was *never* a priest, Indy. Dom was excommunicated sometime after I entered the seminary. He pulled me out, told me I had a calling, that he had special dispensation to ordain me himself. And I believed him." He lowered his head. "I think he told us he was going to that memorial service and then went and killed Jonathon instead. I think that document Jonathon translated was the same story you found in those scrolls. Dom didn't want us to know the truth."

It all made sense. I was weakening. My heart was swelling.

"Indy, how can you be afraid of me? How can you believe I would . . . kill you?"

"It wouldn't be the first time, would it, Tomas?" I spat the words in pure self-defense. After all, he'd only killed me then at my own bidding. But even as I said them, there was a flash behind my eyes. Memory, the past, playing like rapid-fire snips from a movie. I was at the edge of the cliff with my sisters, facing the vast distance to the ground, and he was behind me. *I feel his hands on my back.*

Do it, my love! You have to do it!

I can't. I can't, Indira.

They'll know.

I don't care. I love you!

"I love you, Indy."

I love you, too. And so I cannot let you die with me. Goodbye, my love.

I was facing the cliff now, in real time, just as I had been in the past. I was leaning forward, as if I would throw myself over the side.

Just as I had done before. To save my lover, because he couldn't do it. He couldn't push me then, even though I'd begged him to. Even though refusing would mean his own life. Tomas had never pushed me. I had thrown *myself* off that cliff so long ago.

"Indy!"

His harsh voice snapped me out of my trance and I spun around, my feet slipping in the slick brown mud. I started to teeter as he lunged toward me, my arms whirling in huge circles, my body rocking, almost going over. He would never reach me in time! Somehow, though, I rocked the other way and fell forward, facedown in the mud.

I heard his relieved sigh as I pushed myself up on my elbows, smiling now, nearly laughing as I looked up at him. He hadn't killed me then, and I knew, somehow knew, that he had no intention of killing me now.

And then my smile died as I spotted a rain-soaked man in black emerging from the woods behind Tomas, and heard the action of the shotgun as he pumped a round into the chamber.

"Get up, witch," Father Dom commanded.

Tomas's face went lax with horror, and he turned, almost losing his footing in the mud. "Dom, listen to me —"

"Shut up, Tomas. I've heard enough from you." He wiggled the barrel at me. "Up."

I pushed myself up on trembling legs. Tomas was in front of me, but a couple of yards to the left. Dom stood dead ahead. I wondered what time it was, whether I could release the amulet from here, whether the demon who wasn't a demon could be of any help to me — to us — now.

Dom shouldered the gun and closed one eye as he pressed his cheek to the stock and peered down the barrel at me. His hand flexed as he tightened his finger on the trigger.

I shouted "No!" and flung out my hand.

A blast of energy hit Dom, but he pulled the trigger even as he was reeling from the impact, and Tomas dove in front of me just as I heard the explosion of the shotgun. I saw it all. Tomas, my beautiful love, threw himself into the path of the bullet. His body jerked in midair, and blood exploded from his back as the slug passed straight through him. I heard it zing past my ear before Tomas's body smacked down on the muddy ground, hitting shoulder-first before he tipped onto his back. He lay still, eyes closed. I stared, stunned, first at him and then at Father Dom, who was jerking on the pump action to no avail. Jammed.

He threw the shotgun aside and strode toward me. Murder blazed from his eyes. Murder and madness.

"No." I tried to harness my power to stop him, but it wouldn't work. I was too focused on Tomas. He was dying! I couldn't back away. There was nowhere to go. Nowhere but down.

Just like before.

"No, Father Dom, *don't.*"

Even if I had never believed in demons or devils in all my life, I would have believed in them then. Because what I saw in his eyes was evil. Pure evil.

I tried to shuffle sideways, toward the cave, but the path between the pool and the cliff was only a foot wide, and uneven. Rocky. Slick now, even underwater in places, because the rainfall had raised the water level.

"We have to help Tomas," I pleaded with Dom. "And Rayne, we have to help Rayne."

"Rayne is fine. The effects of the drugs only last a day. As for Tomas, first I have to save the world. Then I'll save him." He kept coming, and I knew he would push me over the side. I didn't want to die that way. Not again.

"Dom, listen to me, it's too late anyway. It's past midnight."

"Liar." He was close, way too close. And then he lunged. I tried to dodge, but one gnarled old hand caught my shoulder, and it was just enough to propel me off balance. I was going over this time, no help for it. "Goddess, protect me!" I shouted as my feet slid from mud into nothingness and my body followed them over the edge. I wasn't airborne. My body was raking over the cliff face, and I clutched with clawed fingers, caught hold of a rock outcropping and held on for dear life.

"You murdering son of a bitch!"

That was Tomas's voice! He was alive!

The rock beneath my fingers was wet and cold, and my face was pressed to the freezing stone. Water from the pond mixed with the rain and flowed over my hands and face, trickles now, but growing. I jammed my foot into the cliff face over and over, in search of a toehold. Finally I found one.

Using all my strength, I managed to raise my head above the lip of the cliff, but all I saw was the evil priest looming over me, smiling maniacally down at me as he held a big rock above his head. He was going to bring it down, crush my skull and send me plummeting to my death.

Then I heard the shotgun's action work again and saw the old priest's eyes widen momentarily before he smiled, and I read his thoughts. He was going to kill me anyway. He didn't care if he died in the process.

He met my eyes, and then suddenly something flew at him from off to one side — a huge wolf, leaping through the air like a monster out of a horror movie. It hit him, knocking him sideways to the ground. Dropping the rock, he rolled onto his back as the beast snarled and growled. He pushed himself backward through the mud as the animal came at him, and just like that, he was gone. Over the edge, falling past me as I hung there. He screamed as he fell, and I heard the horrible sound of his body hitting the rocky shore.

My arms, trembling from the effort of holding me up, gave out, and I started to fall, too. But a strong hand closed around my left wrist. And then another hand grabbed the right. And as I pushed with my feet, Tomas pulled me slowly, inexorably, up the cliff face and — finally — into his arms.

He held me so hard I could barely breathe. I couldn't tell which of us was shaking more fiercely, or whose tears I tasted all mingled with mud and rainwater as we kissed there again and again.

"I said I love you, Indy."

"You saved me. You saved me." I was sobbing, nearly incoherent.

"Karma. Full circle. Rule of Three. Whatever you want to call it. It's what I should have done last time."

"It's what you *did* do last time. Or tried to." I pulled back enough to meet his eyes, then looked away, past him, around us, afraid of the wolf. But there was no animal in sight. My sobs kept breaking up my words, but I had to tell him. He had to know. "You d-didn't push me then, Tomas. I threw myself off that cliff to protect you. And I'd do it again, just like you did for me tonight, when you threw yourself in front of —"

And then I stopped and realized that the warmth seeping between us was coming from blood, not passion. "Oh, God, no!"

"You have five minutes, Indy," he told me. I was surprised to see his cell phone in his hand. I hadn't thought of them when I'd been so cleverly changing clocks. And he nodded toward the cave.

"I'm not sure you do, though." I yanked off my blouse, wadding it up and pressing it

457

to the wound in his chest. I stood there in my soaked jeans and my bra, shivering with cold, willing him to live.

"Do you think we found each other again after three thousand years just to have it end like this?" he asked. His voice was tight with pain. His smile was the bravest, phoniest thing I'd ever seen. "No way, Indy. That would be a sucky ending to a really long story. Go on, get it done and then get back here."

"I can't leave you. I won't leave you. Nothing is more important than love, Tomas. I realize that now. Nothing. Not my mission, not justice for Demetrius, not a promise I made to my sisters, noth—"

"Not my vows to my God, not my belief, not my faith, not my dogma," he said, cutting me off. "Rayne's been trying to tell me that all along. Nothing is more important than love." He frowned. "Because love is the only thing that is, that's what she said. Love is at the heart of all of those other things. Love's the core. Everything else is man-made, beliefs and theories and rules and religions made up to try to explain the inexplicable, to know what can't be known. But if you strip it all away, love is what you have left. That's what Rayne's been trying to make me see, all this time."

I was crying as I stared at him, and then I gasped as two of my teardrops seemed to fall in slow motion, expanding and glowing so brightly that neither of us could look away. They fell to the ground, those two glowing tears, and hardened into diamonds. The amulet formed around them, and when I picked it up, it didn't disappear.

I closed my eyes. "That's the answer." Then I opened them again and looked toward the cave. "It's his answer, too." And then I rose and ran toward the entrance, but before I crossed through the water and went inside, I lifted my head skyward. "Lilia!" I cried out loud. "I know you're out there watching, sister. I'm leaving my man to save yours. You'd damn well better return the favor!"

Mere bullets cannot defeat love.

The voice was a whisper that came from nowhere and everywhere, and it was also the sound of the rain stopping all at once.

I nodded and entered the cave, walking quickly all the way to the source of the glowing light. I did not see the sad form with his longing eyes as I had before. But I knew what I had to do. I stared into the swirling colors, and I called out to him.

"Hear my words and know me! I am Indira, the sister of your woman. Your name is

Demetrius, and you are not a demon. You are a man. Seek love, and remember. Seek love, and do no more harm. Seek love, Demetrius, and be restored!"

I hurled the amulet with all my strength.

There was a flash of light from somewhere on the other side, and then the Portal popped and vanished. Just like that. I'd done what I had come here to do.

Turning, I moved as fast as I could through utter darkness until I found my way back outside. And as I emerged from the cave, I saw a beautiful woman leaning over Tomas, glowing like some ethereal angel. She glanced my way, and I saw her smile before she vanished.

I ran to Tomas's side and knelt, then gently tugged my wadded up blouse away from his flesh. He blinked down at his chest as I dabbed the blood away with rainwater. But there was no wound. No wound at all.

He lifted his eyes to meet mine. "I love you, Indira. And I'll never lose you again. Never again."

I smiled down at him. "I love you, Tomas. Always have." My heart was nearly bursting with the power of what was between us. "Always will."

The employees of Thorndike Press hope you have enjoyed this Large Print book. All our Thorndike, Wheeler, and Kennebec Large Print titles are designed for easy reading, and all our books are made to last. Other Thorndike Press Large Print books are available at your library, through selected bookstores, or directly from us.

For information about titles, please call:
    (800) 223-1244

or visit our Web site at:
    http://gale.cengage.com/thorndike

To share your comments, please write:
    Publisher
    Thorndike Press
    10 Water St., Suite 310
    Waterville, ME 04901